The Third Coin

J. A. Howard

ISBN: 1500550914
ISBN-13: 978-1500550912

DEDICATION

To my amazing daughters Phoebe and Georgia. You are my
reason and my heart.

CONTENTS

ACKNOWLEDGMENTS

My deepest thanks:

To my husband Ted for his endless patience, love and support.

To my sister Abby who believes in me more than I believe in myself.

Also:

To my nieces Madeline and Eloise who were the original inspiration for this story.

CHAPTER 1

THE NEW GIRL

New York City: not at all as expected, Bea wrote in her notebook. She sighed, slumped back into the dark leather of the hired limousine and watched the city slip by the car windows. Where was the gleaming, teeming metropolis she'd imagined so many times? Even the skyscrapers were a bland shade of gray and the yellow taxi cabs faded and dirty. She yawned. Ever since they'd landed at the airport, Bea had felt both tired and uneasy. Normally she was neither. Normally, when she arrived in a new place, she could barely contain her curiosity. Now here she was in New York - the city she'd been longing to see her whole life - and she could scarcely muster enough interest to write a decent observation in her notebook.

As the car inched its way through the slow-moving traffic, Bea doodled unconsciously, another inky cluster of interlocking circles filling up the corner of the page. Finally, after what seemed like hours, the car made a wide left turn.

"This is your street," the driver announced. "It's just a few blocks down."

Bea pulled herself up and peered out the window again. Her eyes shifted restlessly over the tightly-packed brown buildings that lined the pavement. The gray afternoon light gave everything the dusty gloom of a graveyard.

As Bea tucked her pen and white notebook into her well-worn travel bag, she caught a glimpse of herself reflected in the car window and sighed again. She was glad her father wasn't there, relieved he couldn't see the grumpy girl who frowned back at her.

Nana Anna, Bea's travelling companion and caretaker, didn't seem to notice Bea's mood. She chatted amiably with the driver, her correct British accent in stark contrast to his rough New York one.

"Isn't it charming, Bianca?" Nana Anna said over her shoulder. "It looks a good bit like London, wouldn't you agree?"

Bea nodded unenthusiastically, though Nana Anna was right. The street did seem familiar, with its dark old buildings and sad little shops. Had she not been so cranky, Bea might have laughed. She should have known it would be just this way; she could have predicted it. Her father was only happy – if you could ever use that word to describe him – when he was in dark, dank places filled with moldy old things. Why had she expected New York to be any different?

Other twelve-year-old girls would never put up with this, she thought with a huff. Other girls would never stand for all the moving around; the dirty, overcrowded cities or the smelly little villages. Bea had seen how other kids pouted and sulked when they were unhappy or uncomfortable, and she thought, for the first time in her life, that her father should be grateful she never behaved that way. He probably never even noticed how pleasant she was or how patient. But even as the thought spun angrily through her mind she knew it was not true. Of course her father noticed. He noticed everything.

Dr. Nathan Brightman, Bea's father, noticed things for a living. He was a doctor of Archeology and Art History and was famous – at least in the world of academia - for his ability to track down lost artifacts. It was in this way that he made a living and that meant that he and Bea moved frequently, often to remote and unusual places. Bea suspected he was paid well for his efforts by the wealthy collectors who commissioned his services. They never lacked for money. However, she also knew that it wasn't money that motivated him. Her father cared little for material things. He chose to live simply, claiming there was far more to learn living among the people than one could ever learn living above them.

It was a strange way to live, moving around the globe like nomads, but Bea actually enjoyed it. Like her father, she was naturally curious and his work gave her the chance to experience things most people only saw on television. It also gave her father the opportunity to educate Bea on all the things he loved the most – art, science, history, and nature – treating her more like a scientist-in-training than a kid.

If his work took them to the wilderness or to the desert, they'd head out into the bush armed with notebooks, pencils and binoculars. Together, tucked in a quiet spot in the trees, they'd sit silently observing the animals, Father breaking the stillness only to ask questions or point out a fact.

In cities he found lessons everywhere they went. He'd even quiz her as they walked down the street. "What type of leather was that woman's handbag?" he'd ask as a well-heeled lady passed, or "What language are those children speaking?" when a group of foreign students clamored by. When they shopped in the markets he would challenge her to identify things using only her sense of smell or touch. "Be specific," he would say. "Is it a peach or an apricot? Are you sure? How do you know?"

And so Bea had learned the art of observation and with it the skill of note-taking. Even before she could write, he'd encouraged her to draw pictures of the things she saw. She took in the details of everything around her and faithfully transcribed it all in her white notebook.

These lessons came easily for Bea. She loved to be challenged but especially loved the look on her father's face when she discovered a small, overlooked detail or solved a difficult puzzle. His eyes would twinkle and his mouth would turn up slightly at the corners. It was the closest he ever came to a smiling.

Nana Anna claimed that he hadn't always been so dour. It was the death of Bea's mother that had closed him up so tightly. Bea knew there was truth in Nana Anna's words but she also knew there was something else in her father's life that haunted him. It was a coin – a precious artifact of some kind - and no matter where they went, or what assignment he was on, Father was always hunting for it. Whenever he got close to finding it he became obsessed; forgetting to eat and even to sleep. And when the searches came up empty – which they always did - he would slip into a black fog that could last for weeks.

Whenever Bea attempted to ask him about either the coin or her mother, sadness would darken his pale blue eyes and he would change the subject or simply not answer at all. He shared nothing about the coin and the only facts she ever got from him about her mother was that her name was Kate and that she passed away the day Bea was born.

After a time, Bea stopped asking questions, choosing to try to make him happy rather than sad. She studied hard, never complained and always did what she was told. She dreamed that one day she would find the coin for him and he would finally be happy and maybe even settle down somewhere. In the meantime, she learned to keep her spirits up for both of them and, though Father never said so, Bea knew it meant a lot to him.

The car slowed down just as Bea was sighing for the third time. Bea pulled herself up again and peered out the window at the row of brown buildings. Without a word from anyone, Bea knew which one was hers.

Squeezed between two lovely, tidy homes was a large, dilapidated stone house so badly in need of restoration that, if not for the propping of the buildings on either side, Bea was sure it would slide to the sidewalk in a muddy pile of rubble. Father had warned her in advance that his family home might be in ill repair. No one had lived there for at least a decade. Even so, it was far worse than she imagined.

"These houses are called brownstones," Nana Anna

explained with a sniff as they stepped out onto the sidewalk into the dull daylight. "And this is considered a very posh address," she added without a hint of sarcasm.

Nana Anna paused for a moment to neatly remove her gloves, then waved a hand at the driver to indicate he should collect their luggage from the boot.

"Your family," she continued, "was once extremely wealthy. Did you know that the east wing of the New York History Museum is named after them?"

The afternoon air was dry and thick, as if someone had kicked up a pile of sand and the smallest particles hadn't yet settled again. Bea nodded, blinking in the dull, dusty light. Of course she knew about the museum. She had researched her family many times, but her searches turned up little more than what Nana Anna was sharing with her now: William and Rose Brightman of New York City, her father's parents, had owned a shipping company that imported antiques. They donated many things to the museum, and in return the museum named a wing after them. And of course there was the fact that they were dead.

As they waited for the luggage, Nana Anna went on to explain that some kind of illness that had caused her grandparents to lose the family fortune. All that was left after they passed was the house and its contents.

"It's still worth a small fortune," Nana Anna insisted, shaking her head at the mess in front of them. "Or at least it will be when Cookie and I get through with it," she added, referring to their cook, who'd also been with Bea since childhood and would be arriving later that day.

Bea squinted up at the house and for a fleeting moment got an impression of how grand it might have been years ago. The most striking feature was the large stone staircase that tumbled from the façade, spreading out as it reached the sidewalk below. Although still impressive, the stone was cracked in many places and the steps worn away, the edges soft and rounded like lumps of sand.

At the top of stairs was an enormous front door, its green paint faded and peeling. In the center was a large brass knocker which Bea barely recognized as the Hand of Fatima, an ancient talisman meant to ward off evil. The curve of the fingers had been so beaten by time and weather that now it looked more like a seashell than a hand. In fact, the whole building gave the impression of a sandcastle that had been partly washed away by the ocean's waves.

Nana Anna tsked with disapproval as she and Bea navigated the worn stairs and seemed even more exasperated as she struggled to open the huge door with a key the size of soup ladle. Finally Nana Anna pronounced her success and with a hard shove they pushed open the door together.

Things inside the Brightman home were even worse than on the outside. The imposing front hall was dank and smelled like old cabbage. Paint and wallpaper peeled from the dark walls and the windows were so crusted with grime that only patches of dim sunlight shone through. There was no furniture in the room except for a faded rug that had turned brown with rot and in some places had disintegrated clear through to the floor.

"Well I shouldn't lack for things to do," said Nana Anna with another sniff, then briskly headed off through the doors on the left to see what challenges awaited her in the kitchen. Bea remained standing where she was, just inside the front entrance. She could hear the sound of closets and cabinets being opened and closed as Nana Anna inspected the inner rooms.

Bea placed her bag on the ground beside her and pulled out her notebook. Then she tugged the cap off her pen with her teeth and wrote: *House is fantastic - may finally have a chance to learn about Dad's past.*

A moment later Nana Anna returned to the front hall. "Out. Out. Out," she barked. "I must clean things up a bit before I can let you take another step inside. Why don't you take a little walk, maybe see if you can find your new school?"

CHAPTER 2

THE STREET

With no other choice, Bea stepped outside again and frowned. She didn't feel like looking for her new school. Although her first day was just two days away, she wasn't ready to face it just yet. Instead, she parked herself about halfway down her lumpy front steps and rubbed her eyes as if she could somehow clear away the dull grayness that hung in the air.

It wasn't that Bea found school difficult – she didn't. She was a Brightman after all, and schoolwork was almost always easy for her. But, as everyone knows, there was a lot more to school than just classes and homework. There was the whole making-friends part, and that always turned out to be far more challenging than getting A's.

When Bea was younger she had tried to explain this to her father, but as brilliant as he was, he couldn't understand why it would matter. "Don't bother yourself with those things" he would say, "it's your studies that matter." But Bea knew better. Making friends mattered. She had seen how things worked at school. The popular children were powerful and respected. The unpopular ones were weak and abused. If social skills were graded, the popular children would have been A students, the unpopular ones, failures.

Determined to be an A student in every way; Bea decided to take a scientific approach. She began by observing the other children. She watched them in the classroom, on the playground and in the cafeteria. And over the years, with time, study and careful note-taking, she eventually made an important discovery. No matter where she went in the world, kids fell into five basic types which she named and categorized:

Top Pops: These were the very most popular and therefore the most powerful children in the school - the ones who everyone wanted to be or to know and who determined who and what was cool.

Almosts: Almosts were almost as popular as Top Pops but not quite. They wore the right clothes and listened to the right music but they didn't have what it took to take the lead. They spent their time following the Top Pops around, emulating their behavior and vying for their attention.

Specialists: Specialists were the kids who spent their time developing special interests like creative writing or violin or math skills. They usually hung out in small groups of two or three, got good grades and stayed out of the Top Pops' way. Although they were often bright, they weren't willing to put the time and effort into their social lives. Bea suspected they lacked confidence. Why else would someone go to the effort of making friends if they weren't the right friends?

At the bottom of the chart were the *Not Pops*, two equally unpopular groups but for different reasons.

First there were the *Clueless Not Pops*. These children were the ones who just couldn't figure out how things worked. They didn't understand why coming to school with extremely dirty hair or carrying an old teddy bear around was not a good idea when trying to get along with others. If anyone bothered to notice them at all, it was usually to make fun of them.

Rogue Not Pops were very different. These kids operated outside the system – in other words, they were unpopular by choice. Everything they did was designed to be off-putting or intimidating. They moved through the school halls looking angry and bored, bullying anyone who bothered them and frequently getting in trouble. Being scary protected them from being tortured by the more popular kids but even so, Bea suspected their lives weren't all that great. They were often alone and never looked very happy.

Once Bea had identified who was who, she would begin the work of making the adjustments necessary to fit in with the Top Pops. Clothes and hairstyles were very important and easy enough to fix. The harder part was suppressing any behaviors that could suggest suitability for a different group. In other words: no joining the Science Club, no matter how much she wanted to.

It's just another new school, Bea thought, squinting out at the street. She had managed to be a Top Pop in every school she'd been to so far. Why should this one be any different? Sure, it was frustrating to have to start again when she'd only just gotten settled in London. She'd have to figure out whether it was cool to carry a backpack or a book bag, what clubs to join, and if she should wear her shirt tucked in or out of her uniform skirt. And of course, most importantly, she'd have to determine as quickly as possible who was popular and who was not. Still, she'd figure it out. She always did. So why did it feel different here?

Is it worth it? Bea scribbled across a blank page in her notebook. *We're probably just going to move again.* She shifted on the cool stone stairs and pushed her pale hair behind her shoulders. Maybe Father will like his job here so much that we'll actually stay a while, she wished. But as much as she wanted it to be true, she knew it wasn't likely. Her father didn't seem capable of staying in one place.

Bea closed her eyes and forced herself to sit up even straighter. She flipped her hair behind her shoulders again and took a deep breath. This is silly, she thought. Wasn't it good enough that she was here, in New York, finally? She wasn't going to sit around feeling sorry for herself.

At that moment, a horn honked and Bea opened her eyes.

She peered down the street through the afternoon gloom until she found the source. There, at the corner, was a dark grey limousine outside a small shop called Perfect Timing. It was just the kind of distraction she needed. So Bea shifted around on her step to get a better view and turned to a clean page in her notebook.

CHAPTER 3

THE FORTUNETELLER

Perfect Timing was a clock shop. The sign over its front door was neat and simple, gray letters on a white background. As Bea watched, a tall, silver-haired man in a gray suit came out of the shop, closed the door behind him, and neatly flipped the OPEN sign to the CLOSED side. The man, whom Bea presumed to be the shop owner, walked quickly from his door to the car. After quickly glancing at his watch, he slipped into the half-open car door. Seconds later the limousine moved silently from the curb and disappeared around the corner.

Odd, Bea thought and wrote, *Since when do clock shop owners get driven around in limousines?* She added an asterisk beside her note, a reminder to investigate further.

She looked up again just in time to see a teenage boy emerge from the shop. He too was tall and thin but his hair was flaxen. Even from across the street Bea could tell his expression was sour. He wore a t-shirt and narrow jeans that made his legs look long and stick-like. A short, oil-smeared apron was tied around his waist. When he was sure the limo had gone, he let himself back inside and reappeared a minute later. His apron had been replaced by a dark green leather jacket, though the weather did not call for one.

For the briefest moment his eyes flickered over Bea. Then, with a sharp tug, he flipped his collar up around his neck and headed to the corner. Bea watched him until he too disappeared around the bend.

A tinkle of bells drew Bea's attention back to the street. The sound had come from the small store next to the clock shop, a pretty little bakery with a pink door and curly gold trim that immediately brought to mind a wedding cake. Above the door was a sign that read, *A Taste of Love*. Each time the door opened a jingle of bells rang out brightening the dull afternoon air.

On the other side of the bakery was an even smaller shop called *The Woven World*, whose narrow front window was almost completely consumed by spools of wool in every imaginable color. In front of the shop, just outside the door, was an old wicker rocking chair and in it a rumpled old woman with wild gray hair and dark brown skin. The woman, who Bea was certain had not been there earlier, rocked slowly, lazily stitching at a large needlepoint spread across her lap. Every so often, when the sky dimmed, the needlepoint lady would look up and frown. Then she'd whistle quietly through her teeth or shake her head in a worried way.

A mangy dog and two skinny cats lay curled at the old woman's feet. Seeds scattered the sidewalk in front of them and Bea watched as a pigeon swooped down for a snack. To Bea's surprise, the bird ignored the seeds and landed on the woman's shoulder instead. The woman barely flinched as it pecked playfully at her ear and then, to Bea's dismay, appeared to pluck something edible out of her mass of gray curls. *Very odd*, Bea noted with another asterisk.

Just next door to *The Woven World* and directly across the street from Bea's front steps was perhaps the most intriguing storefront of all. It was not a proper shop, but a ground floor apartment that had been converted into a place of business. In the small picture window of what should have been the living room was a delightfully mysterious sign made of neon tubing and shaped like a hand: palm out, fingers together. Above it, in capital letters, was the word FORTUNETELLER. Underneath, in smaller letters, were the words *Tarot & Palm Readings*. On the sidewalk in front of the shop was another sign propped against the wall. In scraggly script it read:

See The Future
Find What's Lost
First Readings $10

Such strange little shops for such an ordinary street, Bea thought, noticing the sun had started to set behind the gray haze. Bea stood up and dusted off her shorts. She assumed enough time had passed that Nana Anna would allow her to come inside. However, just as she turned to head up the stairs, the neon sign in the Fortuneteller's window flickered to life. Bea sat back down immediately and reopened her notebook.

A moment later, a person emerged whom Bea had to assume was the fortuneteller herself. She looked as Bea had imagined she would, small and dark with shiny black hair pulled tightly into a braided bun. Woven through the heavy twist of hair were ribbons in varying shades of blue. She wore a simple tunic for a shirt, which shone vivid white against her coffee colored skin, and a full skirt with so many different colors and patterns it looked as if it had been pieced together from old clothes. She briskly swept the sidewalk in front of her shop, stopping only once to nod at the needlepoint lady next door. When she'd finished sweeping she held her hand out, palm up, as though testing for rain. Then she shook her head disappointedly and went back inside. She'd done nothing unusual and yet Bea was enthralled. *A real fortuneteller*, she wrote, adding an asterisk and then another.

As Bea stood up again, a dark-haired boy approximately her age rolled by on his skateboard. Bea had noticed him pass by a few times already that afternoon. Each time, Bea had made a point to look in the other direction. She had, however, made some notes to herself. The first one read: *Boy on skateboard - highly self-assured, maybe a Top Pop.* The second time he passed she added, *No afternoon sports practice and very into the skateboard thing, most likely a Specialist.* Yet after his third pass, he shot a white-toothed grin in her direction and she was forced to reconsider yet again. *Trying too hard,* she wrote, *probably an Almost.*

What she didn't write down was how tall and graceful he was, with the pink cheeks of a farm boy and shoulders already stretching wide under his t-shirt, as though he couldn't be more than fourteen. She could tell just by the way he moved that he knew he was handsome – and worse still, he lacked the decency to pretend that he didn't. In fact, on his next trip past her stairs, he skidded his skateboard to a stop, flicked his dark hair from his eyes and winked at her. Then he kicked off down the street to do some silly trick obviously designed to impress her. Bea added another note to her page: *Show-off. In love with himself. Ignore at all cost.*

CHAPTER 4

THE FIRST DAY OF SCHOOL

As if first days weren't bad enough, Bea's first day at Miss Huntington's School for Girls fell on Halloween. According to a letter she'd received days before, students were invited to attend class in costume. Of course this only added to Bea's concerns. Should she wear a costume? What if she chose something that the Top Pops considered silly or strange? Or what if they thought costumes were too babyish for seventh grade and she turned out to be the only one wearing one? And of course there was another problem. If the girls did choose to wear costumes, would she still be able to tell who was popular and who was not?

On Halloween morning Bea's jitters woke her up before the alarm went off. She had decided the night before that her safest course of action was to wear her uniform. It hung on her closet door, pressed to perfection by Nana Anna. Bea noted with a sigh how much it looked like every uniform she'd worn before: white shirt, blue plaid skirt, white socks and black shoes. After washing up, she pulled on the familiar garments and hurried downstairs for breakfast.

When Bea arrived in the dining room, she was delighted to find her father home and seated at the far end of the long table. After a brief welcome-home hug, Father began his daily ritual of reading newspapers from all over the world. He held an Egyptian paper in front of him as he ate, and although it blocked most of his face, Bea could see his forehead and the deep crease of worry that stretched across it.

Bea knew her father preferred to eat breakfast in silence, but she was feeling nervous and wanted to talk to someone. Hoping to get his attention, she scraped her plate with her fork loudly. She also tried bumping her chair around and slurping her juice, but nothing worked. Finally she blurted, "Father, do you think all the other girls will be wearing costumes?"

"I believe your school requires you to wear a uniform," he answered without taking his eyes from the paper.

"I know that, Father," she replied, trying not to sound exasperated, "but today is Halloween."

"Is that so?" he answered, laying his paper down beside his tea cup. "I've always been fascinated by Halloween."

"Really? Why?" Bea asked, genuinely surprised. Her father was rarely interested in childish things.

"Well," he answered, picking up another paper and scanning it briefly before continuing to speak, "Halloween has an interesting history. It has been celebrated in some form or another for hundreds of years. Around the eighth century, the Christians chose the first day of November as a holy day in honor of the saints. On the eve of that hallowed day, they honored the dead. This night became known as Hallows Eve, which in time evolved into what we now call Halloween." With that, he shook the paper open and began to read again. So much for chatting, Bea thought as she gathered her still-full plate and glass and headed towards the kitchen. As she passed her father, he put his paper to the side once more.

"Come here, Bianca," he said quietly.

"Yes, Father?" she said, setting her plate down on his end of the table.

"Are you alright?" he asked.

"I'll be fine," she replied, forcing herself to smile brightly. "You know me, I'm always fine." Bea didn't want her father to worry about her on top of whatever else he had on his mind.

He nodded and a pained expression passed over his face. He looked away.

"Are you alright?" she ventured, knowing he did not like to share his concerns.

"I'm fine," he answered with forced brightness. "Everything will be fine… and you, well, you are going to be more than fine. You are very rare and very special, Bianca, truly one of a kind." Then he cleared his throat and turned his attention back to the paper once again.

Bea dropped her dishes off in the sink and made her way to the front door in a daze. She was confused by her father's comments. He rarely spoke to her in such a fatherly way and instead of reassuring her it had somehow made her even more anxious.

At the front door, however, Nana Anna was her usual chatty self. "No need to be nervous, Bianca dear," she said, as if reading Bea's mind. She handed Bea her lunch bag. "Everything will go just as swimmingly as it always does. You are simply a wonder at making friends." She added smoothing Bea's hair. "And Halloween is a perfect day to go to school for the first time. I read somewhere that, without knowing it, people select costumes that reveal their true nature. So you see you'll be able to tell so much about the girls just by the costume they've chosen."

It was an interesting thought, and as Bea headed down the front steps she hoped very much that Nana Anna was right.

Miss Huntington's School for Girls was only a few blocks from her new home. As Bea expected, it was small and pristine with ivy running up the brick façade. Its appearance gave the impression that the students inside were all fresh-faced girls who ate oatmeal and apples for breakfast and who sat straight up in their chairs reciting their lessons in unison. Bea's father always selected schools that had this look to them, though Bea thought it foolish. As a scientist, he should know that things were not always what they appeared to be.

The main lobby of the school was painted a deep salmon color, with a large sweeping staircase that encircled the hall. The walls were adorned in keeping with the season, bright orange and black Halloween decorations interspersed with brown and yellow construction-paper leaves. It all looked quite cheerful and inviting and Bea hoped it was true.

She followed the large and somewhat lumpy headmistress up the oval stairs and down a long hall until they arrived at the door of her homeroom class. Bea tossed her hair behind her shoulders and braced herself. She knew from experience that it was important to look confident regardless of how she felt on the inside.

Bea stepped into the classroom and looked around for a seat, careful to avoid eye contact with anyone. Choosing the right seat was critical – not too far forward, not too far back, best if it was on one side of the room or the other so she could scope out the other students without appearing to look. Also, it was important not to sit in a seat normally occupied by a Top Pop. That could cause trouble early on. Since most of the girls had already arrived, Bea had only a few seats to choose from. She selected one about halfway back and close to the door. Once settled, she took the opportunity to observe her surroundings as she pulled her white notebook from her pack.

The girls were clustered in pairs and small groups and all of them were in costume. There was a cat talking to two princesses, a genie copying some notes from a superhero Bea didn't recognize, and two ballerinas, one in black and the other in pink, who seemed to be having a debate over a lunch bag. Nearby a witch was whispering something to a cheerleader who passed a note to a baseball player who was practicing clarinet with a baloney sandwich.

Bea smiled as she considered Nana Anna's theory. What could a baloney sandwich really reveal about someone's personality – that they were full of baloney? Bea giggled to herself and dug around in her bag for a pen so she could make some notes. When she looked up again, she found the two princesses were standing in front of her desk.

"Hi," said the smaller of the two.

"Hello," Bea answered with a friendly but guarded smile.

"So, what's so funny?" the taller princess asked.

"Pardon?" Bea answered.

"You were laughing just now and we'd like to know what the joke is."

"Oh, uh, nothing, just a funny thought," she answered carefully.

"Well, let's hear it then," the tall princess pressed.

Bea took a breath and thought about how to answer. She could tell immediately that these two girls were Top Pops. She needn't have worried that the costumes would confuse her. It was perfectly apparent in the way they stood, the tone of their voices, the shine of their hair. It seemed that no matter where she was in the world, popular girls looked exactly the same. For one thing, Top Pops were almost always pretty and these two princesses were no exception, particularly the smaller of the two. She was of Asian descent, probably Chinese or perhaps Korean, with a smooth flat face and a regal air. Her glossy black hair was expertly cut in a sharp, high-fashion bob that perfectly complemented her high cheekbones. On top of her flawless hair was a simple, porcelain tiara that appeared to be anchored in place by magic. Her gown, which was truly more like a gown than any costume Bea had ever seen, was a soft, off-white satin that fit her as if it were made for her, which it probably was.

The small princess flashed a fake but dazzling smile, complete with dimples and blindingly white teeth.

"Never mind that," she said, saving Bea from having to answer the uncomfortable question. "I'm Charlotte Wang and this is Amanda Whitehead."

Amanda, although tall, was a slightly chubby, blandly pretty girl with a round face. Her thick honey blond hair was curled and carefully arranged in a pile on top of her head. She wore an ornate silver crown encircling her curls and a puffy pink dress with dozens of bows in various shades of pastel. Although Bea

19

suspected the costume had cost as much as Charlotte's, the effect was totally different. Charlotte looked like a real princess and Amanda looked like a drugstore Easter basket.

"You must be the new girl," said Charlotte authoritatively. "So sorry you didn't get the letter that said you could wear a costume today. We so rarely get to dress in anything but our Huntington plaids."

Before Bea could make any reply, Amanda said in a falsely sweet voice, "Why, what do you mean Charlotte? She is wearing a costume. She's the ghost of Huntington School." Charlotte and several other girls nearby began to laugh.

Bea did not laugh, but she did not mind as much as this Amanda girl might have hoped. She was used to comments such as this from Top Pops like Amanda. Bea had always been tall, thin and very pale. Her skin was so light that in the winter she was frequently compared to milk or snow or the moon or cream cheese or sugar or paper or just about anything white you could think of. Her eyes were large and pale blue and her long, straight hair was the very lightest shade of yellow. On Halloween there was never a shortage of ghost jokes. She'd heard them all.

Bea flipped her hair back behind her shoulders and sat up straight. This insult was her first test. She took a deep breath and considered her options. There were three.

Option One: Try to ignore the comment. This was the parent and teacher favorite but despite their insistence, Bea found that this approach almost always led to further and more intense teasing.

Option Two: Try to laugh along with your assailant and maybe even make a joke at your own expense. The goal here is to make them think you're a good sport. This option works well, at least at first, but Bea had discovered it had an unfortunate down side - no one wanted a friend with no confidence. So making fun of yourself often backfired in the long run.

This left Option Three: To say or do the very thing you wished you had said or done a million times in a million situations but didn't because you were too scared. Option Three was not for everyone. It was always risky and in some schools even dangerous, but for Bea it was almost always superior to Options One and Two. So, looking directly at Princess Amanda, Bea summoned her courage and, with as much of her mild British accent as she could muster, she spoke.

"Well then, my turn is it? Now don't tell me… So if Charlotte here is Cinderella that would make you one of the ugly – I mean the wicked step-sisters, right?"

Charlotte and a few other girls sitting nearby burst into another round of laughter. Amanda's cheeks glowed fuchsia with anger.

Bea was more than a little grateful when the teacher appeared a moment later and instructed everyone to find a seat. She knew that although she'd gained the respect of several girls in the class, she had also made an enemy of Amanda Whitehead and that was going to come back to her for sure.

As soon as Charlotte and Amanda were safely across the room, Bea took a couple of deep breaths to calm herself. Option Three always took a bit out of her. She looked down at her notebook, and let her hair fall in front of her face.

From somewhere nearby she heard a whisper. "Don't cry, for Spirit's sake. That would just ruin it." Certain the voice had come from the girl behind her, Bea turned around. She was surprised, however, to find the seat unoccupied. When she turned back to the front she accidentally knocked her notebook to floor. There were giggles from the other side of the room.

Her notebook had landed under the chair of the girl in front of her. The girl, whom Bea had not noticed until now, was dressed as a gypsy with long black braids that hung three quarters of the way down her back. Oddly, the girl didn't move. She seemed totally unaware that the notebook had fallen.

"Pardon me?" Bea whispered. The girl did not turn around.

"Pardon me?" Bea said in a louder voice. Still she did not turn around.

"Ahem," Bea said, falsely clearing her throat. "Would you mind handing me my notebook? It's under your chair."

Finally the girl turned and their eyes met. Hers were startlingly black and as shiny as olives. The expression on her face was unreadable. After a moment the girl picked up the notebook and slid it silently onto Bea's desk.

"Thanks," Bea said, but the girl didn't answer. She just turned back towards the front of the classroom. It was only then that Bea noticed that the girl was not wearing a gypsy costume at all – just her plain plaid uniform, the same as Bea.

CHAPTER 5

THE FIRST FRIEND

Thankfully the rest of the day was uneventful. Bea moved through her classes – Social Studies, Math, and even PE – keeping a low profile, observing the other students and taking notes. Her impression was that Miss Huntington's School wasn't very different than any other. There were Top Pops and Almosts, Specialists and Not Pops in varying degrees and numbers. By the end of the day, Bea felt with some certainty that, with the exception of Amanda Whitehead, most of the girls would be easy to win over.

After school Bea rushed home, eager to get back to her spot on the front steps so she could see what the fortuneteller might be up to. She opened her white notebook to review the day's events, but as she flipped to a clean page, she noticed the skateboard boy rolling towards her. This time however, instead of rolling by, he stopped just inches away from the bottom step. He jumped gracefully from the board, kicked it up onto one end and caught the other in his hands.

"What's in the notebook?" he asked.

"Schoolwork," Bea answered, closing the book quickly.

"Homework on Halloween? Tragic."

Bea shrugged and opened the notebook again, hoping that if she looked busy he might go away. He didn't.

Instead, he tossed his hair from his eyes with a quick jerk of his head and raised one eyebrow in challenge, "The way I see it," he said, "you have a couple of choices here. You could come trick-or-treating with me or you could sit on your stoop all night doing homework."

"Sitting on my what?" Bea asked, thinking he might have said something rude.

"You know, the front steps here. Why?" he added with a smirk. "What did you think I meant?"

Bea felt a smile push at the corners of her mouth but she quickly suppressed the urge. She didn't want him to get the impression that she found him amusing. "I thought trick-or-treating was for little kids," she replied, using her most mature, not-impressed voice.

"Suit yourself," he said, "I mean if you think you're too old or something…What are you, about twenty-two, twenty-three?"

This time Bea almost smiled in spite of herself. "I'm twelve, almost thirteen," she answered. Then, before she thought long enough to stop the words from coming out of her mouth, she added, "And even if I wanted to go, I don't have a costume." Realizing what she had done, she braced herself for the inevitable ghost joke. To her surprise, none came.

Instead the boy said, "No, not too old then, though you are close to the limit. The bigger problem is the no-costume thing. Grownups really don't like it when you show up without one. But, hey no big deal, it might be just as entertaining to sit here on your stoop and watch the little kids freak out when they walk by."

Bea frowned. "And why would they do that?" she asked, thinking, Here comes the ghost joke. But again none came.

"You mean you don't know?" he asked, sounding genuinely surprised. He let out a low whistle and began flipping his skateboard from hand to hand. Bea didn't answer, but he continued anyway. "You just moved in here, right?"

Bea nodded.

"And no one told you about this place before you bought it?"

Bea shook her head. Whoever this kid was, he certainly had her attention. "Why, is there something we should know?"

"Aw, come on," said the boy, who was now grinning mischievously. "You never heard? This building is Barnacle Brightman's Brownstone. It's haunted, and that's a fact. Most kids wouldn't dare come to the door on Halloween night – or any other night, for that matter."

"Haunted?" Bea replied skeptically. Her family's home was definitely creepy but it had never occurred to her that it might be haunted. "And who haunts it exactly?"

"Well, Barnacle Bill of course."

"Do you mean Admiral William Brightman?"

"I guess that's his real name," the boy answered. "I do remember something about him being in the Navy."

Bea shook her head in disbelief. "My grandfather?" she said mostly to herself.

"What?" The boy let his skateboard fall to the ground with a loud thud. "Did you say *grandfather*?"

"Well, yes," she answered. "My name is Bianca Brightman, but everyone calls me Bea. This is my family's home."

"Wow," said the boy, staring at her with new interest.

"And you are…?"

"Oh, sorry," the boy answered, flipping his skateboard back up on end and catching it in his left hand. He brushed the other hand against his pant leg several times before sticking it out to shake. "People call me Indy. I live down there," he added, tipping his head towards the end of the street.

"Nice to meet you," Bea said, surprised to meet someone her own age that shook hands.

The official introduction seemed to make Indy feel even more comfortable because without being asked, he leaned his skateboard against the stairs and took a seat on the step next to her.

"So how do you know so much about my grandfather?" Bea

asked, having given up on trying to get rid of him.

"Well," said Indy, "I've lived around here my whole life, and pretty much everyone who lives around here knows about Barnacle Bill."

"And they think he was crazy?"

"Well, that's what people say anyway," Indy replied, suddenly hesitant. "I mean, I didn't know him or anything..."

"You won't offend me," Bea assured him. "I've never met him either. I mean, he died just after I was born, I think."

Indy studied her face for a moment and then nodded. "Well…the way I've heard it, your grandfather was nuts. And not just ordinary crazy but like major-sized-hole-in-his-bag-of-marbles crazy."

Bea felt her cheeks get hot and knew she was blushing. Despite what she had promised, part of her was a little insulted. *What did this boy really know about anything, let alone her grandfather?*

"Go on," she said, making sure her voice still sounded friendly.

"Well, the story I've heard is that he spent most of his life traveling on ships, going to all sorts of places to buy old stuff, worth a lot of money. But something went weird on his last trip and when he finally got home he had pretty much lost it."

"Lost the stuff?" Bea asked.

"No, not the stuff," said Indy, grinning. "His mind – he lost his mind. He would walk up and down the street going on about how he was a knight of the realm, you know, like from old storybooks. It probably wouldn't have been so bad but sometimes he would grab people walking by and try to knight them with this old sword he carried around. People complained, tried to get him locked up."

"Oh my," Bea heard herself say, half-enthralled and half-embarrassed.

"Yup," Indy agreed, "definitely rowing with one oar. Anyway, before they could get him committed, he kicked. It was Halloween night. He came down the stairs here shouting and carrying on. He got a pretty good crowd going since people were out trick-or-treating and all. Then he just died – had a heart attack right here in front of the house." Indy got up and stood in a spot on the sidewalk right in front of where Bea was sitting. "Ever since then, people say he haunts the house."

Bea nodded slowly. She couldn't think of an appropriate response to the news she had just received. It wasn't that she doubted it. The opposite was true. It made perfect sense. It explained why Father hadn't returned to New York in such a long time and why he had never told her about his parents.

"Are you all right?" Indy asked.

"Sure," she replied, straightening herself up and flipping her hair behind her shoulders.

Indy sat back down and looked around at the street. "You've got a pretty good view from here" he said. "You can even see Mr. Green's clock shop."

Bea looked back at Indy and smiled a genuine smile. Maybe this Indy kid was alright after all. At least he knew when to change the subject. She was just about to share her observations on the Clock Shop Man when Nana Anna stuck her head out the front door.

"Dinner time, Miss Bea. Would your friend like to join us?"

Indy accepted immediately.

Bea wasn't sure she was entirely comfortable with the idea of having Indy to dinner, having just met him, and she grew even more uncomfortable as they stepped across the threshold. Although Nana Anna and Cookie had been cleaning the house diligently since the day they'd moved in, Bea was embarrassed by how old and run down it was. Indy would surely think it was haunted as soon as he saw it. However, when Indy walked in, he looked dazzled.

"This place is fantastic!" he exclaimed. "I can't believe you actually live here. My dad told me these places used to be single-family residences but I've never seen one in its original state before."

"It certainly is in its original state," Bea replied. "I don't think anyone has done anything to care for it in years."

"It's a little beat-up but the bones are great" he replied. "My dad could do wonders with it."

"The bones?" Bea asked, thinking he might be referring to her crazy dead grandfather.

"You know, the frame of the house, the shape of the rooms and doorways, the high ceilings, these moldings over here. Oh and that fireplace," he said, pointing into the dining room. "I've never seen anything like it."

"Oh, *those* bones," she replied, relieved. "How do you know so much about old buildings?"

"That would be interesting to hear," her father agreed as he entered the room.

Bea's father was strikingly tall and slender. Like Bea, he had pale skin and sharp features that made his face look older than he was. As always, he was dressed in a dark suit and in the dimly lit hallway, he looked very much like an undertaker. Bea saw Indy take an unconscious step backward as he approached.

"How do you do? I'm Dr. Brightman," her father said, holding out his hand to Indy.

Indy took a breath and bravely stepped forward again to shake it.

To Bea's astonishment, her father and Indy seemed to get on quite well. Through dinner they talked about old houses and the methods and materials used to build them. Although Bea wasn't particularly interested in the topic, she was relieved that Indy could carry on a respectable conversation. He even had decent table manners, although he ate more than Bea thought a person could or should. When dinner was over, Bea walked Indy to the front door.

"This was fun," he said. "I've never had dinner in a haunted house before."

He pulled opened the huge front door and it creaked loudly as if to punctuate his joke. When he got to the stair they had been sitting on earlier, he turned around.

"I have to help my dad at work tomorrow, but maybe I'll see you on Friday."

"Okay," Bea answered hoping to sound nonchalant.

When he was gone, she closed the door and opened her notebook. *Not a total idiot after all.*

CHAPTER 6

THE FAVORITE TEACHER

The second day of school started out much better than the first. Just seeing the girls in their uniforms instead of their Halloween costumes made Bea feel more like she belonged. Also, Charlotte, who Bea determined was the top Top Pop, made a point to say hello to her that morning and Amanda, although not friendly, seemed to have lost interest in her altogether.

Just after Art and before lunch, Bea was scheduled for English Literature, which, along with Science, was her favorite subject. She was even more excited because according to the girls at her Art table, the new English teacher, Mr. Morton, was amazing. In fact they were so gushy and giggly when they were speaking of him that at first Bea thought they were discussing a boyfriend or perhaps a celebrity.

Unfortunately, Bea got lost somewhere between the Art room and her locker and by the time she found the English Lit classroom, class was already in progress. The students were silent as she opened the door and all eyes watched her as she made her way to the only available seat which was, of course, in the front row.

As Bea got herself settled, she studied Mr. Morton out of the corner of her eye. She couldn't help but be a bit surprised by the look of him. The way the other girls had spoken, she had expected someone handsome. Mr. Morton was not. Not that he was ugly. He wasn't. It was just that there was nothing exceptional about his looks at all. He was neither tall nor short; his skin was neither dark nor light, his hair was neither blond nor brunette. He wore plain pants and a white shirt and was, overall, so completely nondescript that had he not been their teacher she might not have noticed him at all. Bea pulled out her notebook and smoothed out the page in front of her; *remarkably unremarkable*, she wrote.

However, as she finished her notation, Bea got a funny feeling. Why was everyone still so quiet? Although she was seated and clearly no longer disrupting anything, the class had not resumed its progress. She looked up to find Mr. Morton looking at her, studying her, with a strangely amused look on his face. After several more uncomfortable seconds he finally spoke.

"You must be Miss Brightman," he said, sounding out her last name as if it tasted bad in his mouth. "I believe I heard something of your enrollment. You are the daughter of Dr. Nathan Brightman. Is that correct?"

Bea nodded. She was not surprised by the question as many of her past teachers had also heard of her father.

"Well," he said gesturing to the class, "We are honored to have such a luminary among us. Aren't we ladies?" A few of the girls giggled but no one spoke. "But let's be clear on one thing," he said turning back to her abruptly, the humor gone from his voice, "just because your father is a well-known archeologist does not mean that we will tolerate bad behavior from you."

Bea could feel her cheeks getting pink. She cleared her throat and said, "Yes, of course not. I'm sorry I was late. I got lost."

"Oh you got lost? How very unfortunate," said Mr. Morton

smiling vaguely. "Apparently you didn't inherit your father's aptitude for finding things."

"I, uh…"

"Please don't explain," said Mr. Morton, cutting Bea off, "I think we've heard enough already," he added rolling his eyes at the class conspiratorially, as if they'd all agree Bea was prattling on. "You've wasted enough of our time already, so if you don't mind, we'll get on with the lesson."

Bea's cheeks burned with embarrassment.

"So," Mr. Morton called out to the room, "who here can tell me anything about King Arthur?"

Bea glanced over her shoulder at the other girls. Most of them were staring mutely up at Mr. Morton, their eyes wide with admiration, not a single hand in the air.

"Come now," said Mr. Morton crossing to the other side of the room, "one of you very lovely ladies must have heard something about King Arthur."

Several of the girls giggled like idiots at being called lovely. Everyone else remained silent. Finally, Bea raised her hand. She knew a lot about King Arthur. It was one of her favorite stories. Perhaps a smart answer would prove she had no intention of riding on her father's reputation.

Mr. Morton nodded enthusiastically when he saw her. "Miss Brightman, how delightful you're feeling confident enough to participate on your very first day."

Bea hesitated. *What was that supposed to mean? Was he setting her up to embarrass her again?* It was too late to put her hand down so she cleared her throat and said, "King Arthur was the King of Briton in the early sixth century. Many stories have been written about him but he was most famous for bringing all the kingdoms of Briton together and leading them to victory against the Saxon invaders."

When Bea finished, Mr. Morton stared at her for several seconds, stroking his clean-shaven chin thoughtfully. "And you are certain of that, Miss Brightman?" he asked, a small smirk dancing around the sides of his mouth.

Bea quickly reviewed her answer in her head. The date was

correct and her facts seemed in order so she nodded.

"Well, then, it's lucky this wasn't a test," he said smugly, "Because you are totally and utterly wrong."

Bea felt another rush of blood color her cheeks and heard a few quiet giggles behind her.

Mr. Morton turned to the class and smiled cheerfully. "Although Miss Brightman did have some sense of the timeline, she left out the most important point of all. Can anyone tell me what that is?"

He paused for a moment. "No, of course you can't," he said smiling adoringly as if looking at a room filled with toddlers. "King Arthur," he continued loudly, "is a storybook character; a myth, a legend. To hear Miss Brightman tell it you'd think he was a real king. He was not. That is why we are studying him here in English Literature and not in History. The story of Arthur's reign is a fabrication created and glorified by authors of fiction."

Without thinking, Bea opened her mouth to disagree. Many people, including her father, believed Arthur had quite possibly been a real person or at least an amalgamation of people. However, a glance at Mr. Morton's triumphant face made her change her mind.

"Do you have more to say, Miss Brightman?" he exclaimed, sounding delighted at the possibility. There was no doubt in her mind that he intended to embarrass her again. She sucked in a mouthful of air and willed herself not to show any emotion. "I'm sure we'd all love to hear your theories."

Bea could feel her face go red for a third time but this time it was anger that rose to her cheeks. *Why was he giving her such a hard time?* She probably knew more about King Arthur than anyone in the room. Hotheadedly, she put her hand up again.

"Yes, Miss Brightman," said Mr. Morton, a nasty look of enjoyment on his face.

"Many people believe that King Arthur was a real person or at least that parts of the legend are true," she said, her voice only a little tighter than normal.

Mr. Morton's eyebrows went up, "Like your father perhaps?"

He grinned and turned to the room. "Does he believe in Santa Claus too?"

The class laughed.

Bea felt her throat tighten with anger, "The Annales Cambriae…" she began, referencing an ancient book on the history of Wales, but then someone whispered urgently from behind her. *Just drop it. You can't win.* Bea stopped talking in mid-sentence and glanced behind her to see who had spoken. All the girls close enough to her were looking at Mr. Morton; all but the gypsy girl whose eyes were riveted to her desktop.

When she turned back to the front of the room, Mr. Morton was standing in front of her, blinking innocently. "Miss Brightman, why did you stop? We're all fascinated. What was it you were saying?"

"Nothing," she answered; her voice barely audible.

"Nothing," he repeated to class. "I see. So, may I take that to mean that we are in agreement that King Arthur was not a real king?"

Bea bit down on her tongue to keep herself from talking. She looked down at her notebook and he took the movement to be a nod.

"Excellent," he said. "If you intend to survive my class, I suggest you keep your silly ideas to yourself."

"Yes sir," she managed, swallowing the queasy feeling that had welled up in the back of her throat.

Then, as if nothing could have pleased him more, he laughed and spread his arms out grandly to the class, "Well, this has been a lively discussion, hasn't it? You know your assignment, four chapters in Pyle's *King Arthur and his Knights* by next week.

Relieved the class was finally over, Bea packed her books into her bag and left as quickly as she could; English Literature officially off her list of favorite subjects.

CHAPTER 7

THE SCIENCE PROJECT

The last class before lunch was double period Science Lab. The teacher was a fish-faced woman with the unfortunate luck to be named Miss Trout. Miss Trout was pleasant enough but painfully boring. She began the lesson with the announcement that the girls would be starting a new project in which there were three topic choices, which she explained in painstaking detail. Although Bea loved Science almost as much as she loved Literature, she was having trouble focusing, for she was dreading what was coming next.

Just as Bea expected, when Miss Trout's lecture finally ended, she instructed the students to select a lab partner. The girls excitedly moved into pairs, shuffling their chairs loudly.

This would not have been a problem if Bea had been at school even a week. By then, she'd likely have her choice of partners. Instead, by virtue of her newness, she had to sit patiently watching the other girls pair up, knowing from previous new-girl experience that she would either end up a third wheel, added to a pair who didn't really want her, or partnered with the most unpopular Not Pop in the class. This time the latter was her fate and Bea was partnered with the one girl no one else wanted. To her surprise, that girl turned out to be the gypsy girl from Homeroom.

Bea glanced over at the gypsy girl. Was she a Clueless or a Rogue, Bea wondered? Physically, she didn't fit in to either category. Though her uniform was a bit too small and noticeably worn, it looked freshly washed and neatly pressed. Her dark hair was clean and carefully arranged in two long tight braids, tied at the bottom with pale blue ribbons. Her nails were well groomed and her dark skin was flawlessly smooth. She had no dandruff or sniffles or hangnails or snotty tissues or funny smells and the only accessory she wore was a pretty circle of tiny rubies on a chain around her neck. In fact, if someone were to notice her at all, which was unlikely, they might think she was one of the prettiest girls in the class.

Consequently, Bea had to assume that Nisha Lakewood, as that was her name, was a Rogue and unpopular by choice. But here again there were no apparent signs. She didn't seem to want any trouble and she certainly didn't make any noise. She looked only at the teacher and her books and between classes she waited for the other students to leave before entering the hallway. It was as if she were trying to attract as little attention as possible.

Once the lab partners were established and everyone was settled, Miss Trout instructed the class to gather their lab equipment and line up at the sink. Each team was to wash, dry and label each piece of equipment with their topic and a team name.

The other girls chatted quietly as they lined up, some whispering their ideas in each other's ears. Bea looked at Nisha as they took their place in line but Nisha was staring at the floor.

"So, what topic do you think we should cover?" Bea ventured. "I think Heredity and Genetics sounds interesting."

Nisha shrugged.

Bea tried again. "I'm not that interested in Weather and Climate, particularly with the weather being so dull lately, but I'd be okay with the Properties of Water if that sounds better to you."

Nisha shrugged again, her movements barely perceptible.

"Okay, then let's go with Heredity and…" Bea began, but at the same moment Amanda Whitehead pushed past Nisha, bumping her into Bea.

The Properties of Water, Nisha blurted suddenly.

Startled, Bea looked at Nisha sideways but Nisha's eyes were still focused on the floor in front of her.

"Okay," Bea said slowly, "The Properties of Water it is."

Nisha lifted her head abruptly and her black eyes met Bea's for a moment. Her expression was a mixture of surprise and curiosity.

"Like I said, I'm fine with either one," Bea continued, assuming Nisha wasn't used to having someone agree with her. "So," she plugged on, "what do you think we should name our team?"

Nisha looked away, shrugging yet again.

"How about the Gypsy Princesses?" Bea said as they stepped up to one of the sinks thinking Nisha looked even more like a Gypsy princess up close.

As they eased their items into the sink full of water, Nisha shrugged yet again. Then suddenly she spoke. *"The Gypsy Princesses? Does she really think I don't get it? She doesn't even know me and already she's insulting me. I should suggest we call ourselves the Angels because that what she looks like, like something from the spirit world."*

How odd, Bea thought as she pulled the magnifying glass out of the water to dry it. She looked at Nisha carefully out the corner of her eye. Nisha was diligently washing a measuring cup. She hadn't even looked up. No wonder she's unpopular, Bea thought. She is seriously strange.

Knowing they were going to be partners for the rest of the year, Bea tried not to overreact. She took a deep breath, dunked the other measuring cup into the water. "I've heard the angel thing a lot. I guess when you're as pale as I am… anyway, I wasn't making fun of you. I meant the gypsy princess thing as a compliment."

Nisha looked up at Bea, her black eyes were round with

surprise. "What did you say?" she asked in a gravelly whisper.

"I said, I didn't mean the gypsy princess thing to be an insult. I mean, isn't that what you said; that you thought it was an insult?" Bea answered.

"No," said Nisha staring at her intently, "I didn't say anything at all."

For several seconds the girls stood looking at each other blankly. Finally, Bea said, "We'd better get this washing done, other people are waiting." Both girls put their hands back in the sink to see if there was anything left behind. *I'm sure she said something*, Bea thought. *Why is she denying it?*

I am not denying anything, Nisha replied, *I didn't say anything.*

Both girls looked up startled. For several seconds, they stared right into each other's eyes. Neither one had spoken yet both had heard the other. Someone in line behind them said, "Hurry up you guys, everyone's waiting!"

With her eyes still locked on Nisha's, Bea thought, *Can you hear what I'm thinking now?*

Yes, Nisha answered without saying a word

Bea's thoughts started spinning so fast she was having trouble honing in on one. *How is this possible…can you believe…it's incredible!* Bea thought to Nisha in a rush.

I…I don't know, Nisha thought back hesitantly.

Suddenly Miss Trout was standing beside them.

"Is there something going on here?" she asked looking from Nisha to Bea and back again.

"No ma'am," the girls replied in harmony.

"Then I suggest you move along, there are others waiting."

"Yes ma'am," they answered.

Bea pulled her hands from the soapy water and quickly moved away from the sink. The girls took their kit back to the desk and dried each piece in silence. Bea kept trying to speak to Nisha with her mind. *Can you hear me?* she asked her over and over again. *If you can hear me blink your eyes twice.*

Finally she gave up. "It doesn't work anymore," she said out loud.

"No, it doesn't seem to," Nisha whispered. Her strange,

sand-covered voice was filled with relief.

Bea's mind raced. *Did that really happen? Had she really heard Nisha's thoughts? Maybe this Nisha Lakewood person had some kind of mind-reading ability? Or maybe it had something to do with the sink and putting their hands in the water?*

When they were seated, Bea turned to Nisha, expecting she'd be equally curious. Instead Nisha was glancing nervously around the room. *She's afraid*, Bea thought. *She's frightened that I'm going to tell the other kids.*

Bea considered her next step carefully. She didn't want to scare Nisha off before she'd learned how the mind reading had happened.

"We still need a name for our team," Bea said hoping that a change of subject would calm Nisha down and get her talking again. "How about the Blue Ribbons? You know like winning a blue ribbon means you're the best and also because you wear blue ribbons?"

Nisha nodded once in agreement.

"Great," Bea said and turned her attention to filling out the labels, trying not to let her expression reveal the intense curiosity that was burning in her head. If she was going to find out more from Nisha, she needed to reassure her that she wasn't going to give away her secret. When the bell rang, Nisha stood abruptly. Bea stood too, stepping in Nisha's path.

"Listen," she said leaning in conspiratorially, "I know we barely know each other but we are going to be lab partners so, um, perhaps we should keep what happened at the sink just between us. I mean at least until we can figure it out anyway. What do you think?"

Nisha's black eyes met Bea's blue ones. She nodded once then stepped quickly around Bea and rushed out the door.

CHAPTER 8

THE FLYING BOY

Bea inched her way down the lunch line, barely noticing the selections. For the last three days she'd been avoiding the lunchroom, asking Cookie to make her a bag lunch which she'd been eating in the library. She'd learned from past experience that it was better to avoid the cafeteria until you were certain of being included at a good table. However, Nana Anna had tired of this arrangement, already having so much to do around the house. She sent Bea to school with lunch money rather than food and Bea found herself exactly where she didn't want to be, on the perimeter of the lunchroom, holding a tray, and scanning the floor for a seat.

Of course all of the tables were packed with girls, and she felt her appetite being replaced with that awful new-girl feeling in her stomach. She looked over the field of faces and felt certain they were all ignoring her on purpose. *Don't be silly*, Bea instructed herself, *they're just eating lunch*. As if she could shake the feeling away, she tossed her head back so her long hair fell neatly behind her shoulders. She scanned the room again. There, in the corner, an almost empty table. She took a deep breath and headed towards it.

As she got closer, she saw that its only occupant was Nisha Lakewood. Bea stopped. Should she sit with Nisha? Although Bea had hoped for another chance to talk to Nisha about what had happened in Science Lab, sitting with a Not Pop was a big risk. Still, hovering between tables with a full lunch tray wasn't doing her much good either. With no other option presenting itself, Bea made her way through the maze of students towards Nisha's table.

Nisha looked up in surprise as she approached. Bea smiled and was about to say hello when someone grabbed her sleeve and began pulling her away.

"I simply can't let *that* happen!" Charlotte Wang whispered loudly enough for Nisha to hear her.

"Wait, what?" Bea asked, trying to hold her tray steady as Charlotte tugged at her arm.

"Trust me," Charlotte said, "you want to sit with us."

Bea smiled to herself. Charlotte Wang was going out of her way to invite her to the Top Pop's table. This was good.

"Well…thanks," Bea said innocently, letting herself be guided to a crowded table at the center of the room.

"Make some room, you guys!" Charlotte called out.

After some shuffling, Bea was squeezed in between Amanda and a small blond girl who introduced herself as Candy. Charlotte slipped into her seat across from Amanda and quickly introduced the girls at the table. "This is Liz and Claire and Becca and Justina and Karen and Gianna and Alex and Lauren and, well, you already know Amanda."

Bea smiled politely as her eyes traveled over their faces. Most were Top Pops with a few Almosts sprinkled in. Not bad for only her second day. She was feeling quite pleased with herself until her glance rested on Amanda. Amanda glared back at her and for a moment Bea thought Amanda might protest to her presence. Instead she turned her back to Bea with a snap of her thick, blond ponytail.

Bea set her shoulders back and forced herself to smile even wider. "How do you do?" Bea said glancing from girl to girl, memorizing their names as she went.

"Oh, I just love your accent!" said Justina.

"Me too!" said Becca, "It sounds so grown up and smart."

"Thanks," Bea said smiling confidently. She knew the next few minutes were critical. She had to play it right. There were too many girls at the table to try to talk to all of them, so she decided to take the quiet approach and let them talk to her. It was a good decision, for Alex jumped in right away.

"Sometimes people think I'm English with my Boston accent and all," she said.

"Oh sure they do, Alex," Liz retorted sarcastically. "And do those same people tell you that Mr. Morton is madly in love with you?"

Everyone laughed.

Alex put her hand to her mouth in mock distress. "You mean he's not?" she said. "Now you've gone and ruined English Lit for me, and it was the only class I liked!"

"I agree," said Charlotte. "Mr. Morton is the only good teacher we've got. Not like boring Miss Trout. Science is the worst and now with Lab it's absolutely endless!"

"Well, at least you have me," said Amanda, turning to face the table again. "I mean, think of poor Bea. She has to partner with Nisha Lakewood! Really, it could not be worse."

With the mention of her name, Bea realized that she'd forgotten all about Nisha. She glanced back over her shoulder and saw Nisha eating quietly, looking down at her tray. A wave of guilt washed through her. She turned back to the table and asked, "What do you mean? What's so bad about her?"

"What do you mean, what do I mean?" asked Amanda incredulously. "Can't you tell she's a total freak?"

"Um, well, she is a bit odd, I guess," Bea agreed. "She doesn't talk very much."

"Take my word for it; she's a freak," said Amanda.

"Oh Amanda, come on. Not this again," said Candy.

"Look, if you had seen what I saw, you would know why I can't get over it."

"What did you see?" Bea asked, intrigued. Was it possible

that Amanda had somehow witnessed Nisha's mind-reading too?

"I saw a kid fly. That's what I saw," said Amanda.

"Fly?"

"Oh, please don't get her started," said Candy.

"Yes, please not again," said Justina.

"Well, why don't we ask Bea if she wants to hear it?" said Amanda, looking over at Bea with one eyebrow lifted in a sort of challenge.

"Well, yes, I suppose I would," Bea answered with an apologetic shrug. "Sorry, but I don't know how I can pass on a story about a flying kid."

Amanda grinned and turned her whole self towards Bea. "It's best you know about it, seeing that you're going to have to deal with her all the time." Amanda took a long breath and looked around. Then she leaned in and began in a whisper. "It happened in kindergarten…"

"Kindergarten?" Bea interrupted in surprise. It was almost impossible for Bea to imagine going to school with anyone for that long.

"Uh, yeah," said Amanda annoyed at being interrupted, "a lot of us went to public kindergarten together because Miss Huntington's doesn't start until first grade."

Bea nodded and Amanda continued.

"Anyway, as I was saying, Nisha and I were in kindergarten when it happened. It was the day that Charlie Campbell got stuck on top of the monkey bars."

At this point, in spite of themselves, the other girls had quieted down to listen as Amanda continued.

"We were at recess and a bunch of kids had formed a circle around him, chanting; *jump, jump, jump*."

"Remind me again why you were encouraging a five year old boy to leap to his death?" asked Liz.

"Well you didn't know him," said Amanda. "He was one of those wimpy little kids, completely annoying."

"Oh, well in that case…" said Liz sarcastically, and Bea did her best to suppress a grin.

"Really Liz, we were five," said Amanda. "We didn't know he could die." Amanda rolled her eyes at Liz and continued. "Anyway, out of nowhere comes Nisha who even back then barely said a word. But there she was, standing by the side of the monkey bars, and she was watching the crowd shout at Charlie. Well, wouldn't you know it; the little freak starts to get mad. 'Stop it!' she shouts at us in her weird frog voice. 'Leave him alone.' Of course everyone thinks this is funny and starts chanting even louder."

"Then, and this is the freaky part, Nisha steps forward with her arm out in front of her." Amanda raised her arm in front of her to demonstrate. "Her eyes were half closed and she had a really strange look on her face. She calls up to Charlie 'Fly, Charlie, just fly!'"

"Suddenly, and I swear this is true, Charlie lifts off into the air and just like that, he's flying. I mean literally flying through the air. Of course, when he realizes what is happening, he freaks out. He starts screaming and kicking his legs and basically going crazy. And who could blame him, really? But then all the kicking gets him really messed up and out of control. He goes crashing into a tree and falls to the ground and we hear this loud noise like a stick breaking. Turns out it was his arm. Needless to say, we were all completely freaked out."

All the girls at the table were listening now, and even a few girls from nearby tables had drifted over to hear the story. Amanda continued:

"When the teachers arrived, we tried to explain to them what happened. We told them how Nisha told Charlie that he could fly and then he did. Of course the teachers didn't believe us. They assumed that Nisha was trying to get Charlie to jump and had convinced him that he could fly. They blamed her for Charlie falling. And if you think about it, it really was her fault. They expelled her and good thing because, like I said, she's a total freak."

"She was expelled?" Bea asked, not entirely believing the story she was hearing.

"Yeah, and she deserved it," said Amanda indignantly. "She

43

disappeared for a while. I think she was home-schooled. But come fourth grade, she shows up here and now we have to deal with her all over again at Huntington's. I just can't imagine how someone like her can be allowed to go to a school like this."

"Mmmm," said Liz, considering the story, "if I didn't know you were the most unimaginative person on earth, I'd say you made the whole thing up."

"Very funny," said Amanda, "but every word of it is true, right, Becca?"

"Well my brother Ben does tell a pretty similar story," said Becca. "He was there and he claims the kid flew."

"What about you, Bea, do you believe me?" asked Amanda.

Bea thought for a moment before answering Amanda's question. She could tell it was a test. And, after the comment she made on Halloween about Amanda's costume, she knew she had to answer yes if she wanted things to smooth out between them. At the same time, Bea didn't like Amanda. She had told the story about Nisha as if Nisha had done something wrong. It seemed to Bea that Nisha was only trying to help a scared little boy. Plus, she was only five at the time. Maybe she believed he could fly. Or maybe ... no, there was no way she could make a little boy fly...*was there?*

"Well, Bea, what do you think?" Amanda pressed.

Bea nodded hesitantly. In spite of the fact that Amanda was awful, it was possible she was telling some version of the truth. Hadn't Bea herself witnessed Nisha doing something extraordinary? "I think you saw what you saw," said Bea trying to appease Amanda without actually agreeing.

Amanda smiled slyly, "Then you agree she's a total freak?"

"Well, uh, no, I didn't say that," Bea answered quickly.

"Well, then what do you think she is?" asked Amanda.

"I'm not sure yet," Bea replied, biting back the urge to say, "but I'm pretty sure I know what you are."

CHAPTER 9

THE FLEA MARKET

On Saturday morning, Bea's father suggested they go on a treasure hunt. What he meant was a visit to an antique shop or flea market looking for artifacts that people had mistaken for junk and of course, looking for the lost coin. Bea supposed other kids would find this sort of thing boring, but she loved it. It was fascinating to peruse all the old things, wondering where they came from and why they were left behind.

Most of their hunts were fruitless. They shopped for hours only to come home with sunburned cheeks and dust on their clothes, but every once in a while it paid off. The summer before last, in Lisbon, Father found an ancient Indian earring; and another time, in Morocco, they found the missing claw from a hand-carved 15th-century Chinese Dragon. For Father it counted as work, but for Bea it was just plain fun.

Saturday was warm, much warmer than a November day in New York should be. There wasn't even a hint of the winter that was due any day. The air was a dull, heavy gray, as if a wool blanket had been placed over the sun. Bea and her father took the crosstown bus and arrived in time to get some apple cider before heading to the back of the market.

They moved past several booths: old clothes, glassware, hand-painted furniture. These items were of little interest to Father. His focus was always the same; jewelry, figurines, pottery, and, of course, coins. In many of their expeditions, Bea and her father would often find a bowl or bin of dusty shekels shoved in the corner or under a table and nothing excited Father more. One by one, he would examine them, holding each coin up to the light, then under a magnifying glass. Sometimes he'd jot a few notes in his notebook or weigh the coins in the palm of his hand. He'd start out eagerly, charged up by the possibility of discovery, but by the time he reached the bottom of the basket, his earlier enthusiasm would be gone as if he'd spent it one coin at a time.

As they headed down the second aisle, Bea's father stopped and knelt to examine several large earthenware pots that were pushed under one of the booths. Bea stood quietly behind him, her eyes wandering over the tables nearby. One held macramé plant holders and the one next to it displayed war memorabilia. A bit further up the aisle Bea spotted a display of jewelry cases on a dark blue tablecloth.

"I'll be down here a bit," she said. Her father nodded distractedly.

The cases were filled with sparkling pendants, bracelets and earrings, and although Bea thought many of the pieces were beautiful, she was less interested than she would normally be. Her mind was elsewhere, her thoughts returning again and again to Nisha Lakewood and all that had happened in school over the last few days.

Bea's logical brain insisted that what had occurred in Science Lab had to have been some kind of a trick. However, when she factored in Amanda's story about Nisha and the boy, Charlie Campbell, in the playground, Bea couldn't help but wonder if there was something more going on, something not easily explained. Was it possible that Nisha Lakewood could really do magical things like make a boy fly or read minds?

Unconsciously, Bea drifted down the aisle to another jewelry booth, glancing unseeingly at the items on display. Although the air was still, she felt a small chill on the back of her neck, and when she lifted her head up, there, across the table, was Nisha Lakewood.

Nisha didn't see Bea. She was facing in the other direction, talking with a small old woman who was dressed in a vibrant colored skirt and an old black sweater patched at the elbows. The woman's dark hair was coiled up into a bun on the back of her head and tied with deep blue ribbons. Though the woman's face was partially hidden from view, Bea was certain it could only be one person; the fortuneteller from her street.

The fortuneteller and Nisha were standing very close to one another and whispering intently. With one hand, Nisha played nervously with the circular pendant that hung around her neck, and with the other, she was gesturing at something small and shiny at the far end of the table. The fortuneteller nodded and began to dig through a small purse. Bea's mind was whirring with questions. Was Nisha somehow related to the fortuneteller? There was definitely a resemblance: the hair, the skin color, the dark black eyes. If she was, maybe it could explain the mind reading. Maybe it was some kind of fortuneteller's trick. As Bea got closer, she could hear pieces of their conversation.

"You must stay right here and don't let anyone touch it. I have to go home and get some money from Graydon," the fortuneteller said.

Bea inched her way further along the table, determined to get a closer look at what they were discussing. It didn't take long before her eyes landed on a large coin lying in a wooden box among some pins and war medallions. The coin was about the size of a silver dollar but golden in color and very, very old. Parts of it were dirty or rusted but the metal underneath was beautiful, almost liquid, and glowing in the dull gray air. There was an engraving of some kind that looked like a braid or maybe a knot. Bea was mesmerized. She stared at the coin, unable to look away. Then, suddenly, she felt an overwhelming desire to touch it.

She reached out to pick it up, and at the same time, Nisha,

who she had nearly forgotten about, also turned and reached for the coin. Their fingers arrived at the coin at exactly the same instant and a powerful jolt shot through Bea's fingertips. Then everything was black and she felt as if she were falling. *I must be fainting*, she thought, but the thought was not her own.

Bea wasn't sure what happened next. She only knew she was no longer holding the coin, and that her fingers were stinging as if they had been burned.

Bea grabbed the table to steady herself, then looked over at Nisha. Had she felt it? Nisha's expression was blank, but her deep eyes were staring hard into Bea's. Bea opened her mouth to speak, but knew from the look on Nisha's face that it would be no use. Her best bet would be to find her father and see what he could make of the unusual coin.

I need to find Father, Bea thought taking a quick glance back at the coin to be sure it was still there.

She spotted him just where she'd left him, crouching beside a stack of pots. However, the narrow aisle was now crowded, and it took her a minute or two to reach him. By the time she got there, she felt panicked, although she couldn't explain exactly why. She just knew they had to get that coin. She tapped him urgently on the shoulder.

"Father, you've got to see this!"

"See what, dear?" he asked, still examining the old pottery. "Look at this one!" he said excitedly, holding up a small bowl. "I think it's Incan." He shook his head in wonder.

"They're nice, Dad," she agreed, glancing back towards the table with the coin, "but you've…"

Without turning around, her father said, "Bianca, you know I prefer to be called Father. Dad is so pedestrian. Not even in the United States for a month and you're calling me…"

Bea sucked in a mouthful of air and tried again. "Father," she huffed at the back of his head. "You know I prefer it when you call me Bea, but could we talk about this later? Right now, you've really got to see this coin."

"I don't…coin?" he said, turning quickly and bumping his head on the table. "What kind of coin? Where?"

"Over here," Bea said, tugging his sleeve.

Her father rushed to follow Bea through the crowd back to the table with the coin. However, when they got there, both the coin and Nisha were gone. Bea wondered for a moment if Nisha had stolen it. Bea knew she didn't have the money, for she had heard the fortuneteller say that she needed to go and get some from someone named Graydon. But the idea of Nisha stealing didn't sit right. For some reason, Bea felt certain that Nisha wouldn't do something like that.

They looked around, but there was no one to ask where the coin might have gone. No one appeared to be manning the booth, and none of the nearby vendors knew anything about it. It was so mysterious, Bea might have thought she'd imagined the whole thing if it wasn't for the stinging in her fingertips.

By the time the bus came, Father was visibly tense. He had already asked her at least a dozen questions about the coin, and they kept coming. He wanted to know how big it was. What kind of metal? What shade of gold? What was the engraving? Could it have been a Celtic knot or was it more like the Indian Shrivatsa?

Bea answered all his questions as best she could, yet she purposely left out the part about Nisha and the fortuneteller. In those few seconds that she and Nisha held the coin together, Bea had felt something she couldn't explain. It was as if the coin had connected them somehow. She had felt Nisha's feelings as if they were her own; her excitement of having found the coin, and more strongly, her fear of losing it. Odder still was the intense urge to protect Nisha, to help her, and she knew in order to do so, she couldn't tell anyone what happened between them – not even her father.

Finally, her father gave up asking questions, but Bea could tell he was even more disappointed and frustrated than usual. For the first time, she shared his feelings. She was sure that the coin she'd touched was *the coin*, the one her father had been searching for so long. What surprised her was the realization of how much she wanted – needed - to find it too. *How could she have walked away from it? And where could it have gone?* The one thing she knew for sure was that Nisha and the fortuneteller wanted it too - *but did they have it?* As the bus headed eastward through the park, Bea made up her mind to find out.

CHAPTER 10

THE BATHROOM

The next morning at breakfast, Bea's father was in a foul mood. He explained briefly that he'd gotten a phone call the night before from his most demanding client. Whoever that person was, they had insisted that her father follow a lead on an artifact spotted in Germany. It was obvious to Bea that her father didn't want to go, and Bea knew why. He wanted to stay in New York and pursue the coin they had seen at the flea market the day before. However, shortly after breakfast, a car arrived and he resignedly carried his bag to the sidewalk.

As he left, he took Bea aside and said, "You're certain you'll be alright?"

"I'll be fine," she assured him. "It's not like it's your first trip."

"No, of course not," he said, and then suddenly pulled her into a tight hug. "You are very special person, Bianca Brightman, even more special than just the part you know about." When he let go, there was a look of affection mixed with sadness in his eyes. Then the car horn sounded outside, and a minute later he was gone. It was as close as he had ever come to mentioning her mother.

All that day, Bea thought about the coin. The more she thought about it, the more she was convinced it was the one her father had been looking for all these years. *But where had it gone? And how did Nisha Lakewood factor into the whole thing?* Each time she thought of what happened at the flea market, or the story of Charlie Campbell, or the episode at the sink in Science Lab, she was even more certain Nisha was the key to the whole mystery. She had to find a way to get Nisha to talk.

Bea knew it had to be in private, but it wasn't easy to find privacy at school. She considered sitting with Nisha at lunch, but if she wanted to keep hanging out with the Top Pops, she couldn't risk it. Her best bet was to pass Nisha a note in the hall when they switched classes between fourth and fifth period. Bea tore a page from the back of her notebook and wrote:

> N,
> *Need to speak to you urgently.*
> *Meet me in the 2nd floor lav at 12:12*
> B.

When she handed it to Nisha as they passed, Nisha looked surprised but said nothing.

Bea was almost convinced that Nisha wouldn't come, but at 12:12 on the dot, the bathroom door was pushed open a crack and Nisha Lakewood slipped silently through it. In anticipation of their meeting, Bea had stopped up one of the sinks with paper towels and had the water running. When their eyes met, Bea lifted her finger to her lips and tipped her head towards the bathroom stalls to indicate someone was there. A moment later a small fifth grader came out. She glanced distastefully at Nisha, rushed to wash her hands, and hurried off.

When she was sure they were alone, Bea stuck her hands into the water and motioned for Nisha to do the same. Nisha frowned but complied and the second her fingers touched the water one of her thoughts popped into Bea's head. *This is crazy*, she said. Even in Bea's mind, Nisha's voice was gravelly and her thoughts abrupt.

Yes it is, Bea agreed, unable to stop herself from smiling, *but really amazing, don't you think?*

Nisha shrugged. She did not form a thought in return.

Unsure of where to begin, Bea tried to make conversation. *So that Mr. Morton certainly doesn't fancy me much. If you ask me, he's a bit of a creep.*

Nisha looked at Bea. For several seconds her dark eyes studied Bea's face. *You asked me here to talk about Mr. Morton?* she asked.

Bea hesitated. She knew Nisha didn't trust her, or anyone for that matter. Perhaps a more direct approach would be better. Bea took a breath and focused her thoughts. *No,* she answered, *the truth is, I asked you to come here because I want to know about the coin we saw at the flea market.*

I don't know anything about it, Nisha thought back quickly.

Didn't you feel something? Bea pressed.

Nisha shrugged. Her thoughts were jumbled and Bea sensed she was hiding something. She tried again.

When we both touched the coin at the same time, I got a shock, and I thought you did, too.

Again, Bea sensed that Nisha's thoughts were scrambled. She was purposely not responding.

I know you remember, Bea pressed, *I can feel it.*

Why don't you ask your father about it? Nisha thought back, challengingly. *He bought it, didn't he?*

Bea frowned and shook her head. *My Father never even saw the coin,* she explained. *When we got back to the table it wasn't there. He probably would buy it though. He collects things like that and would probably pay a lot of money for it.*

Nisha black eyes flashed. *I can't help you,* she thought sharply. *We don't have it and even if we did, we don't want your money.*

As soon as Bea heard Nisha's reaction, she realized she'd made a mistake. She hadn't meant to suggest that Nisha needed money. She only wanted to find the coin. She cleared her mind again and asked, *But if you didn't buy it, who did?*

I told you, I don't know anything about it.

Bea shook her head in frustration and took another tack. *What about the woman you were with? Could she help us find it?*

No! Nisha's reaction was so strong Bea felt as if she had been struck. Nisha's eyes were blazing. *My aunt can't help you and neither can I,* she replied, and began to pull her hands of the water.

Wait! Bea thought urgently. *I know you can feel it too…our connection to it, to each other. We can't just ignore it, can we?*

Nisha paused a moment and looked at Bea. *What do you mean, 'we'? We don't even know each other.*

That's true, Bea replied quickly, seizing her opportunity, *but there are so many coincidences. For instance, why are both your aunt and my father interested in the same coin?*

Nisha shrugged. *Lots of people collect coins.*

Well, how can you explain that we ended up finding it at the same time? Or how we both felt a shock when we touched it? And why, if I'm wrong, can we talk to each other by putting our hands in a sink of water? Don't you think these things might mean something?

Without waiting for an answer, Bea continued. *I think we should ask your aunt about it. She is a fortuneteller, isn't she? Maybe she knows about this sort of thing?*

The communication between them went fuzzy again. Bea tried to make out Nisha's thoughts swirling inside her head, but there were too many of them and they were coming too fast. After a few moments, Nisha's mind slowed down and Bea got a cohesive message. It was not what she expected.

How did you know my aunt is a fortuneteller? Nisha's thought was strong and high-pitched.

Bea hesitated. She did not think it would be a good idea to tell Nisha she had been watching their apartment from across the street.

Uh, I don't know, Bea thought hurriedly, *I think someone told me.* But as soon as she thought the reply, she knew she had made another mistake. Now Nisha thought Bea had been talking about her with other girls in their class.

Nisha's mind went quiet, and then Bea got a very clear message.

No.

But I'm sure she knows something, Bea pleaded, knowing she was losing ground. *Maybe we could help each other.*

"No," Nisha said again in a loud whisper as she pulled her hands out of the water. "You should not approach my aunt. Fortunetelling is not a game to her. And besides, she doesn't read for children." Nisha collected her books and walked quickly towards the door.

"Wait," Bea said urgently, "I know you have no reason to trust me, but I think this might be important. I mean, I feel like we're supposed to do this…to find this coin. It's our destiny or something."

Nisha looked back at Bea, and for a moment she hesitated. Then she shook her head and said, "We don't have a destiny."

At that moment the door swung open and Amanda Whitehead came in, her clogs clomping loudly on the tile floor.

"Hello Bea," Amanda said, her eyes darting between Bea and Nisha suspiciously.

Bea felt her chest tighten. Leave it to Amanda to show up at the worst possible moment.

"Hi Amanda," Bea replied casually. "Nice clogs. A bit noisy in here though."

Amanda clomped over to the sinks. "Well, some people don't mind making a little noise," she said, not taking her eyes off Nisha as she fluffed up her hair in the mirror. "Not everyone goes sneaking around whispering in bathrooms, you know."

"Huh? Oh, yeah, well, I guess not. So," Bea said, trying to rush Amanda along, "what do you have next period?"

"P.E.," she said, and watched herself blow a small pink bubble with her gum. She popped it with a snap of her teeth and added, "And so do you. Better hurry. We're late."

Bea looked down at her watch, and as she did, she heard the door close. She looked up to find that Nisha was gone. "Rats!" she said, forgetting Amanda for a moment. When she turned back, she saw that Amanda was watching her with a strange smile on her face.

"What's the matter, Bea," Amanda asked tauntingly, "having trouble making friends with the freak?"

CHAPTER 11

THE CUPCAKES

Bea's heart was pounding loudly in her ears as she carried her tray into the noisy lunchroom. She already knew it was going to be awful. Amanda had told everyone what she'd supposedly overheard in the lavatory the day before. Most of Top Pops had been avoiding Bea since homeroom. If Bea tried to smile at them or catch their eyes, they glanced away nervously.

Bea took a breath and pressed her shoulders back. She lifted herself up from the waist so that she was standing at her full height. *Convey confidence*, she told herself sternly. With a shake of her head she flipped her hair behind her shoulders and set a course for Nisha, who was sitting in the far corner silently curled over her lunch.

"Bea, over here."

Bea looked up to find Charlotte Wang waving enthusiastically at her from the center table. She slowed down for a moment but did not stop. She was thrilled that Charlotte was still interested in her, even after whatever horrible things Amanda must have said. However, instead of going over to Charlotte's table, Bea just smiled and waved back nonchalantly.

It was a huge risk not going over there, and perhaps a huge mistake, yet Bea kept moving towards Nisha Lakewood, her heart pounding wildly in her chest. She simply had to find out more about the coin. She'd deal with the Top Pops later.

"Mind if I sit here?" Bea said, as she approached Nisha. Her hands were shaking slightly as she slid her tray onto the empty lunch table. Nisha looked up, her dark eyes wide with surprise.

Nisha glanced uncomfortably over her shoulder at Charlotte and Amanda. Then she said in her whispery voice, "I've already told you. I don't know anything about the coin."

"I know," Bea said, sitting down and opening her milk container.

Nisha stared at her hard and shook her head. "Don't you get it?" she rasped, "you don't want to sit with me." Bea looked back at Nisha with a blank expression.

Nisha went on nervously, "And if you're sitting with me because you think I'm going to change my mind about you seeing my aunt, I'm not."

"Okay," Bea said, with a shrug.

The girls sat in silence for several seconds. Bea could feel Nisha's eyes on her, but she didn't look up from her food. Finally Nisha asked, "So why are you sitting here?"

"I'm not entirely sure," Bea replied, with a grin. "I was going to sit with one of the other girls who can read my mind, but I can't seem to find any."

Nisha stared at her a moment longer. She appeared to be deciding if Bea were telling the truth or making a joke at her expense. Then she turned back to her lunch and said, "Suit yourself."

Nisha was clearly uncomfortable, but Bea also thought she detected a look of amusement in Nisha's black eyes. They ate quietly for a while, neither one of them saying or eating very much. Bea took a few furtive glances at Charlotte's table and was relieved to see that no one appeared to have any interest in her or Nisha. To Bea's surprise, Nisha broke the silence.

"So, you really don't like Mr. Morton?" she asked shyly, her eyes focused on the food in front of her.

"Not even a little bit," said Bea. "I think he's rude and pompous and I don't understand his personal vendetta against King Arthur. He gives me the creeps."

"Yes," Nisha agreed quietly.

"I've been to eight different schools and I think he's the creepiest teacher I've ever had."

Nisha looked up. "Eight?"

"We move around a lot," Bea replied, putting down her dry turkey sandwich. "Eight different schools and I've yet to find one that has good food. Though these look quite nice," she added, picking up her cupcake. "But, I wish they had chocolate frosting instead of vanilla; you know, the really buttery kind?"

"Mmm," Nisha agreed picking up her own cupcake. "They never have chocolate. I wish they did ..."

Her words were interrupted by a shriek, and then another.

"Oh my god, look!" shouted a third.

Bea looked around the room, trying to find out what was happening. The shouts seemed to be coming from all different tables.

"My cupcake!" another voice squealed from a nearby table, and then everyone began talking at once.

Bea looked over at Nisha. She was staring at the cupcake in her hand; her face frozen in horror. Then Bea saw it. Instead of the white vanilla frosting that had been there just moments before, the cupcake was now topped with a swirl of rich chocolate icing, exactly the kind Bea liked.

Bea looked down at the cupcake in her hand. It too had transformed. Just then, the bell rang and Nisha jumped to her feet and rushed out of the room.

No matter where Bea went for the rest of the day, she overheard girls talking about the cupcakes. Some people swore the frosting was chocolate the whole time. Others claimed that there had been two kinds to begin with and that people were just confused about which one they had chosen. Still others thought it was some kind of practical joke, like birthday candles you can't blow out. However, there was no doubt in Bea's mind that it had something to do with Nisha Lakewood.

CHAPTER 12

THE FREAK

Disappear, Nisha thought to herself as she moved noiselessly down the hall towards her locker. As usual, nothing happened.

You have to concentrate, she told herself firmly and took a breath. *Disappear!* she thought again, more emphatically this time, squeezing her eyes tightly closed. Still nothing happened.

The floor had been recently cleaned and the hallway reeked of ammonia. The swirled streaks from the old mop head left a gritty pattern on the cement. As usual, the janitor had accomplished nothing but stink up the halls and move the dirt around. Nisha was sensitive to smells and her stomach clenched in revolt. She wasn't sure if it was the ammonia or the fact that she had just left a note in Bea Brightman's locker.

Just because Bea Brightman is the only other person in the school that doesn't like Mr. Morton doesn't mean she's trustworthy, Nisha thought, admonishing herself for acting so hastily. But as soon as she thought it, the memory of Bea's scent washed over her; chamomile and buttered toast. It was a good smell, an honest smell. Maybe it won't be so bad, she thought hopefully.

Ahead of her, on the left, a door opened and two tenth grade Horribles came out. Huntington Horribles was Nisha's name for the girls at Miss Huntington's school, and it suited these two perfectly. Even the ammonia couldn't hide their sharp, cloying stench.

Keeping her head perfectly still, she continued to walk towards them; her eyes fixed on the ground in front of her. She hugged her books tightly to her chest. She was in no mood to have her papers spilled over the damp floor.

Most of the time, if she didn't speak and kept her movements to a minimum, the Horribles just walked by as if she were a shadow; as if she didn't exist. And, on the rare occasion that one of them did notice her, she found that having no reaction to their advances was usually enough to get them to move on. Sometimes they teased her for her silence, taking it for stupidity, as though withholding your thoughts meant you didn't have any at all. But Nisha did have thoughts. She just knew better than to share them with Horribles. If they knew what she was thinking, it would only confirm what they already suspected: that she was weird and maybe even dangerous…because she was.

For one thing, she could smell things, people mostly; and not just in the usual way. Nisha could smell *them*, their personalities; each one a mix of their unique chemistry, their bloodlines, their emotions. With a single whiff she could tell what they were feeling, and it was often more than she wanted to know.

As the two tenth grade Horribles came towards her, Nisha could smell the shorter girl quite strongly. A typical, Horrible kind of odor emanated from her; the harsh clash of entitlement and insecurity.

Don't notice me, Nisha hoped, but she could already feel the small girl's eyes on her. She steeled herself for the inevitable.

As they passed, the girl's hand darted out towards her. Though she saw it coming, Nisha did not flinch. She would not allow the girl the satisfaction of frightening her. The girl's hand connected with one of Nisha's braids and it swung up into the air behind her like a whip.

"Where ya goin', Freak?" the girl sang in a mocking voice.

Nisha didn't answer, and the Horribles weren't expecting one. All they wanted was to appear tough for one another. They liked to prove they weren't afraid of the strange seventh grader with the long braids who, it was rumored, tortured a little boy back in kindergarten.

The familiar, bitter taste of anger filled Nisha's mouth and in spite of her efforts to keep still, she turned to look the girl in the face. The girl stared back boldly for a moment. Then her eyes grew wide and she took a small gasp of air as if the wind had been knocked from her lungs. Nisha smelled a sharp tang of fear. The taller girl grabbed her friend by the sleeve and they hurried off down the hall. Nisha wasn't sure why, but whenever she looked a Horrible in the eye it had the same effect. It worked on all of them, with the exception of Bea Brightman.

Nisha could hear the girls whispering as they moved on. A few seconds later came a burst of laughter, ringing with cruelty and relief. Nisha's ears, like her nose, had special talents.

Nisha felt her own relief pulse through her veins. As long as they were gone, the laughter didn't bother her. She had grown accustomed to it - expected it even. And compared to the way things used to be, being laughed at seemed like nothing at all.

It was seven years since the Charlie Campbell incident, yet she still shuddered when she thought about it. No matter how much she tried to bury it, the memory of day stayed with her like a cut that would never heal.

Recess had been outside that afternoon despite the morning rain. The playground was wet and the misty air seemed to amplify the children's voices. Nisha heard them before she saw anything. She heard the mercilessness in their shouts. She had been so frightened for Charlie. He was so small and delicate, like a baby bird. She hadn't planned to do anything. She just wanted to help him. She thought, if he could fly away, he'd be safe.

Even now, she wasn't sure what had happened, but she remembered feeling a great swell of energy like a wave crashing through her, and the next thing she knew they were both on the ground, she and Charlie. Everyone stood around him, but their eyes were on her. She got up and tried to move towards him. She wanted to see if he was all right, but someone grabbed her jacket and pulled her back. After that, everything went hazy; the sequence of events unclear in her memory. Aunt Faye was there, in the principal's office, holding her hand. Faye's expression was fierce, her black eyes shining. Then the playground again, a teacher's cheeks flushed with anger.

"Don't you move a muscle," the woman commanded.

Then the principal's face, twisted tightly like a fist. Her gaze was nervous but unwavering as she spoke to Aunt Faye, her voice stern and superior. Nisha remembered every word from her frosty pink mouth.

"Your niece is a menace," she said, hissing on the s-sounds. "I cannot allow her to return to the school. I have to think of the other children."

Nisha remembered the metallic scent of control mixed with the putrid smell of the woman's disgust. It was all there in the room, as if the principal had spoken her feelings out loud. Nisha watched Aunt Faye's face change from anger to confusion and then sadness.

"She's just a baby," Faye had said quietly. "She can't contain it. She doesn't know how."

Even though Nisha was only five at the time, she knew something very bad was happening. She had done something wrong, something that other people didn't like. She also knew that she was frightened, frightened because what Faye had said was true. Whatever it was she had done, she couldn't control it. She wasn't even sure what it was. What if it happened again? What if another child got hurt because of her?

As the principal had promised, Nisha was not allowed to return to school, which meant there were only two alternatives: private school and home schooling. They were too poor for the former so Faye had no choice but to educate Nisha at home. It was lonely, since Nisha had no contact with other children, but she didn't mind it so much. Other children never liked her anyway.

For a while, Faye had followed the lesson books carefully, but she soon got frustrated.

"It's a good thing you're not in that school anymore," she said. "These are not the lessons that a girl like you needs to learn.

You need to be prepared!"

Nisha wasn't sure what Faye meant. She only knew that all of a sudden she had a whole bunch of new subjects to learn. They had strange names like Tarot Card Reading, Water Whispering, Palmistry and Spellbinding, and lessons came from books that looked even older than Faye herself. The lessons, Faye explained, were to prepare Nisha to someday return to a place called Annwn (pronounced Ann oon), the ancient and secret island on which Nisha was born. According to Faye, the island was home to the powerful magic on earth, and it was ruled by a great enchantress, The Goddess or Great Lady, who hid the island from the rest of the world to protect its mysteries.

"Someday, it will be your duty to return and serve The Great Lady," Faye told her. "That is why we are given special Gifts; magical Gifts. It is these Gifts that bind us to the island and to one another. In this way, every girl of Annwn becomes a Daughter of the Lake. When your time comes, you must be ready," she said.

At first, Nisha thought her Aunt was making these things up to entertain her. But the more she challenged her, the more real the story became.

"What kind of Gifts?" Nisha had asked.

"There are five: Healing, Telling, Seeing, Knowing and the most coveted of all, Wishmaking."

"Those don't sound like very good Gifts," Nisha said.

"Ah, but they are the very best Gifts of all," her Aunt had replied, smiling, "for each one is a different kind of magic! A Healer can restore the body and even the heart when it breaks. The Teller can speak for The Spirits, to share the wisdom of those who are gone from this world with those who are still here. The Seer can see what lies ahead and The Knower can sense the thoughts and feelings of those around them. Sometimes Knowers can even communicate with animals and other creatures. And then there is The Wishmaker, the rarest of The Gifted. A Wishmaker has the ability to summon the Powers of The Lake at will."

"Where does the magic come from?" Nisha had asked

skeptically.

"From the water, of course. It flows within all women. It is the power of birth and life and the life beyond."

"Every woman?" Nisha asked.

"Yes, every one of us, even the women of Man Kind, although they can no longer call upon it. Long ago, they chose to ignore it and so it has faded away. But we, the daughters of Annwn, have not forgotten. We have worked and studied for centuries to strengthen and perfect our Gifts. Then we pass them down, mother to daughter, or in our case, aunt to niece."

"Will I get them?" Nisha asked.

"You already have at least one of them. You proved that in the playground, didn't you? You may even get more than one, for they sometimes come in pairs or even threes. The Great Lady herself has all five. But whatever you get, I'm sure it will be very special indeed."

"What Gifts do you have, Aunt?"

"Me? Oh, I have a few, although none of them are very strong." She smiled to herself. "I am a Seer mostly, and a little bit of a Knower, and sometimes, though rarely, I have the gift of Telling."

"What about boys? Don't they get any Gifts?"

"Well, no dear, they don't, but that doesn't mean they do not have their own magic. Some possess great strength and some great skill. Many are talented in the ways of practical magics like alchemy and spellbinding. Those with patience and ability can become very powerful indeed. However, they cannot make life, and therefore they will always depend on the Goddess in us. I will teach you some of these practical magics while we wait for your Goddess Gifts to come."

And so her preparation continued. They fasted on the nights of the Harvest Moon in the early fall and knelt beneath the stars in the dead of winter. Nisha memorized the twelve blessings of the Goddess and the seemingly endless list of the ancient daughters whose names she must learn if she were to one day call upon the Spirits herself. She studied the lines of the palm of her hand and learned the meaning of each cross and break.

She learned to make a common healing salve of bones, apple seeds and fish oil; and a sleeping tea of goose feathers, tears, and ash from a fire that had burned itself out. She learned to recognize the different cards in the tarot deck, though she never quite mastered the interpretation of their mystic pictures. She was a good student and did her best to absorb all she could as she waited for her Gifts to come.

Then, one hot spring night when the windows were open in hopes of catching a breeze, Nisha was awakened by the sound of familiar voices: Aunt Faye and her friend Gloria from next door. They were in the backyard, talking. It was a soothing, everyday sound, and Nisha had just turned herself over to go back to sleep when she heard Aunt Faye say her name. There was concern in Faye's voice. Nisha's sensitive ears pricked up like a dog's.

"I don't know what's wrong with Nisha," Faye was saying. "She's almost nine and the magic just isn't coming. When I eight years old, I could already Water Whisper, and make no mistake, I was not an early learner."

"Perhaps it's because she has no twin?" suggested Gloria.

"Maybe," Aunt Fay conceded, "but when she was a babe, she was showing all the signs. I'm afraid that after what happened with that boy in the playground, all the magic was scared out of her. I don't know if she'll ever get it back."

"Spirits forbid! Don't say such a thing," replied Gloria, as if no worse a fate could befall anyone.

"But it is possible. The experience was quite a shock for her. I'm not even sure if she's one of us anymore."

Nisha was now fully awake. What could Faye mean? She lay in her bed and repeated the conversation back to herself. *If she wasn't one of them, who was she?* No matter how much she tried, she did not fall asleep again that night.

CHAPTER 13

THE REQUEST

Night after night, Nisha lay in bed wondering what would happen to her. It seemed that everything, the whole direction of her life, depended on whether or not she got her Goddess Gifts. However, as time passed, she became less and less certain she wanted them.

Nisha began to see things she'd not noticed before: the way people in the neighborhood watched her and Faye wherever they went, and how they whispered behind their hands; words like gypsy, witch and freak.

Even at home, Nisha was uncomfortable. Faye's friends, though pleasant enough, seemed to avoid her. When they did speak to her directly, there was always the soft look of pity in their eyes.

Several times a week, when they thought Nisha was asleep, they would gather to talk about Annwn and a mysterious lost coin. Their voices were often tight with concern and the smell in the air was the sticky syrup of worry. The nights when the moon was high and round, they would come together wearing long robes and arrange themselves in a circle around the small pond in Faye's garden. They'd chant in a language Nisha had not yet learned. Sometimes the ceremonies lasted long past midnight, longer than Nisha could keep her eyes open. Her Aunt referred to those nights as "Council Nights", and on the mornings after, Faye was quiet and preoccupied.

Most nights, though, Nisha would lie in her bed listening to the sounds of the city and imagine she was a regular girl. In her fantasy, she had a mother and father and they all lived together in one of the beautiful buildings across the street. They had all sorts of things Aunt Faye would never allow, like computers and potato chips and fancy, uncomfortable shoes. Nisha would wear her hair down instead of in braids, and she'd attend a real school where she had friends to talk and laugh with. And even though she'd be super popular, she'd never be mean to anyone.

Although Faye continued to push Nisha in her studies, still the Gifts did not come and Nisha knew, though Faye never said it to her face, that she doubted they ever would. But what did it matter? Maybe Faye and her friends were just a bunch of crackpots like the people on the street said they were. Nisha had never seen Faye do anything magical; at least nothing more than a few parlor tricks for her customers.

Without really planning it, Nisha began to avoid being seen in public with Aunt Faye. She hated the way people glared at them and was embarrassed by Faye's clownish skirts and silly blue ribbons. Nisha even tried going without her own pale blue ribbons once, but when she arrived at the breakfast table without them, Faye broke down in tears. Why did Faye have to be so strange?

In short, Nisha was miserable, and there was little doubt she was making Faye miserable as well. So, on her ninth birthday, when Faye presented her with The Necklace of the Blood Spring, a circle of tiny rubies set in gold hanging from a thin gold chain, Nisha turned it down. The necklace was the symbol of Annwn, and as beautiful as it was, she had no business wearing it.

Nisha then went on to explain that she no longer wanted to study the ways of Annwn. They both had to accept she wasn't going to get any Gifts and that a normal school would be a better place for her to prepare for a life in the world of Man Kind.

Nisha had braced herself for a storm of anger but got something far worse: the heartbreaking, guilt-inducing, unbearable flood of Faye's disappointment.

"Sometimes you are so unlike your mother, I can hardly believe you are her daughter," Faye said, knowing how much the words would sting. "I know you have not yet received your Gifts," she went on, "but you must give it time. Sometimes the powers don't reveal themselves until a girl's moon days. You will see, when you start to change from a girl to a woman, the powers will come."

"We both know I have no powers," Nisha had replied, bravely looking into her Aunt's liquid black eyes. "Like you just said, I'm not like my mother."

The next morning, Aunt Faye was different. She was no longer angry, just a quiet kind of sad. She agreed to send Nisha to a regular school, with two conditions. The first was that Nisha would attend a girls-only school, to follow at least in some small way the ways of the Goddess. The second was that Nisha was never, under any circumstances, to attempt any Gift magic at school: most particularly, Wishmaking.

Faye selected Miss Huntington's School for Girls, and Nisha did well enough on the entrance exam to secure some financial aid. However, the money offered was not enough to cover the whole tuition. Paying the difference would be a great strain on her Aunt. Nevertheless, Nisha sincerely believed that she had no other choice. She convinced herself that if she studied hard and got good grades it would be worth it and Faye would be proud of her.

Nisha started school in the September of her fourth grade year and if there was ever a hopeful moment, she could not recall it. From the minute she stepped into the entrance hall of Miss Huntington's, she knew she had made an awful mistake. Everything about it felt wrong. She was overwhelmed by the crowded hallways and claustrophobic in the stuffy classrooms. The teachers were impatient and dismissive, openly favoring the wealthier students. Nisha could smell the dirty-water scent of intolerance on their breath.

Worse still, the girls at Miss Huntington's were horrible in every way. Each one was, in various measures, rude, spoiled, bored and cruel. At first, they took little notice of the quiet new girl with long black braids and ugly second-hand shoes. And if that had been all, Nisha probably could have managed. However, one day, in only her second week, a girl named Amanda Whitehead made the dreaded discovery.

"Hey," Amanda had called out loudly as Nisha walked past her lunch table, "I know that girl." Her fat pink finger was pointing directly at Nisha's heart. "She's the witch from kindergarten."

After that, the story had spread at an alarming speed. In a few hours, the fourth, third and fifth grades had been alerted to her presence and by the end of the day, the word "FREAK" had been painted across her locker in sparkly blue nail polish.

From then on, the girls of Huntington School had a new pastime: torturing Nisha Lakewood. On a good day, they excluded her from all activities and teased her about her long braids or thrift store backpack. On bad days, they threatened her, shoved her to ground at recess, stole her gym clothes, put garbage in her locker, or followed her home calling her hateful names.

In short, Nisha was more miserable at Miss Huntington's than she ever imagined possible. When she thought of how hard her Aunt was working to find the money to keep her there, it made her sick to her stomach. Faye could never know how awful it was. So Nisha put a smile on her face, hid the evidence, and acted as if everything was alright.

CHAPTER 14

THE WISHMAKER

On her tenth birthday, Aunt Faye presented Nisha with same the lovely necklace Nisha had rejected the year before.

"It was your mother's," Faye explained, "Perhaps I didn't tell you that last year. The circle gives you strength. It holds your mother's love inside it." Despite her protests, Faye fastened the necklace around Nisha's neck and as she did, a large tear fell from Nisha's left eye and then another from her right. Before she knew it, she was crying with great heaving gasps.

Faye stroked her hair and said, "There, there my little Goddess. The power of The Lake is within you, I'm sure of it. Look at your tears, how big they are! Only a Daughter of the Lake can cry such marvelous tears."

Though the next day was bitter cold, several of the Horribles had the bright idea to follow Nisha home. She tried to walk quickly, but the sidewalks were slick with slush from a recent storm. The girls trailed her, just a few steps behind, laughing each time she lost her footing. At an intersection, Nisha decided to make a run for it. She made it across the busy street, but as she rounded the corner, she slipped and fell, tearing her tights and scraping her knee badly. The Horribles caught up to her a moment later. One girl reached out to help her up, only to twist her arm behind her and force her into a nearby alley.

The alley was narrow and dark, not much wider than a sidewalk. Along one side were a dumpster and a cluster of overflowing trashcans. Long soot-blackened icicles hung from the fire escape above.

The girls forced Nisha to the ground and began to bury her in the filthy snow. Several times, she tried to get up, but they held her down until they were finished. Then, one by one, they stepped back, laughing at their handiwork, their faces in shadowy contrast to the bright winter sun above them.

"That's just where you belong, you hideous little freak." Even through the trash, Nisha could smell the noxious odor of Amanda Whitehead.

As Nisha looked up into Amanda's round, ruddy face, she felt tears pushing at her eyelids. *Please don't cry*, she begged herself, and, oddly, the feeling vanished. At the same time, she noticed a tingling at her throat. She reached up and felt her new necklace. It was surprisingly warm to the touch and her freezing fingertips thawed a little as they traced the ruby circle. The ache to cry was slowly replaced by a pounding in her heart. Her blood began surging through her until she felt almost hot. It took her a moment to recognize the feeling, for it was one she had denied for so long. It was anger, and it was suddenly so strong she felt she could barely contain it.

"Leave me alone," she heard herself whisper, but her words were lost in a cold snap of wind.

"Did you say something, freak?" said Amanda, jeeringly. Her voice echoed slightly on the brick alley walls.

"I said, leave me alone," Nisha repeated, less meekly this time.

"Yeah, well, how are you gonna make us do that?" a tall girl asked, wiping her runny nose with the back of her gloved hand. Then she flapped her arms up and down and laughed. "Are you going to make us all fly away like little Charlie Campbell?"

Nisha took in a slow breath. Normally, any reference to that day in the playground brought tears to her eyes. But today she noticed something she hadn't before; something in the girl's voice. Underneath her words, Nisha heard or perhaps sensed the undeniable tremor of fear. Despite her predicament, she almost smiled. They hate me because they are afraid of me, she thought. *They're* afraid of *me*.

Nisha touched her necklace again and felt another surge of warmth, stronger than before. She felt oddly calm as she pushed her way through the trash and stood up, slowly brushing a sticky ketchup packet from her skirt. Then, she lifted up her eyes to face Amanda directly.

Amanda chuckled. "Well, look at you," she said. "What are you gonna do, witch girl, curse us or something?"

"No," Nisha answered quietly, "just you."

Nisha knew Amanda was the leader, and though she hadn't planned exactly what she would say; her intention was to frighten Amanda Whitehead into backing down. She could tell by the hush that had fallen over the alley that it was working already.

"Yeah right," the tall girl ventured, but no one else chimed in.

Nisha said nothing, but continue to stare directly at Amanda.

"Are you threatening me?" said Amanda loudly. Nisha could smell the fear coming off her skin.

"Yes," Nisha answered, forcing herself to step forward.

"You can't do anything to me," said Amanda, trying to keep her voice steady.

"Are you sure about that?" asked Nisha, stepping forward again, never taking her eyes off Amanda. *If only I could do something that would really scare her.* Suddenly, there was a sharp cracking noise above them. Then, as if she'd planned it, one of the huge icicles from the fire escape came crashing down. Amanda jumped back just in time, and the icicle smashed on the ground between their feet.

They all just stared at the shattered ice until Nisha spoke. "I've asked you to leave me alone and I suggest you do," she said, glancing from Amanda's face to the broken icicle on the ground, as if she had somehow commanded it to fall. She looked around at the other girls. "I suggest you all do."

The girls were genuinely frightened now. The tang of fear was potent in the cold air. Amanda turned to the others and said, "Let's go. She's seriously creeping me out."

After that day, things improved for Nisha. Sure, the kids still taunted her as they passed in the halls and certainly no one would even consider befriending her, but if she kept to herself, and out of their way, she could go about her life without incident.

Interestingly, Nisha's small victory in the alley had done more than just help her manage through the school day. Soon afterwards, Nisha began to notice a change in herself. At first, she thought it was her imagination, but she couldn't deny what was happening. All of a sudden, Nisha's everyday wishes, the kind everyone makes, began to come true. For instance, the street lights would turn in her favor whenever she needed to cross, or someone would inexplicably vacate their bus seat if she felt like sitting down. She told herself these were just coincidences, but the feeling in her stomach told her it was something else entirely. As weeks and months went by, the coincidences came more frequently, and by the time she started her seventh grade year, magic, for there was no other name for it, flickered around her like butterflies in a flower garden.

Despite the evidence that her Goddess Gifts had actually arrived, Nisha did her best to ignore them. She was scared that it might not be true, but even more concerned that it was. And her greatest fear of all was that one of the Horribles would figure it all out. Her only hope was that she might be able to use the magic to hide the magic. *If I could just make myself disappear,* she thought as she watched the two tenth graders turn the corner at the end of the hall, *I'd never have to deal with any of them again.*

The hallway was quiet now, except for a few second graders near the water fountain, so Nisha took a deep breath and tried to concentrate. *I should have paid more attention to Aunt Faye's lessons.* She squeezed her eyes shut as she tried to recall the three steps of Wishmaking.

"First," Faye had instructed, "you must form a detailed picture of the Wish in your mind." Nisha breathed deeply and pictured her body fading into the stale air of the Huntington's School hallway. She imagined that with her next step, her foot would move out in front of her but she wouldn't be able to see it because it would be gone.

"Step two: Move your wish into the center of your body where it can gather strength from your feelings. For your mind and heart must be in harmony for the wish to work."

Nisha did her best to imagine her wish moving to somewhere just above her bellybutton. She had never been completely clear on where her "center" was, but she figured the bellybutton had to be close.

She closed her eyes and concentrated again on her Aunt's words. "Once you are certain that your Wish is in place, summon the Power of The Lake within you and release your Wish out through your fingertips." This was step three and it always tripped her up. She could never get it right. How could a person summon the power of some mystical lake that might not even really exist?

Still, she tried again. *Power of The Lake make me disappear*, she whispered, squeezing all her hope into the words. Nothing happened. Nisha huffed with frustration. She tried again, scrunching up her face and holding her breath as if she could force the wish down her arms and out through her fingertips. Still nothing.

I'm an idiot, she thought, exasperated. *This is never going to work. There is no such thing as Wishmaking.* But somewhere deep inside her she knew that it did exist. She knew it as certainly as she knew the difference between chocolate and vanilla frosting.

CHAPTER 15

THE NEW CUSTOMERS

At seven-thirty that evening, while Nisha and Aunt Faye were having dinner, the front buzzer rang. Nisha nearly choked on her soup. She'd been hoping with all her will that Bea had forgotten about their plans, or perhaps changed her mind.

"Ah," said Aunt Faye, "a customer. Thank the Spirits; we could use the money." Then she looked over at Nisha. "Someone you know?" she asked, suspiciously.

"Why would you think that?" Nisha replied, asking a question in place of an actual lie. It was eerie sometimes, the way Aunt Faye knew things.

Faye took another long look at her and said, "Alright then, why don't you get the door while I clean up a bit."

Nisha walked hesitantly to the front door. On her way, she passed the entrance to her small, shabby front room, and felt a sinking feeling in her stomach. As if seeing it for the first time, her eyes travelled around the room. She glanced at the ancient bookshelf nearly overflowing with Aunt Faye's old books and potion bottles. In the corner, she noticed the rainbow of crystal balls that filled the top of a dingy wooden chest. The couch, which Faye and Nisha had found on the street last spring, was a faded orange-brown color splattered with ugly green flowers. It clashed dreadfully with the vivid red velvet cloth that covered the round table in the center of the room. Nisha felt her throat go dry. *Was it possible to actually die of embarrassment?*

The buzzer rang again and a rush of anxiety coursed through Nisha's veins. She couldn't imagine what had made her think having Bea Brightman over was a good idea. Had she been temporarily insane? What did she actually know about this girl besides that fact that they could, somehow, sometimes read each other's thoughts? And that was certainly no guarantee she wasn't just as awful as the rest. *What if the whole thing was a horrible Horrible trick, or worse? Even if by some miracle Bea turns out to be okay, what if she saw right through Faye's routine? What if she could tell it wasn't magic?*

Nisha reached for the pendant around her neck, and just the touch of it reassured her. *Faye's been doing this a long time*, she told herself. Her Aunt knew how to impress her clients. She always followed the same steps. She'd begin by flattering them, making them feel special and smart. Then she'd ask them a few questions and before they knew it, they were telling her everything; their secrets and hopes and fears. Once she'd collected enough information, she'd spread the tarot cards or reach for their palms. For a little extra money, she'd pull out a crystal ball. Then Faye would sell their dreams back to them, one at a time. It was impressive to watch, masterful even, but it definitely wasn't magic.

Nisha swallowed hard as she approached the door. *How could she have been so foolish? Faye couldn't help Bea find the coin she was looking for. If Faye was capable of finding coins, she would have found the one she'd been searching for herself all these years.* With no other choice, Nisha pulled the door open a crack, leaving the chain loop in place.

"Nisha, it's me!" Bea whispered through the small opening.

"It's not a good time," Nisha replied. "You should go."

At that moment, Faye swept by and called out, "Let them in, Nisha, dear. Let's not keep them waiting. And make them comfortable. I'll be there in just a moment."

Nisha hesitated again, but couldn't think of any way out. She unlatched the chain and opened the door.

Bea stepped inside, followed unexpectedly by a boy about their age whom Nisha recognized. She'd occasionally seen him riding up and down her street on a skateboard. Both Bea and the boy were dressed in strange-looking outfits. Bea had somehow colored her blond hair a dark sticky red and arranged it in a stiff bun on the back of her head. She wore large black-framed glasses, reddish lipstick and a brown tweed suit at least two sizes too large. She wobbled on her high heels as she stepped inside. The boy wore khaki pants and a blue blazer. On his feet, in place of his high-top sneakers, were shiny loafers. Wide comb marks were distinctly visible in his normally messy hair. He also wore large glasses with lenses so thick his eyes looked twice their normal size. Despite his get-up, he was undeniably the handsomest boy Nisha had ever seen up close. She felt dizzy with panic.

"What are you…why is he…why are you dressed like that?" Nisha could barely keep her voice steady.

"You told me your Aunt didn't read for kids so we dressed like adults," Bea said, smiling smugly as if this was a clever idea.

"You… you're not going to fool…" Nisha stammered, finally managing to ask, "And why did you bring him?" But before Bea could answer, they heard Faye enter the front hall. Her long braids and blue ribbons were piled high on her head, creating the illusion of a much taller person and her eyes were ringed with a black line of makeup that made her look mysterious and even a bit frightening.

Faye walked over to Bea and the boy and studied them both for an uncomfortably long moment before gesturing them into the front room. She invited them to sit at the table, and once they were settled, Nisha turned to leave.

"Please join us, Nisha," Faye said softly, smoothing the red velvet tablecloth in front of her. Nisha turned around, startled. She hadn't expected this.

"This is my grandniece, Nisha," Faye said, turning to Bea. "She is a fortuneteller-in-training, so she will be observing us this evening if that is acceptable to you."

Nisha felt as if her cheeks had been lit on fire.

"Oh, of course!" replied Bea, enthusiastically. "Well, Nisha was it?" Bea continued, smiling at her, "you must be thrilled to be learning such a fascinating art."

Faye grinned with pleasure, but Nisha couldn't speak. Her throat felt like flypaper. She could feel Skateboard Boy staring at her.

Nisha slipped into a chair, trying hard not to look at Bea or the boy. Faye hummed a little as she lit the candles, oblivious to Nisha's discomfort.

"Let's begin," Faye said, turning and placing a single candle directly in front of each of them, including Nisha. "Please, tell me your names and how I can help you this evening."

"Well," began Bea, overplaying her mild British accent, "my name is Clarisse and this is my twin brother Clarence. Several years ago, we lost our mother, and ever since, we have been searching for a lost pendant of hers. It meant a great deal to our family. We've asked every relative and friend and no one seems to know where it's gone. We were hoping you could help."

Although Bea delivered it well, the fishy odor of the lie hung heavily in the air and Nisha wondered if her Aunt could smell it.

"Of course I can…Clarisse," Faye responded, pausing on the false name for a moment. "I'm sure your mother would want you to have the pendant. She must have been very proud of you two; you're so lovely and your brother, so handsome." Faye smiled warmly at them. "Don't you think he's handsome, Nisha dear?"

Nisha's stomach did a full back-handspring but she managed to make a small squeaking noise. Luckily, Faye was into her routine and didn't expect a real answer. She continued, with enthusiasm.

"Of course, you realize that finding lost things is not easy. It will take a great deal of effort and a real commitment on your part," Faye said, adding extra emphasis on the words *real commitment*.

"Oh, we're very committed. We'll do anything to find it," Bea answered in her exaggerated accent.

"Excellent. It will be one hundred dollars, in cash, before we begin."

"A hundred dollars!" Nisha heard herself blurt out. "Aunt, that's..."

"Not a problem at all," Bea interrupted. "It's well worth it," she added, as she dug through her large crocodile handbag for the money. Smiling, Bea handed the money to Faye, who tucked it into a pocket somewhere in the folds of her skirt. Then Faye got up and went to the shelf behind her. She fussed for a few seconds, then turned back to the table with something in her hands.

"We'll consult the cards," she announced.

"Ooooh!" said Bea excitedly.

Faye ceremoniously placed the oversized deck of gold-edged tarot cards on the table in front of her. She smoothed out the tablecloth again, then slowly laid the cards out one at a time to form a large H. As Faye placed the last card on the table, Nisha noticed her Aunt's expression darken. "Very unusual," she said, her eyes moving from card to card.

Although this was all part of the routine - Faye frowning with concentration in order to build the suspense - Nisha sensed something was different this time. Faye looked as if she might truly be perplexed, and she was taking a curiously long time. Finally, Faye looked up at Bea and Skateboard Boy.

"Things are not revealing themselves just yet," she said glancing, back and forth between them.

Nisha held her breath. Was Aunt Faye going to call them out on their silly disguises? Or worse, was she going to ask them for even more money?

Faye looked back at the cards and shook her head. "What else can you tell me about the pendant?"

"Well," Bea answered, "it's in the shape of a coin."

Faye lifted her eyes up from the cards and looked directly at Bea. Again, Nisha held her breath. Was it possible her Aunt recognized Bea from the flea market?

"What kind of coin?" Faye asked, her eyes locked on Bea's face.

"Well, I can't be certain, uh… I mean, I don't really recall," Bea stammered. "As I said, it has been lost for many years. It's about the size of an American silver dollar, I think, but it might not be silver, perhaps more of a sort of gold color."

"I see," said Faye, still not taking her eyes off Bea, "Well, then, I will need your help for the next part. Please join hands and try to picture the coin in your mind."

Nisha looked at her Aunt in surprise. This was definitely not part of the usual program.

Suddenly, Nisha was acutely aware of herself. Her mouth went dry and her mind blanked. She looked around the table. Aunt Faye, Bea and the Skateboard Boy were already holding hands. She had no choice. Slowly, she reached out and grasped her Aunt's bony hand in one of her own, and then, trying her best to keep herself from turning bright red, she slipped her small fingers into Skateboard Boy's large outstretched palm.

CHAPTER 16

THE TELLING

Bea could barely contain her curiosity. Everywhere she looked in Nisha's odd little apartment were things begging to be investigated. Behind the fortuneteller was a shelf filled with tiny dark bottles; brown, blue and green. Above them, stacks of ancient, leathery books overstuffed with ill-fitting pages. To the left was a large fish tank that held a slender, silvery snake, a species Bea had never seen before; and to the right, a dozen crystal balls of various sizes and colors sat on top of an old bureau. They glinted mysteriously in the candlelight.

Bea wasn't naïve. She knew that although they had been around for centuries, there was no proof that tarot cards or crystal balls could predict the future. In fact, Father had explained to her years ago that the people who used such things were usually frauds, selling hope to people in despair. However, this knowledge did little to curb Bea's interest. She had always been fascinated by myths and stories of magic. And now, in Nisha's small living room, Bea found herself captivated. The fortuneteller, with her piercing black eyes and smooth smoky voice, was mesmerizing. Bea was already convinced she could see right through her disguise.

As instructed, Bea grasped the Fortuneteller's hand. It was

small and bony but her grip was tight and strong, and Bea felt a strange, gentle tug from the center of her palm as if they were magnetically attached. In contrast, Indy's hand was large and a bit sweaty. He must be nervous, too.

He's probably just uncomfortable in those clothes, was the reply that popped sharply into Bea's mind.

Bea's head shot up and her eyes met Nisha's. *What? How? Why now?* Bea asked her in rapid succession.

I don't know, Nisha thought back, with her usual curtness, and then, with a small shake of her head, she added, *Just don't say anything.*

The fortuneteller spoke, and both of them looked up, startled. "Are you two... ready?" she asked, looking at them curiously.

Bea gained her composure. "Yes, of course," she answered. "My brother and I are anxious to hear whatever you can tell us."

The fortuneteller nodded, but looked back and forth between the two girls again.

Do you think she can hear us? Bea asked Nisha.

Nisha didn't answer, which was answer enough. Bea turned her attention to the fortuneteller, who had started chanting. At first, her words sounded like a mumbling of odd sounds and syllables. Slowly, however, Bea began to sort out some recognizable words.

"I call to the Goddesses of the Other World: Keridwen and Ana, Cerridwen and Morgana, Hecate and Morrigeu, Igraine, Elaine and Lunesa. We seek to be heard and to be answered." Her list of names went on, never repeating the same one twice. Some seemed familiar to Bea, as if she'd heard or perhaps read them somewhere before.

What is she doing? Bea thought to Nisha.

She's trying to contact the Spirits, Nisha replied, glancing nervously over at her Aunt.

"Is she really going to?" Bea started to ask, but her thought was interrupted by a strong *shhhh!*, and she wasn't sure if Nisha had thought it or had hushed her out loud.

"Picture the coin," Faye commanded. She sounded irritated,

as if the girl's thoughts had somehow interrupted her.

Bea closed her eyes and tried to focus, forming a picture of what she could remember of the coin - the soft luminous gold, the curled engraving - but she couldn't concentrate. Everything in the room was vying for her attention. On top of that, her suit, which she'd found in a closet in her grandparents' house, smelled unpleasantly of mothballs, and was starting to get itchy.

"Let your mind go," said Faye, holding to the rhythm of her chant, as if she sensed Bea's unrest. "Relax and let the spirit of your mother speak to us from the Other World."

Bea felt a small chill sneak up her neck as if a breeze had passed through the room. Was this woman really capable of contacting her dead mother? Bea hadn't really imagined it could be done until then. *Impossible*, she thought, as she listened to Faye's soft song-like voice. *But was it?* Some cultures believed the spirits of the dead were always there, watching them. Maybe Faye could actually reach them. As Bea listened to the woman's rhythmic words, another thought struck her. *What if the coin her father was looking for had actually belonged to her mother?* How had she not considered it before? She had always assumed it was just another precious artifact, but what if that wasn't the case at all? It would certainly explain her father's obsession. She tried to remember if he'd ever said anything to suggest it might be so. Then she felt it for sure; a breeze on the back of her neck.

Bea forced her eyes open and looked around, wondering if anyone else had felt it too, but Indy's eyes were closed and Nisha was slumped in her chair as though she were asleep. Bea sat up straighter, and peered around. Nothing seemed to have moved or changed. The room was still. Then, just as she was about to let her eyes close again, the candle in front of her flickered.

Bea looked over at the fortuneteller. She was still chanting, but her voice was a whisper now, and her words were jumbled together like pebbles in a stream. Indy was sitting perfectly still, his eyes closed, and she wondered if he too had nodded off. She squeezed his hand, and he opened his eyes just in time to see the candles flicker again. He frowned, and looked back at her, confused. A moment later, the fortuneteller stopped talking entirely, and Bea felt the woman's wrinkly fingers loosen their grasp on her hand.

When Bea turned to the fortuneteller, she was startled by her appearance. Something was terribly wrong. Nisha's Aunt was shrinking, shriveling before Bea's eyes, growing both smaller and older at the same time, curling inward like an autumn leaf. Her skin had turned yellow and her hair was fading from black to a colorless brown. It was awful to watch, but Bea couldn't take her eyes away. Nor did she dare let go of the hand that lay lifelessly in her palm. Had the fortuneteller died?

After a moment, to Bea's enormous relief, the woman slowly opened her eyes, exposing foggy orbs. Then she took a breath, which made her small body shutter, and began to speak in a voice that sounded like sand against metal. "Fetch me some water," she said, locking her gaze on Nisha.

Nisha, who was wide-awake now, looked terrified. She quickly pushed her chair out and rushed out of the room. Seconds later, she was back with a glass of water, which she set down in front of the old woman.

"Aunt Faye?" Nisha whispered, uncertainly.

With a great effort, the woman held up her hand to shush Nisha. "I am so dry. I must drink. Help me, please."

Nisha moved closer to her and helped her lift the glass to her papery lips. Nisha's hands were shaking and most of the first sip ended up on the old woman's chin. Nisha's eyes blazed in concentration as she tried again, tilting the glass further until the woman was able to swallow several noisy gulps.

Nisha placed the glass back on the table, and the woman nodded at her gratefully. The water appeared to revive her a bit, because she suddenly raised her hands up in front of her. Both Indy and Bea leaned back as she took a deep, rattling breath.

"As the vision has foreseen," she croaked, "three have come."

Then, without so much as a sneeze, the candles went out. The only light in the room was the dim glow of the streetlamps pushing through the edges of the front window curtains.

For several moments, no one spoke. It had to be some kind

of scam, some kind of magician's trick. Still, she couldn't figure out how Faye had changed her appearance so drastically right in front of their eyes.

Then, in the darkness, the old woman raised herself up and began to speak.

"Three Finders will come if Coin is lost,
The brave and true to stand the test,
Seeking the treasure at all cost,
As all depends upon their quest."

The woman paused, and in the dim light, Bea saw her foggy gray eyes scan their faces. Bea wasn't sure if the woman could even see them, but she went on. "The Dark to see what cannot be seen." And with her words, her eyes rested on Nisha. Bea gasped with surprise when the candle in front of Nisha re-lit itself; the flame flickering gently in the windless room.

"The Light to guide the way," the old woman continued, as she turned her gaze on Bea. Bea's candle ignited into flame. "And The Third to keep them both safely until the Passage Day," she said. With her words, the flame of Indy's candle jumped to life with a tiny popping sound.

The old woman paused again as she strained to catch her breath.

"The Book of Charms will take the Three
To The Room of Truth in misty waves;
Unlock the gate with Vesica's Key,
Return the Coin and all is saved."

The woman sat down with a sigh of exhaustion. Her withered face crinkled into a horrible grimace that Bea presumed was a smile.

No one spoke and several minutes went by. Finally, unable to contain her curiosity any longer, Bea softly cleared her throat and said as politely as she could, "Pardon me, but I'm not really sure I understand what is going on. You see, I came here tonight simply to find my mother's coin."

The woman nodded, but said nothing. Exasperated, Bea tried a more direct approach.

"I'm sorry, but what did your poem have to do with my

mother's pendant?"

The woman turned to face Bea directly. Her eyes were half closed and she tilted her head back slightly so she could look up at Bea from under the lids. "I am here to help the three of you begin your quest," she said. She spoke slowly in a way that suggested she thought Bea wasn't very bright.

"But there are only..." Bea began to respond, but was interrupted by Nisha.

"Who are you?" Nisha asked, staring hard at the woman.

The woman's wobbly head turned to Nisha. "I am the Goddess Ninane," she replied, as though they should have figured it out. "I have much to share with you, but before I do, I must have more water."

Bea watched Nisha closely. She had assumed Nisha was a part of the whole thing, but the look on Nisha's face told a different story. She looked genuinely frightened. But it couldn't be real...

Nisha picked up the glass from the table, and returned a few moments later with it filled. This time, the woman managed to curve her bony hand around it and drank the liquid hungrily.

"Death is so very dry," she mumbled to herself. Then she sat up a little straighter and spoke as if she were reading. "I am Ninane, daughter of Nimue, honored messenger of The Prophecy of The Three Finders. And although you are very late, we offer our gratitude that you have finally arrived."

None of the children spoke, and the woman continued. "I am here to assist you, but I cannot stay long in this form. Faye of The Lake has not vesseled a Spirit in many years. She is unpracticed in the art of Telling and is drying quickly. It is not safe for her to sustain my presence for very long."

Bea frowned. There had to be some kind of logical explanation. "Uh, I'm sorry," she ventured again, "but I think you may be mistaken. It's just my brother and..."

The woman's head pivoted towards Bea. "There is no mistake." Her voice grew louder. "I am Ninane, Teller of Annwn. I am here to share The Prophecy with The Three Finders; The Dark, The Light and The Protector, as the vision has foretold. Are there not three of you seated here?"

"Well, yes, but…"

"And did you not proclaim to be searching for a lost coin?"

Bea looked from Indy to Nisha, hoping for some support, but they both stared back at her, bewildered. So she turned back to the old woman and said, "We came here to find a coin…yes."

The expression on Ninane's face grew dark.

"My time is short," she croaked impatiently. "You must decide. Do you accept the quest the Lady has bestowed upon you?"

The room was silent. Bea turned again to Indy. He raised his shoulders and eyebrows in a gesture that said, 'I'm game if you are.'

Bea smiled at this. Most kids would have been scared to bits by now.

Suddenly, the old woman gasped and grabbed for the glass, accidentally, knocking it over. The small spoonful of water that remained in the bottom spilled out and beaded up on the cheap velvet tablecloth.

Nisha immediately stood up to get more water, but Ninane grabbed her forcefully by the arm, pulling her back into her seat. Nisha's eyes were wide.

"There's no time. If this is to happen I must bind you now," she gasped, "but you must swear the oath first. Do you accept?"

Bea looked at Indy. Her heart was beating hard. She nodded and he nodded back.

"Nisha?" Bea whispered.

Nisha swallowed hard and blinked. She pulled her eyes away from her Aunt and looked at Bea. The fear in her eyes was real. "I don't think I have a choice," she answered.

Bea turned back to the woman. "Well, I guess we'll do it then," she said.

"No guessing!" the woman hissed. "You must be sure! Swearing The Oath means that you are bound to fulfill The Quest regardless of the consequences. Are you agreed?"

"And if we can't, you know, fulfill it?" asked Indy, speaking for the first time.

"Then you will suffer like the rest of Man Kind," Ninane answered simply. "But if you choose to help, we will help you. And in time you will be rewarded."

Real or not, Bea could feel the curiosity pulsing through her, and since no one said anything in reply, she spoke for them.

"Yes," she said. "Yes, we accept."

Apparently satisfied, Ninane raised a gnarly hand to her head and slowly pulled one of the dark blue ribbons from Faye's hair. Then she rose unsteadily to her feet.

"Place your left hand on the table in front of you," she commanded.

They did as they were told, as Ninane began to chant softly. It was a list of names, like the ones Faye had used, only Ninane's list was even longer. As she chanted, she slowly, shakily wrapped one end of the ribbon around Nisha's outstretched wrist. Then she tipped dangerously forward and slipped the middle of the long ribbon around Indy's wrist. Finally, she pulled the end of the ribbon around Bea's wrist. Then she tied the ends of the ribbon loosely together, her knotted fingers fumbling with the slippery fabric.

When she was satisfied, she said, "Repeat my words... From this moment forward."

The children looked at each other, but no one spoke.

Ninane sighed loudly. "Repeat my words," she commanded. "From this moment forward."

They repeated, "From this moment forward."

"We are sworn and bound," said Ninane.

"We are sworn and bound," they echoed. Indy glanced over at Bea with one eyebrow raised. She almost laughed, but Ninane's authoritative voice forced her to restrain herself.

"To search the World of The Living."

"To search the World of The Living."

"Until The Coin is found."

"Until The Coin is found."

"Once a Finder, one of three." Ninane's voice rose as if in triumph.

"Once a Finder, one of three," they said.

"Always a Finder I will be," she finished.

"Always a Finder I will be," they mimicked, their voices trailing off into the silent room as they repeated the last line of the oath. As the last syllable exited their mouths, Bea expected something to happen. She looked around, but there was nothing, not even a flicker of candlelight.

Ninane collapsed back down in her seat. "There, it is done," she rasped. "The Finders and The Coins are bound together in The Oath. Now you must make haste, Finders, and bring The Third Coin back to us."

"The *Third* Coin?" asked Indy.

"That is your quest," she continued, sounding calmer now that they had sworn The Oath, "to find The Third of The Five Eternal Coins of Annwn."

"The Five what?" Indy asked.

"The Five Eternal Coins," the old women repeated impatiently. "But it is the Third, The Coin of Balance that you seek. It is the most precious of all, for it binds the others together, just as the Lake binds the Two Worlds."

"But how will we find it? We don't know where to look or even know what it looks like," said Bea, forgetting it was supposed to be her mother's coin.

"You will know it by its perfect duality: one side made of silver from The White Waters of The Other World, the other forged in gold from the Blood Spring of the Great Hill. It is marked by the eternal circle that connects all the magic of the worlds into one. And in regard to where to look – I suggest you start with the last Caretaker," the old woman answered, her words coming more slowly now, in short broken breaths. "We know with certainty that The Coin was passed to her on her thirteenth birthday, as is the custom."

"Who is it?" asked Indy. "And why doesn't she still have the coin?"

"I…am sorry," Ninane said, gasping as she turned towards him. "I have helped as much as I can… I have no time left."

"But how are we supposed to…?" Nisha began. "You said you would help us."

89

Ninane began to speak, but instead coughed painfully, each crackle in her throat shaking her small body. Finally, she caught her breath and whispered, "Ask Faye. She knows much more than you think she does. But be quick in talk. If the Third Coin is not passed on to the rightful Caretaker on Passage Day, the balance will be destroyed and the two worlds will become one."

"Wait!" Bea cried. "When is Passage Day?"

With a deep sigh, Ninane slumped back in the chair.

"Aunt Faye?" Nisha called, as she jumped up and rushed over to the small figure slumped in her Aunt's chair. "Aunt Faye? Aunt Faye? Are you alright?"

CHAPTER 17

THE RETURN OF AUNT FAYE

Nisha's heart finally stopped pounding when she saw her Aunt's skin smooth out and the blackness return to her hair. After another minute or so, Aunt Faye had recovered enough to notice Nisha standing over her.

"For Spirit's sake, what are you doing, child?" she asked, waving Nisha away. Then, to herself, she said, "I must have been in a trance of some kind."

"Are you alright?" Nisha asked again.

"Well, I don't feel… exactly like myself," Faye answered, smoothing the braids that had loosened during the séance. She picked up the dark blue ribbon from the table and looked at it curiously. Then she turned towards Bea and Indy and said, "I am very sorry; I don't know what came over me. Please, let me give you your money back."

"Oh, uh, that's not necessary," Bea answered, forgetting to play up her English accent. "But… thank you." Then she added, "We got much more than we expected."

"So we found the pendant, did we? That's wonderful," answered Faye, absent-mindedly. "I'm so pleased I could help. Now, if you lovely young people will excuse me, I must get some water. I'm terribly thirsty. Nisha, help me to the kitchen, then

91

you can show your friends out."

Nisha looked at her Aunt sideways then answered her carefully, "Um, Aunt, these people aren't my friends. You must not be feeling well."

"We have discussed this, Nisha," Faye said tiredly. "I will not tolerate lying. I may be old but I know much more than you think I do." She turned to Bea and Indy then and said, "Now if you'll excuse me, children." Faye gripped Nisha's arm for support and began to walk shakily from the room.

"Wait!" Bea called out. Faye slowly turned back to her, frowning with fatigue.

"What is it, child?" she asked.

"Well, I...I thought you might want to know that Ninane said the same thing."

Faye's eyebrows rose slightly. "Pardon me?"

"Can't you see that my Aunt is not well?" said Nisha. "She needs to rest."

However, instead of agreeing, Faye patted Nisha's hand gently and said, "Just a moment dear." Then she looked at Bea again, "What did you say?"

Bea cleared her throat nervously. "The Goddess Ninane said the same thing about you during the séance," she repeated. "She said that you know more than we think you do."

Faye was silent. She stood, frozen to the spot, with her mouth half open and her eyebrows deeply knitted together. Then, slowly, her expression changed. Her mouth formed a kind of half smile and she shook her head from side to side.

"Well, of all the mysteries of The Lake!" she exclaimed. "Was I a Teller tonight? Great Spirits, is it even possible?" She shook her head again in disbelief. "But what could I possibly have to tell you two?"

"We three actually," said the boy, stepping forward. "You included Nisha. You said we were the Three Coin Finders and we're supposed to find The Coin of Balance before Passing Day."

"The Pass*age* Day," Faye corrected. But then her eyes grew wide with realization. She abruptly let go of Nisha's arm and took two or three stunned steps backwards. "It can't be," she said in a whisper to herself. "As the vision has foreseen, three will come."

"You chanted a rhyme," he explained.

Faye nodded and asked, "I mentioned a coin, specifically?"

"Yes." Bea and the boy answered at the same time.

Faye nodded again, but her eyes looked dazed.

"You called Nisha The Dark and me The Light," explained Bea.

"The Light to guide the way…" said Faye, nodding slowly, "and The Third to keep them both safe," she continued, turning to Indy, her lips tucked in around her teeth in a worried grimace.

"Yes, that's it," said the boy enthusiastically, "until the Passing Day. That's the rhyme."

"It's Passage Day," Faye corrected again. "And it is more than a rhyme, dear boy, it is a prophecy. But how is it possible that you heard it here? The Prophecy is meant as a guide for the Coin Finders and that couldn't be you. Could it? Of course, Nisha's connection is clear, but why the two of you?"

Faye continued to mutter to herself as she made her way slowly to the couch, where she stood for several seconds as though she'd forgotten how to sit down. "Oh, great Spirits, I made a promise, but this? I did not foresee this. I will have to consult The Council immediately."

"The Council?" Bea asked.

"Mmm, The Council of The Five Coins," said Faye, nodding distractedly. Then she looked from Nisha to the boy and then to Bea. "You're certain I was a Teller?" she asked.

Bea and the boy nodded.

"And I said that the three of you are The Finders?"

They nodded, and Faye began to mumble again. "It must be true. How else would they know The Prophecy unless a Teller was here? Yet it doesn't make sense. They're too young and it's too…" Then her eyes lightened a bit. "Maybe it was a mistake," she said hopefully. "And as long as you didn't take The Oath then…"

"Oh," said the boy, interrupting her, "we swore we'd find the missing coin if that's what you mean."

At this news, Faye grasped about for the arm of the sofa and, upon finding it, lowered herself slowly into the cushions.

"You took The Oath?" she said weakly.

They nodded again in harmony.

Faye began a series of long breaths. "I need some water," she said. "And then I think perhaps we'd better make some tea. I'm going to need to know everything Ninane said. Everything. And there are a few things I'm going to have to tell you as well."

As soon as Nisha and Aunt Faye were alone in the kitchen, Nisha pleaded with Faye to send Bea and the boy home. She could only imagine what they might tell people about the experience they'd just had. However, her Aunt flatly refused.

"They cannot leave yet," she said, "I need to find out why they were chosen."

"But it must be a mistake," Nisha insisted. "You said so yourself. And the whole Ninane thing was pretty weird. They probably want to leave."

"Perhaps," she said, "but even if they want to, they can't, not really, at least not for good."

"What do you mean? Of course they…"

"Bring the tea tray into the living room and I'll explain more. Come now, this is important."

Frustrated and more than a little nervous, Nisha followed her aunt back to the front room.

Once the tea was poured and Faye had settled back into the cushions, she turned to Bea and said, "Now, I need you to tell me what Ninane said; everything you can remember."

Behind her oversized glasses, Bea's blue eyes sparkled and Nisha could smell the fizzy scent of enthusiasm bubbling in the air around her. If Bea was faking her feelings, she was darn good at it. Nisha was even more impressed when Bea proceeded to recount Ninane's words verbatim.

When she was done, Faye nodded, then shook her head, then nodded again. "You are quite a remarkable girl, aren't you? What else can you do?"

"Excuse me?" said Bea.

"Your powers of observation are remarkable," Faye replied. "I was wondering if you have other Gifts?"

"Oh, I don't know, not anything special. I like to read. I mean I read a lot," said Bea. Faye nodded but looked dissatisfied. "Well, that's a fine interest to have," she said. Then she turned her attention to the boy. "And you? Do you have any special talents?"

"Uh, I'm pretty good on a skateboard and I'm okay at basketball, but that's about it, I guess," he answered with a shrug.

"I see," Faye said, smiling vaguely at Indy, and Nisha wondered if her Aunt even knew what a skateboard was. "Well, honesty is a noble quality," she added politely, though Nisha could smell the stale scent of disappointment in the air.

"Because you know little of our ways, you cannot know how significant it is that one of the First Nine Sisters was here in this room," Faye said looking, at each of them in turn. "It is made more extraordinary by the seriousness of the circumstances, but I suppose that is the way of these things."

"Serious circumstances?" the boy asked.

"Very," answered Faye, "You have been asked to take on an exceedingly dangerous task and it appears that you have willingly accepted. Did Ninane explain that you have made a promise that cannot be undone?"

Nisha saw the boy and Bea exchange a confused look, but again, neither spoke.

"As I suspected," said Faye. "You don't fully understand what you've gotten yourselves into, do you? And to think, you only came here looking for a lost necklace."

Faye's eyes landed on Bea, and a touch of pink rose in Bea's cheeks. *Don't admit anything*, Nisha thought to her urgently. *Please just thank her very much and get out of here.*

When Bea did not respond for a moment, Nisha was hopeful that she might have received the message. However, instead of getting up to leave, she leaned forward and said imploringly, "But you are going to help us, right? Ninane said you would. She said you knew a great deal about The Coin."

Nisha felt her mouth drop open. Bea sounded so sincere. She even smelled sincere. *Does she really believe all this?*

"Of course," said Faye, reaching over to pat Bea's hand with her own, "but even with my help, it won't be easy. My knowledge has not been enough to help me and I have been searching for The Coin for the last twelve and some years."

"Well, one thing's for sure," said Indy, "you know more than we do."

"I suppose that's true," said Faye softly. "So I must tell you all I know if you're going to solve anything. And it all begins with Annwn."

"Who is Ann Oon?" asked the boy, pronouncing the word as Faye had said it. "Ninane said something about her, too."

"Annwn is not a person; it is a place," Faye replied, smiling at his mistake. "It is an island and it has been called by many names, though Annwn is its oldest and most secret." Faye looked dreamily into her teacup as she spoke. "It is a beautiful place with soft green hills, apple orchards, lush forests and in the center, a vast and deep lake. It's a peaceful place, ruled by The Great Lady, and I miss it very much. I'm sure Nisha would too if she could remember it, but she was so small when we moved."

Nisha cringed at the mention of her name. She glared at her Aunt, willing her to stop talking, but to no avail.

Bea, on the other hand, was concentrating on every word Faye said. *She's got to be faking it*, Nisha thought. *She's probably trying to memorize everything so she can tell the other Horribles all about it in the lunchroom tomorrow.* Nisha could just imagine the look on Amanda Whitehead's horrible face and she felt sick at the thought. She pressed her eyes closed.

"Where is the island?" Bea asked.

"Well, that's the thing about it; it's very hard to say because it is never exactly in the same place, and I have not been summoned home in many years."

"A moving island? That's impossible. I mean if it moves, how could you get there if you wanted to?" asked the boy.

"It's a very good question, but it would take too long to explain tonight. Besides, it's getting quite late. Perhaps it's best if you both go home now. I don't want your parents to worry."

Nisha opened her eyes hopefully, only to see a stricken look on Bea's face.

"Oh no, please go on," Bea said "We don't need our parent's permission to stay out," she added stressing her accent again and sitting up straighter. "Besides, Ninane said it was very important we hear the whole story as soon as possible. She said we need to hurry because it's almost Passage Day."

"It's true we have very little time," said Faye, "and if you truly are the Finders…" Her eyes drifted over the three of them again and landed on Nisha. Nisha looked back at Faye, trying to convey her feelings through her expression. *'Please stop talking right now or I might die'* was what she hoped her face said, but if Aunt Faye saw it, she ignored it entirely. She turned back to Bea and the boy and said, "Well, alright then, but what I am about to share with you may be very difficult for you to believe."

"Actually," said Bea, giving Nisha a quick, knowing glance, "I've just recently started to believe that anything is possible."

CHAPTER 18

THE THIRD OF FIVE

"It is usually best to start at the beginning," Faye began, setting her teacup down and tucking her bun into place, "but in this case I cannot, for there is no beginning to this story. No one knows for sure where The Coins came from, and the truth is so old it has become legend. I can only tell you what I have heard and hope that you will make sense of it." Faye paused a moment to make sure her audience was with her, before continuing.

"There are and have always been five Coins. Each is unique and incredibly powerful, for they hold within them the most elemental requirements of all living things. The First is the Coin of Life and it represents the earth and all the living creatures. The Second, Death, contains the consciousness of all that has come before and is now past. The Fourth coin is Love as vital as the air we breathe. And the Fifth is The Coin of Time, without which nothing could exist."

"What about the third one? You left that one out," said Bea.

"Yes," Faye agreed, "I left it for last on purpose, for it is The Third Coin that has brought you, The Finders, together tonight. It is The Coin of Balance, the center of the five, and it keeps the others in harmony, balancing the delicate tension between them. That is why it is so important that we find it. For without it -

without The Third Coin - all The Coins are at risk. If they are not all together in The Room of Truth by Passage Day, I'm afraid that nothing in our world will remain as we know it."

No one spoke, and Faye nodded in understanding. "I realize it is a lot to take in," she said, "but now at least you understand how important this quest is." Then she turned her attention to Bea. "I must ask you about your mother's pendant. You said it was shaped like a coin. Is it possible you have found your way here because your mother's pendant is The Coin we seek? Could your mother be a daughter of Annwn?"

Bea looked down at her lap and appeared to be seriously considering the question. When she looked up, her eyes had a damp softness to them, as if she were about to cry. "The truth is," she said, "I really don't know anything about my mother except that she was English and that her name was Katherine. I don't even know if the coin we're looking for, or the pendant, I mean, was actually hers."

Nisha looked closely at Bea. Again, her feelings appeared genuine. Nisha could detect no fishy smell in the air. *She must be telling the truth*, Nisha decided, for she couldn't imagine anyone, even a Huntington Horrible, who would lie about their own mother being dead.

"Well, I'm sorry to hear it," said Aunt Faye. "I was hoping your mother might provide us a clue. You see, the whereabouts of The Coins has been a secret ever since The War of Logres."

"The what?" Indy asked.

"The War of Logres," said Faye. "I didn't expect they'd teach you about it in school. It happened a very long time ago, before people wrote things down. However, it was so terrible and dangerous that The Lady was forced to hide our island and its treasures. It has been drifting in The Mists ever since."

"Treasures?" asked Indy.

Faye nodded solemnly. "Almost every known magical object, or majects as we call them, is kept on our island, for Annwn is known as a place of peace and protection. Like the island itself, all of the majects were carefully hidden away during the war. Some went to the Green Wood where the elves live and others to the dark caves of the Druids. The more valuable and dangerous things were secreted away in the depths of The Lake itself, for few mortal men can endure its cold waters and live. But the most precious of all, The Five Coins, had to be safeguarded with the greatest care. It was then that the Order of Caretakers was created. Five young girls were selected, one from each of the five houses of Annwn, to serve a new role: Caretakers of The Coins."

"I don't get it," said Indy. "Why would The Lady give The Five Coins to a bunch of girls?"

Faye smiled at Indy. "Man Kind always makes that mistake; underestimating women, and girls even more so. The Lady is wise. She knows the minds of men. She knew their logic would lead them in other directions. And, wiser still, she knows the hearts of women, fierce and loyal as lions. The Lady knew that no man would protect The Coins with as much devotion as the young Caretakers would."

"And it remains true to this day. When a girl becomes a Caretaker she willingly swears to give up her life for her coin if need be. And she carries out her commission until the day that one of her own daughters turns thirteen. On that day, Passage Day, The Coin is passed to that chosen child and the child becomes the new Caretaker. And so it has gone ever since."

"How did the war finally end?" asked Bea.

"It ended only when The Lady sent her most trusted advisor to intervene, a Druid and master spellbinder by the name Myrddin. He used his magic to put the one true king on the throne, and finally there was peace. But ever since…"

Faye was stopped in mid-sentence when suddenly Bea gasped and clapped her hand across her mouth. She began to bounce up and down in her chair.

"What is it, child?" asked Faye.

Bea's words came out in bursts of excitement. "Myrddin? A great king? The Lady of the Lake?" Nisha could see a look of epiphany in Bea's bright blue eyes as she put the pieces together. "Are you saying… are you talking about Merlin and Arthur? King Arthur? Are you telling us that you come from Avalon?"

Faye shifted in her seat uncomfortably. "It is a bit too much for one evening isn't it?" she said. "I should have seen that sooner. Tomorrow is better, perhaps. We can take the story up again then."

Instantly, Bea was subdued. "No, I'm sorry, I didn't mean anything… I just…please continue. I promise I won't interrupt again."

Nisha's heart was now pounding in her ears. *Is Faye insane?* Why would she trust these strangers with secrets Nisha was barely able to believe herself? To Nisha's great dismay, Faye nodded at Bea.

"Alright, just a bit more, but then you must promise to go home and get some rest."

Bea nodded eagerly, and Faye continued.

"Unfortunately, the magic that was necessary to bring Arthur to the throne also brought unwanted attention to Annwn, or Avalon as you call it. Men began to hunt for the lost island and its treasures. And although The Lady pulled the island even farther into The Mists, the Caretakers' job grew more daunting with time. They began to travel the world looking for the safest hiding places."

"So let me get this straight," Bea said, pulling a white notebook from her handbag and beginning to write. "You and Nisha are part of the family that was protecting one of these coins, right?"

"That is correct," Faye answered.

Bea nodded enthusiastically as she wrote. "So how did you lose the coin? You said, I mean Ninane said that we should start with the last Caretaker. Where is she?"

Faye hesitated, and Nisha saw her Aunt's eyes suddenly brighten with tears. "The last Caretaker is dead. She died trying to protect The Coin."

"Oh… I'm sorry," said Bea.

"Who was she?" Nisha demanded, surprised to hear her own voice so loud in the quiet room.

Faye looked at the ground and shook her head slowly back and forth. "Oh, my dear Nisha," she said softly, "you already know the answer, don't you?"

"Who?" Nisha demanded, but Faye was right: Nisha already knew the answer. It was her mother, Caitria.

After promising to return the next night, Bea and the boy finally left but Nisha was barely aware of their goodbyes. Her head was pounding and questions stormed through her brain. *How could Faye share such important and personal things with people they barely knew? How would she face the Horribles tomorrow if Bea Brightman decides to tell them any part of what she'd just heard?* And perhaps the most confusing of all, *Had her mother really died trying to protect some magical coin?*

Nisha felt tears spring to her eyes. She turned to her Aunt. "Do you have any idea who those kids are? That girl…she…"

"Goes to your school."

"You knew all along?" Nisha cried, tears now sliding down her cheeks. "If you knew, then why would you tell her that stuff? Can you imagine what my life will be like if she tells the other kids at school?"

"She won't."

"You don't know what those girls are capable of," Nisha replied desperately.

"She took The Oath, didn't she?"

Nisha nodded, wiping the hot tears from her cheeks with the back of her hand.

"Then you can stop worrying. Once The Oath is taken The Finders cannot speak of The Coin to anyone except The Council and each other."

"You don't understand," Nisha almost shouted. "Just because she said some silly rhyme does not mean that she won't go blabbing all over the school. This isn't Annwn or Avalon or whatever you call it. Girls at Miss Huntington's have no code of honor. She's probably on the phone already."

"Nisha," Faye replied, her face pale with exhaustion. "Have you considered that it might be you who does not understand? When I say they cannot talk about the quest, I mean it. They cannot. It is impossible. The Oath is enchanted. Its magic takes effect immediately. So, if that's all that you are worried about, then I'll say good night." Faye turned and headed off down the hall, but Nisha stopped her.

"No, wait..." Nisha hesitated. Faye paused expectantly. Nisha knew her Aunt had seen through to her deeper feelings as usual. There was much more to it all than just Bea keeping her mouth shut, but Nisha didn't know where to begin.

"I...I still don't understand," Nisha stammered, her voice shaking. "Why would you bring my mother into this?" She said, a sob escaping with the words. "My mother died during childbirth. End of story."

Faye sighed and stepped forward. She reached out for Nisha's hand but Nisha pulled it away.

"Nisha dearest," she said, undaunted, "your mother's death is not the end of the story. Look inside yourself and you will know what's true. For Spirits sake, child, do you really think you are a Wishmaker so you could make little boys fly? Don't you think there might be more to it?" Faye looked deeply into Nisha's eyes. "Nisha, you have those powers so you can help people. And right now I need you to help me, to help us, The Council. We cannot do it without you."

Nisha stopped and stretched out her senses. Every one of them: her eyes, her ears and even her nose was telling her that Faye's words were true. She steadied her breath and wiped her face dry with the sleeve of her shirt. Her heart was still pounding, but the tears had stopped.

"Okay, so let's say I believe it all?" Nisha said, "The powers I have are useless. Even if I wanted to help, I doubt I could."

An expression of relief passed across Faye's face and she smiled. "You will practice. You will learn."

Nisha nodded. "Fine, I'll practice. I'll learn everything you want me to learn and I'll do my best to find your coin, but we have to leave the others out of it."

Faye raised an eyebrow. "I'm sorry, Nisha, but I cannot leave them out. For some reason, The Lady has chosen them just as she has chosen you. Our only hope to find The Coin is if the three of you work together."

CHAPTER 19

THE BIRTHDAY PRESENT

It was difficult to get through school the next day. Bea hadn't slept well. And when she did finally fall asleep, dark, confusing dreams awakened her throughout the night. She tried her best to pay attention to her lessons but she couldn't focus. Her only clear thoughts were of the previous night's events; Nisha's strange Aunt, the candles, The Oath.

To make things even more complicated, Charlotte Wang and Amanda Whitehead seemed to be everywhere. In fact, ever since the day Bea had chosen to sit with Nisha in the lunchroom, they were friendlier than ever. Bea knew that being unavailable often intrigued popular girls but she was surprised at how determined they seemed. However, knowing how much they disliked Nisha, she couldn't help but wonder if their intentions were genuine, especially Amanda's.

Normally, Bea would have been pleased by the attention, but for some reason she just couldn't seem to muster any interest in Charlotte or any of the other Top Pops. All she wanted to do was make it till lunchtime so she could talk to Nisha about The Coin. Unfortunately, when lunchtime came, Charlotte appeared beside her, linked her arm in Bea's, and demanded that Bea sit at the Top Pop table. There was just no way to turn her down.

When the last bell of the day finally rang, Bea still hadn't seen Nisha. Frustrated and tired, she headed home. When she arrived, she was happily surprised to find her father in the front hall, his suitcases were lined neatly against the wall.

"Welcome home, Father!" Bea said, hugging him briefly and even in his woolen suit, he felt thinner than usual.

"It's good to see you, Bianca. How are you?"

"Me? Just fine. Did you just get in? Are you hungry? I think Cookie's making a roast tonight." Bea hadn't realized how much she'd missed him.

Father frowned and pulled at his cuffs nervously.

"What is it Father? Is something wrong?"

"No. All is well. It's just that I'm afraid I'm not even staying the night. I'm flying out on the eight o'clock to St Petersburg. There's a contact there who has an interesting lead on the… on an artifact I'm looking for."

"But you just got home," Bea said, forcing herself not to whine.

Father cleared his throat. "I know, but I'm very close to finding something; something I've been after for many years."

"Oh…cool," Bea said quietly, wondering if he might be talking about a coin or even The Coin. Her father raised an eyebrow.

"Cool?" he repeated as if the word were another language. "Well, we still have a few minutes before the car gets here."

Bea shrugged. "We could sit on the stoop," she suggested.

"The stoop?"

"The stoop, you know, the front steps."

"Yes, I know the colloquialism. It's from the Dutch word 'stoep', which means small porch. And thank you, yes. I'd be happy to join you on the stoop…It would be cool."

It was rare her father made any effort at humor so Bea forced herself to smile at his weak attempt. They stepped outside into the thick, warm evening air.

"It's been like this every day," Bea said. "Depressing, isn't it?"

Bea's father looked up into the hazy sky. "Highly unusual,"

he answered as if noticing the strange grey weather for the first time.

When they were settled on the top step, Bea took a deep breath. "I'm glad we have a moment to talk, Father. I've been meaning to ask you something."

"Is there something you need?"

Bea glanced quickly across the street at the flickering neon sign in Nisha's front window.

"No, it's ...well, it's..." She hesitated. "I was wondering... do you believe in the existence of magic?"

Her father looked at her sideways. "You're serious?" he said.

"Quite."

He leaned back and scratched the back of his head. There was an odd look on his face. "Many cultures have believed in magic throughout the ages," he said slowly.

"I know, but what about you? Do you believe magic exists?"

Instead of answering right away, he picked up her hand and dusted off the tiny cement pebbles that clung to her palm. Then he squinted out towards the street as if straining to see something far away. "Bianca," he said, with a small squeeze of her fingers, "I am absolutely certain of it."

Bea's mouth fell open. She had expected a long-winded history of magical practices or perhaps a lecture on how she shouldn't let her imagination get the better of her. She waited for him to say more, but he did not.

Just then, the hired car pulled up, and Father stood up to get his bags. When the car was packed and ready to go, Father returned to the stoop where Bea was still perched. "I may not be back for some time," he said, "so I wanted to give you this."

He reached into his jacket pocket and pulled out a small box. The paper wrapping was a pale gold, faded and creased as though it had been wrapped a long time ago. Bianca stared at the present in his hand.

"It's for your birthday," he said.

Bea nodded. "So, you won't be home until my birthday?" she asked, unable to hide the disappointment in her voice.

"I'll try my best to be here, but just in case I'm not, I wanted you to have it so you can open it on that day."

"You've never given me a present before," said Bea, confused. "Not a traditional one anyway…"

"And I still haven't. It's not from me. It's from your grandmother. She gave it to me a long time ago with instructions that you were to have it on your thirteenth birthday."

"Oh…" said Bea, not sure what to make of a present from someone she'd never met. "Thanks," she added.

"Remember, not until your birthday," her father said.

Bea nodded solemnly. Then, moments later, he was gone, and Bea went back inside with the box in her hand.

Surprisingly, Bea didn't feel curious. She felt sad. She wasn't interested in an ugly old heirloom from a grandmother she never knew. All she really wanted for her birthday was to have her father back home.

CHAPTER 20

THE COUNCIL OF THE COIN

Bea placed the present on the bookshelf in her room and glanced at the clock. Five minutes to seven and she was still in her school uniform.

For a moment, she froze with indecision about what to wear. Should she try to maintain the charade of Clarisse Worthington? She knew she hadn't fooled the fortuneteller and she doubted she could get Indy to wear a costume again, so what was the point?

Bea decided on jeans and a t-shirt. With her hair flying behind her, she ran down the staircase two steps at a time. She hadn't thought to bring a sweater, but luckily, it was another unusually warm night.

Indy was already there, standing across the street in front of Nisha's building, and seeing him made Bea smile. He hadn't even questioned whether they would be returning to Nisha's or not. Of course they would be. He was as curious as she was. And, if the whole thing turned out to be real, well, even better.

"So, what do you think?" he asked, as they stepped up to Nisha's front door. "Is all this stuff real or what?"

"I don't know," Bea answered thoughtfully as she rang the doorbell. "I mean, it seems unlikely but somehow it feels real. I can't explain it."

"I know what you mean," said Indy enthusiastically. "This afternoon I…" But before he could finish, the door opened and Aunt Faye was in front of them, looking startlingly different than she had the night before. Her hair, which Bea had only ever seen twisted up in a bun, was loose and hung down around her almost to her knees. Some strands were woven into narrow braids, laced with blue ribbons and arranged in an intricate crown around her forehead. She wore a long deep blue dress made of a rich material that softly reflected the front door light, giving her a phantom-like glow. Silvery ropes crisscrossed the front of the gown, and pulled it close to her small frame. The impression was regal; as if she were some kind of queen, and Bea suddenly felt a self-conscious in her jeans.

Aunt Faye smiled at them distractedly and Bea realized that despite her elegant attire, Nisha's aunt was a bit frazzled. She didn't seem to notice how different they all looked compared with the previous night.

"Good, you're here," she said as she ushered them past the living room and down the narrow hall. "Right on time for the meeting."

Indy looked at Bea and she knew what he was thinking. *What meeting?*

"Wait here," Faye said when they got to the kitchen. "Nisha will join you in a moment." She exited out the back door and a minute later Nisha walked in carrying a tray of empty glasses. When she saw Bea and Indy, the glasses on the tray rattled slightly. She hurried over to the table to set them down.

"Hi," she said quietly, glancing nervously at the back door. "I wasn't sure if you were coming."

"Are you kidding, this is really important," Bea assured her with a grin.

Indy nodded his agreement, then asked, "But… are there other people here?"

"Didn't my Aunt explain?" Nisha said, looking nervously from Indy to Bea. "They're her friends, well not just her friends. She says they're…" Nisha looked down at her hands. "She says that they are The Coin Council that she was talking about last night."

"Really? They're here? Now?" Bea said. The astonishment was evident in her voice.

"Yes," answered Nisha, frowning at her.

"Who are they?" asked Indy.

Nisha's eyes moved to Indy's face and Bea saw her expression grow softer. "They're others from…" Nisha hesitated, then continued in a whisper, "they're all a bit…I mean they're dressed up like…well, you'll see." Nisha turned towards the door, and at the same time, Faye came in.

"The Council is waiting," she announced formally. Then she leaned closer to the three of them and added in a conspiratorial voice, "I'm sorry to spring this on you children but when they heard about The Telling and The Oath they were insistent on meeting you immediately. The story of Caitria will have to wait until later. I promise this won't take long."

It was after sunset and the sky was dark. The only light came from a dim moon and a few strings of white Christmas bulbs draped haphazardly around the wooden fence that enclosed the small yard. Bea could make out the shapes of people sitting and standing around what appeared to be a small rock pond in the center of the lawn.

As her eyes adjusted to the light, she saw that seated on a large stone to her left was a very pretty woman in a long pale dress much like Faye's. A light blue satin cord wound around the garment, pulling it close to her curvaceous figure. A small golden band encircled her head and glittered softly from between her smooth brown curls. In her arms was a beautiful child, about two years old, dressed exactly like her mother except for the crown. She was sleeping peacefully. On the ground by the woman's feet was another child identical to the first one, happily chewing the hem of her mother's long skirt.

"She's owns the bakery," Indy whispered. Bea nodded and her eyes moved to a man who was standing behind a low picnic table. He was tall and slender and wearing a pale, pearly gray robe tied around the middle with a black cord. The large hood of his garment hung halfway down his back and his silvery hair looked luminescent in the moonlight. After a moment, he pulled his wide sleeve up to check his watch and as he angled his head to catch the light, Bea confirmed what she had already suspected. It was the man from the clock shop.

On the right side of the small pond, in her familiar white wicker chair, was the needlepoint lady, wearing a heavily embroidered gown of earthy colors. Her curly black and grey hair, which she normally wore in an untidy bun, was loose and wild around her dark, round face. An odd tiara of golden leaves stuck out from above her forehead. On her feet were pink, puffy bedroom slippers.

"Do you think this is some kind of cult or something?" Indy whispered.

"It's possible," Bea said, nodding, having already considered this. "But I doubt it's dangerous. I mean, Nisha seems to be alright, and anyway, if something suspicious happens, I'm pretty confident we can outrun most of them."

"Seriously, that's your plan?" asked Indy, looking around uncomfortably.

Bea grinned. At the same moment, the clock shop man sniffed loudly. "Well, what are we waiting for? If everyone's here, then let's get on with it."

"Yes, we should," said Faye, who was standing at the front of the group. She lifted her arms to the sky and said, "Everyone, please form a Water Circle so I can begin to summon The Spirits."

As everyone began to gather around the small pond, Bea thought she saw someone else, a dark presence in the back of the yard, but when she looked again, the figure was gone. She was startled moments later when a man dressed in a long cloak similar to that of the clock shop man took a place beside her in the circle. His hood was pulled so far forward that his face was not visible. A small shiver ran down Bea's back. No one else seemed concerned except for Indy, who took Bea's arm and pulled her closer to him. Everyone else continued to arrange themselves around the small rock pond until the circle was complete.

When everyone was still, Faye nodded at the clock shop man, and he reached back and brought his hood up over his head so that, like the man next to Bea, it covered his face entirely. Then he clasped his hands in front of him, bringing the long flowing sleeves of the robe together until all of his skin was hidden by fabric.

The women struck a different pose. They stood with their eyes closed and their chins tilted up so their faces were turned towards the sky. Their hands hung at their sides; palms open and facing forward as if waiting for an embrace. Faye began to chant and Bea peeked at Indy to see how he was doing. He appeared curious but unfazed, and Bea smiled to herself. Most people would be completely freaked out by now, but not Indy. He looked back at her and shrugged as if to say, "I'm okay if you are."

Faye's chant was fuzzy and whispery but there was something soothing and familiar about it. Bea watched the reflection of the tiny lights on the still water of the pond, and before she knew what was happening, things around her began to change. The air had grown thicker and the lights from the small Christmas strings softened. She felt calm, yet at the same time strangely conscious, aware of each person's heartbeat and breath coming together into a single connected rhythm.

When the air was so dense and misty that Bea could not see beyond the circle, Faye stopped chanting and spoke in her normal voice.

"We have formed our circle tonight around the Waters of Life, in the light of the November moon, to welcome The Finders, bound by The Oath in The Quest of the Third Coin."

Bea shifted uncomfortably as she felt the attention of the group turn towards her and Indy.

Faye took Nisha by the hand and pulled her gently into the circle. "One in darkness she will see." Faye glanced around the circle as if expecting someone to say something. Everyone remained silent, so she continued.

"One to light the way," Faye said, gesturing to Bea to move

forward. Not knowing what else to do, Bea took a small step forward and then quickly stepped back. Again, there was no response from the group but she could feel their eyes appraising her.

Then Aunt Faye grasped Indy's hand and raised it into the air. "And the Third to keep them both safely until the Passage Day." Her voice was loud and determined.

The group was silent for several seconds. The air hummed around them, and Bea thought for a moment that something truly magical might happen. Instead, the figure next to her suddenly threw back his hood with a loud huff. Bea was startled to find that he was a boy; the same boy she had seen come out of the clock shop just a few weeks ago. He was no more than fifteen, with sharp, almost feminine features. His ears were particularly odd, so pointed that their tips poked out through the strands of his fair hair. He might have been handsome, beautiful even, but his face was full of anger.

Indy leaned over and whispered in Bea's ear. "I know him," he said. "He goes to the high school. Kids say he's crazy; put some seventh-grader in the hospital last year."

"Really?" the boy said incredulously, and for a horrible second Bea thought he was addressing Indy, but his eyes were on the other council members. "I mean, I know you said they took The Oath," he continued, "but them? We are supposed to believe that these three kids are The Finders?"

"They were named as Finders at my own table," Faye said sternly. "Do you doubt this?"

The clock shop man slid back his silver hood and glared at the boy. The boy sighed loudly and checked his tone. "No, of course not, Lady Faye. I'm sure you thought…or that is, I'm sure that's what it seemed… but don't you think maybe we should discuss it? It's got to be some kind of mistake. I mean with the exception of Nisha of course," he added quickly. "They just seem so… so… *ordinary*," he finished.

"Our purpose here tonight is to share our mission with the Finders," Faye replied calmly, "not to discuss the validity of The Lady's choice. I will note your concern for the record, but this decision is not for us to question." She turned to the group and announced, as if speaking to a large audience, "The Apprentice Councilman of the Second Coin has voiced concern about the age and... ability of the chosen Finders."

"And you are sure they've taken The Oath?" The boy spoke again, before Faye had finished.

"They have," she answered. Her voice was now icy. "As I have already..."

"And has it taken effect?" the boy interrupted.

"I don't know," said Faye sharply. "And it's not necessarily something we can know."

Had what taken effect, Bea wondered? She shot a look at Indy. He looked back at her with one eyebrow raised quizzically and she knew he was wondering the same thing.

Faye continued, "According to The Great Book, the change is very personal, very subtle. We may not even know when it happens."

"Well, maybe we should ask them" said the boy. "Or better yet, we should test them."

"Penn," the clock shop man interjected sternly, "this is not an interrogation. Faye has already explained the events of last night."

"I know, I know, but be reasonable, Uncle," the boy moaned. "We need to know if they have the skills. You know as well as I do what The Finders will be up against." His voice was rising now as he gestured towards Indy. "The Third, The Protector, is supposed to be a great warrior; not some kid who rides around on a toy all day. And the Dark, the Dark is supposed to have the Spirit Gifts of Knowing and Wishmaking that are beyond all our powers combined, and we all know that..." He stopped himself, and turned suddenly to Bea. "And, well, what about her?" he said. "The Light is supposed to be a great Seer, one with the vision to lead us to The Coin. Blondie O'Cheerleader here can't possibly..."

"That's enough, Penn," said the clock shop man. Then he turned to Faye. "I beg your pardon, Lady Faye," he said, bowing his head respectfully. "Despite his inappropriate behavior,

Penn's concerns seem legitimate. I, myself, find it difficult to believe that these ordinary children of Man Kind are adequate for our purposes."

"How are you so sure they're ordinary?" the needlepoint lady asked, speaking for the first time. "We should never be quick to cast judgment based on appearances. We all know the ways of The Lake aren't always plain. Take our Nisha here. She just got her Spirit Gifts when we'd all but given up hope."

Bea glanced over at Nisha and could almost feel her blushing, though it was too dark to tell for sure.

"Yeah, but how strong will they be?" Penn grumbled angrily. "She doesn't even have a twin."

"You will stop now, Penn Ludd," Faye commanded, her voice echoing in the small yard. "The discussion is over. Gloria is right. It matters not what we see or do not see. The Lady has made her choice. These are our Finders. Though, I, more than anyone else, wish it were not so."

CHAPTER 21

THE INTRODUCTIONS

"We are, as always, grateful for the Lady's wisdom," said the clock shop man, glancing sharply at the boy. "And we will *all* cooperate and work with what we have been given. But now," he said, checking his watch, "if we could get on with things, I would deeply appreciate it. I only have another eighteen minutes."

"Clock emergency," said Indy, out of the corner of his mouth. "Not a minute to waste!" Bea stifled her laugh and poked him with her elbow, hoping no one had heard him.

"Another appointment, Graydon, really?" said Faye. "Please tell us what could be more important than this?"

"Another delayed sunrise," he answered grimly. "Point one six five seconds behind schedule again yesterday."

The Needlepoint lady gasped.

Indy leaned toward Bea, "Point one six five seconds doesn't sound all that serious to me," he whispered.

Suddenly the clock shop man's head spun in their direction and his eyes met Indy's. "Well, apparently you're no wizard at math."

"Not a wizard at all, in fact..." said Penn, to no one in particular.

Indy looked over at Penn for a moment; his eyes slightly squinted. The boy stared back challengingly.

"I do okay in math," said Indy, slowly turning his attention back to the clock shop man.

"Is that so?" said Graydon, tilting his head back slightly so he could look down his nose at Indy. "Well excellent. Then you'll have no problem telling us what will happen if each day gets *point one six five* seconds shorter for one year."

Indy looked stricken and Penn chuckled.

"Don't worry," Penn sneered, "I'm sure your skateboarding skills will more than make up for what you lack in intelligence."

"What is your problem?" Indy said, stepping forward in front of Bea so he could face the boy directly. He had an expression on his face Bea hadn't seen before: his eyes had gone flat and the muscles in his jaw flexed. The blond boy matched Indy's stare. He pushed back his cloak and stepped forward so they were inches apart.

"Are you sure about this, skater-boy?" he said.

The clock shop man took two long strides forward, grasped both boys by the shoulders, and shoved them back into their places in the circle. "It would mean," he said, continuing the conversation as if it had not been interrupted, "that in one year's time the day would be …"

"One minute shorter," said Indy, sounding as if he were surprised by his own voice.

"That's correct," said the clock shop man, appraising Indy with a look of surprise. "And if the daylight hours continue to shorten it would mean devastating effects on productivity."

"Not to mention eventual poverty and famine," added The Needlepoint Lady.

"Another reason the sooner we find The Coin the better," Faye interjected. She turned her attention back to Indy, Nisha and Bea, and cleared her throat. "Tonight we welcome you, Finders, to our Council Circle and offer you our help. The Council that you see before you is made up of members from each of the Five Houses of Avalon and each member has sworn to protect the Five Coins and their Caretakers. Let us begin with

Graydon."

The clock shop man stepped forward and gave a short bow. "I am Graydon Green of Greenstone, the Councilmember for the Fifth Coin, The Coin of Time."

"So are you a Caretaker of a coin like Nisha's mother?" asked Bea.

Penn chuckled.

"Indeed not," said Mr. Green, ignoring Penn, "our jobs here are to protect and care for our respective Caretakers. In addition, we must also monitor all that our Coins represent. You have heard the expression time is money, I presume? Well it's true. Time and money are one and the same, which means, in essence, that I am also responsible for monitoring the world's financial structure."

"That's cool," said Indy, sounding genuinely impressed.

Mr. Green raised an eyebrow. "If by cool you mean important then, thank you," he replied stiffly.

"Wonderful," said Faye brightly, "Bridget, perhaps you could go next."

The pretty bakery lady nodded and carefully shifted the sleeping child in her arms over to one hip. Then, stepping delicately over the other, she walked up to Indy and Bea.

"How do you do, my dears?" the woman said, smiling a wide, dimpled smile. "I am Bridget of Maidenhair Glen, the Councilwoman of the Fourth Coin, The Coin of Love."

Bridget stepped up to Indy and grasped him by the chin. For a long moment, she held his face and stared into his eyes. Indy blushed a deep shade of red and Penn chortled. When Indy was released, he looked down at his shoes.

Then Bridget turned to Bea. She stood so close that Bea could hear the toddler in her arms breathing. Then she placed her hand on Bea's cheek and Bea felt a gentle heat radiating from her fingers. After a moment she smiled. "You have a beautiful heart," she said. "And a beautiful face as well. Don't you think so, Penn?" she asked, gently turning Bea's face towards the boy.

Penn cheeks went pink and he shrugged uneasily. Bridget gave Indy a quick wink and Indy grinned back at her gratefully.

"There is a great deal of love in all of you," she said grasping Nisha's hand. "Don't forget to listen to your hearts. You will need love's guidance on your quest."

"That and much, much more, I'm sorry to say," said Gloria, the needlepoint lady, who padded towards them from the other side of the small pool, her large form bumping into Penn as she passed. "I am Gloria of Redspring, the Councilwoman of the First Coin; the Coin of Life. I am pleased to finally meet you, though I fear it may be too late. I'm afraid I can't remember a time when the weather was this bad."

Indy looked upward and shrugged. "It doesn't seem that bad to me," he said.

Suddenly, the needlepoint lady's eyes flashed. "Do you see bright stars in the heavens?" she asked angrily. "Do you feel the cooling winds of autumn? And what about rain? Where is the rain? For Spirits sake boy, it's November!"

"I've noticed it," Bea said, agreeing with her quickly. "Actually, I was just noticing it tonight on my way here. It has been much nicer than usual for this time of year."

"Nicer?" said Gloria, her voice deep and rumbling.

"Well I didn't mean nicer as in *nice*. What I meant was it hasn't been raining or…"

Suddenly a gust of wind whipped through the circle, leaving ripples in the small pond and knocking over one of the lawn chairs. "This weather is not *nice*," the Needlepoint Lady growled. "It's the opposite of nice. Don't you feel the dryness? No rain means no water and no water means no life." She glared at Bea. "Does that sound nice to you?"

"Alright now," said Faye as she and Bridget rushed forward to take Gloria by the hand. "Calm down, dear," Bridget said soothingly. "You mustn't get so emotional. You're frightening them. They don't yet understand what this weather means."

Gloria nodded slowly and Bea could see the anger begin clearing from her face. After a few seconds, she turned back to them and put her hand to her mouth. "Oh, I am sorry. It's just, well, things are so much worse than they appear."

As Faye and Bridget led Gloria back to her place in the circle,

Mr. Green turned to the group. "Allow me to wrap this up. This," he said with a wave of his hand, "is my nephew Penn Ludd, Apprentice Councilmember of the Second Coin, The Coin of Death. When he completes his apprenticeship, he will also be responsible for monitoring the gate between the two worlds. For the time being, however, Penn lives with me, under my supervision, until he has proven himself worthy of full duty."

Penn huffed loudly.

"Penn," said Mr. Green impatiently. "Every one of us went through a trial period. You are no exception."

"But I am an exception," said Penn angrily. "I have exceptional skills and I'll be happy to prove it. Make me a Finder and I'll find Sahwin. I'll hunt him down and I'll get The Coin back."

"We have been over this," his uncle snapped back at him. "We don't believe Sahwin has The Coin, so tracking him would be a waste of time.

"How can you say that? Didn't you hear Gloria? Things are worse than ever. It hasn't rained in over a month and we all know why. The Lost are seeping through the cracks and sucking up all the moisture. Stop pretending you all don't know what I'm talking about. Without The Third Coin we won't be able to stop them. If we don't get it back by Passage Day the wall may crumble completely and The Lost will be free."

"We are all aware of the situation," said Mr. Green, his jaw tense with controlled anger.

"If that's true, then how could you possibly think they're going to solve it?" he said, gesturing towards Bea and Indy. "Hasn't it ever occurred to you that the Lady doesn't live in this world? She doesn't know how things work here. But Sahwin has been here a long time. He knows how to manipulate things outside of The Mists. Maybe he's responsible for giving us these kids instead of real Finders."

"Enough!" Faye commanded. Her voice was bigger than Bea thought possible, coming from such a tiny woman. Everyone went silent.

"Go!" she commanded, pointing to the back door of the

apartment, her outstretched hand shaking slightly with anger. Penn hesitated. "Go," she said again, "and calm yourself. I know you are in the changing years but it is no excuse. You will not speak of The Lady that way; not within The Water Circle; not ever. You will respect The Cloak of Merlin you wear or I will take it and return it to its makers. Now go and pray to The Spirits for some self-control."

Penn boldly met Faye's eyes, but only for a moment. Then he bowed his head and said, "As you require, Lady Faye." But even then Bea thought she heard a hint of sarcasm in his voice. He pushed his way between Bea and Indy. "Good luck, kiddies," he hissed. Then he crossed the lawn and disappeared into the house.

Everyone remained silent until the door slammed behind him. Then Faye turned back to the group, her face full of sadness. She moved towards Indy and Bea and took their hands.

"I am Faye of Lakewood," she said quietly. "I am responsible for The Third Coin, which guides and protects the balance between all the forces of our world and The Other. But as you can see, I have failed at my task, and that is why you are here."

No one said anything at all, and Faye sighed miserably. "The circle has been broken. Our meeting is ended."

Bea looked around and saw that the misty air had cleared and everything looked much the way it had when they arrived.

When they were back inside, Mr. Green neatly removed his cloak. "I apologize for Penn," he said. "He's having a lot of trouble with all this."

"Is it true, the stuff he said?" asked Indy. "And what did he mean by the walls between the two worlds cracking? What two worlds?"

"The World of the Living and The Other World," said Bridget. "The world of The Spirits of those who have gone before us."

Indy nodded as if he understood, but Bea knew he must be as confused as she was. "So who are The Lost? And why are they dangerous?" Bea asked.

"Most Spirits are harmless," Bridget explained, "gone to the Other World to live out eternity in peace. But there are some, The Lost, who made ill use of their lives and therefore do not deserve their deaths. Their punishment is to be forever trapped between the two worlds, guarded by walls on either side. The balance of The Coins keeps those walls and everything else in check. If The Third Coin is not found by Passage Day and The Lost find their way into this world, it would be bad."

"How bad?" said Indy. "I think we ought to know what we're dealing with."

Bridget glanced at Mr. Green, who took a large breath and said, "It would mean the end. The Lost would suck up all the water on earth trying to live again. The Living would parch and die. We've heard that the walls are already cracking, and some believe that this dry weather we're experiencing isn't weather at all, but some of The Lost who have squeezed out through the cracks and are drinking the moisture out of the air." Mr. Green sniffed sharply. "I know it's a lot to take in, but I'm afraid I have to leave now. Come to my shop on Sunday at 2:00 pm and I will explain further."

"Uh, I'm not sure I can," said Indy. "I'm supposed to work, so I'll have to ask my dad."

"Ask him what?" said Mr. Green checking his watch.

"For permission, of course."

Mr. Green looked up from his watch with a perplexed look. "Haven't you heard what I've been saying? The world is in peril. You are The Finders sworn to find the lost Coin. It's too late to ask for permission. You took The Oath. It's an ancient druid enchantment. It is unbreakable, unalterable, unquittable and *unutterable*.

Indy nodded solemnly. "I get it, sir. I'll do everything I can to be there and I promise."

Mr. Green shook his head. "Well, do whatever you feel you have to do," he said. "Just be at my shop, Sunday, 2:00 pm, and don't be late."

CHAPTER 22

THE MIRROR OF AVALON

Nisha was relieved when the last of The Council had left. It had been a strange and difficult evening. Penn had been awful, not that she was surprised. Any time the Council gathered in the backyard he was always rude and conceited. She would overhear him bragging about his Elfin grandmother, how clever she was and how powerful. Nisha couldn't figure out why he went on about it so much. As far as she could tell, the only thing he inherited from her was his pointy ears and a snooty attitude.

Indy, on the other hand, was so polite. Whenever he spoke to someone, he looked them in the eye as if they were important, as if they mattered. Nisha realized, to her dismay, she was blushing at the thought of him. She cursed herself. She'd seen how idiotic the Huntington Horribles behaved when any of them liked a boy, and she'd promised herself that she would never act that way. Yet whenever Indy was around, her brain went haywire.

Nisha righted a tipped-over lawn chair and took in a sharp breath. She knew it was hopeless to think about someone like him; a normal boy with a normal family. Besides, the more she thought of it, the more obvious it became that it was Bea he cared for. *Hadn't she seen him hanging around Bea's stoop? Hadn't he gone along with wearing that silly costume to make Bea happy?*

She picked up the last of the glasses and brought them to the backdoor, but stopped when she saw Bea and Indy through the window. They were standing side by side talking quietly. Nisha's heart fell into her stomach.

Nisha waited until Aunt Faye returned to the kitchen before she letting herself in. Aunt Faye had changed her clothes and pulled her hair up into her everyday bun. "I'm sorry about the suddenness of the meeting," she said, as she ushered the three of them into the front room. "It's all been a bit of a shock... you finally turning up. I'm sure it's all a bit confusing for you too."

"Very," Bea admitted. "In fact I was just wondering about what Penn meant when he asked if The Oath had taken effect yet?"

"Yes, that, well, I was planning to share that with you earlier but didn't have the chance," Faye replied. "You see, some believe that when The Oath is taken, The Finders will change."

"Change?" Indy asked.

"Perhaps change is too strong a word," she clarified quickly. "It is more of a small enhancement, so to speak. The Oath brings out The Gifts each Finder already possesses. So, for instance," she continued with a glance at Bea, "if you are smart, you will be smarter or," her eyes moved to Indy, "if you are strong, you will be stronger."

And what if a person doesn't have any Gifts, or can't control the Gifts they have? Nisha thought with a pang. It hadn't occurred to her until then that she might be the least useful member of this small team.

"But that's not important right now," Faye continued. "If it's alright with Nisha, I'd like to tell you all more about Caitria. I think it will help you to understand what it is that you're really up against."

It took Nisha a moment to register what Faye was asking her. Was she ready to hear about how her mother had died? And maybe more importantly, was she okay with Indy and Bea hearing it too? She looked at Bea and Indy for a moment. They had seen so much already.

Nisha shrugged.

"Alright then," said Faye gently. "I think the story will be better told if you can see some of it. It's a bit dangerous of course, but serious situations often call for a bit of risk."

Once the candles were lit and the shades drawn, Faye went over to the chest of crystal balls which glowed in the darkened room. She picked up the largest and carried it carefully to the table. The ball was a deep blue-green and when she placed it on the table, the candles reflected in its surface like stars in the night sky. It was all very magical looking, and Nisha could see the anticipation in Bea's eyes.

"Oooh, I've never seen into a crystal ball before," Bea said. "I've always wondered if they really worked."

"Oh my, no!" said Faye with a chuckle. "But they're very good for business. My customers just love them. Now if you'll take your seats, we'll get started."

Bea sat, but her brows were crossed with confusion. "Then why are we…" she began, but Faye wasn't listening. She was focused on a shelf behind the table. On it was a cluster of colored bottles, dark blue, amber and green. After examining several, she finally selected one and turned around.

Bea's eyes brightened again. "What's in that?" she asked.

"Water, of course. What else would it be dear?"

Bea's look of confusion grew so comical that Nisha nearly laughed out loud.

Faye smiled and patted Bea's arm. "Sometimes it's best to observe first and then ask questions."

"Oh, of course," said Bea, her cheeks turning pink with embarrassment. "No more questions."

"Lovely," said Faye pleasantly. Then she held out the tiny blue bottle so they could all see it. "This," she said, with dramatic flourish, "is the purest water in the world, drawn from The Lake of Avalon; the source of life itself and that which connects all things." She pulled out the cork stopper with a small, hollow pop. "Tonight we use it to see the past." Then she slowly tipped the bottle over the deep turquoise ball, allowing only a single drop to fall. Instantly, the droplet was absorbed into the glass, and Nisha saw Bea and Indy look at each other in astonishment.

Faye then unraveled one of the dark blue ribbons from the end of her braid. She wrapped the ribbon gently around the ball and when it was completely encircled three times, she raised her hands out over the table and began to chant. "Mirror of the Avalon, reveal yourself. Water of The Lake, show us the past. Mirror of Avalon, reveal yourself. Water of The Lake, show us the past."

After a few moments a strange bubbling gurgled through the room and Nisha had to hold in her laughter again as she watched Bea and Indy looking around for the source of the sound.

The noise grew louder and louder, and Bea and Indy finally realized it was coming from the orb in front of them. Bea and Indy watched, transfixed, as the ball of glass began to churn and boil shifting itself into a new shape. The top sunk into the center as the bottom began to spread, and then, after another minute, it stopped entirely. With a small cracking sound, like water turning suddenly to ice, the glass hardened again. The ball had become a bowl.

It was low and wide with a thick rim. The outside surface was ropey and layered as if it were made of translucent seaweed, but the inside was smooth and shiny, and the flames from the three candles flickered in its mirror-like surface.

Faye laid the end of the ribbon on the table and looked up at them. "This," she said, with a dramatic pause, "is one of the Five Mirrors of Avalon."

"Wow," said Indy, whose mouth was agape, his eyes shining in the candlelight. "That's the coolest thing I've ever seen. What is it again?"

"It's a Mirror," said Faye, "one of five ancient vessels, created by the Elves as a Gift to The Lady. "

"It looks like a bowl," said Indy.

"Yes," Faye said patiently, "but not an ordinary bowl, for it holds the Water of The Lake in such a way that it becomes a mirror. The surface of the water can show you reflections of the past or the present and sometimes even the future. Of course, one must be worthy in order to see into it."

"Are we worthy?" Bea asked hopefully.

"Quite," answered Faye. "You have a worthy quest. But be warned, you must be trained to handle its power, for worthy or not, The Mirror is very dangerous."

"How can it be dangerous if it just shows you stuff?" said Indy.

Faye leaned over the bowl and said quietly, "If used incorrectly, this mirror could show you things you should not see. It can show you things that no one should ever see. People have gone mad from visions they were not prepared to witness, and that is not all you should fear." Faye leaned over further and whispered, "The mirror is like a window to another time or place, so not only can you see out, but sometimes, if you're not careful, others can see in."

"If it can do all that," said Bea, "can't it show us where The Coin is?"

"That is an excellent question, dear girl," said Faye, sighing, "but unfortunately, so far, the answer has been 'no'. I have tried all the magic I know but The Mirror will not reveal to us the whereabouts of The Coin. I believe The Lady enchanted The Mirrors so they could never reveal that information. So," she continued, looking imploringly at each of the children, "you must promise me you will never attempt to use The Mirror without me here."

Bea and Indy nodded and Faye said, "I will take your answer as a vow. Now, please rejoin your hands. It is growing late and there is a story to be told."

CHAPTER 23

THE STORY OF CAITRIA AND SAHWIN

Nisha, Bea and Indy watched in silence as Faye uncorked the bottle again and carefully allowed a single drop of liquid to fall into the bowl. Upon touching the glass, the drop sizzled and multiplied until water filled the bowl to the very rim. It was silvery and luminous like the center of a raindrop.

"Show us the beginning of our story," said Faye, with her arms stretched out in front of her. As soon as she spoke, a misty fog appeared and hung over The Mirror like a tiny cloud. As it dispersed, the face of a woman appeared on the surface of the water. She looked very much like a younger version of Faye.

"Ah," said Faye, "it begins with Danu, Nisha's grandmother, who was my sister." Nisha looked at the surface of the water and felt a sudden rush of anticipation. She had never seen another of her relatives other than Faye before. "Like all the girls on the Isle of Avalon," Faye continued, "I was a twin. My sister and I were the daughters of The Caretaker of The Coin, born on Passage Day. Therefore, it was to be that one of us would take our mother's place when we turned thirteen. Though we were both blessed with the Spirit Gifts, Danu's powers were much stronger than mine. When our thirteenth birthday came, it was no surprise that she was chosen."

"So, were you mad?" Indy asked, "You know, when you weren't chosen?"

"Not at all," said Faye, smiling. "It was Danu's dream to be The Caretaker, never mine. I was offered a place in the House of The Lady to study and serve, a position I desired and loved. Things went well for many years. I was very happy in my life of service, and Danu was a wonderful Caretaker, very dedicated and very skilled."

"When she was old enough, Danu was matched with Tages, a druid and a good man, and eventually she gave birth to her own twin daughters, Caitria and Kesara. They were born on December twelfth, Passage Day just like their mother and me, and all the Caretakers before us… and now Nisha."

"Wait…December twelfth is Passage Day?" Bea said, interrupting again.

Faye frowned.

"Sorry" Bea said quickly. "No more questions, I promise."

Faye nodded patiently. "Passage Day is the twelfth day of the twelfth month, just a few weeks from now. It was on that day many years ago that Danu chose Caitria to be the next Caretaker. Ah, here she is," said Faye, pointing to the bowl. The small cloud had returned, and as it slowly evaporated, Nisha, Indy and Bea leaned in closer.

Nisha could see a girl walking down a dirt path in the woods. She was a little taller and perhaps more narrow than Nisha, but so much like her that it would be hard to tell them apart.

Nisha sensed both Bea and Faye looking at her, gauging her reaction, yet Nisha wasn't sure what she should feel.

"She's really pretty," said Indy.

"Yes," Bea agreed. "She looks just like Nisha."

Nisha felt her cheeks turn pink and her fingers moved instinctively to the small circle of stones that hung from her necklace. However she stopped abruptly when she saw that Caitria, her mother, was wearing the very same necklace in the reflection in front of her.

"Some were surprised by Danu's choice of Caitria to be Caretaker," Faye continued. "On the surface, Kesara, an excellent student, seemed better suited. Caitria was more of a dreamer, always fascinated by things beyond the shores of Avalon. However, when the choosing was done, both girls accepted their fates gracefully."

"As the years turned, choosing Caitria proved to be a good decision. Like her mother, Caitria took her charge very seriously. She practiced her skills and studied her lessons so devotedly that Danu was worried she would never find the happiness of a partner and children."

Faye paused and the water in the bowl darkened; a dark grey mist appeared and lingered over the surface. Slowly it dispersed, leaving behind the image of a young man. His features were straight and sharp with black eyes and equally black hair. He might have been handsome but for his mouth, a thin whitish line; fleshless lips pressed together in an angry grimace.

"Sahwin" said Faye gravely. "Even then, we all had some trouble understanding why Danu chose him," Faye continued. "Yes, he was a good student, well-practiced with spells and potions, and a powerful magician. But Sahwin was a quiet and lonely boy. He came from the Family of The Second Coin, the Coin of Death, and there was no doubt he carried his family's burden."

"What burden?" Bea asked, apparently unable to control her curiosity for more than a minute at a time.

'Well, the family of the Second Coin is..." Faye paused, trying to select her next word. "Strange," she said, with a small shrug as if no other word would do. "It can't be helped, really. You see, the family of The Coin of Death is required to guard the gate between the two worlds. This task necessitates that they behold the faces of death, and even meet with Avalloc, The King of The Dead. It is said that some are not strong enough to bear it. Their hearts dry up and their capacity to love is replaced by a constant thirst that can never be sated." Faye sighed. "Of course these are only rumors, and obviously Danu never believed any of it or she would not have arranged the union between Caitria and Sahwin."

Faye shifted in her seat as if uncomfortable with what she

was about to say. She took a breath and looked at Nisha questioningly. Nisha nodded back, encouraging her to go on. She wanted to hear it all.

"Unfortunately, there was much about Sahwin Ludd that Danu did not know at the time. Even at his young age, he was cursed with the thirst of the dead, and, in his madness had convinced himself that his family alone should rule the island and all that was Avalon."

A sense of dread crept up the back of Nisha's neck. Until this point, Nisha had always thought her mother had died in childbirth, yet the mention of Sahwin involvement suggested something else, something darker.

"Sahwin readily accepted the arrangement, for he saw it as an opportunity to lay claim to our Coin and secure more power for the Ludds. Caitria, on the other hand, was not at all happy with her mother's choice. When Danu insisted they marry, Caitria and her mother argued fiercely. Caitria left the house in tears."

The scene in the bowl shifted again and when the cloud cleared, the surface of the water showed the figure of a young woman walking down a deserted, narrow beach, her long pale dress whipping in the wind around her brown legs.

"But The Spirits bent the path of fate that day," Faye continued, "and Caitria's life took an unpredictable turn. As she walked along the beach a blind mist rolled in and she was forced to find cover in a hollowed tree. It was late in the day and she fell asleep waiting for the weather to pass. When she awoke, she was surprised to find it was morning."

"Knowing her mother would be sick with worry, Caitria set out in a hurry down the beach, but was stopped by the sight of a sailing ship wrecked upon the shore. It was manned by a young explorer and his crew. They had been caught in a squall and had found the island quite accidentally."

"I supposed you can guess what happened then," said Faye with a small smile. "Caitria and the young captain fell in love at first sight. In only a few weeks, he proposed and Caitria begged her mother to allow their marriage. Danu had no choice but to agree. Her daughter's happiness came first in her heart."

"Who was he?" Nisha demanded, realizing for the first time that Faye must have known him. "Was he my father? What was his name?"

"Oh Nisha, my dearest," said Faye, her voice soaked with sadness, "I am so sorry to say that I don't really know. I never knew him very well. I was deep in my studies at that time and sworn to silence and prayer. The awful truth is none of us tried very hard to know him. He loved Caitria and that was all that seemed necessary to know. I don't think even Danu ever learned his real name. We simply called him Captain."

"Captain?" Nisha asked, shaking her head with confusion.

"I know it sounds strange to you, but in Avalon it is our custom to call people by a name that describes them, what they do or where they live. Like us. We are the Lakewoods because we come from the wood by the lake. We called your father Captain because that is what he was."

"That's a stupid custom," Nisha whispered, looking down at her hands. The feeling of hope had surged and fallen so quickly within her that she felt as if her insides were upside down. Hot tears gathered in her eyes.

"Perhaps it is," agreed Faye sadly.

Another mist gathered and cleared above the bowl and Caitria appeared, radiant in long silver robes. She stood on a green slope between two rivers. The pale blue ribbons in her long black hair lifted in the soft breeze.

"The Day When Two Rivers become One," said Faye. "Your mother was so beautiful, so happy. It would have been a perfect wedding day but for Sahwin. He nearly ruined it, bursting in on the ceremony in a rage. He accused Danu of robbing his family of their rights to The Third Coin claimed that Caitria was a traitor. That same night he ran away and no one heard from him or saw him again for almost a year."

"Your mother and father lived quite happily during those months. Your mother spent most of her time learning the ways of The Coin and your father spent most of his time repairing his damaged boat and taking care of your mother."

"Taking care of her?" Nisha asked. "Was she sick?"

"No, dear," said Faye, with a small smile, "she was pregnant."

However as Faye spoke, the mist came again over the bowl and this time it was thick and dark like a storm cloud. When it cleared, Bea and Indy leaned forward to get a better look, but Nisha closed her eyes. Her heart was pounding. She knew Aunt Faye had come to the end of the story.

When Nisha finally forced herself to look, she saw Sahwin in a long black coat. He was still recognizable but his long sharp features had become harder and uglier. His skin had taken on a sickly yellow tone and his black hair, which was once lustrous, was thin and oily, scraped back into a narrow braid.

"Sahwin returned to the island," Faye said, as she too stared into the bowl, her eyes dark with anger, "which is nearly impossible to do unless The Lady summons you. Only those willing to bargain with the dead can get back without her blessing. Who knows what promises he made to get through The Other World alive?" She sighed. "Yet there he was, on Passage Day; the day of your birth. In fact he arrived only minutes after you had fallen asleep for your very first nap."

The water changed again and there was Caitria in a large low bed with pale linens. Her eyes were closed, her face peaceful and shining with happiness.

"Danu was in the next room caring for you," Faye continued, "and your father was down at the beach working on the boat, trying to distract himself as he waited for your birth. A messenger had been sent to collect him but they had not yet returned."

"It was at this moment that Sahwin burst in on your mother. He demanded The Third Coin in the name of Ludd." Faye frowned. "I can only imagine Caitria's despair at that moment - sworn to protect The Coin and desperate to protect you. Thank The Spirits she was able to keep her wits about her. She did the one and only thing that could protect both you and The Coin. She lied. She told Sahwin that The Coin had been stolen."

Faye paused and Nisha could feel her heart pounding in her

ears and throat. She needed Faye to go on. She needed to hear what it was that Faye had kept silent all these years.

"The news that The Coin was lost infuriated him. Without a second thought, he vexed Caitria with a deadly plague. Having given her powers to the lie, Caitria had no defenses. She was consumed by the curse almost instantly.

"Danu rushed into the room but she was too late, Sahwin was gone and Caitria was fading quickly. Danu might have gone after him but instead she did what any mother would do. She tried to save Caitria." Faye was crying now as she spoke. "Danu used all of her Gifts, but nothing worked.

"Your father arrived not long after, expecting the joyous news of your birth, only to discover that Caitria was gone."

Faye paused for a moment, trying to regain her composure. "He went crazy, tortured with grief and anger. He left and went after Sahwin that night, though his boat was not yet seaworthy. Danu tried to stop him but he could not see reason. He promised Danu he would return for you as soon as he had avenged Caitria's death.

"When he was gone, Danu called for me. I arrived to find her so weak from trying to save Caitria that death was close. Still her thoughts were of you, her newborn granddaughter, and your safety. She was terrified that it would be Sahwin, and not your father, who would find his way back to Avalon for you, and that he would try to stake claim to you in place of The Coin. We decided that night that I would take you away from Avalon and make a new life someplace safe."

The Mirror had been swirling with images: Sahwin casting his curse, Danu with a baby wrapped in blankets, the silhouette of a young man on his knees on the beach, his face in his hands, a ship several yards from shore.

"Where is he now?" Nisha asked, her voice barely a whisper.

"We don't know where Sahwin is," said Faye, "but there is a rumor he is in New York."

"I don't mean Sahwin," Nisha said, choking on her words.

"Oh," said Faye looking down with shame. "Well we can only assume he must be... he's almost certainly dead. His ship wasn't ready to sail and he left in such a rush…It is doubtful he survived very long."

"Did you look for him?" Nisha asked, through clenched teeth.

"I did. We did. But we didn't have much to go on."

Nisha felt so many emotions at the same time that they blended together into one numb ache in her chest. She and Faye had never really talked much about her father before. She wasn't prepared for this whole new pain in her heart…all because of a stupid coin.

Thankfully, Indy changed the subject. "Do you think Sahwin has The Coin?" he asked.

"Well, that's what we thought for many years. We assumed he had discovered Caitria's hiding place, but he never came forward. Then rumors began to circulate of Sahwin at auctions and markets around the world. We believe now that he too is looking for The Coin, and as Passage Day approaches, it's more urgent than ever that we find it first. We have to unlock its power before he does."

Bea frowned. "Unlock its power?" she asked. "You mean we don't just have to find it? We have to figure out how to use it?"

"I'm afraid so," answered Faye. "Only The Caretakers are allowed to learn the ancient rituals. Only they know what must be done on Passage Day, and they are sworn to secrecy, much like the three of you."

"But this is urgent. Couldn't Nisha ask another Caretaker how it works?" asked Bea.

"It is a good suggestion, but not possible," said Faye. "Even if we wanted to ask them, we have not been able to contact them in some time."

"Why not?" Bea asked "Where are they?"

"Well, we don't know for sure, but it is not uncommon for a Caretaker to seek privacy and contemplation before Passage Day."

As her Aunt spoke of The Caretakers, the image of her father faded and was replaced by a foggy darkness and the sound of voices crying out to her. Nisha pointed to the bowl. "What's that?" she asked. But no else could see what she was looking at. She shuddered. It was them; the other Caretakers. They had been taken. Nisha was sure of it.

CHAPTER 24

THE TAROT

"Going out again?" said Nana Anna, as Bea reached for the front door. Bea froze. She had been so distracted by all the events of the day before that she had forgotten all about asking permission to go out that evening. "What is it this time?" asked Nana Anna. "The boy with the skateboard again?"

Bea hesitated. She was quite sure Nana Anna would frown on the idea of her seeing a fortuneteller, but she didn't want to lie.

"Actually, I've become friends with the niece of the fortuneteller across the street," she said, but to her surprise, the words that came out of her mouth were, "I've made a new friend named Nisha." And when she tried to say "We are on a quest to find a secret coin," what she said instead was, "There was a sign-up sheet and Nisha and I joined a club."

By the end of the conversation Nana Anna looked pleased. "A Science club? Well that certainly sounds like your sort of thing. Have a good time. And call if you need a car sent for you. I don't want you walking home in the dark."

That was totally weird, Bea thought as she watched Nana Anna head off down the hall. It was a thought she was having quite a lot lately. There was no other way to describe the remarkable coincidences that kept coming up between herself and Nisha. Last night's discovery – that they shared the same birthday, December twelfth – was the weirdest of all, especially because that same day also happened to be Passage Day. She wondered what it all meant and what the connection might be between them.

Anxious to discuss it all with Indy, she hurried across the street where he was waiting in front of Nisha's building. However, as she walked up behind him, she found Indy deeply engrossed in a dialogue with himself.

"Hey Nisha, how's it going?" he said to the air in front of him. Then he cleared his throat and said, "Hey Nisha, so are you okay after last night? I was thinking about you. No, damn, I can't say that."

Was Indy practicing saying hello to Nisha? Bea was amused but not surprised. She hadn't missed the way Indy blushed whenever Nisha was around.

She was just about to tap him on the shoulder when suddenly he spun around, startling her instead.

"Hey!" he said angrily.

"Wow," Bea said laughing. "How did you know I was here? I mean, I didn't think you could hear anything but your heart talking."

"What? I wasn't... I was just..." Indy stammered, his cheeks turning pink.

"Oh, don't worry about it. Your secret is safe with me," Bea said, trying to keep the giggle out of her voice.

They rang the bell and Nisha answered with her usual solemn expression. She nodded hello and stepped aside to let them in. "My Aunt will be ready in a minute,"

"Hi," said Indy, following Nisha into the living room.

"That was brilliant," Bea whispered following Indy into the darkened room. "Simple is best, don't want to overdo it."

Indy turned around and glared at her, which made Bea laugh. At the same time Faye came rushing into the room.

"Hello, hello," she called out. She was back in her fortuneteller clothes, her long colored skirt sweeping around her as she took her place at the table. "Take a seat, please," she said, smiling. "There is very little time and so much more to do!"

Once they were seated, Faye paused and looked around at their faces. "So," she said, "before we get started, do any of you have any questions?"

"Oh yes, loads of them!" said Bea, relieved to have a chance to ask.

"What a surprise," said Indy sarcastically.

Bea ignored him with a grin and said. "Well, for starters, I'm not sure how are we supposed to find this Coin if you couldn't. And even if we do find it, how will we figure out how it works, or find The Room of Truth or Vesica's Key or the Book of Charms? I mean, it stands to reason that with all your wisdom and powers, you would have found it by now. And what about Sahwin? Why hasn't he found it if he's so powerful? Oh, and there's my father and probably dozens of other collectors and historians who have likely heard the legend. If none of you have found it, what chance do the three of us have?"

Faye nodded in understanding. "These are all rational thoughts, dear," she said patting Bea's hand, "but let's not let reason get in the way. You must rely on things beyond that now."

"Beyond reason?" Bea asked. "Like what?"

"Truth, faith, magic," Faye answered with a sweeping wave of her hand on each word. "The three of you have advantages that none of us have ever had. For one thing, you are The Finders, which means you are *meant* to find The Coin. It is your destiny. The Oath connects you to The Coin and The Coin to you. Plus," Faye said with a smile, "you have me and The Council and even Danu to help you."

"How can Danu help us?" said Nisha in her raspy whisper. "Isn't she…" Nisha's voice became almost inaudible "I mean I thought she was…"

"Dead? Well yes she is, but Danu would never let that stop her. The proof of that is here, dear," said Faye, turning around to take something from the shelf behind her. "You see, Danu knew she was going to die. So she prepared for it," Faye continued over her shoulder. "She selected five of her most useful majects to help The Finders should they need it, and this," she said, turning around, "is one of them."

In her hands was the loveliest box Bea had ever seen. The top was a shimmering gold and the sides were encrusted with blue stones.

"Nice!" said Indy.

"Actually," said Faye, "it's what's inside that is truly incredible."

Faye placed the box on the table and sat back. "Who wants to open it?" she said, looking from one child to the next.

"Well, if it's from Nisha's grandmother, shouldn't she open it?" Indy suggested.

"I don't know," said Faye. "It could be for any one of you really."

Bea looked over at Nisha, who looked slightly terrified. Indy must have noticed as well because he said, "Why don't I go first?"

"An excellent idea," said Faye, smiling.

Indy picked up the box from the center of the table and set it squarely in front of himself. Slowly he lifted the lid. Inside was the large deck of cards that Faye had used the first night they had met.

"They're Danu's tarot cards," said Faye, her eyes sparkling. "Each card has a meaning and when laid out in a pattern can tell a story. I have been using them these many years, but I believe their true power has never revealed itself to me. I think it's because they were meant for you, The Finders, though only one of you can use the magic they offer." She turned to Indy and smiled. "Go ahead, pick one."

Indy hesitated but only for a second, then he reached out, picked the first card off the top of the deck and turned it over. On it was a picture of a young knight in a golden chariot pulled by two beautiful horses, one black and one white. Faye looked at the card and made a tsking sound.

"What is it?" Bea asked. "Is there something wrong?"

"It is the card of the Chariot," Faye said, as if the problem should be obvious. "It is a card of conflict and struggle. The person who draws it may face a difficult battle of one kind or another." Everyone was quiet for several seconds until Indy broke the silence.

"Well, who doesn't like a good battle every once in a while?" he said with a forced grin. "Who's next?" he asked brightly as he carefully returned the card to the deck.

Bea glanced over at Nisha. Her eyes were even darker than usual and she played nervously with the small circle of rubies at her throat. "I'll go next," Bea offered, sensing Nisha's hesitance. "But if I pick one off the top the way Indy did, I'll just get the same card."

Faye nodded. "Yes, of course. You should take them out and spread them on the table. Then pick the one that calls to you."

Bea followed Faye's directions and took the oversized deck out of the box and placed it on the table face down. She could see these were not the ordinary kind of cards that Nana Anna and Cookie used to play gin rummy. They were much larger and a dark liquid blue, each one edged in gold. With one hand on top of the deck, she fanned the cards out across the table.

"Go ahead," Faye said encouragingly. "It is not necessary to think hard on this. It is best to go with your first instinct."

Bea nodded and selected a card from the center of the deck. The card showed a picture of two men each holding a golden cup. Bea looked up at Faye questioningly.

"It's the two of cups," she said, "a fine card; a positive card. It means the beginning of a new relationship or perhaps a reconciliation of some kind. I'm not sure how it applies here but I'm sure its meaning will be revealed."

Bea nodded. Perhaps it was a reference to her relationship with Nisha or maybe with Indy, she thought as she collected the cards from the table and put them back into the box. Or maybe it was just a card. Despite all she had seen, there was always the possibility that none of this stuff was true. However just as she placed the lid on top of the box, it suddenly began to shake, then slowly, silently, it slid itself across the tabletop and stopped directly in front of Nisha.

Bea gasped and looked over at Nisha, whose mouth had fallen open. Even Faye looked a bit surprised.

"What…? How…?" Indy began, but Faye held up her hand to quiet him and turned her attention to Nisha.

Nisha took a deep breath and said bravely, "Looks like it's my turn."

With trembling fingers, Nisha opened the lid. She lifted the deck and fanned the cards out in front of her in the same way Bea had. Then she reached out and hesitantly picked a card from the pile.

Faye was visibly tense. It was clear that she feared what Nisha's card might reveal. But, when Nisha placed her card in front of her for all of them to see, even Indy and Bea could tell that it was a good one. The picture showed a woman kneeling on the ground. Her arms were stretched over her head, reaching for a vivid silver star in the night sky. On the ground beside her was a small collection of books in a pile and a bow with a quiver of silver arrows. The image was beautiful and peaceful, and Faye sighed audibly with relief.

"It is The Dark Star," she said, "a very good card. It represents hope; light in a time of darkness."

"Is that why they used it for the cover?" Nisha asked.

"What do you mean, dear?" asked Faye.

"The picture on the card matches the one on top of the box. Do you think that means something?"

"The box has no drawing on it," said Aunt Faye with a frown of confusion.

Nisha frowned in return. She picked up the lid and turned it around so it faced Faye. "But it does, see?" she said quietly.

Faye squinted at the box top. "Really dear, there is nothing there. I have had these cards since… well, a long time, and I'm quite certain there is no picture."

Nisha set the lid on the table and ran her finger over it.

Bea leaned forward and squinted. "I see it too!" she said excitedly, "I didn't at first but now I do."

Faye leaned back in her chair and looked from Bea to Nisha

and back again. Then she leaned forward and peered at the box carefully. "I don't see it," she said with a disappointed huff. "Of course that doesn't mean it's not there. Perhaps it's something only Finders can see. Do you see it?" she asked Indy.

Indy seemed a bit surprised to be included. He looked over at the box top and shook his head. "No Ma'am, I don't see it," he answered, sounding a little worried that it might be the wrong answer.

Everyone was silent for several seconds, giving Faye time to think. "Well," she said finally, "I can only imagine that the picture on the lid is significant in some way; particularly to you, Nisha, as these cards were always meant to be yours; a thirteenth birthday Gift from Danu. I suggest you consult the cards each day and perhaps more will be revealed."

Nisha placed the lid back on the box and let her fingers move over the surface again. "Thank you, Aunt Faye," she said.

"You need not thank me, the Gift is from Danu. They are the first of five majects that will help you on your quest. Graydon has one for you, as do Bridget and Gloria, and I assume Penn as well. Remember, you have an appointment with Graydon on Saturday. The others will pass their majects on to you as they see fit."

"You should also know that The Council has put a protective enchantment on this home and yours, Bea. It's a necessary precaution and you should be safe as long as you are on the premises. However, we cannot count on these enchantments alone. There are always ways around them if you know enough magic. The sooner you get the magical objects, the safer you will be."

CHAPTER 25

THE CLOCK SHOP

Saturday finally arrived but the appointment with Mr. Green at the clock shop was still hours away. To distract herself, Bea began working on a paper that was due for creepy Mr. Morton's class. The assignment was to write an essay about one of King Arthur's adventures. Bea chose the story of Excalibur, hoping to discover more about The Lady of the Lake and Avalon. Although Bea checked out every library book with any mention of the tale, she was disappointed to find little about The Lady. Any references to her or to the island of Avalon were vague at best.

When Bea finished her paper, she was surprised to see that it wasn't yet noon. She had done her paper in record time even for her. Had The Oath somehow improved her ability to study? Faye said that they might get better at the things they were already good at. Pleased with her newfound ability, Bea picked up one of the library books and began to flip through it. Almost immediately she came across something she'd missed the first time. It was an drawing of two overlapping circles carved out of metal, and it was labeled Vesica Piscis. Could it be related to Vesica's Key in the prophecy? Bea searched through the entire book and the rest of them but could find no other reference to the symbol. When she finally looked up, an hour had passed. She had just three minutes before she was supposed to meet with Mr. Green.

Nisha and Indy were standing in front of her stoop as she rushed out the door and down the stairs. "C'mon," she called as she hit the sidewalk, "we're going to be late!"

"And whose fault is that?" shouted Indy as he sprinted after her with Nisha close at his heels.

"Sorry," Bea called out breathlessly over her shoulder, "but I found something really interesting. I'll tell you about it after we meet with Mr. Green."

They arrived in front of the shop just seconds before two o'clock. Bea put her hand on the doorknob and then turned to Indy and Nisha. "Ready?"

"Sure," said Indy.

"Yes," whispered Nisha.

Bea nodded and slowly opened the door into a dimly lit, ticking room.

"Well, come in, for Spirit's sake," Mr. Green called from somewhere in the back of the shop. "We certainly don't have all day. In, in, in," he commanded.

Bea, Indy and Nisha clustered together inside the small shadowy store just as the clocks inside struck two. Bea jumped a little as the large grandfather clock to her left let out a loud clang. Then, as if the large clock had awoken the rest, every clock in the room chimed in. A battalion of smaller clocks on the far wall began to ring, peal and bong. Even some of the watches in the cases beeped and chirped the time.

"That was awesome," said Indy, when the room finally quieted again to a low tick.

"If by awesome you mean well-executed," replied Mr. Green, who had come out to greet them, "then I agree. Perfect synchronization is the sign of a well-run system. But there's not time to chat about the merits of organization, I have another appointment in…" he lifted his arm to check his watch, "twenty-six minutes."

The children followed Mr. Green to the back of the small store, around the counter, past a workroom, through a door, and down a long, tightly-wound staircase. As they descended, the loud tick-tock of the cluttered shop grew softer, and the sharp smell of oil and metal that was so pungent in the workroom was replaced with the lemony richness of wood polish. When they reached the bottom, Mr. Green touched the wall by the last stair and the room lit up with a warm golden glow. Indy let out a low, approving whistle.

"Whoa! Cool office!" he said appreciatively.

"If, by cool, you mean well-appointed, then thank you," said Mr. Green with a self-satisfied smile.

Bea nodded her agreement as she looked around. The room was perfectly round and had the hushed, expensive feeling of a fancy hotel lobby. In the center was a round, golden table surrounded by four sleek chairs. A plush banquette ran the circumference, luxuriously upholstered in green and gold. Above it, the walls were polished wood and embellished with gold inlays of sundials, hourglasses and megalithic ruins. But it was the floor that was the most incredible, for the whole thing was a large, softly glowing clock; its slender golden hands pointing to the twelve and the two.

"Please take a seat," instructed Mr. Green.

Mr. Green glanced furtively around the table as they settled in and, once they were still, he pressed what appeared to be a random spot on the tabletop. To Bea's surprise the polished walls began sliding silently down, slipping behind the banquet. They revealed several screens which were lit up to display the stock market tickers from around the world. Directly behind Mr. Green was a large wall safe.

"Some Avalonians don't like technology, but I've always felt it's, well… cool, wouldn't you say?" he asked, looking at Indy.

Indy nodded in awe, "totally double-O-7."

"Double oh what?" Mr. Green asked. However, when Indy started to answer, Mr. Green interrupted. "Never mind, I'm certain I don't care." Then he cleared his throat in an official way and said, "I have invited you here because I have something for one of you, though I don't know what it is or even which one of you it's for."

With that, Mr. Green touched the tabletop again in a sequence of different spots. Then, with a small click, the door to the safe swung gently open. He stood up and walked over to it. From his vest pocket he produced a silvery silk handkerchief which he wrapped around his hand before reaching into the safe.

Carefully, he pulled out what looked to Bea like a small rock. There was nothing unusual about it as far as she could tell, yet as Mr. Green carried in his wrapped hand, he had a strange, pained expression on his face. He walked back to his seat with two long strides and quickly deposited it on the table. Then he removed the handkerchief and briefly examined his palm before returning to his chair.

"What are you waiting for?" he asked, turning to Indy. "Pick it up."

Indy looked taken aback. "Me?" he said, looking back and forth between Mr. Green and the rock.

"Yes you. Or perhaps you'd like one of the girls to go first?"

Indy shot a look at Nisha and quickly put on a braver expression. "Uh, okay. Sure. Here goes…"

Indy reached out and picked up the rock, but a second later, he dropped it back on the table, cursing under his breath and shaking his hand as if it were burned.

"What the heck…?" he said, looking at Mr. Green suspiciously.

"Well, don't blame me," said Mr. Green indignantly. "I didn't do anything to you. There's obviously a protective hex on it."

"A hex?" said Indy, confused.

"Yes a hex," said Mr. Green slowly, as if speaking to an idiot, "so the wrong person won't open it. Faeries are quite smart despite what people say." Then he took a silver pen out of his pocket and used it to push the stone towards Nisha.

Her eyes became round but she didn't hesitate. She lifted the rock and held it for a few seconds before quickly putting it down and rubbing her hands rapidly against the top of her legs.

"Did it burn you?" asked Indy.

"No," she answered, "it's more like ice."

"Interesting," said Mr. Green. "For me, it's like broken glass."

"Sounds great!" Bea said with sarcastic enthusiasm, "and it looks like it's my turn!"

There's no reason to be frightened, Bea told herself. *If the rock wasn't meant for Nisha or Indy, then it must be meant for me.* She clenched her teeth, reached out, and picked it up. It felt rough and cool in her hands, exactly like a rock.

"Just right!" she sighed with relief. "I feel a bit like Goldilocks," she added with a giggle.

"Who?" Mr. Green asked.

"You know, Goldilocks and the Three Bears?" said Bea. "It's a children's story," she added when she saw the perplexed look on Mr. Green's face.

"I fail to see how that is relevant here," said Mr. Green. "And, in the interest of time, I suggest we continue if you don't mind." Without waiting for an answer, he went on. "That part was self-explanatory enough. Can you open it?"

Bea looked down at the rock, perplexed. It was a rock. It didn't look like something a person could open.

"Go ahead, give it twist," Mr. Green urged with impatience.

Bea picked up the rock again skeptically and grasped the narrower end. She gave it a slight turn and it sprang open so quickly that she sat back with a startled jerk.

"Amazing!" cried Mr. Green shaking his head. "That certainly settles one thing; you are *definitely* a Finder. I've tried to get that thing open at least a hundred times and I..." He stopped suddenly and looked around the table. "Because...I...I felt it was my duty to know what I was protecting of course," he explained hastily.

"Of course," agreed Indy, but one of his eyebrows was raised in doubt.

Mr. Green sniffed indignantly and said, "The important thing is that it is open now. So..." he said, turning back to Bea, "tell us dear girl, what's inside?"

Bea peered in, but the opening was too small for her to see

anything. With no other choice, she carefully tipped the rock upside and let its contents fall into her open hand. Then she held it out over the table so they could examine it together. Lying there in the center of her palm was a small, slender, rectangular piece of gray metal slightly wider but no longer than a straight pin.

"Mmm," said Bea.

"Yeah," Indy agreed, "I'm not sure what it is, but I'm pretty sure it's not what I was expecting."

"Perhaps we shouldn't judge it until we know what it does," said Nisha.

"Very wise," said Mr. Green in agreement. "It is possible for remarkable things to be very unremarkable-looking." He glanced around at the three of them, smugly. "I think perhaps this is one of those things." Then he turned to Bea and asked politely, "Would you mind if I took a closer look at it upstairs?"

The children followed him back up the winding staircase and into his small, tidy work room in the back of the shop. Bea wondered for a moment if this was where Penn worked and where he might be that afternoon.

Mr. Green plucked the object out of Bea's hand with a pair of tweezers and laid it on a small glass tray, then placed it directly under an elaborate system of magnifying lenses used for intricate clock repairs.

He positioned his eye over the eyepiece. "Ah," he said after a moment, "remarkable indeed."

"What is it?" all three of them asked in harmony.

"A minute," said Mr. Green triumphantly.

Nisha frowned. "A minute?"

"Exactly," Mr. Green replied.

"You mean like on a clock?" Bea asked, as if she'd heard him wrong the first time.

"Yes, a minute," Mr. Green repeated impatiently, "sixty extra seconds."

"An extra minute?" asked Indy as though there still might be a more logical answer.

"Yes," Mr. Green huffed, "and make no mistake, they are

exceedingly rare. You see, when time was first invented, it was free. But as people began to recognize its value, it became the most precious and coveted thing on earth. This could quite possibly be the very last extra minute on the planet. I myself have never seen one before, although I have heard they existed. To actually have one to use at your discretion; why, it's a Gift above all others."

"What am I supposed to do with it?" asked Bea.

"Well, that I can't tell you, because I don't know. I suggest you spend it wisely as it may be your salvation. But..." he said, pausing before handing the minute back to her. "I must caution you to use your words very carefully."

"Why, what do you mean?"

"Well, said Mr. Green, "you certainly don't want to waste it by accidentally saying something like 'wait a minute' or 'give me a minute', or even 'just a minute' might set it off. If you do, you'll use it up and never even know it. I'm sure it doesn't seem like much to you now but a minute is quite a bit of time. It can make all the difference in the world."

"I certainly don't want to waste it," Bea replied, thinking about what kind of situation she might find herself in where an extra minute could change everything. "I will be careful."

CHAPTER 26

THE WALK HOME

For three days, Nisha and Bea had walked home together after school. It was Bea's idea, of course, insisting that they needed every available second to work on The Quest. At first Nisha had resisted, still worried, despite Bea's enthusiasm, that she might be playing some kind of Horrible trick. But so far, Bea had acted (and smelled) as genuine as can be. She waited for Nisha every day by the back steps, and no matter how many girls waved to her or called her name as they walked by; Bea simply nodded in return and linked her arm more tightly through Nisha's.

Bea also spent every available moment in the school library, for each day she had more information or a new theory about Avalon or The Coin. And it was nearly impossible to doubt her commitment when her backpack was loaded down with books on the subject. So far she hadn't found much about The Coin itself, but she had discovered an ancient symbol called Vesica Piscis, a geometric sign in which two circles overlapped. Bea's theory was that Vesica Piscis had something to do with Vesica's Key from The Prophecy, and she was determined to figure it out.

Indy also seemed committed. On each of the last three

afternoons, by the time Nisha and Bea made it to Bea's stoop, Indy was already there waiting for them. Bea would dutifully record the time in her white notebook before reading the prophecy aloud. Then, together, they would try to decipher what it all meant.

Although it was nice to have Indy there, it turned out he wasn't much good at the deciphering stuff. He was clearly more interested in the extra minute Mr. Green had given to Bea, and spent most of the time theorizing about what kind of circumstance could possibly call for them to use it. He was convinced that they were going find themselves in at least one very dangerous situation. "It's in the prophecy, plain as rain," he maintained when Bea teased him about it. "It seems to me that if there is a Finder just to keep the other two safe, there must be something you need protection from." Unfortunately, neither girl could find a flaw in his reasoning.

It was hard to believe that not even a week had past. Things had changed so much in such a short amount of time that Nisha hardly recognized her life or herself. Although she went about each day as if everything was the same, on the inside her blood raced and her heart pounded with energy and purpose she had never known before. It was nearly impossible to focus on anything but Bea, Indy and The Coin. So, when the end-of-the-day bell finally rang on Thursday, Nisha found herself rushing to her locker in anticipation of the afternoon ahead. Some eighth grade Horribles harassed her as she passed the gym, but it didn't bother her nearly as much as it would have a week ago. In fact, it didn't bother her at all. She just kept going, her mind too occupied to register the tired taunts she had heard so many times before.

At her locker, Nisha gathered her things and quickly stuffed them in her knapsack. Then she swallowed her old anxiety and headed directly out the main door.

The front of the school was even more crowded than usual. Clusters of girls in sports uniforms waited for buses to pick them up. Bea was not there yet, and the familiar feelings of fear and self-consciousness began to rise in Nisha's chest. Unsure of what to do, Nisha edged over behind a large bush to avoid being noticed.

Several minutes went by and the crowd began to thin, but still there was no sign of Bea. Then, as she started to consider the possibility that Bea might not be coming, the door burst open and out came Charlotte Wang. Her distinctive giggle cut sharply through the din and Nisha knew that if Charlotte was there, Amanda wasn't far behind, so she wedged herself more tightly between the shrub and the building to ensure she wouldn't be seen. As expected, Amanda Whitehead came bursting through the door a moment later with another girl. The flick of long blond hair was unmistakable, yet it still took Nisha several moments to absorb what was happening. Was Bea really walking down the steps with Amanda Whitehead? All three girls were laughing loudly in that way that makes everyone else feel left out.

At the bottom of the stairs, Bea paused for a moment. She scanned the steps and sidewalk, and then looked up and down the street. Nisha's stomach did a full flip at the thought of being discovered. There was no way she could allow Bea to see her, not when Bea was with the two most horrible Horribles of all.

With a shrug, Bea followed Charlotte and Amanda to a large car parked across the street. A driver got out and opened the back door, allowing the three of them to climb in. As the car pulled away, Nisha caught a glimpse of Bea peering through the tinted window of the back seat. It seemed for a moment as if she'd seen Nisha, for she looked directly at the shrub where Nisha was hiding, but a moment later she turned back towards Charlotte and laughed.

For several minutes, Nisha remained behind the bush, too confused to do anything. *Was Bea really a Horrible after all?* Nisha couldn't believe it. Bea had seemed so genuine; so interested in finding The Coin. Was it all a lie?

All of Nisha's worst fears came rushing up into her throat, and she felt as if she might cry, or throw up, or both. She swallowed as hard as she could and forced herself to take a breath. *Why had she been so foolish? Had she wanted a friend so much that she let herself be completely deceived?*

With no other choice, Nisha adjusted her backpack on her shoulders and headed home. The sky was overcast and grey and the air was warm and thick. Nisha walked purposefully, concentrating on breathing. She would not let herself cry. Her focus was so intent it took several minutes before she noticed someone was following her.

The Horribles hadn't followed Nisha since she'd threated Amanda Whitehead in the fourth grade. *As if today isn't bad enough already,* she thought angrily. She shrugged her backpack higher onto her shoulders and determinedly picked up her pace. If the Horribles were going to follow her, she wasn't going to make it easy for them to catch her.

As Nisha approached the corner, she willed the light to change, but oddly, it refused. A wave of dizziness passed through her as she waited, nervously listening for footsteps behind. Strangely, none came. Trying to appear nonchalant, she turned as if checking the traffic and glanced up the street. There were no Horribles to be seen. *Were they hiding?* Unconsciously, she lifted her head and sniffed the air. She didn't detect the scent of anyone she knew, but there was something else, something foul and old. And more than that, there was a feeling; the distinct sensation of being watched, eyes burning into her cheek. A terrible chill crept across Nisha's shoulders. If it wasn't the Horribles, who was it?

When the light changed, Nisha began to walk more quickly, but no matter how fast she moved, she couldn't shake the feeling of the eyes burning on the back of her head. By the time she reached the next corner, the presence was so intense that she felt dizzy. She wanted to stop and steady herself, but it wasn't worth the risk. Better to keep moving. Whoever was following her was getting closer.

Without consciously deciding to, Nisha started to run. She ran right into the next street and heard the cars screeching to avoid her. She didn't stop. She had to keep going. The gaze slid to the back of her neck. She ran faster.

Nisha willed herself to move forward. She knew that she needed to get home before those eyes could see where she lived. She raced down the avenue but couldn't seem to gain any ground. When she reached her block, she hesitated. She couldn't go home and put Faye in danger. She needed someplace to hide. Panting for breath, she darted across the street and ducked down the short dark stairs that ran along one side of Bea's stoop. Nisha crouched in the dark space beneath the staircase, and held her breath. The shadow of the house stretched out above her.

Nisha could hear her own breathing in her ears, and at the same time sensed the presence growing closer. Then someone was there on the sidewalk above her, and she held her breath. Several seconds went by, but there was no sound, only the strong smell of an emotion. Frustration? Exasperation? The scent was followed by a quiet rustling, then nothing.

Nisha waited, stretching her senses out over the street. Whoever had been there was gone. She took several breaths before she let herself stand up. Who was it, she wondered? And then a stranger question popped into her mind to replace the first one. *What* was it? What kind thing had eyes that could burn her skin?

The creepiness of this new thought forced Nisha to move. She wanted to be safely inside her apartment with Aunt Faye. Nisha trembled as she stepped out into the gray light of day. She made her way across the street and let herself into the apartment, locking all three of the door locks carefully behind her.

A moment later, Aunt Faye came bustling out of the front hall closet, startling Nisha. Faye took one look at her and said, "What happened, child?"

"It's, it's ..." Nisha began, not knowing how to explain. "It's nothing..." she finished unconvincingly. What could Nisha tell her? Nothing had actually happened. She hadn't seen anything. She had only felt a presence; burning eyes. One hand moved self-consciously to the spot on her cheek where the eyes had burned her skin, and the other reached automatically for the pendant around her neck.

"Nothing?" Faye asked, knowingly.

"I thought something… I mean, I think some kids were following me." Nisha said.

Faye frowned and walked over to the narrow window by the side of the door. She reached her hand out to pull back the thin curtain.

"No! Don't!" Nisha said quickly

Faye stopped. She turned back to Nisha.

"Do you know who it was?" Faye asked.

"Um, no, not exactly. I don't think I know the kids. Maybe they were eighth graders."

Faye nodded with a deeper understanding. "From now on, Indy will come and meet you after school."

"What? Indy? No, Aunt, please, I'm not a baby, and besides, Indy has school too and he has to work for his father most days."

"His school lets out twenty minutes before yours," Faye interrupted. "That is more than enough time for him to get there. He'll drop you off and then go to work."

Nisha was about to argue when the small window suddenly darkened with a gray shadow. The air became thick and hot and Nisha could sense something was out there again. Faye sensed it too, for Nisha could see the fear in her Aunt's eyes. They looked at one another.

"It's settled, then?" Faye asked quietly.

"Yes, settled," Nisha whispered in reply.

CHAPTER 27

THE MAKEOVER

As the car pulled away from the curb, Charlotte turned to Bea with a broad, perfect smile. "This is going to be so much fun!" she bubbled, and Bea couldn't help but smile in return. It was easy to see why Charlotte was so popular. She had the uncanny ability to make you feel as if you were the most charming person in the world, yet at the same time lucky to be in her presence.

Bea knew she should be excited and even flattered to be spending the afternoon with the very top Top Pops. But the truth was, she would have rather been with Indy and Nisha on the stoop trying to figure out The Prophecy. Unfortunately, there hadn't been any way out of it. She'd already cancelled on Charlotte the week before, and there were only so many times you could say no to someone like Charlotte before your popularity status was downgraded to Almost or worse.

"My parents always send the car for me," Charlotte saying as they turned the corner onto Park Avenue. "Mother and Father are worried I'm going to be kidnapped or something... you know, because my father is so rich," she added, as if it needed clarification.

When they pulled up in front of what Bea presumed to be

Charlotte's building, Charlotte turned to Bea and clapped her hands together delightedly. "I have the best surprise," she said, pausing dramatically. "Today, we are going to have the most awesome makeover party ever."

Bea smiled politely in response. She wasn't sure what a makeover party was exactly, but she gathered it had something to do with makeup, required only three people, and carried the not-so-mild suggestion that Bea needed some fixing up in the looks department. She allowed herself to be pulled from the car, but was now wishing more than ever that she were walking home with Nisha instead of heading into Charlotte's building.

Bea wondered again where Nisha was. She'd been planning to explain about Charlotte when they saw each other after school but oddly, Nisha hadn't been there. Was something wrong?

As Bea expected, Charlotte's building was very fancy. A pleasant doorman in a dark red uniform greeted them as they entered. Another, dressed in blue, operated the elevator that took them upstairs. Bea couldn't imagine what purpose he served. *Was pressing a button really too difficult for someone to do themself?*

Charlotte's apartment was larger than any Bea had ever seen, and walking into to it was like stepping into a vacuum. Sounds of the city outside were silenced by the soft soothing hush of luxury. The only colors were creamy shades of beige and white. Bea felt the sudden desire to wash her hands for fear of accidentally dirtying something.

Charlotte led the girls to the kitchen for a snack. Green grapes and ripe strawberries were waiting for them, freshly washed and piled high in a pretty white bowl.

"I never eat processed sugar; mother says it makes you bloated," Charlotte explained. Amanda nodded sagely in agreement.

"Not that you have anything to worry about, Bea. You're an absolute toothpick!" Charlotte said approvingly. Then she gave Amanda a critical glance which caused Amanda to put down the strawberry she was eating. Turning back to Bea, she said, "But

I think we could definitely do something with your hair."

"Definitely," Amanda agreed with a condescending smile.

When they'd finished their snack, Charlotte announced that it was makeover time. The girls padded in their stocking feet (no shoes allowed past the front door) down the beige-carpeted hall to Charlotte's room, which looked like a picture from a catalog. The shades of cream and white had melted into tones of cotton candy and bubble gum. In the center of the room was a huge, four-poster bed piled high with pillows. The curtains were billowy pink chiffon, and the rug, a deeper shade of cherry, was so thick that Bea's feet nearly disappeared in the rich pile. Everything in the room was in perfect order, not a single book or article of clothing was out of place. Bea felt grungy standing there in her Huntington plaids.

"Before we get started, you'll need to wash," Charlotte announced, and Bea was startled for a moment. thinking Charlotte may have read her mind.

"We must do the makeover on totally clean skin," she explained.

Bea followed Charlotte back down the hall and around a few corners to the guest bathroom. Charlotte reached into a nearby closet and took out a fluffy white towel. "Be gentle, don't scrub. Then pat dry," she advised. "People with skin as pale as yours can get very red," she added, as she shut the door, leaving Bea to her ablutions.

Beau dutifully cleansed her face per Charlotte's instruction and made her way back towards Charlotte's room. As she walked down the wide beige hallway, her thoughts shifted to Nisha again. Nisha's strange little apartment was only a few blocks from Charlotte's but might as well have been on another planet. Nisha's home was tiny but warm and welcoming, where as Charlotte's, with all its luxuries, felt cold and untouchable.

Lost in her thoughts, Bea got a bit mixed up and found herself in a big beige living room. Confused, she glanced around, looking for something that might point her back in the right direction. She walked into the center of room and noticed a large archway that led into another big beige living room, almost a mirror image of the one she was standing in. As she marveled over the idea of having twin living rooms, something caught her eye; a flicker of light coming from a display case at the far end of the other room.

Curious, Bea tiptoed over to investigate, and as she drew closer her heart began to pound in her chest. The case was made of wood, with glass on three sides and three shelves within. Incredible treasures were displayed on all three; the type of things her father scoured the world for. On the first shelf was a small golden dog with emerald eyes, probably from Tibet, and next to it a marble carving of a man on horseback that looked like it might be from India or Morocco. Beside the carving was a gem-encrusted cup that definitely dated back to the Middle Ages, and at the end of the shelf, a brightly colored mask inlayed with an intricate pattern of polished seashells and turquoise.

When her eyes moved down to the next shelf, however, all the other objects might as well have turned to dust, for there in the center of the middle shelf was a large, luminous coin. Bea thought for a crazy, thrilling moment that it was their coin; the size was very like the one she had seen at the Flea Market. But it couldn't be. *How could it have gotten here?* Besides, the coin she had seen at the flea market was gold and this one was silver.

Bea knew Charlotte and Amanda must be wondering where she was, but she just couldn't make herself turn away from the coin. It was displayed standing on its edge on a slowly turning platform so that the viewer, if they watched long enough, could see both sides. It glowed so brightly it seemed unnatural, and Bea watched it in fascination as the shining silver surface slowly completed its turn toward her.

"There you are," said Charlotte from behind her, and Bea jumped. She had been so entranced that she had forgotten where she was. She quickly regained her composure and turned around to face Charlotte.

"Sorry," she said with a giggle, "I got a bit lost. I figured if I stayed in one place, eventually you would find me."

Charlotte laughed, but Amanda, who was standing right behind her, rolled her eyes to the ceiling.

"Well come on," said Charlotte, in her sugary sweet voice. "It's time for your makeover."

"It certainly is," said Amanda, not nearly as sweetly.

As they headed out of the room, Bea took a last glance at the coin. It was just coming around to reveal its other side. Then there was a soft flash of gold as the metal caught the light. *Gold!* Bea stopped and squinted. She could just make out what looked like a pattern of loops of overlapping lines.

It took a single heartbeat for the realization to hit her and then she gasped. The Teller Ninane's word came rushing back to her. "One side made of silver from The White Waters of The Other World, the other forged in gold from the Blood Spring of the Great Hill. It is marked by the eternal circle that connects all the magic of the worlds into one."

It wasn't just a coin; it was The Coin, their coin, the very coin she and Nisha had seen at the flea market … *but what was it doing in Charlotte's living room?* Of course the Wangs must have bought it somehow. It was obvious they had an interest in collecting precious antiques. *Did they know what it was? How it worked?*

Bea cleared her throat and, trying to sound nonchalant, she asked, "That stuff in the case back there was so pretty. Where do you get things like that?"

"Huh?" said Charlotte. "Oh, that stuff? Who knows? Daddy has buyers all over the world who find it. He gets all excited about something, pays a fortune for it, and then gets bored and sells it for an even bigger fortune. It's a hobby of his."

The rest of the afternoon went by in a haze. Bea knew she could not ask any questions about The Coin without causing suspicion, yet it was all she could think of. As Charlotte and Amanda fussed over her hair and face for what seemed like hours, Bea wracked her brain trying to figure out a way to get back in the living room.

Finally, they finished. The results of the makeover were less than successful. The makeup looked harsh and unnatural on her pale skin and her pin-straight hair would not stay in place no matter what they did. The only thing that worked was the mascara, which turned her pale lashes black and made her pastel-blue eyes even bluer.

When it was time to go home, Charlotte and Amanda congratulated themselves on their work, agreeing that it was a vast improvement. They even made a list of all the products they used so she could buy them. She thanked them politely, though she was certain she wouldn't buy any of it. Nana Anna would never let her even if she wanted to, which she didn't. Bea had far more important things to think about than mascara.

CHAPTER 28

THE SKATEBOARD

On Friday, Nisha did everything she could think of to avoid Bea. In Homeroom, she claimed she had to study and moved to a seat in the back of the room. At noon, she circumvented lunch entirely, hiding out in the library. In Science Lab, where she and Bea were partners, she claimed she wasn't feeling well and spent the double period in the nurse's office. It hadn't been easy, but she had managed to steer clear of Bea the whole day. Nisha breathed a sigh of relief when she finally heard the end-of-the-day bell. However, when she arrived at her locker, she found a note stuck in one of the vents.

Dear N,
I know you are avoiding me. I am sorry if I have upset you. I have some very important news to share about our "project." Please meet me after school so I can explain everything. I'll wait for you at the front door.
B.

Nisha wasn't sure what to think or how to feel. The note sounded genuine and Nisha could smell the fresh-bread scent of sincerity coming off the page as if had been baked into the paper. But every time Nisha thought of Bea getting into that silver car, she felt sick to her stomach. Maybe Bea was just really good at lying, the same way she was good at everything else.

Nisha looked at the note again. If Bea's news was so important, she could have shared it with Nisha yesterday, but instead she chose to go to Charlotte's after school. Nisha stomach lurched again. Trust wasn't something she did easily, and Bea was going to have to do more than write a note to earn it back.

After school, instead of heading out the front door where Nisha knew Bea would be waiting, she made her way out the back like she had so many times before. To her surprise, she saw Indy waiting for her. She was so busy worrying about Bea that she'd forgotten about Indy and Aunt Faye's arrangement.

When Indy saw her, he raised his hand in a simple wave, and Nisha had no other reasonable choice but to head towards him and try to calm the pounding in her chest. As she approached, he smiled a mischievous half smile, bowed slightly like a gentleman. "At your service m' lady."

"Hi," she managed. But before either of them could say anything else, Nisha heard a familiar laugh behind her.

She turned to see Charlotte Wang and the rest of the Horrible volleyball team standing in a circle nearby. Charlotte looked perfect, her light blue gym shorts showing off her pretty legs, and Nisha immediately felt short and awkward in comparison. She glanced quickly at Indy to see if he had noticed the girls, but he appeared to be checking the spin on one of the skateboard's wheels. Nisha's relief was short lived, for when she looked back again, Charlotte was walking towards her.

"Well, hi there," Charlotte said cheerfully, sidling up to Nisha. She nudged her teasingly in the ribs and asked, "Who's your friend?"

Nisha looked back at her blankly, too stunned to respond.

Several of Charlotte's friends had wandered over to see what was happening. Nisha felt hot and lightheaded, as if she might pass out. *Please don't do this*, she silently begged, *not here, not in front of Indy.*

"I'm Indy, a friend of Nisha's," said Indy, answering for her.

"Well, helloo," Charlotte said in a flirty, sing-song voice. Then her pretty eyebrows crossed for a moment and she said, "Haven't we met before? Aren't you one of Justina's friends from tennis camp?"

"Sorry, you must have me confused with someone else. I don't play tennis."

"Mmm, I could have sworn…oh well, I'm Charlotte," Charlotte tossed her shiny hair and flashed her dazzling, dimpled smile. "I'm a friend of Nisa's too," she said unconvincingly. Then she turned to Nisha and said, "Nisa, why didn't you ever tell us you had a *boyfriend?*"

"I, er, we're not…" Nisha stammered helplessly, her cheeks blazing.

Then Indy saved her. He turned to Charlotte. "Well not yet, not officially anyway," he said with a wink, "but I'm working on it." Then he reached out and took Nisha by the hand. He slipped his fingers between hers and pulled her free from the circle of Horribles.

"C'mon, Nisha," he said, emphasizing the pronunciation of her name, "we've gotta go." And as they walked away, he called over his shoulder to the group, "Nice meeting you."

Nisha allowed herself to be drawn away and she and Indy fell into step, still holding hands. The blood was now pounding in her cheeks and she was having trouble taking whole breaths. When they finally got around the corner and out of sight, she quickly dropped Indy's hand.

"Thanks," she mumbled.

"Hey, protecting you is my job," said Indy seriously, and then he added, "And don't worry about her. That girl is a… well she's just one of those girls. Is she the one Bea hung out with yesterday?"

"Yes," Nisha answered. "How did you know that?"

"Bea told me about her. Said you didn't like her and that you were mad that Bea went to her house after school. Bea didn't want to go, you know. She told me to tell you that."

"She said that?"

"Yeah, but I told her, I didn't want to get in the middle of whatever's going on with you two. So, how bout we talk about something else, like why is your Aunt so worried about you? What happened?"

"Oh, well nothing really, but sort of something I guess."

"Tell me," said Indy, and Nisha detected the bittersweet smell of concern in the air.

Once Nisha started talking, the words flooded out. It was a relief to describe what had happened and she could tell Indy believed every word she said, even when she explained the feeling that whatever was following her might not be human. In fact, by the time she was through, Indy was on high alert. He kept looking over his shoulder and spinning around unexpectedly.

She finished the story just about the same time they reached her front door.

"I'll wait for you to get inside," he said.

"No need," said Nisha. "I don't think anything is following us today."

Indy nodded and dropped his skateboard onto the road in front of him. "You sure you're okay?" he asked.

Nisha looked up and down the block and nodded. "Yes, I'll be fine."

Indy nodded in return, then turned to go. He took a few quick steps towards his skateboard, but just as his foot was about to make contact, the board sped up and rolled out from under him.

He stumbled and almost fell. "That was weird," he said, tossing his hair out of his eyes and regaining his composure. The board was now several feet ahead of him, and he took a few running steps towards it to jump on. Again, it moved out from under him, and this time he fell backward onto the ground.

"Impressed?" he asked jokingly, though his face was flushed with embarrassment.

Nisha frowned. She looked at the board and then at Indy. "It's not you," she said as she walked up next to him. "It's the skateboard."

Indy laughed. "Of course, right, and the sun's in my eyes and the dog ate my…"

"No, I mean it. I think it's been enchanted. I think it wants us to follow it."

Indy dusted off his pants and looked at her sideways.

"Let's just try," she said, "slowly this time."

Indy shrugged and took several steps toward the board, and just as Nisha predicted, it moved again. He stopped and the board stopped. He walked and the board rolled forward.

Indy scratched his head then took another step towards the board and it moved forward again. He stopped and looked back at Nisha.

"So, you coming?" he asked, smiling.

"I don't know," Nisha said slowly, "I mean, my Aunt probably wouldn't want me to after yesterday and all."

Indy nodded. "True," he said, "but she seems to think you'll be safe with me. Besides, you're a Finder. You've got to follow the clues, right?"

Nisha hesitated. She knew Indy was right. She also knew that if Bea were there, there would be no question about whether to go or not. The thought of Bea kindled Nisha's anger again. She didn't need Bea Brightman around to be brave.

Nisha squared her shoulders and forced herself to smile. "Let's go," she said.

CHAPTER 29

THE PLAYGROUND

Once around the corner, the skateboard picked up speed and Nisha and Indy quickened their pace to keep up. After several turns, Indy said, "I think we're heading to MS 118."

A few minutes later, they were standing in a nearly-empty playground behind the public middle school. The skateboard had stopped moving near the swings and refused to budge. Both Indy and Nisha took several turns trying to get it going again, but finally gave up and sat down on a nearby bench.

"Where is everyone?" Nisha asked.

"Most kids clear out of here right after the bell unless they're looking for trouble. Unfortunately, this is not the safest place to hang out."

Nisha self-consciously smoothed out her Miss Huntington's plaid skirt and nervously looked around. She sensed her prim private-school uniform would not be appreciated here. The air was still and heavy and everything was quiet except for the sound of a ball bouncing. Three teenage boys were playing basketball by the outer fence.

Indy leaned back and stretched out his legs in front of him. "Well, I guess we wait then," he said with a half yawn.

Nisha *mmm*ed in agreement, but she was not as calm as Indy. Perhaps it was paranoia from her experience the day before, but she was certain she felt the presence of someone nearby. She stretched her senses across the playground but could not pinpoint the source. She glanced at Indy to see if he was also on alert, but he didn't appear concerned at all. His hands were behind his head, and his eyes were closed. Nisha couldn't help but notice his dark tangled eyelashes and the tiny teardrop in the corner of one eye. The afternoon sun painted soft shadows across his face, emphasizing the smooth, pronounced line of his top lip, and the hint of a dimple in his left cheek that still showed though his face was relaxed. Indy was handsome. Everyone could see it, but Nisha saw so much more than that in his face. His generous nature showed in his smile, and there was courage and concern in his eyes. Just being near him made her feel stronger and more confident.

Nisha forced herself to look away. She wouldn't want to be caught staring, but a moment later, her eyes drifted back to his face.

Why him? Why was he chosen as a Finder? Was it just his friendship with Bea? Or was there more? He did seem brave but even so, Nisha couldn't imagine how he could protect them against someone as powerful as Sahwin.

Suddenly, Indy opened his eyes and looked right into hers. He smiled, and she felt her stomach do a somersault. She quickly turned back to the playground. The basketball players were gone, and she realized with a sudden jolt that the skateboard was nowhere to be seen. "It's gone!" she said, standing up, mortified that she allowed herself to be so distracted.

"What?" said Indy jumping to his feet. "Where did it go?"

She scanned the playground, and to her relief she spotted the skateboard near the side of the building. "It's there," she said, pointing across the asphalt, "by that alleyway."

"Let's go," said Indy, who was already moving.

They caught up to the skateboard and followed it around the side of the building, until they found themselves standing in front of a dark alley closed off by a large black gate.

"This place looks cheerful," said Indy.

"It's called, "The East Hill Cemetery", said Nisha, reading from a plaque on the building wall. "My Aunt told me about it once. I think it's supposed to be cursed."

"Of course it is," said Indy, with a grin. "I would have been disappointed otherwise."

"Unfortunately, I can't remember why it's cursed," said Nisha.

"Because some idiots built the school right over it; practically covered the entire thing," said a voice from behind them. Both Indy and Nisha spun around in surprise.

It was Penn Ludd, whom they hadn't seen since the last Council Meeting. He was wearing jeans and a dark t-shirt, on it a picture of Legolas, the elf from The Lord of The Rings. An old backpack was slung over his shoulder.

"By the time someone stopped them," he continued, ignoring their startled expressions, "they had already covered the doorway to Avalon."

"The doorway to the Avalon?" said Indy skeptically. "Here at the Middle School? So, it's like buried under the gym or something?"

"The art room, actually," replied Penn humorlessly.

He reached into his gym bag and pulled out large iron key-ring with a single ancient-looking key hanging from it. Penn struggled with the lock for several seconds, but it finally gave in with a loud clank. Slowly, he pushed the heavy gate open, and it screamed on its hinges as if no one had opened it in a hundred years. Penn walked through without comment. "C'mon," he said impatiently, holding the gate open, and motioning for them to step inside.

Nisha hesitated. She hadn't known Penn very long, and what she did know, she didn't like very much. He seemed just the type to sneak up on people. Her Aunt assured her that Penn could be trusted, but she was never entirely convinced, and she could tell by the expression on Indy's face that he wasn't either.

Indy hesitated, "How can there be an entrance to Avalon here? I thought it was almost impossible to get to there."

"It is if you're alive," said Penn, in a tone that suggested that everyone with a brain knew what he was talking about. "But Avalon is the gateway to the Other World. Every soul has to pass through, so every cemetery has a door for the dead."

Indy shot Nisha a look, as if to say, "Do you believe this?" She shrugged. She remembered something like this from Aunt Faye's old books.

The cemetery, or what was left of it, was no more than a long rectangular patch of ground between two brick walls. It was distinctly colder and darker than the playground, as most of the daylight was blocked by the side of the school. The dozen or so headstones were so old that they jutted out at strange angles, and between them, a few ancient, knotted trees twisted up out of the earth.

"Scared?" Penn asked her, teasingly.

"I'm not afraid of the dead," Nisha replied defensively, and then with a furtive look at Indy she added, "I'm from Avalon, just like you."

"If that was true," Penn replied with a snarl in his voice, "you would know that these people aren't the dead, they're the *un*dead. Their souls are trapped here, and believe me, they aren't very happy about it."

"So, why are *we* here?" Indy asked curtly.

"To get the Finders Gift, not that you'll know what to do with it," Penn said over his shoulder as he led them deeper into the graveyard.

"And you're sure it's in here?" asked Indy, not bothering to hide the suspicion in his voice.

"Of course I'm sure. It was made by goblins with the darkest magic, incredibly dangerous for the living, so when it's not with its true wielder it needs to be with the undead for protection."

Penn stopped at a small, dark headstone. "Here she is, old Morgana le Mer, my dear departed great, great grandmother. She was about as nasty as they come," Penn said, with a note of respect in his voice. "Danu was smart to leave the Finder's Gift with her. You'd have to be crazy to mess with Morgana, alive or dead."

He dug in his backpack again and pulled out a small

gardening shovel. Then he bent down behind the dusty stone and began to dig. Nisha couldn't see what he was doing, but she could hear the shovel scraping against the rock. After a minute or two, Penn stood up, holding a small, dirty wooden box. Without any ceremony, he held it out to Indy.

"How do you know it's for me?" Indy asked, surprised.

"Because it's Drae Mord. The Dragon Killer."

Indy looked mystified.

"It's a knife," said Penn, shaking his head, "and you're the protector, remember?"

"How do you know what it is?" asked Indy, accusingly.

"Because I looked," said Penn. "Got a problem with that?"

"Maybe," said Indy. "How can I be sure you didn't do something to it?"

Penn raised one of his sharp eyebrows in disgust. "Drae Mord is Goblin magic. If I tried to hex it I'd be dead right now." Penn held the box out to Indy again. "Go on; take it, even though you don't deserve it."

Indy cautiously took the box from Penn. Carefully, he slid the lid back. He reached inside and pulled out a pale knife handle that appeared to be made of a green stone or metal of some kind. He held it out for Nisha to see it. Carved into the surface were letters of some ancient language. The only words Nisha recognized were the ones Penn had just spoken. The name "Drae Mord" was centered down one side in long, low letters.

"A jackknife?" said Indy .

"Something wrong with that?" said Penn.

"No. I don't know. I just expected it would be a dagger kind of thing."

Penn smacked his hand to his forehead in frustration. "This is an ancient Goblin weapon made in a time before Man Kind. The handle is made of dragon skin and its blade can cut through anything known on earth and beyond. In the right hands, it could be a powerful weapon against Sahwin, and you're disappointed it's not some fancy dagger?"

"Drae Mord," said Indy to himself. "The knife has a name,

that's kinda cool." Indy flipped it open with an easy snap of his wrist and ran his thumb gently across the blade to test for sharpness. It wasn't until he folded the knife again that Nisha saw the red stain across the handle.

"You're bleeding," she said. She felt a strange dizziness come over her, and in her mouth, the taste of apples. Then she spoke. "He who bears the cut shall bear the blade," she said, surprised to hear her own voice.

"What did you just say?" said Penn, peering at her curiously.

For a second, Nisha could not remember, but then the words came back again. She spoke them more clearly, "He who bears the cut shall bear the blade."

Penn nodded thoughtfully, then turned to Indy. "It means that the one who can cut himself with the knife is its true wielder. I tried to cut myself at least a dozen times. I was denied," he added bitterly.

"Too bad," said Indy, with a smirk.

Penn ignored him. He was looking at Nisha. "How did you know the Legend?"

Nisha shook her head. "I don't know," she answered truthfully, "I just saw the knife and I knew it."

Penn nodded again. "Well, well, it seems little Nisha is not completely without Spirit Gifts."

"I told you, I'm a Daughter of The Lake," Nisha replied, raising herself up to be more commanding, as she had seen Faye do.

"Don't kid yourself," Penn replied dismissively. "You are a twin-less half breed. A moment of The Sight does not make you a Daughter of Avalon."

Nisha felt anger boiling up in her chest. But at the same moment, she felt something bump up under her feet.

"What was that?" she said anxiously.

"What was what?" asked Indy.

"I think I felt the ground move."

Penn looked up at sky. "It's the curse. It comes with the darkness. We need to leave, like... now."

"The curse? What curse?" asked Indy.

"The curse of Drae Mord. Anyone who tries to take the knife from this cemetery is doomed to stay here forever."

"But I thought it was meant for me," said Indy.

"It is, but even the rightful wielder has to take the knife in daylight. When darkness comes, you're at risk like anyone else."

"Why didn't you bring us here earlier then?" asked Indy angrily.

"It's not my fault it took you forever to figure out that your little wheelie toy was enchanted."

Indy looked as if he might take a swing at Penn, but then suddenly his eyes grew wide. "Something's got hold of my leg," he whispered.

"Not good!" said Penn. His eyes darted toward Indy's ankles.

Indy looked down too. "Holy… "

"What is it?" Nisha asked. She could barely see what was happening in the shadow of the tombstone.

"It's Morgana!" said Penn, "She's got his ankle!"

Nisha squinted in the dim light. There, wrapped around Indy's ankle, was a bony, decaying hand with pink plastic fingernails.

"Try to get her fingers off him while I pull!" said Penn urgently. "We've got to get out of here before they all wake up!"

"All?" said Indy looking around as he desperately tried to tug his leg free.

Nisha knelt on the ground and began to pry at the disgusting fingers around Indy's ankle. A pink fingernail still attached to the real fingernail came loose in her hand and for a moment she thought she might be sick. Indy and Penn tugged as hard as they could, but the hideous hand only tightened its grip.

The earth rumbled again, and Nisha screamed when another hand shot up through the ground; this time it was a man's knobby bones. Flesh hung off one side of it like hairy, moldy cheese. It caught Nisha by the wrist and pulled so hard she tumbled over sideways. The smell of dried blood made her gag again.

"Nisha!" said Indy, forgetting that his leg was being held to the ground. He lunged for her and fell forward on to the ground with a heavy thud.

"Drae Mord!" shouted Penn, who was now on the other side of Nisha, trying to pull the hand away, "use Drae Mord!"

"Trying!" said Indy, twisting around to avoid a third hand that had burst up through the earth and was grasping blindly at the air beside his shoulder. Indy frantically shoved his hand in his front pocket and pulled out the box. His fingers fumbled as he struggled to open it, but it appeared to be locked shut. "It's the curse!" said Penn, breathing hard from pulling. "She's probably resealed the box. Keep trying."

Nisha looked up at Indy's struggling face and suddenly she knew what to do. With her right hand still trapped in the hairy grip of the dead man, she twisted around so she could point her left hand at the box. Then, with all her might, she wished. "OPEN!"

The box popped open and the knife went flying. Miraculously, Indy caught it in mid-air. Then he flipped open the blade and with a single swipe severed the pink-finger-nailed hand from its wrist.

A loud shriek of pain came up out of the earth, and for a few seconds the hand remained fixed to his ankle. Finally, it lost its hold and flopped lifelessly to the ground. Indy moved quickly to Nisha's side. She turned away as he sliced effortlessly through the man's thick wrist bone, setting her free.

"Run!" Penn commanded, but Indy and Nisha were already in motion. They ran as fast as they could out of the small graveyard, the ground rumbling and buckling under their feet. Nisha stumbled and Indy caught her under the arms. In one easy movement, he scooped her off her feet as if she weighed nothing at all. In a few seconds, they burst through the gate and into the playground.

"Keep going," Penn shouted, as he slammed the gate behind them and locked it.

Indy put Nisha down, grabbed his skateboard, and they took off through the playground, not stopping until they had reached Nisha's front door.

CHAPTER 30

THE CATS

At 3:55, Bea picked up her notebook and headed outside to the stoop, even though she was quite certain Nisha would not show up. As it had been for weeks, the sky was gray and the air unseasonably warm. Bea's sweater was tied around her waist, and she scooped it under herself before sitting on the rough stairs. She checked her watch: 3:57. She looked across the street. No one was out except for Gloria, who was so engrossed in her needlework she did not notice Bea's presence. Bea's eyes moved from Gloria, down the street to Nisha's front window. It was still and quiet in the dimming afternoon light; the large neon hand had not yet been lit for the evening. Bea cast her glance further down the street, wondering where Indy might be; probably somewhere with Nisha, she thought miserably.

It was so frustrating to think of them both somewhere without her, especially when she finally had something real to tell them, something more than a clue or an idea. *Why was Nisha so mad?* Sure, Bea had gone to Charlotte's house when she probably should have been with Nisha and Indy working on finding The Coin, but everyone knew it was nearly impossible to say no to Charlotte Wang. Plus, saying no would have been the final snip to the thin thread of popularity she had left. *What should she have done, just let it all go and given up her seat at the Top Pop table forever? Besides,* Bea thought, shifting uncomfortably on the step; *it isn't like she had fun with Charlotte and Amanda.* She hardly knew them and only barely liked them. *Wait.* Bea rubbed her head in confusion. *That wasn't right. Why would she be hanging out with people she didn't even like? Who would do that?* Bea pulled a strand of her pale hair forward and studied the ends. *Me,* Bea thought with a new, queasy feeling in her stomach, *hundreds of times. It's part of being popular.* Bea disgustedly brushed the strand of hair back and frowned.

So, okay, going to Charlotte's had been a bad decision, but it had been the best bad decision she'd ever made. If she hadn't gone, she never would have found The Coin. Bea looked up the street again; no sign of Indy or Nisha. Her watch told her it was 4:01. She shook her head. Nisha and Indy weren't going to show up. She was going to have to figure this thing out on her own.

Bea sighed and opened the notebook on her lap. *November 22,* she wrote at the top of the page, *3 weeks (21 days) until Passage Day.* Bea pushed down the swell of lonely tears that were rising up behind her eyes. She refused to let herself get emotional about this. Emotions didn't solve problems.

Forcing herself to focus on something practical, Bea pulled out a page from the back of the notebook and folded it half to use as a straightedge. Then, carefully, she began to draw a map of the Wang's apartment. It wasn't long before she was deep in concentration, so much she didn't notice she was no longer alone.

A soft mewing sound right by her ear made her jump. She turned to see a pretty, mostly-brown calico cat with golden yellow mark on its forehead and vivid green eyes. She was startled a second time when she felt something rub against her leg. It was another cat; also calico, also with vivid green eyes, but this one had mostly-gold fur and a brown marking on its forehead, the perfect opposite of the first cat. She looked around to see if there was someone nearby to whom the cats belonged.

"You're so pretty, you must belong to somebody," she said, stroking the brown one down its narrow back. "Let me see your collar."

Both cats, she noticed, were wearing beautifully embroidered collars, gold for the brown cat and brown for the gold cat. She looked closely from one cat to the other. "You're twins, aren't you?" she cooed, scratching the mostly-brown cat under its chin. Then she smiled.

"Twins…well that's a clue, isn't it? I'll bet you belong to the Needlepoint lady, Gloria, don't you?" Bea looked across the street, but Gloria was gone.

The gold cat snuggled against her legs and the brown cat began to purr softly. It rubbed itself against her hand and looked up longingly into her face. "Do you want me to pet you some more, kitty?" she asked, looking into the cat's intense gaze. To her utter amazement the cat shook its head no.

Bea looked around and then back at the cat. *That didn't just happen,* she thought as the cat circled around, rubbing its soft fur against her arm. *Or maybe it did.*

"Do you want me to pet you some more?" she asked the cat again, this time pointedly watching to see what it would do. The cat turned purposely towards her, looked up at her face with its yellow-green eyes, and shook its head again.

"What do you want me to do, then?" Bea said quietly, looking around to be sure no one was passing by.

The cat again ducked its head and slipped it under her hand, turning slightly so her fingers fell on the embroidered collar. It was then that she noticed something tucked inside the collar, something made of a soft cloth. Bea gently pulled it out of the collar, taking care not to drop it. It was a tiny brown drawstring pouch, the kind that was used for a fine jewelry or gemstones. She rolled the pouch between her fingers and felt a few small hard objects inside.

The brown cat purred loudly, and Bea's heart began to race a little as she carefully pulled the pouch open. The gold cat bounded silently up the stairs and parked itself beside her shoulder, as if trying to get a better view. Slowly, she turned the pouch upside down to let the contents fall into her open hand. She held her breath, expecting something wonderful; star sapphires or emeralds or fire coral from Tibet; but instead of gemstones, into her palm fell four grayish brown seeds.

"Seeds?" she said aloud to the cats, not hiding her disappointment. "What am I supposed to do with these?"

With this, the gold cat stepped delicately onto her lap and pushed its nose against her open hand.

"What is it, kitty?"

The cat pushed its nose against her hand again. Bea lifted her hand closer to her eyes and saw that she had missed something. There were actually only three seeds. The fourth was a tiny, rolled-up piece of parchment.

Bea carefully balanced the three seeds on her knee. Then, after a third glance up and down the street, she unfurled the small scroll.

It said:

Seeds of Magag – USE IN CASE OF EMERGENCY –

And in smaller type:

To use:
1. Say what you need
2. Mix earth and seed

"And then what?" Bea asked aloud, re-rolling the paper and placing it back in the bag along with the seeds. "Well, whatever they do, I'm glad to have them." She gave the gold cat a grateful rub behind the ear. Then she tore a tiny piece of paper from her notebook and wrote:

Dear Gloria,
Thank you for The Gift.
Yours very sincerely,
Bea Brightman (Finder)

She rolled up the note and tucked it between the collar and fluffy neck of the brown cat. With this, the cats seemed to understand that their job was done. They stood up and stretched, the way cats do. Then they slipped noiselessly down the steps and trotted side by side across the street, until they disappeared behind the cars parked across the road.

Bea held the pouch in her hands, feeling the seeds and the note inside. *Say what you need. Mix earth with seed.*

Bea looked up and down the street once more and sighed aloud. Where were Indy and Nisha? They should be there with her. She knew Nisha was angry, but The Quest was more important than all of that. Bea's eyes filled with tears. Why was Nisha so stubborn? Tears slipped down Bea's cheeks and she pushed them away with the back of her hand. Then she tightened the opening of the pouch and tucked it deep into the front pocket of her jeans.

"Emotions don't solve problems," she said out loud. Then she took one last glance up and down the street, picked up her notebook, and went inside where she could draw a map of the Wang's living room in better light.

CHAPTER 31

THE KISS AT THE FLEA MARKET

Bea awoke the next morning almost as tired as she had been when she went to bed the night before. For the fifth night in a row, she had been up late worrying. She was worried about The Coin and how she would ever get it out of the Wang's living room. She was worried about the weather, which seemed to be getting grayer and drearier with each passing day. Even more, she worried about Sahwin, whose invisible presence haunted her dreams, and about her father whose voice over the phone seemed sadder than ever. She was worried about the shift in the balance of things as Aunt Faye had predicted; more earthquakes and fires, and floods on the news every day. She was worried about the midterm exams she'd been neglecting because there were so many other things to worry about. But most of all, she was worried about Nisha.

It had taken her a while to figure it, out but Bea finally saw how much her visit to Charlotte's had damaged the delicate trust she'd been trying so hard to build between them. *How had she not realized it before?* There was no way Nisha could trust her when she'd been hanging out with the girls Nisha trusted least. It occurred to Bea that, although she was good at observing people, she had a lot to learn about seeing things through someone else's eyes.

She knew that more than anything else, she needed to fix things with Nisha. Time was slipping by and they had to get back on track with The Quest. But there was something else; more to her feelings than just her desire to find The Coin. Bea really missed Nisha. When Nisha was around, Bea could be herself in a way that she couldn't with the Top Pops. With Nisha she didn't have to pretend to care about things she didn't give a fig about or pretend to dislike things she actually loved. And now that Bea had experienced that kind of friendship, no one else's company seemed to matter as much.

It was Saturday however, which meant no school, making it even easier for Nisha to avoid her. So, instead of wasting time, she'd asked Indy to go with her to the Flea Market and to her relief he had agreed – at least one Finder was still talking to her. She hoped they might find the person who'd sold The Coin to Mr. Wang. Maybe they could learn something about how it worked or where it came from. It was a long shot, but it was better than staying home alone.

Indy and Bea took the cross-town bus to the West Side and on the ride over Indy told her all about the night at the cemetery and about Drae Mord. In turn, Bea told Indy about the cats and the seeds. She held off telling him about The Coin in the Wang's apartment, however, for she was still hoping Nisha would come around. It didn't seem right to tell Indy without Nisha knowing too.

It was still early when they arrived at The Flea Market. Indy followed Bea as she wove her way through the tables towards the spot where she and Nisha had seen The Coin for the first time. Traditionally, most Flea Market vendors chose the same location week after week, so Bea was fairly confident she knew where she was going. She recognized the table with the macramé plant holders and the one next to it with the war memorabilia. However, when they got to the spot where The Coin should have been, there was a vendor selling bonsai trees instead.

"It should be right here," Bea said, frustrated. "I'm sure of it."

"Maybe it's somewhere nearby," said Indy, squinting over the neighboring tables. "Hey, isn't that Brigit from The Council?"

Bea looked up and followed his gaze. Behind the bonsai tree man, a few tables down, was a woman in a red dress surrounded by racks of old clothes. Even with her back to them, it was unmistakably Brigit.

"Let's go talk to her," said Bea.

"Uh, you go, I'll keep looking around here," said Indy.

When she frowned at him, he added, "What? She kind of makes me nervous, Okay?"

"Oh, don't be ridiculous," Bea giggled. "She's not the only beautiful woman on earth. You're going to have to get used to them sometime," she added, grabbing him by the sleeve and dragging him toward the booth where Brigit was standing.

When they reached her, Brigit smiled at them warmly as if she'd been expecting them. Her black hair was pulled back with a dark blue satin ribbon and the red of her dress set off the pink in her cheeks and lips. Around her neck were ropes of beaded necklaces in all colors and shapes. Similar necklaces and beads were displayed on the table in front of her. They shimmered in the dull sunlight. Behind her were racks of colorful clothes, and Bea spotted her two beautiful daughters napping comfortably in a large basket of fabric.

"Hello!" Brigit said brightly, "I was wondering when I'd see you here."

"You expected us?" said Bea, surprised.

"Well, let's call it a hunch," said Brigit. "It's lovely to see you both again," she added with a smile so warm and sincere that Bea couldn't help but smile in return.

"We didn't know you were here," Bea said honestly. "We came to see if we could find The Coin vendor, but no luck."

"Yes, me too," said Brigit. "I've been here every week since Faye told us about it, keeping an eye out. Unfortunately, the merchant who sold The Coin appears to have disappeared."

Bea nodded and looked down at the table in front of her. There was a pile of beaded bracelets on a tray. "I thought you were a baker, not a jewelry maker," she said.

"I enjoy making all kinds of lovely things," said Brigit. Then she turned to Indy and said, "Have you found something you like?"

Indy was standing closer to the other end of the table. He looked down at his hand and appeared surprised to find he was holding something. It was a smooth, deep red bead attached to a black leather cord. He looked up, confused.

"I..." he began, somewhat dumbfounded.

"Well," said Brigit, smiling, "it seems to like you. Look how it glows in your hand!"

"Huh?" said Indy, idiotically, looking down again at the bead.

"That is a very special bead you're holding," said Brigit. "It is called The Kiss of the Moon Goddess." She took a few steps towards Indy and picked up the bead from his open palm.

"It doesn't look like the other beads," said Bea.

"That's because it's not a bead at all. It's a stone and more." Then she lifted the stone to her lips and kissed it. "And now it belongs to you, Indy," she said turning back to him and placing the stone in his still-open palm.

Indy blushed and nodded dumbly.

"Is it a Finder's Gift?" asked Bea, moving over to Indy to examine the stone more closely.

"Yes. It is a Healing Stone; perhaps the most precious of all the Gifts."

"What does it do?" asked Indy who was finally composed enough to speak.

"Once activated, it bestows upon its owner the power to save a life with a single kiss."

"How do you activate it?" asked Bea.

"A kiss from the last person who the stone has saved is the only way."

"So," said Indy, "Are you saying I can save someone's life by kissing them?"

"Yes. But listen well. The Kiss only works in the few short moments between life and death. It only works once and it only works on someone you love."

"Oh," said Indy, who glanced quickly at Bea and then back down at the stone, looking more uncomfortable than ever.

Bea, too, looked at the stone again with fresh curiosity. "But that means that your kiss activated the stone which must mean that you are the last person the stone saved."

"Clever as always," said Brigit with a sad smile. "It was my husband who saved me with The Kiss, just before he was killed. But that is another story for another time."

They were distracted for a moment by one of Brigit's daughters, who yawned loudly in her sleep before turning over and settling back down.

"Wow," Bea said, swallowing hard. Then she looked over at the stone, which was still glowing softly in Indy's palm.

"I'm not sure Indy should take this. What if something happens to… I mean you have children… How can you give up something so powerful?"

Brigit nodded slowly and took Bea's hands between her own. "That is both kind and wise of you, Bea, but I really don't have a choice. None of us do. Now is the time for sacrifice. We must do whatever it takes even if it means putting ourselves at risk, even if it means we are frightened. In the end it will be worth it."

Unexpectedly, Bea's eyes filled up with tears, and Brigit leaned forward to whisper in her ear. "You and Nisha must resolve your differences. The fate of us all depends on you working together."

"But she doesn't want to make up!" Bea blurted out, with another unexpected rush of emotions.

"Remember what I said, Bea. Now is a time for sacrifice even if it means you must give up something that you think you can't live without. In the end, it will be worth it."

Brigit turned to Indy and said, "Put it on, around your neck, and don't take it off unless you have to."

On the bus ride home, Bea told Indy about The Coin in the Wang's apartment. After the strange conversation she'd had with Brigit, she somehow didn't feel comfortable keeping a secret from him any longer. *After all, weren't they in it together?* For a few minutes, he seemed angry she had not shared the news sooner. However, when she explained how she hoped she and Nisha would make up so she could tell them at the same time, Indy softened up a bit.

"Maybe if I tell her…" he suggested, "maybe she'll realize…"

"Do you think so?" Bea asked hopefully. "If you think it could help, then please…"

Indy nodded his agreement. "Have you given any thought to how to get into their apartment again?"

"It would be easiest if I could get myself invited again, but I can't really count on that. And even if I do get back in, I haven't figured out how to get The Coin out."

"I'm sure you'll think of something," said Indy, in a tone of voice that sounded surprisingly sincere.

The delicious smell of something baking greeted Bea as she walked through the front door, reminding her she hadn't eaten all day. She kicked off her sneakers and headed toward the kitchen. However, as she passed the front hall table, she was distracted by an oversized pink envelope sitting on top of a pile of mail. On the front was her name drawn in curly pink letters.

With mild curiosity, Bea slid her finger under the thick flap of the envelope. She pulled out the sturdy card and a tiny tornado of silvery pink sparkles came out with it and fluttered to the ground at her feet. The card was pink with a pattern of dark pink roses around the edge.

Miss Charlotte Wang
invites you to
A Party
in celebration of her
13th Birthday
Saturday, December 3rd
3:00 pm

Bea smiled. Finally, things were coming together. Here was the chance she'd been hoping for; a reason to return to Charlotte's apartment. But as quickly as her spirits lifted, they sank again. Even if she could get close to The Coin, how on earth was she going to get it out of the Wang's living room in front of all those people?

Bea made her way to the kitchen so deep in thought that she nearly walked into Cookie, who was pulling a baking tray out of the oven. "Afternoon, dear, you're just in time to ice the cupcakes."

"Cupcakes?" Bea said, another smile forming on her lips. "What a great idea."

CHAPTER 32

THE RISK

On Monday in homeroom, Bea purposely chose a seat near the window close to where Nisha had been sitting lately. Bea hoped that the closer proximity would allow her to hear Nisha's thoughts and maybe get her talking. Of course, it meant Bea would not be sitting near Charlotte, as she'd been doing lately. It was risky, but as Brigit said, it was time to take risks.

When Nisha arrived, she headed towards the windows as Bea had anticipated, but as soon as she spotted Bea, she stopped short. Her face showed surprise and then puzzlement. She glanced over to the spot where Charlotte and her friends usually sat. Some of the Top Pops and Almosts were already parked in their usual seats. Nisha turned back to Bea. Bea smiled, but Nisha did not acknowledge it. Instead, she hurried to a chair in the front of the room.

A moment later, Charlotte came in and Bea's stomach clenched nervously. *Get over it*, Bea commanded herself, forcefully. *It isn't important if Charlotte gets annoyed. The Coin is what's important.* Bea flicked her long hair behind her shoulders and sat up straighter in her chair. Charlotte headed towards her usual seat, but as she put her books down on the desk, she spotted Bea. To Bea's amazement, Charlotte smiled at her and waved enthusiastically. Then, she restacked her books, marched across the room and slid into the seat beside Bea.

"Hi," Charlotte said, smiling cheerfully. "What's up?"

"Thought I'd sit near the window today," Bea answered, trying to sound nonchalant.

"Excellent idea," Charlotte replied, "I always prefer the window seat in airplanes, don't you? Without waiting for an answer, she asked. "So, did you get my birthday invitation?"

"Yes, thanks," Bea replied.

"And you're coming, right?"

Bea paused for a moment. "I'd like to, but, I was wondering, did you invite Nisha?" Bea tried to sound as if it would be the most ordinary thing in the world.

"Nisha?" Charlotte frowned. "You mean the fre…I mean, the uh, girl with the braids?"

"Yes, Nisha Lakewood."

"I couldn't," Charlotte said in her best sing-song voice. "I mean I'd like to, of course. I would like to be able to invite the whole class, but my mother insists I set some limits. You understand, right?"

"Sure," said Bea, "but unfortunately, I can only go if Nisha is going."

"What? Why?" said Charlotte.

Before Bea could answer, Justina and Candy came over and noisily settled in around them. Shortly after, Gianna and Lauren relocated themselves from the other side of the room. Nobody mentioned the change in seating arrangements. They chattered and gossiped as if nothing had changed.

If only she'd had another minute with Charlotte alone. She might have been able to get Nisha invited to the party. But with a single glance at Nisha, Bea realized her plan was doomed. Even if she could convince Charlotte to invite Nisha, she'd never get Nisha to agree to come.

As always, Nisha sat still as a stone with her focus on the book in front of her. Bea sighed. If only there was a way to get Nisha to trust her. She had to do something drastic, something risky; an act of solidarity that would prove to Nisha that Bea was truly her friend. At that moment, Nisha lifted her hand to smooth one of her already flawless black braids, and as she did, an idea popped into Bea's mind.

As soon as the bell rang, Bea headed for the girl's lavatory. She dug around in her bag until she came up with two elastic bands. Then she proceeded to twist her hair into two long blond braids. She wasn't very practiced at braiding and it took her longer than she'd planned to get it right, but when she was finished, the result was perfect: from Top Pop to Not Pop in five minutes. She gave herself a quick smile of encouragement and headed for her English classroom.

When she walked in, she got exactly the response she was hoping for. Nisha's eyes went round with surprise and Amanda Whitehead burst out laughing. Bea controlled her face and headed to an open seat in neutral territory.

After her initial shock, Nisha did not look at Bea again. Bea tried to read her thoughts, but there was no connection. Amanda made her thoughts known to everyone by bursting out in periodic fits of noisy giggles. Mr. Morton did nothing to quiet her and even chuckled to himself once or twice.

To keep it from bothering her, Bea focused her attention on writing and rewriting The Prophecy in her notebook. She got so lost in concentration she didn't notice Mr. Morton reading over her shoulder until it was too late. She shut her notebook as quickly as she could, cursing herself for being so careless.

"Something you want to share with the class, Miss Brightman?" he said. He was smiling, but his eyes were steely.

Bea shook her head nervously.

"I see. Well then, I'm forced to assume that you were not taking notes on my lecture. Am I right?"

Bea nodded once. She shot a furtive look at Nisha, but Nisha's eyes were glued to her desk.

"See me after class, and bring the notebook."

After the bell, Bea waited apprehensively by Mr. Morton's desk, flicking her new braids nervously with her right hand. How was she going to explain The Prophecy to Mr. Morton?

"The notebook, please," said Mr. Morton holding out his

pale hand.

Bea handed him her red science notebook hoping he would not notice the switch.

"The white one, Miss Brightman," he said impatiently.

Bea pulled out her white notebook and handed it to him, trying to keep her hand from shaking. Why was she so nervous? There was no way he would understand what she had written. Would he?

He opened the notebook to the last few written pages. He read one page and then the next.

"What is this?" he asked, looking up at her sharply.

He looked back down at the notebook and, without waiting for an answer, he read from it aloud.

"The Little Bird, by Bianca Brightman

Once I saw a little bird

It stood upon a hill

A head of red

A tail of black and

Spots upon its bill."

For a moment it was Bea's turn to be confused. She hadn't written any poems about birds. But then she realized what had happened. It was the concealing charm; the same one that changed her words when she spoke of The Quest must also change her words when she wrote about it. She was so relieved that she almost laughed.

Mr. Morton however was not amused. He glared at her suspiciously, then did something odd. He lifted the paper to his nose and sniffed it. His expression slowly changed from suspicion to a sort of wicked amusement. "How fascinating!" he said turning to her. "Where did you find this…poem, Miss Brightman? Did your father give it to you?"

"No, sir," Bea replied, shifting on her feet uncomfortably. She didn't like the look on Mr. Morton's face.

"Did you steal it from him, then?"

"No, sir," Bea answered again, trying to control her tone.

Mr. Morton turned back to the page in front of him and sniffed again. "And what about the notebook? Did your father give you the notebook?"

"Yes, sir," she answered honestly.

"I see," he said, snapping the book shut and making Bea jump.

"Well, it appears, Miss Brightman, that we have something in common."

Bea held her breath, afraid of what Mr. Morton might say next.

"You see," he said, smiling his wicked smile; "I too am quite fond of birds."

Then to Bea's surprise, Mr. Morton handed her back the notebook and excused her without so much as a reprimand. Bea rushed from the room, relieved to be let go, but with a sick feeling in her stomach. Had Mr. Morton smelled the spell on the paper? If he had, then that meant that Mr. Morton knew something about spells, and if that were true, did he also know about The Coin?

By the time Bea made it to the lunchroom, Nisha was nowhere to be found. Bea ignored the waves from Charlotte and the loud laughter from Amanda and headed down towards the Library. No sign of Nisha. From there, she checked the girl's lavatories, but again she had no luck.

Bea spent the entire lunch period searching for Nisha, but when the bell rang for the next class, she still had not found her. After school, she ran to Nisha's locker. She waited for some time but Nisha never showed up.

Tuesday was a repeat of Monday, and by Wednesday morning, Bea was exhausted. She continued to wear hair in braids as a sign to Nisha that she wanted to make up, but still Nisha seemed determined to avoid her. Every day that went by, she became more and more frustrated. Time was running out and she wasn't any closer to getting The Coin back than she had been before she'd found it.

Charlotte wasn't in school on Wednesday, having left a day early for Thanksgiving break, so when the Top Pops and Almosts came into homeroom, they clustered around Amanda. Bea sat near Nisha again, but to no avail. Nisha wouldn't even look at her, and when the bell rang, she was out the door like a shot. Bea ran after her, but as she pushed her way through the crowded doorway, she felt someone tug on the back of her sweater. It was Amanda.

"I don't know why, but Charlotte wanted me to remind you that her birthday party is going to be on December 3rd. It's Saturday. You haven't RSVP'd."

"Oh," Bea said. "I want to come but I told Charlotte on Monday that I couldn't go unless Nisha is invited. Would you remind her of that?"

Amanda stared at Bea for what felt like a full minute. Finally, she said. "You really want me to tell Charlotte Wang that you're not coming to her party unless that little freak comes? You're kidding, right?"

"Not at all," said Bea, flipping a braid behind her shoulder and trying to sound confident.

"Guess I won't be seeing you there then," said Amanda with a smug snort.

"Perhaps not," Bea said, "but you will remind Charlotte, won't you?"

"Course I'll will. I can't wait to see her face when I do."

"Thank you," Bea said politely, and turned to go.

"Hey," said Amanda, tugging Bea's arm sharply.

When Bea turned around again, Amanda face was only inches from her own. "I don't know who you think you are with those stupid braids," Amanda breathed into Bea's ear, "but if I were you, I'd choose my friends more carefully."

"Thanks for the advice," Bea said, smiling calmly at her. "That's exactly what I'm trying to do."

Bea walked home slowly. She was tired and the air was so thick and warm she felt she was walking through glue. It was another miserable reminder that things were getting worse; that she was running out of time. She pulled her sweater off and stuffed it haphazardly into her backpack, her footsteps matching the heaviness of her thoughts. She rounded the corner of her street in a daze, so she was almost knocked over when Indy whizzed by on his skateboard. A sleeve of her sweater was dangling from her backpack and Indy grabbed it as he passed, pulling the sweater from her bag as he did.

"Oh, a Miss Huntington's sweater," he called out in a high-pitched, girly voice. He waved the sweater over his head, "I've always wanted one," he cooed.

"Hey," Bea shouted, laughing for the first time in a week, "give that back."

"Never!" Indy squealed.

Just seeing Indy gave Bea a charge of much needed energy. She took off after him, but he was too fast on his skateboard. Finally, he came to a sharp stop in front of her stoop and she ran up to him, breathing hard but still laughing.

"Looking for this?" he said innocently, holding out the sweater.

"Why yes, I was, thank you," Bea answered as if she hadn't just chased him halfway down the block.

"Looking for me?"

Bea turned. It was Nisha. She was sitting on the steps, smiling up at Bea. Her black eyes and glossy blue ribbons seemed bright against the dull afternoon light. In her hands was a large pink envelope.

CHAPTER 33

THE BEGINNINGS OF A PLAN

"I didn't know what to think," Nisha blurted, standing up. "It looked like... well, that day you got into Charlotte's car...it was like you cared more about the Horribles than finding The Coin."

"The Horribles?"

"Those girls, Amanda Whitehead and Charlotte Wang, it's just something I call them because they can be..."

"Horrible?"

"They sound pretty horrible to me," chimed Indy. Bea and Nisha turned to look at him as if they'd forgotten he was there.

"I'm just saying..." he said with a shrug. "Never mind, forget I'm even here."

Nisha nodded. "I didn't trust you and I'm sorry."

"And you trust me now because...?"

"Well, first, when Indy told me about you discovering The Coin at Charlotte's house, I didn't really believe it; that is until today. You see, I got Charlotte's invitation by messenger yesterday and I thought it was just part of some big plan to make me look... well, to make fun of me somehow."

The color in Nisha's cheeks intensified and Bea could tell how embarrassed she was to admit any of this in front of Indy.

"But then, after Homeroom," Nisha continued, "you told Amanda that you wouldn't go to the party unless I was invited too, and I could tell by her reaction that there wasn't any plan and well, I also realized what a big risk you were taking saying that to her. It was very…well, it proved that you're genuinely committed to finding The Coin no matter what. So I'm sorry. I'm sorry I was stupid and that I wasted all this time."

Bea smiled. It was more than she had ever heard come out of Nisha's mouth at one time, and she could tell it wasn't easy for her.

"It's me who should be sorry. I shouldn't have gone in the first place. I know I act like I know everything sometimes, but I don't. The truth is, I had no idea that I would find The Coin at Charlotte's apartment. It was just luck."

"Or fate," said Nisha.

"Or fate," Bea agreed uncertainly. "But just because the outcome was good doesn't mean it was a good decision. And those girls, The Horribles, they don't matter to me anymore. It was me who wasted time."

"We both have," Nisha said.

"Very true," said Indy, nodding solemnly. Both girls looked at him again.

Indy held up his hands in surrender. "Staying out of it."

Bea turned back to Nisha. "Before we get back to looking for The Coin, could you just explain something? How is it you avoided me for almost a week? I looked for you everywhere. And how did you know I spoke to Amanda after Homeroom?"

Nisha shrugged and glanced over at Indy. "I can sort of sense where you are all the time so I just didn't go there."

"You just sense it?"

Nisha nodded, and Bea knew Nisha's strange explanation was all she was going to get.

"Well, Ladies," said Indy, interrupting again, "I, for one, am thrilled we've patched all this up. What say we get back to Coin hunting now, okay?"

This time, both girls looked at him and smiled. Bea pulled out her notebook.

"Oh no, not the notebook," said Indy, laughing. "I didn't miss the notebook! I've already memorized the prophecy, I swear!"

Nisha laughed.

"Speaking of that…" said Bea. Then she went on to tell them the story of how Mr. Morton had smelled the words on the page.

"It's possible he could have smelled the spell. I mean I can smell all sorts of things," said Nisha.

"Like what?" Indy asked.

"Nisha's amazing!" said Bea enthusiastically. "She can actually smell what people are thinking and even feeling sometimes."

"Really? That's… that's really cool," said Indy, his cheeks pinker than Nisha's. "Can you do it with everyone?"

"It's easier with people I don't know very well. When I'm around people a lot, my own thoughts and feelings confuse the smells. But," Nisha continued, turning back to Bea, "I'll ask Aunt Faye if people can smell magic. I've never heard of it but that doesn't mean much."

"Well, if it's true," said Bea, "it means that Mr. Morton knows about Avalon and about us and possibly even about The Coin. I've seen him talking to Charlotte after class a few times. I wonder if she's involved too, somehow."

"He's definitely hiding something," Nisha agreed, "He doesn't have any odor at all. It's not natural."

"You're going to have to be very careful around him," said Indy, looking concerned. "Don't give him any more reasons to suspect anything."

Both girls nodded their agreement, and Bea shook her braids back as if she could shake off the creepy feeling Mr. Morton always gave her.

"Well at least he didn't take my notebook," Bea said, to change the subject. "I've recorded everything we've done so far and all the Spirit Gifts we have received. We have Caitria's tarot cards, The Minute, Drae Mord, The Seeds of Magag and The Kiss of the Moon Goddess. That makes five, one from each

197

family. Still, as brilliant as they might be, we still don't have a clue what we're supposed to do with them. I've looked in every book I can find."

"These are secret magical objects. Maybe nothing's been written about them," said Indy.

"Don't be silly, there is something written about everything," said Bea.

Indy shrugged. "Did you find any books on how to steal something from a rich girl's apartment? Because that would be really helpful."

Bea smiled. "Funny you should mention it," she said, "because I have a few ideas about that. It seems obvious that Charlotte's birthday party is our best chance at getting The Coin… that's why I was so anxious to get Nisha invited and now that we know we can get into the apartment, the only real challenge will be getting The Coin out. I'm fairly sure I can break into the curio cabinet," Bea continued, ignoring Nisha's worried expression. "From what I could see, a small lock held it closed at the front, and I think I can pick it with a hair pin or piece of wire."

"You can pick a lock?" Indy, sounded impressed.

"As a matter of fact, I learned how from a book," said Bea. "You know, you really should try reading some time, it can be quite enlightening."

"Whoa, that's a big word, en…light…en…wait, what was it again?" Indy said, sounding the word out as if he'd never heard it before.

"The more difficult part," Bea continued, swallowing her amusement, "will be to create a diversion big enough to distract everyone at the party so I have time to do it. But with Nisha going, I think we've got that part solved."

"What do you mean?" Nisha said, frowning.

"Let's not worry about that now," said Bea, knowing Nisha wasn't going to like her plan very much. "We have one even bigger problem to sort out first. How do we keep the Wangs from discovering that The Coin is missing? There's no doubt they'll suspect someone from the party has stolen it."

The three Finders spent the rest of the afternoon trying to solve their dilemma, without much progress. Nisha rejected every idea that Bea came up with, as most of them involved Nisha performing some kind of magic. And Bea nixed most of Indy's, as they all required incredible feats of daring and strength.

When the light started to fade, they were still without a plan, but both Indy and Nisha had to leave. The next day was Thanksgiving and Indy had cousins coming to visit. Nisha's Aunt had invited the entire Council over for what she called The Spirit's Feast of Thanks. Thanksgiving, she claimed, was an Avalonian tradition that Man Kind had adopted centuries ago.

Bea was scheduled to visit some distant cousins living on Long Island whom she'd never met. She would have much preferred a quiet evening with Nana Anna and Cookie, but her father had insisted she go to observe an authentic American tradition.

Nisha and Bea agreed to meet again on Friday evening, and though they had not figured out a plan to retrieve The Coin, Bea went inside that night feeling better than she had in weeks. She climbed into her bed with a book on Arthurian legends, but exhausted as she was, she fell asleep before she made it through the first chapter.

CHAPTER 34

THE SLEEPOVER

Nisha had been sitting on Bea's stoop for more than an hour when the car finally pulled up. The driver got out and collected Bea's bag from the trunk.

"Hi," Nisha said, trying not to sound nervous. She twisted her necklace anxiously between her fingers. Had Bea forgotten about their plans? Changed her mind?

Bea's huge grin completely quelled Nisha's fears. "Hi!" she replied, bounding from the car. "Sorry I'm late. I'm so glad you waited!"

"How was it?" Nisha asked politely.

"Sort of awful, but fine I guess," said Bea, with a shrug, her big smile fading a bit. "The food was good but all they talked about was football, *American* football, and after dinner, we actually had to watch it. Then, of course, there was the earthquake."

"The earthquake?"

"Yes, didn't you hear about it? It was on the news everywhere. There was a big earthquake, during the game. Twelve people died when part of the stadium collapsed and dozens more were injured. I can't believe you didn't know."

"There's not a whole lot of technology at my house," said

Nisha. "Unless I buy the paper, I don't hear much. Do you think it was connected to The Coin?"

"It had to be. Earthquakes are incredibly rare in that part of the country," said Bea as the driver set her bag in front of the stoop.

"I don't think we're going to have much time to work on solving our puzzle," Nisha said, dropping her voice so the driver wouldn't hear them. "It's getting late and Gloria insists we are inside before the sun goes down."

Bea looked at the sky. "But we have to," she said, frowning, "we're running out of time." Then Nisha saw an idea light up Bea's face. "Hey!" she said. "Why don't you sleep over?"

As Nisha expected, Aunt Faye didn't love the idea, but, when Nisha explained they needed every available minute to work on The Quest, she hesitantly agreed. Nisha rushed to her room to pack a bag before Faye had a chance to change her mind.

"If anything happens, call me," said Faye, as Nisha opened the front door.

"Auntie," Nisha said, with a smirk, "you hardly know how to use the phone."

Faye smiled and then laughed at herself. "I just can't get used to holding that silly thing up to my head. But it doesn't matter; you and I don't need a phone. Just call me with your heart and I will hear you.

Nisha looked over at her Aunt. "Really?" she asked.

Faye smiled. "Really. When two daughters of the Goddess are deeply connected, they are often able to communicate without words," she said.

Nisha immediately thought of Bea, and for the millionth time, she wondered about her new friend. Bea was not a daughter of the Goddess, yet Nisha could read her thoughts. Then, also for the millionth time, she reprimanded herself for not learning all she could about the powers of The Lake. There was so much she didn't know about her Spirit Gifts and how they worked. She had wasted so much time worrying about what other people thought of her that she had missed everything important about herself.

Nisha gave her aunt a long hug goodbye. "I promise to call you if I need to," she said. Then she tugged her bag onto her shoulder and headed across the street.

Nana Anna answered the door and invited her in with a warm smile. Then she went off to find Bea, leaving Nisha alone in the large foyer. It was darker than Nisha had expected, and a bit run-down, but it was impossibly big and elegant compared to her own little home. At the back of the room was a grand staircase that rose up at a slow, gracious angle and split at the top into a balcony that wrapped all the way around the room. In the corners of the ceiling were carvings of angels and vines, some chipped and faded but splendid just the same, and the rug, though worn through in a few spots, was lovely, with a pattern that looked like water beneath Nisha's feet. In the center of the hall was a large, round table that had been rubbed to a shine. On it was a vase filled with fresh, fragrant orchids, their scent mixing pleasantly with odor of the polished wood.

Nisha walked over to the table and carefully placed her bag down. Then she turned slowly around, trying to take the whole room in at once. It was all she could do to keep herself from spinning on her heel like a little girl.

"I swear it's not haunted," said Bea, coming down the huge staircase. "Though that might actually be interesting," she added with a grin. "And it might be quite nice if it were really fixed it up, but Father doesn't care a fig about such things. I'm afraid Nana Anna and Cookie have done the best they can with it."

"Have you forgotten where I live?" said Nisha who could not imagine anyone complaining about living in such a house. "This place is a palace."

"It's big," Bea conceded, "but I much prefer your apartment, it's so cozy and happy."

"If you say so," Nisha replied.

"Father says it is human nature to want what we don't have. If we don't want for things, we don't progress, or something like that. Speaking of wanting things, are you hungry? Dinner's ready," she said. "C'mon, I'm starved."

Nisha followed Bea into the dining room and nearly gasped in amazement. The room was long and dark and so opulent that everything in it seemed in competition for Nisha's attention. Finally her eyes settled on the three glittering chandeliers hanging in a perfect row down the center of the ceiling. Making them even more dazzling were two enormous golden-edged mirrors hung at either end of the room. They were positioned in such a way as to reflect each other's reflection, creating the illusion that both the room and the chandeliers went on forever. Beneath the chandeliers was a long dark table. Eight tall chairs stood at attention on either side with a more elaborate chair at either end.

It was only as the girls headed towards the far end of the table that Nisha noticed the fireplace. It was unlike any she had ever seen: carved out of a pale blue speckled stone and shaped like a circle rather than a square. It was so large that Nisha was quite certain she could step inside it without ducking down.

Before she even knew she was moving, Nisha found herself standing in front of it, running her fingers along the cold polished stone.

"That's my grandfather," said Bea, who mistakenly thought Nisha had crossed the room to look at the huge portrait that hung above the fireplace. Nisha looked up. There was something in the man's smile that was familiar; a glint in his blue eyes that reminded Nisha of Bea. "Father said he was a prankster who was always kidding around. But most people say he was crazy," Bea added, looking over Nisha's shoulder at the wall behind her.

Nisha turned around to see a mirror, reflecting the portrait on the opposite wall. It was arranged so that it appeared the same painting hung on both sides of the room; Bea's grandfather smiling back at himself as if he had a secret or perhaps a private joke.

"He liked mirrors," Bea said. "He thought they were magical."

"Magical?"

"He collected antiques and artifacts from all over the world like my father, but he particularly loved anything to do with ancient myths and sorcery; that sort of thing."

"Is that why they thought he was crazy?" Nisha asked.

"I suppose that's part of it," said Bea.

"Well, maybe he just knew something they didn't." said Nisha. "Maybe he knew something about us; about The Lake or about the Mirrors of Avalon. Perhaps that's why…" Nisha stopped.

"Why, what?" Bea asked.

"Well, why you're involved," she answered carefully, worried she might insult Bea. "I've been wondering what the connection might be; why you were chosen to be a Finder. Maybe it has something to do with your grandfather."

"I've considered that as well," Bea replied, matter-of-factly. "There must be a connection, but I've hunted through this entire house and I haven't found a thing about Avalon or even King Arthur. If he did have anything on the subject, he must have sold it or given it away."

Dinner was delicious but Nisha could barely concentrate on eating. The excitement she felt being away from home, combined with all the worrying she'd been doing about The Coin, tightened her stomach into knots. And on top of it all, her eyes kept returning to the strange fireplace and the portrait above it. By the time dessert arrived, Bea seemed to have run out of appetite as well. She took a small bite of chocolate cake and put her fork down. "Maybe we should go upstairs and get to work," she suggested.

Bea's bedroom was almost as fascinating as the dining room, for it was not like a child's bedroom at all. The room was large and the ceiling very high with tall windows along the far wall. Heavy, blue curtains hung between them, straining against the thick gold cords that held them open. In the center of the room was an enormous bed with four posts that nearly reached the ceiling. The bed was so high off the floor that there was a tiny staircase beside it so Bea could climb in.

"I hope you don't mind sharing. The bed should be big enough for both of us."

"No problem," Nisha said, "I think half your bed is bigger than all of mine."

Nisha found her bag set neatly on a chair by the window. Accidentally, she knocked a small box from off a nearby shelf. "Sorry," she said, picking the box from the floor. It was a gift, wrapped in gold paper. Not sure where it had fallen from, she turned around and held it out to Bea.

"It's a birthday present from my grandmother," explained Bea. "My father probably won't make it back for my birthday so he gave it to me ahead of time."

"Your birthday?" said Nisha.

Bea nodded. "It's in a couple of weeks," she said. "Actually," she added with a slight hesitation in her voice, "it's on Passage Day."

"What?" Nisha said, unsure if she had heard Bea correctly.

"My birthday is on Passage Day, the same as yours. I've been trying to figure out what it might mean but I keep coming up blank. It could just be a coincidence of course, but then, it might be the reason I was chosen to be a Finder, to be like... your surrogate twin or something."

"Surrogate twin?" Nisha said, shaking her head in confusion.

"You know, like a substitute. Isn't it true that most Daughters of The Lake have twin sisters? Penn said something about it when we met with The Council. He said you weren't powerful because you were twinless. Maybe I was chosen to be a Finder to make you more powerful."

"Why didn't you say something before?" Nisha asked.

"Well, I tried the night Faye told us the story of Caitria, but it just seemed like too much information at the time and, well, then we got in that fight... Anyway, it doesn't really change anything, does it? I mean, it's been made clear in a hundred ways that we are meant to be in this together, this is just another coincidence."

Nisha nodded. Bea was right. As remarkable as it was, it didn't change anything.

"So this," Bea said, taking the small box from Nisha's still-outstretched hand, "is a birthday present from my grandmother.

I'm not supposed to open it until my birthday."

The girls brushed their teeth and changed into their pajamas, then climbed up into the covers. Bea got out her notebook and pulled a pen out from a side table drawer. She turned to Nisha like a waitress ready to take an order. "So, can you do anything besides turning icing from vanilla to chocolate?"

Nisha caught her breath. She and Bea had never spoken of the cupcake incident and her first inclination was to deny it. *But why?* She knew that if they were going to solve this thing, she was going to have to start being totally honest. Nisha let her breath out slowly and said, "I don't know. I haven't really mastered Wishmaking. Most of the time stuff just happens, like the cupcakes." She shrugged. "I wish it would stop. People already think I'm a freak."

Bea shook her head in amazement and said, "I think it's totally brilliant."

"You do?" said Nisha.

"To be able to do actual magic; are you kidding me?" said Bea.

"I guess it could be, if I could really do it, but I can't, at least not when I want to. So if you're thinking I could wish The Coin out of that cabinet in the Wang's living room, I'm afraid it's not a very good plan."

"Well, I was thinking you could create a distraction. Remember how crazy everyone got when the cupcakes switched to chocolate? A bomb could have blown up and no one would have noticed."

"I don't know, Bea," Nisha said, "I don't think I could do that kind of thing on cue. That was just an accident."

"Why don't you try something now?" said Bea. "See if you can make those books fall off the table over there," she said, pointing to a stack of books by the window.

"Really? Now?"

"Sure. As practice. I mean, imagine how useful it could be if you could master it?"

Nisha hesitated. She had never tried Wishmaking in front of anyone but Aunt Faye before. *What if nothing happened? Or something did happen, but not what she meant to happen? Or what if she broke something? Or she made a weird face when she was concentrating like Aunt Faye sometimes did? No, she couldn't do it.* However, when she turned back to Bea and saw the flickers of excitement lighting her blue eyes, she said, "Oh alright. But don't expect much."

"Take your time," said Bea, smiling.

Nisha sucked in her breath and shifted herself around on the bed so she was directly across from the books. They looked heavy, and Nisha's felt her throat tighten with self-doubt. She swallowed hard and concentrated on the steps of Wishmaking.

She began to form a picture in her head as Faye had instructed, but even as she did, she knew it wasn't right. In every case that she had made something happen, she hadn't needed the steps of Wishmaking at all. When she was in the graveyard with Indy, all it took to open Drae Morde's box was a single word. And with the cupcakes in the lunchroom, she'd changed the icing to chocolate without even thinking about it. In fact, in all of those incidents Nisha was barely thinking at all. It was much more about how she was feeling at the time. *Could that be it? Could it be that feelings made the magic happen?*

She looked at the books again and frowned. She didn't feel anything at all about them. But then she smelled something. It was the scent of lilacs; the smell of hopefulness – one of the loveliest smells of all - and it was coming from Bea.

Nisha breathed in the scent. She too felt hopeful. If she could do this then maybe they actually had a chance to get The Coin. She let the feeling build inside her and then closed her eyes. Hesitantly, she stretched her hand out in front of her. Almost immediately, Nisha felt a surge charge through her body. She opened her eyes just in time to see the book on top of the pile move. It was only a tiny shift, but it moved.

"Did you see that?" Bea said, breathlessly. She pointed at the book pile. "It moved!"

Nisha nodded, but she wasn't as enthusiastic as Bea. It wasn't much of a result.

"Try again!" Bea commanded. "Try it one more time."

Nisha turned back to the books and tried again, but she knew it wasn't going to work. Bea's excitement was too distracting.

Nisha tried again several times, but nothing happened. "I'm sorry," she said, "I think I'm too tired."

"You just need to take a break. Maybe if you just wait a…"

"Stop!" Nisha gasped, and Bea was stunned into silence, her brows crossed in confusion. Then her eyes widened and a smile spread across her face.

"That was close," said Nisha admonishingly."

"You mean it could have been close."

"What do you mean could have been? You almost said wait a minute! You almost used the Finder's Gift."

"You're right," Bea said, still grinning. "I almost said it. Or at least I would have almost said it if we had been talking. But we weren't talking, were we? We haven't said a single word this whole time."

Nisha's eyes opened wide and Bea smiled at her. Their smiles turned into giggles and when they finally quieted, Bea said. "Whatever we are; it's really amazing. We just have to figure out how to use it."

CHAPTER 35

THE NIGHT VISITOR

The girls got back under the covers, and Bea flipped the pages of the notebook until she found the one she wanted. She smoothed the page and read aloud:

"Three Finders will come if Coin is lost,
The brave and true to stand the test,
Seeking the treasure at all cost,
As all depends upon their quest.

The Dark to see what cannot be seen,
The Light to guide the way,
The Third to keep them both safely
Until the Passage Day.

The Book of Charms will take The Three
To The Room of Truth in misty waves,
Unlock the gate with Vesica's Key;
Return The Coin and all is saved."

"The first part is clear," continued Bea. "Three Finders have come to seek The Coin and pretty much everything depends on us finding it. The second part is fairly obvious as well. The Dark is you, the Light is me and the Third is Indy, right?"

"Yes, but we've been over this a thousand…"

"So it's really the third part that is the mystery," Bea continued, handing Nisha the notebook. "Read it again," she requested, although they both knew it by heart.

Nisha cleared her throat and read:

"The Book of Charms will take The Three
To The Room of Truth in misty waves,
Unlocked only by Vesica's Key;
Return The Coin and all is saved."

"Vesica's Key," said Bea stifling a yawn. "We need to find more about this." Bea turned over with a sigh.

"Definitely," Nisha said, with a yawn of her own. "I wish there was someone who knew more, someone who could help us," she added but there was no answer except the soft rhythm of Bea's breathing. The sound was soothing, and before Nisha knew it, she was asleep as well.

It was the smell that woke her – something rich and savory cooking on an open fire. She attempted to turn herself over and go back to sleep, but as she had not eaten dinner, the scent was too tempting to resist. Bea's bed was much further from the ground than Nisha was used to, and her feet made a loud thump as they hit the floor. The wood felt cold under her bare toes. She thought of looking for some slippers, but the smell beckoned her. It was baked ham, she was sure of it, but more than that, she could smell a hint of mustard and cranberry. There was even the buttery smell of baked potatoes and the waxiness of candles lingering at the edges of the aroma. Before she knew what she was doing, Nisha found herself padding down the long staircase. Moments later she was in the dining room standing in front of the large fireplace. The dim light of the street lamps filtered in through the windows. The smell was so strong it made her mouth water. She walked from one end of the long table to the other but there was no food to be found.

"It's fantastic, isn't it?" said a man's voice, just as Nisha returned to the fireplace. "It's the smell of my in-laws house at the holidays. After weeks at sea, nothing smelled better than that ham. Best ham I ever ate. Sadly for you, it's just a memory – there's no ham here tonight – just a little trick to get you out of bed. However," he added, brightly, "the good news is that my in-laws aren't here either." He chuckled. "Truth be told, your great grand-parents were a bit of a snore. Could barely get a smile out of them, let alone a laugh. Me? I enjoy a good belly laugh. There's nothing like a hearty chuckle to put things in perspective."

"Who are you? Where are you?" asked Nisha nervously, looking around for the source of the voice.

"I am your grandfather, dear girl. I have been hoping to meet you for some time but it wasn't until you finally requested my help that I was allowed to make contact."

As soon as she heard the word grandfather, Nisha looked up at the painting of Admiral Brightman above the mantle. Her eyes searched the image.

"Turn around, child," the voice said.

Slowly, Nisha turned around and looked into the mirror that hung directly across from the painting. In it, the reflection of Bea's grandfather shimmered across the mirror's surface like light on a lake. "Mirrors are marvelous, aren't they?" the image said. "I, for one, always thought I looked quite good in them," he added with a chortle and a wink.

Nisha nodded, a bit stunned by what she was seeing.

"So, dear Bea," said the image, with a more serious tone, "you seek to know more about Vesica's Key?"

"Well, yes," Nisha replied hesitantly, "but I'm afraid there has been a bit of a mistake. You see, you woke up the wrong girl. You meant to wake up Bea. She's your granddaughter. I'm just her friend. I'm sleeping over."

"Just a friend? Not possible. If you're just a friend, then explain how you can hear me?" he commanded, sounding more like an admiral than a grandfather.

"I… I'm not sure, but I can go get her if you'd like?" Nisha suggested, thinking she wouldn't mind if someone else were awake to witness this.

"Negative!" commanded the image abruptly. "I am only allowed to speak to one of the living tonight," he continued, more quietly. "If you wake her up, the window between the worlds will close."

"Uh – well - okay," Nisha said, softly. "Perhaps since I'm also a Finder and we're both looking for the Third Coin, I can pass on the information to her."

"You're a Finder?" the image sniffed. "Well, I suppose that will have to do - might as well get on with it then. I'm not getting any younger," he added, the giggle returning to his voice. "Not getting any younger," he repeated. "Get it?" He hooted. "It's funny because I'm dead, so of course I'm not getting younger."

Nisha stood quietly and waited for him to recover his composure.

"Well, you were right about one thing," said the image, wiping away a tear of laughter from the corner of his eye, "you're definitely not a Brightman. Brightmans have a sense of humor. On the other hand, I couldn't agree more that this is not the time for joking around." He straightened up and pushed his shoulders back rigidly. His voice was serious again. "This," he announced, "is the entrance to my secret library."

"I'm sorry," Nisha said, unsure if he were joking again or not, "but isn't this the dining room?"

"Indeed it is," he said, his eyes twinkling.

"So the secret library is in the dining room?"

"Of course the library is not *in* the dining room. The *entrance* is in the dining room."

"So the entrance to the library is in the dining room."

"Precisely," he replied with an exasperated sigh. Then he mumbled to no one in particular, "Doesn't have the Brightman brains either."

"This is a dream, isn't it?" Nisha asked, shaking her head, trying to wake herself up

"Negative," said the image, who was back to acting like a ship's captain, "so pay attention. If I'd put the entrance to my secret library in the library, it wouldn't be much of a secret now would it?"

"No sir," said Nisha, scratching her head. "But why have a secret library at all?" she asked. "What's in it?"

"Secret things, of course," said the image, with an exaggerated eye-roll, "secret books, treasures…You understand I made my fortune searching the world for …" Suddenly the image let out an enormous burp. "Oh no, It can't be! I'm out of time already!" He turned to Nisha with a look of panic eyes. "Don't forget to tell my granddaughter. She'll figure it out. Got the Brightman brains, I'm sure of it."

"But what do we do? How do we get in?" Nisha asked, desperately.

"It's simple," said the image, which was growing hazy in the mirror's surface. "Just do what I do. Stand in front of the mirror and think of something…" And then the living reflection of Admiral Brightman was gone, and there was nothing but the still reflection of the painting over the mantle.

CHAPTER 36

THE DOOR IN THE DINING ROOM

The next morning, when Nisha woke up, she sensed someone was watching her. She opened her eyes cautiously, the weight of sleep still heavy on her lids. To her relief, it was only Bea, propped against the pillows with her notebook on her lap, looking at her eagerly.

"Morning," Bea said brightly. Nisha groaned. Bea was clearly a morning person. All the sleepiness of the night before was gone from her voice. "I was hoping you'd wake up soon. I know it's early but I've been dying to ask you something."

Nisha rubbed her eyes and pulled the blanket up around her. She stifled a yawn.

"What?" she asked sleepily.

"Did you dream about the painting in the dining room last night?" Bea asked, "Because I had the weirdest dream about the painting of my grandfather."

At the mention of the painting, Nisha felt a jolt of memory. She sat up and rubbed her eyes.

"You did, didn't you!" said Bea excitedly, "I knew it."

"Was it a dream?" Nisha asked, speaking to herself more than Bea.

"Of course, but what's really amazing is that it was your

dream," said Bea excitedly. "At first I couldn't figure out what was going on. Everything was fuzzy around the edges; but then I realized what was happening. I was dreaming your dream."

"Are you sure?" Nisha asked.

"Don't you remember, we were reading each other's thoughts all night?" said Bea. "It must be the same kind of thing."

"No, I mean, are you sure it was a dream?" Nisha asked.

Bea smiled. "You are remembering the same thing, right? My grandfather was talking to you from the painting?"

"Yes" Nisha replied, nodding, "actually, it was from the mirror but I don't think he was a dream."

Bea giggled. "A reflection of my dead grandfather was talking and cracking jokes from a mirror in our dining room. Now, how could that be anything but a dream?"

"Well," Nisha said, smiling a little at Bea's indignation. "Didn't we see images in the Mirror of Avalon at my Aunt's apartment? And didn't you see me move those books last night? And what about the mind reading and the cupcakes? "

"I suppose it could be…," said Bea hesitantly. But if you're right…" She trailed off.

"If I'm right what?" asked Nisha.

"If you're right," said Bea scrunching up her nose, "that mean my grandfather could actually be here, haunting this house."

Nisha laughed. "Don't tell me you're afraid of ghosts?"

"No, of course not. It's just well…I don't want them in my house, that's all."

"If it makes you feel any better, I don't think it was a ghost. It was more like a spirit visit like when the Teller Ninane took over my Aunt's body during the séance," Nisha explained.

"I feel much better about it when you put it that way," Bea said sarcastically.

Nisha laughed. "The important part is that your grandfather was here. He came to help us, to give you a message, but he accidentally woke me instead of you. Luckily I could hear him, I think because we're both Finders."

Bea shook her head in amazement. "So what did he tell you?"

"He wanted to show us his secret library. It's here in this house."

Bea's eyes brightened. "I should have guessed it. Houses like this always have secret rooms. Where is it?"

"I was hoping you already knew. He tried to show me last night but ran out of time before he could finish. But I did find out that the entrance to it is in the dining room."

"You ran out of time?" said Bea, who was out of bed and already pulling on her jeans.

"Well, he talked a lot," Nisha added, starting to feel a bit guilty that she hadn't gotten the whole story.

Bea nodded thoughtfully as she rifled through her drawer for a shirt. "You're going to have to concentrate. Try to remember everything, exactly what he said and how he said it. Walk me through it step by step." She pulled a sweatshirt over her head and when her face reappeared through the neck hole she said, "What are you waiting for? Get up!"

Over breakfast, Bea wrote down everything Nisha could remember. When they finished eating, they positioned themselves in front of the fireplace where Nisha had stood the night before.

"We're supposed to say something?" said Bea.

"Yes, I think so. He said 'just think of something'…"

"Like what?"

"I don't know."

"Well, he must have said something that might be a clue. Think!"

Nisha sighed. "He talked a lot but didn't say very much. He wasted a lot of time laughing."

"A very excellent way to waste time, I'd say," said Indy, who walked in from the front hall, startling both girls.

"Sorry, I didn't mean to scare you," he said flashing his but-I-know-you-love-me-anyway smile. "Nana Anna let me in. Said you were in here having breakfast and, yes, I'd love some, thanks."

Indy sat down at the table, and pulled the platter of pancakes towards him. "Who are we talking about, anyway?" he asked, reaching for the butter.

"My grandfather," said Bea, who proceeded to fill him in while he ate.

Indy eyed the fireplace carefully. "Well there's definitely something unusual about that fireplace. I've been in dozens of these old places and none of the fireplaces look like this one. Your grandfather must have had it put in." Indy doused a second stack of pancakes with syrup. "Who knows, maybe it does open up somehow? Do you think it's like a magic word?"

"Unfortunately," Bea said with a huff, "Nisha didn't get the details. All she got was that we're supposed to stand in front of the mirror and think of something… It could be a word, but for all we know it could be a phrase or even an incantation of some kind." Bea turned to Nisha. "Do you know any magic that opens doors?"

Nisha glared at Bea. *It wasn't her fault that Bea's grandfather didn't get to the point faster. And why did Bea always insist on pointing out her magic-ness in front of Indy? It was almost as though Bea wanted him to think she was a freak.*

"Uh, no I don't," Nisha answered curtly, "but let me give Harry Potter a call and see if he can figure it out for us."

"Actually, that would be great," Bea snapped back, "certainly more useful than us just sitting here guessing."

"I swear you two fight like sisters," said Indy pushing back his empty plate. Bea looked over at Nisha, and Nisha knew they were both thinking about the conversation they had the night before.

"Arguing isn't helping," Indy continued, "and I don't think I can handle another fight between the two of you. We need to work together here. We've got a secret room to find."

Indy got up and began to arrange three of the giant dining room chairs in front of the fireplace.

"Ladies…" he said, gesturing for the girls to sit down.

The three Finders sat in silence for several minutes, all wracking their brains trying to figure out what Bea's grandfather wanted them to do.

"Tell us again exactly what he said," said Indy.

"He said to do what he does; stand in front of the mirror and think of something, but he didn't finish."

"Do what he does," Indy repeated. "Okay, well, what did he do?"

"He imported antiques from around the world," said Bea.

"Mmm," said Indy, smirking. "So, you're saying that every time he wanted to get into his secret library, he imported something?"

Bea laughed. "I thought you meant-" Bea began, but her sentence was interrupted by a soft rumbling noise.

"Did you hear that?" she whispered.

Indy and Nisha nodded.

"What was it?" Nisha asked.

"I think it might have been the fireplace trying to open," said Indy.

"But why?" Bea asked. Then she turned to Nisha and said, "Did you do something?"

"No" said Nisha, glaring at Bea. "Don't you think if I knew what to do I would do it?"

"I'm not sure. Sometimes you get...well..." Bea shrugged.

If Nisha was irritated before, now she was fuming mad. *How could Bea think she wouldn't help if she could?* It was true she didn't like to do magic in front of Indy, but Bea should know that it would never stop her from trying to find The Coin.

The three of them went back to staring at the fireplace as the minutes ticked slowly by. The tension between Nisha and Bea made it impossible for Nisha to concentrate. Then, all of a sudden, Indy jumped to his feet raised his arms over his head and said in a booming voice, "Abracadabra."

It was so silly and such a relief to the uncomfortable silence that, despite their spat, both Nisha and Bea burst into laughter.

A moment later, Bea leapt forward, waving her hands in front of her. "Alakazam," she shouted. They laughed even harder.

"Open sesame?" Nisha whispered when they'd finally caught

their breaths, and that cracked them up all over again.

Then they heard it. The rumbling had started again from somewhere behind the wall.

"It's the fireplace," said Indy, pointing to the blackened brick wall behind the andirons. "It's moving."

And it was. The back wall of the fireplace was shifting. There was a groaning, crumbling sound, and then slowly the black bricks began sliding upward to reveal a dark, dank passageway.

For several seconds, no one said anything. Then Bea giggled. "Indy, you're a genius!"

"I am?" said Indy, raising a quizzical eyebrow.

"You figured it out!" said Bea, giving him a celebratory punch in the shoulder.

"I did?" said Indy.

"Okay, well maybe it was just luck, but it doesn't matter. I figured it out because of you and now we know how to get in."

"We do?" said Indy.

Bea laughed again. "Yes, we do. We laugh."

"We laugh?" said Nisha

"That's what I'm trying to tell you," said Bea. "My grandfather said, 'Do what I do, just think of something...' Well the missing word is *funny*. Just think of something funny. Laughing makes the door open."

Indy nodded in understanding. "Well then, it's lucky I'm hilarious," he said with a grin.

CHAPTER 37

THE LIBRARY

Bea went first, and then Indy. Nisha followed, stepping carefully over the brass andirons and through the marble arch of the mantle. After the first few steps, the floor angled upward and Nisha found herself at eye level with Indy's jean-clad backside. The path turned sharply left then right again. The light from the opening in the fireplace below them cast tall moving shadows against the curving walls. Nisha could see sticky gray spider webs clinging limply to the cracked plaster and caught a whiff of something like old dry leaves. There were several more turns, but always they moved steadily upwards. With each twist in the path, it grew harder and harder to see.

"This is really weird," said Indy, when the light had disappeared completely. "It seems like we've climbed enough to have passed the second or even the third floor. But that isn't really possible. This house isn't that tall."

"It does seem odd," Bea agreed. "But we might as well keep going. It's dark but there is only one way to go. I don't think we'll get lost."

Nisha was far less enthusiastic, and as the stale air closed in around them, she felt a wave a panic crash over her.

As if reading her mind, Indy turned and whispered, "Grab

my hand."

Nisha reached out in front of her and her fingers found his in the blackness. She felt herself blush when they touched and was suddenly grateful for the dark.

"There doesn't seem to be any end" said Bea but her comment was followed a second later by a loud bump.

"Ouch!" she said with a giggle. "Scratch that, I've found a door."

There was a creak of hinges, and suddenly the narrow passageway filled with a strange bluish light. Nisha followed Indy through another fireplace and into the most amazing room she had ever seen.

It was so large that at first, Nisha thought it might be a church of some kind. But then, as her eyes grew accustomed to the light, she saw the books. Every inch of every wall was packed from floor to ceiling. Piles seemed to grow up out of the floor, twisting like helixes, some as tall as a grown man.

Everything was bathed in dim, dream-like light that filtered in through five round stained-glass windows that ran the length of the far wall. Again, Nisha was reminded of a church, but unlike a cathedral, the windows depicted battle scenes, men with shields and swords and blood-stained armor.

Two enormous circles of iron hung from the ceiling; medieval chandeliers. Stubs of thick, old candles were still there, burned down to the metal.

There was very little furniture in the room. A large wingback chair was turned to face the fireplace with an old, stuffed ottoman in front of it, its needlepoint cover faded with time. Next to the chair was a small table with an oil lamp on it; and there were several trunks randomly scattered among the piles of books.

At the far end of the room was the only other real piece of furniture. A huge desk, buried in a mountain of books and papers. It was placed under the windows, and a shaft of dusty, multi-colored sunlight played across the yellowing pages.

The room smelled as it should, of old paper and tobacco, much like a grandfather might smell, a bit musty but pleasant and comfortable. It was apparent the room had not been used in a long time. Nisha slid her finger over a nearby book, carving a clean arc in the thick dust that covered it.

"No way," said Indy, turning around in a circle and shaking his head. "There is no way that *this* room is in *this* house."

"What do you mean?" asked Bea, sounding delighted, as she too turned to take in the whole environment. "This is exactly the kind of house that would have a room like this."

"But it doesn't make sense," said Indy emphatically. "It's structurally impossible. First of all, you would be able to see it from the outside. The house would be taller. And where are those windows? They're facing north. You should be able to see them from...well from somewhere. It's just not possible."

"We're standing in it, so it must be possible," said Bea. "Isn't funny how we can accept some things but not others," she added, with a wink at Nisha. Then she turned to Indy and said, "You had no problem believing that a mirror image of my grandfather's painting told Nisha how to find this room, yet now that you're in it you don't believe it's real. I think in order to get this Quest accomplished we're going to have to agree to expand our definition of what is and isn't possible."

"I suppose..." agreed Indy, his eyes still running over the walls and windows, "but I just can't figure it out."

"Well let's not waste time trying. It stands to reason that my grandfather wouldn't have gone to all the trouble of coming back to life if there wasn't something here worth finding. I'm guessing it's The Book of Charms."

The Finders set to work immediately, each in a different spot, and spent the next hour and then another digging through the volumes looking for some kind of clue. Nisha had just finished looking through a large shelf of books about the bubonic plague when she got a prickly sensation that they were being watched. She closed the book she was flipping through, and tried to focus on the source but the feeling vanished almost instantly.

"Over here," Bea called out, shaking Nisha out of her trance. Bea's voice wavered with excitement. "There's a whole section of books about Avalon." She began to read some of the titles out loud. "A Pathway Through The Mists, Druids from the Beginning, Medieval Symbols and Signs, The Lady of the Lake. Oh, and here's one for mean Mr. Morton, King Arthur: Legend or Truth."

Bea sat back on her heels, looking pleased. "I'll start with the one about symbols and signs. Maybe it will have something about Vesica's Key."

"Look at this one," said Indy, holding up a small, ancient-looking book. "Coins Through the Ages, now that sounds promising."

Nisha selected an enormous volume called 'Finding Avalon'. Inside were beautiful paintings by different artists all depicting Avalon. One showed a women's arm protruding from a glimmering blue lake; in her hand, a silver sword. Another showed three beautiful women surrounding a sleeping knight. Nisha stared at it for several minutes, wondering if the women might be Daughters of the Lake like Aunt Faye.

She was so engrossed in the book that without thinking, she sat down on a small wooden chest nearby. It creaked so loudly when she put her weight on it that she jumped back up, fearing she'd broken it.

The chest was very old. The black leather straps that bound it on either side were worn and crumbly. On the top was a large leaf-shaped symbol with the rose in the center. 'Brightman Import Company' was written in gold script below it. Nisha ran her fingers over the words and as she did, she suddenly smelled the bright sweetness of apples.

"I think there's something in this trunk," she said.

"Probably more books," said Indy, who had put down 'Coins Through the Ages' and was now reading 'Weapons of Camelot'.

"No," said Nisha, shaking her head, "something else; something I think we want to see."

Bea walked over to the trunk and tried to open it. "It's locked," she said, after several tugs. She reached into her front pocket and produced a hairpin. "I've been practicing," she said, smiling.

For several minutes she worked on the lock, but couldn't get it open. Finally, she sat back with a frown.

"Let me try," said Indy, who entwined his fingers and stretched his arms as if warming up for an athletic event. "It looks pretty old. I'm thinking if I give it a good yank the leather hinge will give out." He squatted down in front of the chest, grasped the lid and pulled.

"There must be something of worth in it if it's locked up so tightly," he said, his face red from the effort, "but it doesn't look like we're going to find out today; it won't budge."

"Or…maybe Nisha could try," Bea said with an encouraging tone in her voice.

"If Indy can't do it, how will I be able to?" Nisha said, knowing fully what Bea was implying. She could not believe Bea was once again pointing out her magic abilities in front of Indy, trying to make her look like a freak. However, when she glared into Bea's face, she didn't see cruelty or malice. The only emotion in Bea's pale blue eyes was hope.

"You could try to wish it open," Indy suggested earnestly. The smell of sincerity coming off him mixed pleasantly with the apple scent in the air.

At that moment, Nisha understood how foolishly she'd been behaving. Both Bea and Indy had seen the freakiest things about her and had accepted them already. She was the one holding onto the idea that she was strange, not them.

Nisha turned her attention back to the chest. "Maybe I could," she said hesitantly.

"You don't have to, you know," Bea said, with a sideways glance at Indy.

Nisha nodded back at Bea attempting to look confident, though her stomach was in a knot. She took a deep breath and tried to concentrate. As usual, she felt the grip of doubt squeezing at her lungs. She couldn't do it. It was impossible. But when she looked up to tell them it wasn't going to work, her eyes met Bea's and she felt a strange swell of energy within her. She swallowed her words and took another breath. *Just focus on the feelings. Don't try to control them.*

She turned her thoughts inward, seeking out her emotions;

her desire to solve The Quest and to prove to Bea, and to herself, that she could master this Wishmaking stuff. Slowly, she lifted her hand towards the lock, fingers outstretched. "Open," she said quietly. A surge of energy, like the rushing of a river, ran through her arm and down through her fingers just as it had the day of the cupcakes, and just as it did on the day little Charlie Campbell flew from the jungle gym. For a moment, everything was silent and then she heard a small click like the sound of a lock opening.

When she opened her eyes, Bea was beaming at her. "That was brilliant!" she said, clapping her hands together.

Though Nisha was pleased with herself, her cheeks burned with self-consciousness. Indy must have noticed, because he quickly said, "Does anybody want to look inside, or is it just me?"

"I do," said Nisha, grateful to shift the attention to something other than herself.

"Here goes," he said as he pulled the lid open. They all leaned forward, and collectively they gasped. Piled inside the chest were hundreds of coins, gleaming softly in the dim light.

Indy let out a low whistle. "Now this is getting interesting."

"Seriously," agreed Bea.

Indy picked up a few coins and let them fall back through his fingers into the chest. "Do you think…?" he began, but Bea cut him off.

"I doubt it," Bea replied, picking up a small handful of coins from the trunk and examining them one at a time. "I mean, it certainly looks like my grandfather was involved in this thing somehow; maybe looking for The Coin himself. And I'm sure these are worth a fortune but I'm also sure that our Coin is in Charlotte Wang's living room," she said.

"How do you know?" Indy asked rubbing one of the coins between his fingers.

"I just do," said Bea. "The Coin in Charlotte's apartment; well it makes me feel…"

"Something," Nisha finished.

"Yes." Bea nodded. "Something like…"

"Electricity," Nisha said, finishing Bea's thought again.

"Exactly," said Bea.

"They all sort of look the same to me," said Indy, with a shrug.

For a few moments, they sat without speaking. Bea picked up another coin and let it drop into the pile with a metallic thud. Then she stopped and picked it up again. She held the coin up to the sunlight. It was a pale gold and almost the exact size of the coin that Nisha and Bea had seen at the flea market. It even had similar geometric engravings on one side.

"You're right," she said finally. "They do all sort of look alike. In fact," she added with a mischievous smile, "I think it would be almost impossible for ordinary people to tell the difference."

CHAPTER 38

THE BIRTHDAY PARTY

Nisha was nervous. Bea could tell by the way she kept adjusting and smoothing her long, colorful skirt and fussing with her braids. If only Nisha knew how pretty she was. So what if her clothes weren't like everyone else's? They suited Nisha perfectly, the way the bright colors stood out against her dark skin. Her petite size made her movements small and graceful, not loping and gawky like Bea sometimes felt. The soft blue ribbons in her hair added to her mysterious beauty, and Bea was reminded of the first time she saw Nisha when she mistook her for a gypsy princess.

"You look really pretty," Bea told her sincerely. "There's no need to be nervous," she added, though she knew her words were not enough to ease Nisha's tension. Bea doubted that Nisha had ever been to a party before, let alone one full of Huntington Horribles. Bea felt for her, but there was no way around it. They had to get The Coin and they had only one chance to do it.

"Let's go over the plan again," Bea said, changing the subject.

They walked slowly so Bea could talk Nisha through it again step by step, carefully reviewing the critical points. When the time was right, Nisha would work her icing trick on the cake to create a distraction. In the confusion, Bea would sneak into the second living room and open the cabinet using a hairpin she had stashed in her small handbag. Then she'd switch the Third Coin for the one from Old Bill's library. It all sounded simple enough, though in the back of her mind, Bea knew any number of things could go wrong. Just the idea of stealing something made her stomach sour. It was against everything her father had taught her. *What if the Wangs had some sort of high security system? What if she and Nisha got caught?* Bea took a sharp breath and forced herself to keep talking, although she sensed Nisha was no longer listening.

"So, are you ready?"

"No," said Nisha, her voice raspier than usual.

"Well, ready or not, we're here." Bea hoped she sounded confident, but as her eyes followed Nisha's gaze up at Charlotte's building, her stomach clenched with apprehension. She swallowed hard and flipped her hair back behind her shoulders. If this thing was going to work, she couldn't let fear or guilt get in the way.

"Now remember, just ignore the other girls and stay focused," Bea said, hoping she sounded calmer than she felt. "We'll get our chance when Charlotte's mother turns out the lights to sing Happy Birthday."

Nisha nodded, but she looked terrified.

"What if I can't?" she stammered, as they crossed the lobby to the elevator. "I mean, it doesn't work if I'm nervous."

"Just stay focused. There's nothing to be nervous about. Remember, Indy will be waiting for us when we come out. Just imagine us coming out of the elevator with The Coin in your pocket, and nodding to Indy just like we planned it. He'll smile that big, dumb smile of his and then he'll walk us home safely, right?"

"Right," Nisha whispered, more to herself than to Bea.

When the elevator arrived, the same elevator man Bea had met at her last visit opened the door.

"Hello there, ladies, I'm Earl, and I'm guessing you are going to the 16th floor to Miss Charlotte's birthday tea?"

"Yes, thank you," Bea replied, feeling as though the guilt of what they were about to do was somehow apparent on her face.

As the elevator doors slid closed, they heard a man call out in a loud, overly cheerful voice. "Hold that!" Then a hand appeared in the small space left between the closing doors.

Strangely, the hand didn't fit with the voice at all. It was yellow and bony and on every finger, even the thumb, was a ring; some with deep red rubies and others pale pastel-colored opals. As the elevator doors reopened, Bea was shocked to see a man she knew. *But how was it possible that he was the owner of such a hand?*

Standing there, in the lobby, was their English Literature teacher, Mr. Morton. As always, he was wearing a light-colored suit jacket and a white shirt. His sandy hair was slightly disheveled, his lips stretched tightly in a wide, forced grin.

As he entered the elevator, he looked curiously from one girl to the other. Then he shook his head slightly as if shaking out a thought.

"Miss Lakewood, Miss Brightman," he said with false enthusiasm, "what a nice surprise." Then he turned to the elevator man and said, "Sixteen please."

Bea felt an odd tingling up the back of her neck. Something wasn't right. *What was he doing here?* She backed up slightly and bumped shoulders with Nisha.

Did you see that? Nisha thought to her.

Bea nodded slightly. Then she thought to Nisha, *Do you think... could it be possible that Morton might be ...*

Sahwin? Nisha responded, finishing Bea's thought.

At the same moment, Mr. Morton's head twitched slightly. *Had he somehow heard them? Was it possible he knew they were talking to each other?* Bea had suspected that Faye could hear them when they read each other's minds. Perhaps people from Avalon could perceive this kind of communication.

Mr. Morton's head twitched again and Bea sensed he was trying very hard to keep himself from looking at them.

That's crazy, right? she thought to Nisha.

Maybe, thought Nisha, *but his hand...*

Again, Mr. Morton twitched. This time his brows knitted as

if confused. Then he slowly looked down at his hand and flexed his fingers self-consciously. Bea glanced at Nisha to be certain that she'd noticed.

Bea swallowed hard. He had definitely sensed something, but it appeared he didn't know what it was. Deciding it was too dangerous to answer Nisha, Bea stepped forward again. Perhaps she could make him think he'd only imagined it.

"Mr. Morton," she said, forcing herself to sound cheerful, "are you here for Charlotte's birthday party?" She pasted a smile on her face and looked up at him, blinking with innocence.

"Charlotte?" asked Mr. Morton, again looking confused. Then his expression cleared. "Is that why you're here? I didn't realize…No, no, I'm here to see her father on business."

Just then, the elevator stopped at the sixteenth floor.

"After you, girls," said Mr. Morton, politely gesturing with his hand, which now looked perfectly in keeping with the rest of him. Nisha and Bea exited the elevator and headed down the hallway towards the Wang's apartment. Bea had to make a conscious effort not to stare at Mr. Morton's perfectly normal hand as he reached over her shoulder to ring the bell. Then, as she listened to the chiming echo into the Wang's front hall, something awful occurred to her. *Was Mr. Morton here for The Coin too?*

A woman, who could only be Charlotte's mother, opened the door. She was an older yet equally perfect version of Charlotte, with smooth black hair and crisp, rich clothes. Her dazzling smile was just as bright and just as fake as her daughter's. When she saw Mr. Morton, she pushed her smile even further out toward her ears and said through clenched teeth, "Ah, Mr. Morton, what a pleasure to see you again." It was obvious to Bea that Mrs. Wang wasn't pleased at all.

"Hello, my dear Mrs. Wang," said Mr. Morton, whose fake grin was equal to his hostess's. "I apologize for my timing. I didn't realize it was Charlotte's birthday."

"Nonsense!" said Mrs. Wang insincerely, the smile barely moving as she spoke. "Herb is expecting you."

Just then, Mr. Wang, who was much rounder and generally

less perfect than Mrs. Wang, came bustling out of the living room. "Morton!" he nearly shouted, "Wonderful to see you. I think you're going to be very pleased!" He grabbed Mr. Morton's hand and began pumping it up and down. "We'll just be a few minutes, darling," he said apologetically to his wife. Then, without even a breath in between, he turned back to Mr. Morton and said, "Pardon the ruckus, but my daughter's having a birthday soirée! Not every day your only daughter turns thirteen, you know. And she wanted to have a tea party. Isn't that a hoot? How could I say no?" As the two men moved off down the hall, Mr. Wang continued to talk, but Bea could no longer make out his words.

Mrs. Wang, who had watched her husband usher his guest away, sighed and shook her head. Then, realizing the girls were still standing there, she said, "Well, then." Her smile beamed as she met Bea's eyes. "You must be Bea Brightman. How nice of you to come! Why, I was just telling Mr. Wang about your father and his very interesting position at the museum. We're big contributors. You must mention it to him. Mr. Wang just loves antiques, as you can see." Mrs. Wang vaguely waved her graceful hand to indicate the many antiques displayed around the foyer. Then she turned her attention to Nisha. For a moment, the tiniest frown crossed her lips. She pasted her smile back in place but when she spoke, her words had lost their friendly tone, "You must be…?"

"Nisha," Nisha whispered, her cheeks blushing to the color of a ripe plum.

"Oh yes, Nisha Lakeworth. You're the one who didn't reply until the day before yesterday. Well, unfortunately you're late," she said speaking to Nisha directly as if their lateness could only be her fault.

"I hope we haven't missed the cake," said Bea with a nervous smile.

"Oh, we're not serving cake dear. You're having tea sandwiches and crumpets just like a grown-up tea party. And not to worry," Mrs. Wang continued, her voice recovering its sing-song quality, "you're just in time for the present opening…" And with that, she scooped the present out of Bea's hands and looked expectedly at Nisha. Bea noticed her glance disapprovingly at Nisha's clothes. *No wonder Nisha was paranoid*, Bea thought; *people could be just dreadful.*

"The gift is from both of us," Bea explained loudly, and Nisha's face turned a deeper shade of purple.

"Of course it is," said Mrs. Wang, once again appraising Nisha. Then she said, "I'll just add this to the pile," and pointed the girls towards a maid who had appeared in the hallway.

"Okay, okay, let's not lose focus," Bea whispered as they headed down the beige hallway behind the housekeeper. "The gift thing is no big deal. There are bigger issues to deal with, like the fact that there's no cake, for one. We'll just have to figure something else out. Let's just find a place to sit so I can think."

Charlotte was seated at the far end of the beige room in a throne-like beige chair. On both her left and right were presents piled up to her elbows. Around her feet, arranged like ladies-in-waiting, were her friends.

Bea spotted a small love seat a good distance away and pointed Nisha towards it. However, just as they were about to sit down, Charlotte caught sight of Bea.

"Bea, you're here!" Charlotte trilled; a perfect parrot of her mother. She jumped up from her chair and rushed over to Bea and Nisha, nearly stepping on several girls in front of her.

"I'm so glad you made it!" Without a glance at Nisha, she grabbed Bea by the hand and dragged her towards the circle of girls. "Come sit by me," she sang, "I'm the birthday girl and I insist!"

As Charlotte pulled Bea towards her throne, Bea caught Nisha by the skirt and tried to pull her along as well.

NO WAY. The thought hit Bea in the back of the head like rock and she felt Nisha yank the skirt out of her grip.

Charlotte, who still had Bea by the hand, was pushing presents and people aside to make a spot for Bea to sit down.

Alright, I get it. So I don't exactly know how to get out of this at the moment. Let me reformulate the plan and I'll make an excuse to come over to you. Bea sent the thought back to Nisha but she didn't feel it connect.

When she glanced backwards, she saw Nisha had moved to the back of the room and seated herself on a small sofa by the door. *Can you hear me?* She called, knowing that Nisha could not. *Why did it only work sometimes?* She thought with frustration.

Bea tried to get Nisha's attention, but Nisha refused to look at her.

Bea sighed and turned her attention back to the task. She knew they couldn't afford to let this opportunity go by, even if Nisha wasn't going to help. *But how?* It was all going wrong. *How was she going to create a distraction when she was practically sitting on Charlottes' lap?*

Once Charlotte had settled Bea next to her chair, she resumed opening presents. She picked up a tiny box from the top of the enormous pile. It was the gift that Bea and Nisha had brought. Charlotte tore the paper off and tossed it aside, where one of the maids quickly whisked it away. Inside was a tiny silver 'c' hanging on a thread-thin silver chain.

"Oh Bea! It's perfect," Charlotte squeaked. "I love it! Thank you!"

"It's from Nisha and me," Bea said pointedly.

"Oh," said Charlotte absently. Her focus had already shifted to a large rectangular box.

Bea didn't dare look at Nisha, whom she knew was probably fuming.

"Excuse me," Bea said getting to her feet. "I just need the loo, I'll be right back."

"Don't get lost," Charlotte called after her, giggling, then, turning to the other girls, she said, "Sorry; private joke between me and Bea."

"Bathroom now," said Bea as she walked by Nisha

Bea found her way to the guest bathroom and filled the sink with water. She waited for Nisha, who took several minutes before knocking softly on the door. Once the door was closed and locked, Bea plunged her hands in the basin and indicated that Nisha should do the same.

Alright, so Charlotte's an idiot. This isn't about her. It's about The

Coin, Bea thought.

You're right. It's not about her. It's about you. You said you wouldn't abandon me, Nisha thought back.

I know. I'm sorry, Bea responded, trying hard to communicate through the water how really sorry she felt. *I didn't know what to do. But, please, don't you realize this may be our only chance to get The Coin?*

Nisha sighed. *Are you even sure it's here? I thought you said it was in the living room. I didn't see it.*

I told you when we went over this. There are two living rooms. The Coin is in the other one. But we have to be very careful. I think Mr. Morton is here for The Coin too.

This seemed to snap Nisha back to the problem at hand. She looked down at the sink and nodded gravely. *You're right. I think he might actually be Sahwin. I think I've always suspected it but couldn't imagine it was possible. But that hand...* She took a deep breath and looked up at Bea. *Okay, where's the other living room?*

It's right next to the one the party is in. That large archway on the left leads to it. We're going to have to hurry. Follow me, I'll show you.

Bea pulled the stopper out of the sink and the girls quickly dried their hands. Then they headed quietly down the carpeted hallway, sneaking past the first living room and ducking into the second. Silently, they crossed the soft carpet until they were standing in front of the curio cabinet that held The Coin.

When Nisha spotted it on the lower shelf, she silently sank down to her knees.

"Oh Bea," she whispered. "It is The Coin!"

"I know," Bea said. "Now would you please get up! What if someone were to walk in here?"

Just then, the girls heard voices coming from another room. It was Mr. Wang and his guest.

"The Coin? Oh yes, I still have it," Mr. Wang said offhandedly. "It's just right in there."

The girls could not hear Mr. Morton's response.

Mr. Wang spoke again. "Certainly you can see it, of course, of course, but I doubt it's the one you've been after. Oh it shines and all, but it's really quite plain. But before we do that, let me show you something really impressive…"

The girls exchanged a look and quietly inched back towards the party. Charlotte was just opening a large box containing a white cashmere sweater.

"Oh Lauren, sweetie!" Charlotte squealed, "Is this the one we saw downtown? You're the absolute bestest!"

With all the attention on Lauren, Nisha and Bea took the opportunity to scoot back into the room without being noticed. They sat at the edge of the circle of girls so Bea could just see the cabinet through the doorway between the rooms.

"I'm pretty sure I can pick the lock but it's got to be now, before Mr. Wang brings Mr. Morton in there. I'm going to need a real distraction. It might take a few minutes," Bea whispered.

Nisha managed a small nod in response.

"Are you sure? It's got to be big."

"Just give me a second," Nisha replied, barely audible in the noisy room.

"Something that will give me some time," said Bea.

"Okay," Nisha said with an irritated glare.

"Sorry," Bea said, and watched as Charlotte picked up a pretty pink shopping bag with pink roses on it.

"Now what could this be?" Charlotte swung the pink gift bag gently from her finger. She reached in and pulled out a box wrapped in pink paper and tied with dozens of pink curly ribbons. "Pretty!" she exclaimed, tugging the ribbons from the box.

"Ready?" asked Nisha.

Bea nodded, and watched Nisha close her eyes. Then, all of a sudden, Charlotte started to scream.

CHAPTER 39

THE ROOF

At first, Bea couldn't tell what had happened, but then she saw them. They were squirming from either end of Charlotte's clenched fist. Instead of curly pink ribbons, Charlotte Wang was holding a large handful of long pink worms.

In horror, Charlotte screamed again, and tossed the worms into the air. They came down on the circle of girls, who shrieked in unison and began to scramble away in every direction.

"Motherrrrr!" "Daddyyyyyy!" Charlotte howled.

Mrs. Wang rushed into the room and looked around at the screaming girls. "What's happening?" she demanded. "What's going on?"

Before anyone answered, Bea ducked into the adjoining living room and made her way to the curio cabinet. With a short intake of breath, she blocked out the noise from the party and focused on her task. Using the hairpin she'd taken from Nana Anna's bathroom weeks before, she began to work the lock. Bea had practiced for this moment and had gotten good enough that she could pick any lock in her house. However, the curio cabinet's door wasn't connected to a sturdy door frame like the ones at home. It was part of a delicate antique. When Bea tried to jiggle the hairpin, the whole cabinet shook making the contents quiver dangerously on their shelves. She took a breath and tried again, but the cabinet wobbled so much that a fragile-looking statue on the top shelf fell over with a small thud. Her heart began to pound wildly. Had someone heard it? She stopped and held her breath.

"Everyone just calm down and tell me what happened," Mrs. Wang pleaded over the din. Bea was running out of time. She flipped her hair behind her shoulders with a flick of her head. Concentrate, she told herself. Using one hand to steady the cabinet, she tried the lock again. She gave the hairpin a tiny twist and to her surprise and relief the door swung open with a soft squeak.

As Bea reached in to pick up The Coin, she hesitated. Would it zap her as it had at the flea market? Mrs. Wang's voice rang out again above the commotion and Bea had no time to think twice. She reached in and grabbed The Coin from its perch. No zap. Quickly, she dropped it in her handbag, pulled out the replacement coin and set it carefully on the display stand. It was a tiny bit larger than The Third Coin but it was close enough to fool someone at least at a distance. Bea righted the tipped statue on the higher shelf, locked the cabinet and carefully wiped away her fingerprints. Then, taking a deep breath, she ran back into the chaos of the other room.

Most of the girls had pushed themselves back to the edges of the room, trying to get as far away from the worms as possible, but not Amanda Whitehead. She was standing in the middle of the room with her fists balled up at her sides in fury. Bright red blotches blazed on her pale puffy cheeks. "It wasn't me!" she shouted repeatedly, her small eyes darting around suspiciously. "One of you set me up and I'm gonna find out who it was!" Some of the girls were crying. Charlotte was sitting on the floor in front of her chair, looking confused and a good deal more rumpled than Bea had ever seen her before. Two maids scurried around the floor with ice tongs, picking up the worms, many of which had been pulled apart or smashed into the carpet during the mayhem.

Mrs. Wang, looking a bit crazed, was walking around from

girl to girl with the Gift bag the present had arrived in, asking, "Who did this? Who put worms in this bag?"

Bea pushed her way through the girls. She had to get to Nisha before Mrs. Wang did. "I think we should go now," she said in Nisha's ear as soon as she was close enough. At the same moment Mrs. Wang approached them.

"Yes," said Mrs. Wang. "Yes, I think that's a very good idea." Mrs. Wang turned towards the room and said loudly, "Attention please, if no one is going to own up to this then I think it's time you all went home. But I want you to know, I'll be speaking to all of your mothers."

"Just stay quiet and keep moving," Bea said in Nisha's ear as she pushed her along towards the front door. They almost made it, but stopped in their tracks when Mr. Wang and Mr. Morton came around the corner.

"What are all you girls fussing about in there?" asked Mr. Wang with a good-natured chuckle.

Before Bea could answer, several girls hurried by all talking at once. And when Becca Peters came around the corner, sobbing, Mr. Wang suddenly looked concerned.

"What the devil is going on?" he asked to no one in particular. "Excuse me, Morton, but I think I may be needed in the living room."

Mr. Morton did not move. Instead he stared down at Nisha and then at Bea and stroked at a non-existent beard on his chin.

"Yes indeed, there seems to be a problem," he said, slowly eyeing Bea's purse, "Tell me girls, what's the hurry?"

Bea shrugged as several girls came out of the living room and pushed by them in the hall. As if sharing the same thought, both Bea and Nisha let themselves be pushed along with the crowd. Bea sensed Mr. Morton was still watching them, but she didn't dare turn around.

After much shoving to get on the elevator, they finally got downstairs and outside. Indy was standing on the corner as planned.

"Is everything okay? What went on in there? Girls have been running out like rats fleeing a fire."

Bea grabbed Indy's arm and pulled him along down the street.

"Could you please tell me what's going on?" he asked. "Did you get The Coin?"

"Yes," she said, out of breath, "but we've got a problem."

"Obviously, where's Nisha?"

"What?" Bea spun around, expecting Nisha to be standing behind her, but she wasn't there. Without thinking, she turned and ran back toward the building.

"Come on," she shouted over her shoulder to Indy, but he was already right at her heels.

"I think Mr. Morton's got Nisha."

Indy and Bea entered the lobby just as the elevator was arriving with a second delivery of girls, none of them Nisha. Bea stepped in and said to the elevator man, "I've forgotten something. Would you bring me back up to sixteen, please?"

"Certainly, Miss, I'm headed that way now," answered the elevator man politely. He nodded to Indy, and Indy nodded back. For a second, it looked to Bea as if Indy knew the man.

The elevator was maddeningly slow, and when it finally arrived at sixteen Bea was panicked that something terrible had happened to Nisha. However, when the elevator doors opened, Nisha was standing in front of them. Bea was flooded with relief until she noticed a large hand on Nisha's shoulder.

"Ah," said Mr. Morton, "we were just coming to find you. He smiled jovially. "It seems you two lost each other." His hand remained clamped around Nisha's collar bone.

"Oh yes, thanks," Bea answered, as though nothing was wrong. "Well, it looks like we've found each other now. Come on, Nisha."

Nisha stepped forward but Mr. Morton came with her.

"Everybody in," sang the elevator man cheerfully.

Bea felt Indy slide his hand into hers. Then he whispered almost inaudibly in her ear, "I'll grab Nisha. Stay close."

As the elevator door started to close, Indy said loudly, "Hey, I didn't get a chance to say Happy Birthday to the birthday girl." He quickly stuck his hand between the closing doors and shoved them open. "C'mon you guys," he said, and with a yank, he pulled both girls out with him.

The doors closed abruptly behind them and as soon as they did, Indy said, "Okay, who the heck was that guy?"

"It was Mr. Morton," said Bea.

"Mr. Morton?" Indy said, squinting at her in disbelief, "You mean your creepy English teacher?"

Nisha nodded. "He's Sahwin," she whispered.

Indy looked shocked, but once he registered the idea, his expression changed quickly to one of concentration. He was formulating their next move.

"We'll take the fire escape out of the Wang's apartment," he said.

"Good idea," Bea said, "but what do we say to them?"

"Maybe Nisha could create another distraction," Indy suggested.

"It won't work," said Nisha. "Mrs. Wang already suspects me of something. I don't think she'd let me back in."

"Well perhaps if you'd screamed when you saw the worms like the other girls, maybe she wouldn't be so suspicious," said Bea.

"Why would I scream? They were just little worms."

"Worms?" said Indy.

"Brilliant, right?" said Bea. "You should have seen it. Nisha was amazing, she…" But Bea's story was interrupted by the ding of the elevator bell. All three of them froze. As the elevator door opened, Nisha gasped. Mr. Morton was there - but it wasn't him; at least not completely. Parts of him had changed. His clothes seemed too large and hung loosely from his shoulders. His normally light-brown hair was darker and fell limply down either side of his face, the beginnings of a scruffy goatee visible on his chin. His skin had sickly yellow cast to it and his hands were gruesomely long and bony. When he saw their startled expressions, he grinned, exposing a mouth full of hideous gray teeth. Behind him on the floor, was Earl, the elevator man.

"Earl!" said Indy stepping forward.

But Mr. Morton, or Sahwin blocked Indy's way. "Earl's off duty," he hissed through his smile. Then he stretched out his hideous hand and said, "You must be The Protector. I don't think we've met."

Indy quickly jumped out of reach. "Run," he commanded. "Move. Now."

The three of them raced down the hall and around two bends. At the end were fire doors. Indy punched them open and pulled the girls into the stairwell.

"Up," he ordered.

"He's not following us," Nisha said breathlessly as she scrambled up the stairs.

"Because he went down," Bea said, "he thinks he can beat us to the ground in the elevator."

Indy got to the top of the stairs first and shoved open the heavy door to the roof. The thick scent of warm tar hit them in the face.

Bea followed him out, and then Nisha, who closed the door firmly behind her.

When Indy heard the door shut, he turned and slapped his hand against his forehead. "Oh no, that door locks from the inside."

"How do you know that? And how do you know Earl?" said Bea.

"Because I… live here," said Indy.

"What?" both girls said at the same time.

"Okay, now don't get excited. I'm not rich if that's what you're thinking. My dad's the superintendent of the building."

"So that's how Charlotte recognized you that first day you picked me up from school," said Nisha.

"Maybe." Indy shrugged.

Bea looked at Indy for a moment and shook her head. It was strange how close she felt to him and yet she never even thought to ask where he lived. "Okay," she said, trying to focus. "How do we get down from here if we can't use the stairs?"

"I don't know… but now that I have this extra strength or whatever it is, I think maybe I could somehow slide over the edge and grab the fire escape. Then I could probably reach you two if you hung over the side."

"Extra strength?" said Bea.

"Yeah, it seems this magic stuff actually works on me too. I'm really strong and fast too."

"That should come in handy," said Bea as she peered over the ledge, "but it's not going to help here. From what I can see, you're just not tall enough. See there, the distance between the top of the wall and the fire escape railing is at least half a meter longer than you are."

"Are you sure?" Indy said, leaning further over the side. "If I reach I think I can …whoa!" Indy jumped back. "He's down there. Mr. Morton or Sahwin or whatever his name is. He's down there and I think he saw me."

For a moment they looked at each other. Then Indy said, "He's going to come up here. We need to hide." Indy pulled the girls from the door and towards the far side of the roof.

"Wait," said Bea, "maybe Nisha can open the door."

She turned to Nisha but there was panic written in her eyes and Bea could see it was no use. Nisha was far too scared to concentrate.

"Okay, forget that," Bea said. "But hiding's not going to work for long. Maybe we can use a Finder's Gift."

"I have Drae Mord," said Indy.

Bea shook her head. "We can't go killing people on the roof of your building. It's bad enough we stole The Coin."

"What do you suggest then?"

"I don't know. Let's see, we have the minute. That could buy us some time…"

"No," said Nisha firmly, "not the minute. There must be something else."

Bea started to argue but Nisha shook her head. "Not the minute," she said again.

"Okay," said Bea, "What about the seeds?" she suggested.

"What are we gonna grow, a beanstalk?" Indy asked sarcastically.

"Something like that could work," said Bea. "We'll grow

some kind of vine and climb down." She headed across the black top to the back of the building. "There," she said, pointing to a tiny patch of earth no larger than a shoebox by some trashcans below.

"He's coming," Nisha interrupted. "I can feel him."

Bea quickly dug into her handbag and pulled out the small pouch. She yanked it open and dumped the three seeds, along with the rolled up piece of parchment, into her open palm.

"The trick will be getting the seeds to land in that spot," she said, hoping she sounded more optimistic than she felt.

"Indy can do it," said Nisha confidently.

"Uh, I don't know. It's not much of a target," Indy said, looking crestfallen at the idea of disappointing her. "Besides, we don't have a lot of time. Even if I do get them in the right place, how is something going to grow …?" The sound of footsteps interrupted him.

"What choice do we have? You have to try," Bea said.

Indy nodded and held out his hand for the seeds. Then he moved to the edge of the roof to throw them.

"Wait!" Bea said. Her hands trembled slightly as she rushed to unroll the small scroll. "It says 'Say what you need. Mix earth and seeds'."

"Uh, okay, what do I need?"

"A way down," she said.

Indy looked doubtful but he lifted the seeds to his mouth and said, "Uh, we'd like a way to get the three of us down from here."

"Safely," added Nisha.

"Yeah, roger that. Safely," said Indy to the seeds.

"Better use just one at a time," said Bea. "I mean, just in case you have to take a practice shot or two."

Just then, they heard the door to the roof crash open, and Indy didn't stop to think. He spun around and with one motion threw all three seeds in the direction of the small patch of ground. Bea gasped. There was no way he could have hit anything.

They could hear Sahwin across the roof, looking for them.

Bea's heart was pounding so hard she couldn't think.

Thankfully, Indy was thinking again, and he pulled them behind a large air conditioning unit close to the wall.

"I can't see if I hit the earth or not," he breathed, trying to peer over the side of the wall without being seen.

"No offense, but I doubt it," Bea said glumly.

"Enough of this," Sahwin hollered from across the roof. "I know you're here. I can smell you."

"Now what?" Bea whispered.

"We'll fight. I'll have to use Drae Mord."

"Too dangerous," said Bea. "Maybe he left the door open. If we use the minute we can sneak past him and down the stairs."

"But what if the door is locked?" said Indy.

"Fine, but if you get killed…"

"I think we should climb down the vine," said Nisha, interrupting them both. She shifted slightly to her left to reveal the tip of a large pale stem curving gracefully over the wall behind her.

"It worked?" Indy said sounding surprised, "I mean, great," he added with more confidence, "let's move then. Quietly now." They inched towards the wall and looked over. The plant was still growing; tendrils slipped and slithered their way up the side of the building like giant snakes. They weaved back and forth; bending themselves around windows and sills, creating a ladder of stems and leafs.

"There you are!" cried Sahwin. Bea spun around but she was not prepared for what she saw. No trace of Mr. Morton remained, and Sahwin was far more horrifying than she'd expected. His face was not much more than a skull, peeling yellow skin stretched tightly across the bone. His eyes, which were somehow too large for the sockets, looked as though they might fall out at any moment. As much as she wanted to, Bea couldn't look away.

"Bea," shouted Indy, as he yanked her from her stunned stance. "Go!" He pushed her towards the vine behind him.

"Nisha should go first."

"Don't argue, just move," said Indy, shoving her again. Bea

nodded, but pushed Nisha ahead of her. As soon as Nisha was over the edge, Bea followed, wrapping her hands tightly around the vine as she swung her leg over the side. Blood was beating loudly in her ears and her breath was coming in short gasps. The height made her dizzy.

She wanted to move, but couldn't leave Indy. As soon as she was sure Sahwin could not see her, she stopped and waited for him to appear over the rim.

"You can't protect them from me," Bea heard Sahwin say. "You can't even protect yourself."

"Maybe," Indy replied, "but I'm going to try." At that moment, Indy must have shoved Sahwin because Bea heard Sahwin swear and stumble back a few steps.

Indy jumped up onto the wall and turned to grab hold of the vine, but Sahwin was there again. He seized Indy by the leg.

"Indy!" Bea shouted.

"Keep going!" Indy shouted back.

Bea didn't know what to do. She looked down and saw that Nisha was nearly to the ground. Bea knew she should be there too. Yet somehow she couldn't. Fear had taken over her body and she was paralyzed.

Bea watched as Indy struggled to break Sahwin's hold, but there was little he could do standing on the narrow wall. If he pulled his leg away hard enough to break Sahwin's grip, he would fall.

Indy took a brave swing at Sahwin, but lost his balance. Suddenly he was dangling over the side and Sahwin's bony grip was the only thing keeping him from falling.

Nisha, who was now on the ground, shrieked with horror.

"Oops," said Sahwin, letting his hand slip further towards Indy's ankle. "I don't know how much longer I can hold on. But not to worry, I'm sure brainy Miss Brightman will figure out a way to save you?" And with a vicious smile he released his grip on Indy's leg.

"No!" Bea shouted. Without thinking, she lunged for Indy. She missed. Her bag tumbled from under her arm and she watched it fall - before realizing that she too was falling. Her hair blew up around her face and she squeezed her eyes shut in terror. She thought she might be screaming, but she couldn't tell. Instead, she heard the hiss of Sahwin's laughter. And then, suddenly, she stopped. Someone or something had grabbed her by the waist and was holding her tightly. Afraid to move, she caught her breath and carefully opened one eye. For a second, she didn't know what she was looking at; a black and white blur against a sea of green. Then her brain oriented itself and she recognized what it was. Just inches from her face was Indy's checked sneaker. Confused, she turned her head slightly to see if the shoe was still attached to the boy. It was. She breathed a sigh of relief. The vines had somehow taken a hold of them, catching them in mid-fall.

A moment later, the shoe was gone. An arm went by and then a knee and Bea realized that the vines were moving, passing Indy slowly from one tendril to another, slipping around his waist and arms so he appeared to be turning cartwheels down the side of the building. Then it was Bea's turn. It was a bizarre sensation and under different circumstances, it might have even been fun. She turned and tumbled and in less than a minute, she was placed gently on the ground, a small tendril-like stem neatly slipping her purse over her arm.

It took a second for her to steady herself, then she looked up. Sahwin was gone from view. The three Finders watched the vine retract from the building and sink back into the earth.

Indy tugged at her arm. "Let's go," he said, "before he gets down here."

CHAPTER 40

THE BIRDS

The sky was darkening as they arrived at the stoop. "We can't stay out here long," Bea observed.

Indy looked up and down the street warily. He nodded. "You're right. We should split up and go home."

"I'll tell Faye and the rest of The Council what has happened," said Nisha "Then we can meet up again in the morning."

Indy nodded his agreement and said, "Okay, but before we do anything, we have to figure out what to do with The Coin." He looked back and forth between the girls. "We need to decide which one of us is going to keep it for the night."

No one said anything for a several seconds, and then they all spoke at the same time.

"It should be me," said Indy.

"It should be me," said Nisha.

"We should do Rock, Paper, Scissors," said Bea.

Both Indy and Nisha looked at Bea in surprise.

"That way there'll be no way for Sahwin to predict who has The Coin," Bea explained calmly. "It's the safest approach."

"The safest approach is that I hold The Coin," Indy replied forcefully. "We were all there today. We all saw how far he'll go to get The Coin. I'm The Protector and I've got Drae Mord. I'm the one who's the most equipped to deal with him."

"Sahwin saw how you tried to protect us today," said Nisha. "He might assume you have The Coin for the same reason. I agree with Bea. Let's not let logic rule us, it's too risky. The best approach is no approach."

Indy looked at Bea imploringly but she balled up her fist, turned to Nisha and said, "One, two, three, shoot." Nisha won both rounds, first with Bea and then with Indy. Nisha didn't tell them, but with her Spirit Gifts, she really couldn't lose.

"That settles it," she said solemnly, "I keep The Coin."

"Yes but only for tonight," said Bea. "Tomorrow, we do it again. That way we'll keep him guessing."

Nisha agreed quietly, knowing she would win again.

Indy's face turned red with frustration. "Fine, you're going to get yourself killed and I'm not going to be able to help you." He walked several paces down the street. Even from a distance, Nisha could smell the bitter, acrid smell of anger coming off his skin. It made her feel awful. But awful or not, she was not going to change her mind. She was The Caretaker. The risk belonged to her alone.

That night, however, Nisha didn't get much sleep. Faye, of course, was thrilled with the news of their finding The Coin, but worried sick that Sahwin now knew who they were and where they lived. Faye was even more distraught at the idea that he'd been with Nisha every day at school and that none of The Council had detected his presence. "He must be extremely powerful to carry a concealing charm that well and for that long," she'd said.

When she got up the next day, Nisha hurried to dress, taking care with The Coin so as not to misplace or drop it. It seemed to shimmer even more vibrantly than it had the first time she saw it, as if it were as happy to have found her as she was to have found it. When Nisha was ready to leave, she looked for her Aunt but Faye was not at home. Nisha assumed she'd gone to share the news of The Coin with the other Council members. Nisha left her a note on the kitchen table before heading out to

Bea's.

Outside, everything remained dry and colorless; especially the trees, which were no longer green but a dull, lifeless brown. Autumn had come and gone without any of its usual spectacle. There was not a hint of a crisp breeze or a single amber leaf to be found.

Nisha quickly crossed the street to Bea's front stoop and was happy to see that Indy was already there. When he stood up to greet her, she could see the relief in his smile. *He must have been worried about me all night.* She smiled in return and tried not to blush.

At the door, Nisha and Indy were let inside by Cookie, who was accompanied by a large ancient-looking vacuum cleaner. "Can I get you something, a glass of juice or maybe some tea?" she asked politely.

"Nothing, thanks," said Indy, and Nisha shook her head. "Nothing for us thanks," Bea echoed as she joined them in the foyer. "We're just going to get some stuff out of my room and then I think we'll head up the hidden passageway to Grandfather's secret library and try to figure out this coin thing."

For a moment, Nisha was shocked. Why was Bea telling the cook about the library? However, when Cookie answered, "All right then, but be sure to bring an umbrella. It looks like it might finally rain," Nisha realized that whatever Cookie had heard, it was not what Bea had said.

"Will do," replied Bea, with a wink at Indy and Nisha.

Cookie pushed the heavy vacuum in the direction of the sitting room, and after several seconds they heard the old machine cough into action.

"Well, let's get to it," said Bea. "You brought The Coin, right?"

Nisha nodded and patted her front pocket. When they got to the dining room, Bea looked over at Indy expectantly.

"What?" he asked.

"Make us laugh," she said matter-of-factly. "We need to laugh to open the passageway, remember?"

"So that's all I'm good for?" He said, gesturing widely. "You know I'm not here to be the court jester. I'm supposed to protect you. Perhaps you haven't figured it out yet, but if it wasn't for me…"

At that moment, Indy stumbled backward over one of the andirons and landed with a hard thud on his bottom.

Because it was impossible not to, both girls burst into laughter, and immediately, the back of the fireplace rumbled open.

"That was genius!" Bea said as she stepped under the mantle.

"Nothing like a good pratfall…" said Indy, with a chuckle. However, when they rounded the first bend, Nisha saw Indy rubbing his backside and it confirmed her suspicion that his fall hadn't been intentional at all. She suppressed another giggle and followed him up the sloping turn.

Nisha was grateful to see that Bea had brought a flashlight this time. She kept her eyes glued on the small beam of light, though it bounced around a bit when Bea spoke.

"It's odd about Nana Anna and Cookie, don't you think?" she said as she rounded another curve. "I mean Nana Anna, who has always been thin, is getting fat, and Cookie who has always been, well, plump, is suddenly slim. I'm certain it's The Coin causing it. It's a shift in the balance of things, just like Faye said, like the earthquakes we've been hearing about."

"Could be," said Indy. "I've noticed some changes too. I mean it doesn't sound possible but I think your street is tilting."

"Oh, right, that," said Bea, as though they had discussed it before. "Are you sure that's not just the world's most elaborate excuse for falling off your skateboard?"

"I resent that," Indy retorted, though Nisha could tell by his tone that he was really more amused than offended. "I've been skating this street since I was six and I'm telling you, it's tilted. I nearly killed myself the other day practicing a backside half-cab heel flip. It's a difficult move, but not beyond my skills, I assure you."

"Of course not," said Bea, laughing. "And we are very impressed, aren't we, Nisha?"

Nisha looked up at Bea, who was flicking her pretty blond

hair over her shoulders, her long legs carrying her gracefully up the tunnel floor, and suddenly she felt like a troll. Bea always knew what to say, particularly to Indy. The two of them joked around all the time. It seemed so natural. Whenever Nisha tried to speak to him, she stumbled over her words or blushed like an idiot.

"Here we are," Bea called out as they reached the door. In the beam of the flashlight it looked like any ordinary door. Yet when Bea quietly turned the knob and they stepped inside, they were once again awed by the amazing room. Finally, Bea broke the silence.

"Okay," she said. "We need to be organized. We have The Coin but there's a lot more we need to know. According to the last part of the prophecy, we need to find The Book of Charms, The Room of Truth and Vesica's Key. Plus, we need to figure out how to make The Coin work. I say we divide and conquer."

"Got it," said Indy. "I'll look for The Book of Charms."

Nisha nodded. "I'll look for anything about The Room of Truth."

"Great," said Bea. "I'll take on Vesica's Key and anything I can find about The Coins."

Like the day before, Bea, Nisha and Indy each took a different wall, and after only a few minutes Bea called out, "I may have something here. Nish, do you have The Coin with you? I want to compare it to this picture."

Nisha stood up and pulled The Coin out of the front pocket of her jeans, and for a moment it flickered like a match bursting into flame.

At the same time, something thumped loudly against one of the five round windows above them, making all three of them jump.

"What was that?" said Indy, looking from window to window anxiously.

"Maybe it was a branch," said Bea. But Nisha's heart began to pound in her chest and her breath was stuck in the back of her throat.

"I'm sure it was nothing," said Bea reassuringly. "Faye said we were safe in this house. No one can get in, remember?"

Nisha nodded slowly, eyeing the windows as she crossed the room. The dull gray light filtered in through the colored glass. Carefully, she placed The Coin on the desk beside Bea. Bea glanced at it. "Not a match," Bea said, disappointed. "It's close, though," she said, turning the book around so Indy and Nisha could see the picture she was looking at.

Suddenly, the room darkened as though a cloud had covered the sun.

"There's something out there," said Indy, his hand moving towards the knife in his pocket.

"A bird?" Bea suggested.

Nisha's eyes widened.

"What's wrong?" said Indy.

"Birds," she said, choking on the word.

Before he could answer, there was a loud smashing sound mixed with the brutal caw of a crow. A shower of glass rained down on them. Instinctively, Nisha's arms covered her head. She peered through the bend in her elbow to see two black birds circling the room, screeching and swooping low enough to knock some of the taller piles of books over with their talons. One of the birds, the one who had broken through the window, was dripping blood.

"Get down!" shouted Indy. "Find some cover!"

Nisha crawled quickly across the rug. Broken glass pressed into her knees and palms. One of the birds swooped by her ear as she ducked behind the chair. To her dismay, the bird circled the room and came back toward her. It flew so close it brushed her shoulder, screeching loudly as it went by. She ducked again, thinking it had passed her, but then her head jerked back and there a sharp pain in her scalp just behind her ear. The bird's talon was caught in her braid. It tugged at her viciously. She cried out.

"It's got your hair," said Indy, his voice coming from somewhere near the desk. "Hang on, I'm coming."

"Untie your braid," shouted Bea from across the room, near the fireplace door.

The bird was screeching, and Nisha could feel its wings flapping frantically against her shoulder. She grabbed onto the back of the large leather chair to stabilize herself. Terrified it would claw her eyes, she used all her strength to turn her face towards the floor. A large pile of books fell over next to her as the bird ripped and tugged ruthlessly at her head. She heard Indy come up beside her, but he couldn't grab the flailing bird without causing her more pain. He was shouting something, and so was Bea, but Nisha couldn't hear them over the bird's angry cries and the flap of its terrible wings.

Without looking, she tried to reach behind and grab the pale blue ribbon that secured her braid, but as she did, a razor sharp claw streaked across her thumb. Bleeding and shaking, she tried again to grab the ribbon, which was now flecked with blood. She reached back and this time got hold of the ribbon's end. She tugged, but the bird's desperate movements had twisted the ribbon more tightly. Nisha changed the angle of her hand and yanked as hard as she could. Finally, the ribbon came loose. It took another second for her braid to untwist and then the connection was broken. Nisha ducked down and covered her face with her arms. Her cheeks were wet with tears.

Then Indy was there, next to her and shouting, "Get away from her!" She looked up through her arms to see him swing at the bird with a large book. The blow sent the bird hurtling across the room, the ribbon in its beak. It hit the wall, slid down, and landed with a thump on the floor below the broken window; one side of its small head crushed and bloody.

"Are you okay?" Indy asked, breathing hard.

Nisha nodded and allowed him to pull her up from the floor. "Where's Bea?" she said. "Where's The Coin?"

"The Coin!" Bea called out, just as Nisha had spoken the same words. Nisha turned to see Bea race towards the desk where The Coin lay shining in own soft glow.

Bea was fast, but it was too late. The second bird had spotted The Coin as well. It rocketed down towards the desk; talons extended, and scooped up The Coin in its claw. Then it was airborne again, screeching in victory as it circled the room heading for the shattered window.

"Get down!" shouted Indy, grabbing for the knife in his pocket.

In what seemed to be slow motion, Nisha saw the knife hurtling through the air. It pierced the flying bird through the side of the neck, pinning it to the wall next to the shattered window. Blood gushed from the wound, spraying out onto the wall like a fan. Nisha, Indy and Bea watched as the creature desperately gasped for air twice, before it finally hung still. Only then, when its body went limp, did it release The Coin.

The Coin flashed as it left the bird's talon and fell towards the ground. But before they could even register their relief, the other bird, the one Indy had hit with the book, somehow recovered itself. It shot up from the floor with the pale blue ribbon still clenched in its beak. It darted upwards with outstretched claws and caught The Coin in mid-fall. The bird and The Coin were through the window before any of the Finders had moved.

When the bird was gone, the room was silent. Indy walked slowly over to the bookcase, climbed up and recovered his knife. Nisha had to turn away as he pulled it from the dead bird's neck, and she winced when she heard its small body hit the floor. Then Indy was back on the ground and insisting that they leave immediately. "I think we're out of danger," he said, "but we can't be too careful."

"Out of danger," Bea gasped in reply. "What if the birds come back?

"They won't," Indy huffed as he hurried them into the mouth of the fireplace. "They got what they came for." Neither girl responded. There was no argument against the plain, painful truth of his words.

When they got out to the stoop, Indy quickly scanned the sky. "The question is: how did they find us?" he said.

"Well, if Sahwin is Mr. Morton, then he has access to all our information in the school files," said Bea.

Indy nodded. "But still, how did they know exactly where to look?"

"They've been spying on us for a while," said Nisha. "I'm pretty sure it was those birds that followed me home the other day."

"That makes sense," said Bea. "But how did they get in? The whole house is supposed to be protected."

"Maybe, but what if Faye and The Council didn't protect the whole house? What if The Council didn't know everything about the house?" said Indy. "I told you when we first found the Library. From the outside, you'd never know it was there."

"I'd better go talk to her," said Nisha.

Bea nodded. "Do you want me to come with you?"

Nisha shook her head. It would be better if she told Aunt Faye the bad news herself. She left Bea and Indy on the stoop with the promise that she would report back to Bea at school the next day.

CHAPTER 41

THE PERFECT FIT

Bea didn't sleep all night. Every sound in her house made her nerves jangle and every time she closed her eyes she had visions of the crow, its small skull crushed on one side, carrying The Coin away. To make matters worse, her father had called that evening shortly after Nisha and Indy left. He sounded tired and far away. He said he would try to make it home for her birthday, but didn't think his business would be finished by then. Bea cried after she hung up. Now that they had lost The Coin, would she ever see him again?

As the dull daylight pushed at the edges of her curtains, Bea gave up trying to sleep at all. She turned the light on and got up in search of something to read. She half-heartedly looked over the books in her bookshelf, not expecting to find anything interesting, when something caught her eye. There on the lower shelf was the small present her father had given her before he left on his trip.

Bea picked up the tiny package and turned it over in her hands. It felt dry and a bit dusty. A small triangle of the wrapping had lifted from one corner. Perhaps it was because she missed her father, or perhaps it was just her curious temperament, but Bea found that she couldn't resist tucking her finger into the small tear and peeling back a wide strip of gold paper. The opening revealed a glimpse of a lovely blue box underneath. Already too far to turn back, Bea pulled again at the paper. It came away in one large piece, which she let fall to the floor.

Bea held up the box and admired it. It was made of milky-blue porcelain with a pattern of willowy silver leaves. She went to open the lid, but hesitated. Perhaps if she didn't open it, she could still keep her promise to wait until her birthday. Then again, the box itself might be the gift with nothing inside at all; and if that were the case the promise was already broken. Bea sighed. It was only a few days until her birthday, she reasoned, and her father would probably not make it anyway. Bea tossed her hair back behind her shoulders and lifted the lid.

Inside, on a soft cushion of blue, was the most beautiful ring Bea had ever seen; a circle of pale silver thread woven around tiny sparkling diamonds. It was so lovely that Bea's breath caught in the back of her throat. Carefully, she picked it up and held it to the light to examine it more closely. It was old, that was certain, and two of the tiny diamonds were missing, but it was exquisite in every other detail. Bea slid the ring onto her finger. It fit perfectly. Almost instantly she felt better; glad she'd opened the box despite breaking her promise. She sighed contentedly and held her hand up to let the diamonds catch the light.

Just then, her alarm went off and Bea's worries came rushing back to her like an icy stream in her veins.

Would Sahwin be waiting for them at school? Bea doubted it, but even so, she still had Charlotte to contend with. Had Charlotte's father discovered the bogus coin? Had someone seen the vine on the side of the building? How would they ever explain it all? And most worrying of all, how would they ever get The Coin back in time for Passage Day?

Nisha was waiting for her across the street when she headed out the door, and even at that distance Bea could tell Nisha was upset. Bea presumed Nisha was plagued by their shared concerns but as they walked to school, Nisha explained that it was something else entirely.

When Nisha had returned home the prior evening, she'd found Gloria there and not Faye. Faye and Graydon had been called away mysteriously and Gloria wasn't sure how long they'd be gone. Nisha was certain something was wrong and though Bea agreed with her, she didn't say so. The air felt heavier than ever and everything looked dirty and old in the dim grey-yellow light. They walked the rest to school in anxious silence.

To Bea's great relief, her prediction regarding Sahwin turned out to be correct. An announcement was made during Homeroom that Mr. Morton had taken a sudden leave of absence. Charlotte came bustling in shortly afterwards, and Bea held her breath as Charlotte slipped into the seat next to her.

"I'm so sorry for my atrocious party," she said with an apologetic smile, which surprisingly seemed to include Nisha as well as Bea. "Some people can be just wretched." As if on cue, Amanda came clomping in with a couple of eager Almosts. She threw her backpack noisily on a desk across the room and laughed loudly, though Bea suspected nothing funny had been said. After that, Charlotte and Amanda spent the rest of the time fiercely ignoring one another, neither of them giving Bea or Nisha another look.

The school day seemed to take forever, but when the last bell finally rang; Bea wasn't sure what to do next. The three Finders headed slowly back to Bea's house. On the way, Nisha told Indy the news of Faye's sudden departure, and Bea felt again the certainty that no good would come of it.

When they got to Bea's, the plan was to go straight to Old Bill's Library. It wasn't easy to get through the fireplace, however, as there wasn't much to laugh about. After several attempts, Indy managed to make the girls giggle, but the mood damped as they stepped inside the dark tunnel.

When they entered into the dim light of the library, they were pleasantly surprised to find that the dead bird had been removed and the window repaired. The only trace of the incident was a pale blood stain that ran down the wall.

"Gloria," said Nisha. "She told me she and The Council would fix things here and make sure the room was protected."

"Kind of her," said Bea. "Now we can get back to work without worrying."

"Back to work?" said Indy glumly. "Why bother?"

"Well, okay, we've had a setback. I'll admit that," said Bea, "but it's not over yet. We've got more than a week to set this straight."

"How do you do that?" he asked, shaking his head in awe. "How do you stay so positive all the time?"

"I don't," said Bea. "In fact, last night I was a total wreck, but then I opened this." She held her hand out and wiggled her fingers. "And I know it sounds silly, but it made me feel better to think that someone somewhere took the time to make something so beautiful. How can we give up on that kind of spirit? We have to keep trying."

"Oh…" Nisha said appreciatively. "Is it your birthday present?"

Bea nodded. "I wasn't supposed to open it but I couldn't help myself, especially after Father told me last night that he probably wouldn't make it back in time."

"It's weird," said Indy.

Nisha frowned at him and he chuckled. "Not the ring, the fact that you guys have same birthday. The ring is really nice." He leaned over to look at Bea's hand. "Hey," he said sounding suddenly serious. "Mind if I get a closer look at that?"

Bea pulled off the ring and placed it in Indy's bear-sized hand.

Indy took it gingerly and held it up to the dim sunlight.

"I know it's missing a couple of stones," Bea said, knowing Indy would notice right away. "But it's so old and it's still lovely."

Indy studied the ring for another minute. "It's not missing any stones," he said certainly. "It was made that way. Look at it again. Nothing is broken and no open prongs. The spaces are an odd design element though. It looks as if it is missing another piece."

He handed the ring back to Bea and she inspected it closely. Indy was right. It seemed as if the empty spaces were there on purpose. With a shrug, Bea slipped the ring back onto her finger. Again she marveled at how perfectly it fit.

The Finders spent the rest of the afternoon trying desperately to figure out a next step. Bea read and reread the prophecy from her notebook, certain that the answer was there somewhere. "Why does it say 'in misty waves'?" Bea asked underlining the words several times. I'm positive that's a clue, but I just can't figure out what it could mean."

"Probably means it's in the mist," said Indy, who was flipping through a large stack of books.

"Obviously," Bea replied, resisting the urge to throw her notebook at him.

Nisha, who had been laying out her tarot cards into different spreads on the library floor, huffed. "What's obvious is that we don't know! We don't know anything. These cards are useless."

"What do they say?" asked Indy, walking over to her and looking blankly at the pattern of cards she'd laid out in front of her.

"They say the same thing that they did yesterday and the day before that," said Nisha, "Look for things that go together."

Indy nodded. "Is that it? Are there any other possible interpretations?"

"Maybe, but not that I can see. I can't figure out why my grandmother left me these cards when I clearly have no talent for them." She tossed the remainder of the deck onto the spread in front of her, her other hand unconsciously moving to her necklace as it often did when she was upset.

"Hold on a minute!" said Indy, suddenly enthusiastic. "I think you might know exactly what you're talking about."

Bea and Nisha peered at him quizzically, and he grinned back at them.

"Hand me your necklace, Nisha."

Nisha looked at him skeptically, but slid her hands to the back of her throat and undid the clasp of the chain. She handed the necklace to Indy, who then turned to Bea and said, "The ring, please?"

Bea handed the ring to Indy and smiled. "Do you really think it will work?"

"Worth a shot," he said with a shrug. It took him a few seconds, but then they heard it; a tiny click. "I knew it!" he said excitedly. Then he stretched his hand out between the two girls so they could both see. He had somehow connected the ruby circle of Nisha's necklace to Bea's diamond ring so that they overlapped to form the symbol of Vesica Pisces.

"Well done!" said Bea.

"It was all Nisha," said Indy, grinning. "She said look for things that go together. And then it hit me."

"This is fantastic," said Bea. "You found Vesica's Key!"

"It is great," said Nisha less enthusiastically, "but how is this all making sense? Why would some present from your grandmother fit with a necklace my grandmother left for me as a baby?"

"Perhaps my grandfather found this ring when he was looking for Avalon and The Coins? He must have given it to my grandmother and she passed it on to me."

"Or maybe someone knew that you two would meet someday," said Indy.

Bea looked at Indy and then at Nisha. She felt a small gleam of hope rekindling between them. "Whatever the reason, the important thing is that you found the key!"

He smiled broadly for a moment and then his eyes dimmed. "Now if only we could find the room," he said.

"Yeah," Nisha agreed quietly, "and The Coin."

CHAPTER 42

THE BOOK OF CHARMS

Day after day, The Finders met after school, and day after day, they discovered nothing new. The excitement of Indy discovering Vesica's Key had long since worn off and with each passing afternoon the thought of their probable failure squeezed the hope out of their hearts. As if to match their growing dread, the sky grew darker and hazier until it seemed as if the sun had given up entirely. In the news, reports of inexplicable tragedies flooded the airwaves.

Bea had all but stopped trying to pay attention in class. She spent most of her time torn between wishing the day would end so she could focus on The Quest and worrying that the hours were ticking by too quickly. And then, suddenly but not suddenly at all, it was Friday, December eleventh. Only one day left.

When Bea and Nisha stepped outside the back door of Miss Huntington's, Indy was waiting for them. His face showed the same worried expression that Bea had worn all day. Without any conversation, they headed home.

The moment they arrived at Bea's stoop, Nisha turned to them and said, "Before we go upstairs, I've got to check something out. I'll be right back."

Bea was confused. She was sure Nisha understood that they needed every possible second to focus on The Quest. "Don't be long," she called after Nisha. Nisha just nodded and crossed the street.

Indy and Bea watched Nisha unlock her door and step inside. Moments later, she reappeared and ran across the street to the stoop where Bea and Indy were waiting.

"I have an idea," she said. She was short of breath and her voice was even raspier than usual. "Gloria mentioned that she had to do some errands today. I just checked and she's not there."

"So?" said Bea.

"So." Nisha hesitated. She avoided Bea's eyes and looked out over the street. "So, I was thinking we could consult the Mirror of Avalon," she whispered.

Bea opened her mouth to speak but Nisha put up her hand. "Before you say anything, just think about it. If we can see the future, maybe we can figure out how to change it."

"You mean that green bowl?" said Indy, "didn't Faye tell us it was extremely dangerous?"

"Yes, she did," Bea said slowly, "but you can't deny it's a tempting idea. Maybe we could ask Gloria to call on The Mirror when she gets back."

"I thought about that too," said Nisha, "but she'll never agree, and besides, you need the gift of Seeing. Gloria doesn't have it."

"Then who's going to do it?" Bea asked, though she already knew Nisha's answer.

Nisha paused. "I have a little bit of the Seeing Gift," she said quietly.

"No," said Indy abruptly. "It's way too dangerous."

"Indy's right of course," Bea agreed, slowly, but she also saw Nisha's point. If they could see the future, perhaps at least they would know what to expect, how to prepare.

Nisha nodded. "I know, but what else can we do? We're out of time and options. I've gotten all I can out of the tarot cards."

"Faye said they were the most precious Gift of all," said Indy.

"Maybe there's something you missed. Maybe you should try again."

"No," Bea said before Nisha could answer. "I mean, Nisha has a point. It's a risk but using the Mirror of Avalon is the only thing we haven't tried. We're not going to get anywhere spending another afternoon in Grandfather's library."

Nisha looked at Bea and nodded once in solidarity. When Bea turned to Indy, he shrugged. "What are you looking at me for?" he asked. "You two already know what I think and you're going to do it anyway."

Bea turned back to Nisha. "Okay Nish, let's try it, but I hope you know what you're doing."

Nisha smiled a small, nervous smile. "Yeah," she said stepping out onto the sidewalk, "me too."

"Aw, hell," said Indy, picking up his skateboard and shaking his head in exasperation. In spite of everything, they all laughed.

Nisha's apartment was dark in the gray light of the late afternoon. Bea carefully locked the door behind them then followed Indy and Nisha into the living room. Indy quickly pulled the curtains over the broad front window and Nisha hurriedly collected her tarot cards, which were spread out on the table in an H formation.

Nisha gestured for Bea and Indy to sit down. Then she returned the tarot cards to their box and set it to one side of the chair that was normally Faye's.

Using a red silk scarf from a nearby lampshade, Nisha carefully picked up the green crystal ball from the bureau and placed it in the center of the table.

"Okay," she said with an audible breath, "now the water." For a few moments, she hunted through the bottles on Faye's shelf. "I think this is the one," she announced, turning around with a small blue bottle in her hand. She placed it on the table in front of her. Then she unwound a pale blue ribbon from her left braid.

Without a word, Bea and Indy reached out and joined hands, wrapping the ribbon around their wrists. Shakily, Nisha uncorked the tiny vessel and positioned it over the ball as Faye had done. As carefully as she could, she tipped it until a tiny droplet hung, suspended from its mouth. With a slight tap of her finger, the drop fell onto the ball and was absorbed instantly. Nisha sighed quietly with relief. Then she extended one end of the ribbon to Indy. "Ready? We don't have much time before Gloria gets back."

Bea nodded and Indy shrugged.

Nisha rubbed the necklace at her throat and took a long breath. Then she stretched her hand out over the green ball and began the invocation; the long list of names Bea had heard Faye use before the séance. It took several minutes, but when she was through, the ball was glowing softly.

Nisha glanced at Bea, and Bea nodded back encouragingly. With that, Nisha lifted her end of the ribbon to her lips. This time she began to chant as Faye had. "Mirror of Avalon, reveal yourself. Water of the Lake, show us the future. Mirror of Avalon, reveal yourself. Water of the Lake, show us the future."

For a long time she chanted, and nothing happened except that Bea began to notice Nisha's voice was getting softer and softer. With the rhythm of the words, Nisha seemed to be hypnotizing herself. Her eyes were becoming hazy and distant, until finally Bea heard what they were all waiting for; the strange bubbling noise from inside the ball. She looked up at Nisha. *It's working*, Bea thought to her excitedly. Nisha nodded almost imperceptibly so as not to interrupt the flow of her words. It took longer than it had with Faye but after a few more minutes, Bea saw the glass begin to roll and bubble deep in its center. Then slowly, as if it were melting, it began to take the shape of a bowl.

Nisha continued to chant, her eyes as reflective as the bowl itself. Then finally, with a quiet but distinct cracking noise, it was finished; the bowl's ropey carvings curled like eels in the green glass. Bea watched as Nisha turned, trance-like, to the shelf behind her. Again, she picked up the small blue bottle. After steadying herself, she uncorked it and tipped it slowly, only allowing a single perfect tear of liquid to fall into the basin.

The three Finders watched intently as the bowl filled with

water. When it was full, Nisha cleared her throat and took a deep breath. She raised her hands over the surface and said, "Mirror of Avalon, show us what will be."

Bea was surprised by the strength of Nisha's voice. She seemed somehow older, even a bit taller.

Bea glanced over at Indy to see if he too were noticing the transformation in Nisha. His eyes were focused on the water instead. It had started to swirl and twist.

"Show us Passage Day," Nisha commanded, with an intensity that made Bea uncomfortable.

Suddenly, a hideously familiar face swam to the surface. It was Sahwin. His face was contorted in a menacing grin. Bea heard herself gasp and she and Indy pulled back sharply.

Nisha remained poised over the bowl. Her eyes were fixed on his face. "It's just a vision," she said dreamily, "just a picture of our worst fears."

"I don't know," said Indy. "Didn't Faye say that other people can look back at you if they also have a Mirror?"

"Show us the Passage Day," said Nisha, ignoring Indy. Her eyes remained focused on the water's surface.

With her command, Sahwin's skull-like face was sucked back into the swirl of the water as if flushed down a toilet, and Indy sighed loudly in relief. Moments later, the water stilled again. This time, in its surface, they saw three figures standing together in a dark room. It was difficult to discern who they were, but from their various sizes, Bea deduced it was the three of them. She tried to note anything she could about their surroundings, but it was all a fog of dark blue. What she could make out was that the three of them were standing in front of a large structure. She leaned in for a better look, but as soon as she did, there was a burst of silvery light on the water's surface. It was so bright that all three of them were forced to look away.

"What was heck was that?" asked Indy.

Bea opened her eyes cautiously and despite the foreboding feeling in her stomach, she forced herself to look back in the bowl. A green glow remained on the surface of the water, making it difficult to see the images there. The surface still showed the strange blue room, but there now appeared to be someone slumped on the ground. The future-Nisha rushed over and fell down to her knees beside the slumped figure. And then the water began to swirl again.

"Did you see that?" asked Indy anxiously. "Who was that?"

But before Bea could answer, the water stilled again and Sahwin's image returned. He lifted his hand and with a long gray finger, he beckoned for them to come closer.

Bea instinctively leaned back, as did Indy, but Nisha leaned forward towards the bowl.

"Nisha, no!" said Indy, grabbing for her arm.

"He's saying something!" said Nisha, shaking him off. "Maybe it's a clue." Sahwin's lips were moving. Nisha eyes were glazed with intensity. She leaned in further.

When she was so close that her breath caused a ripple on the water, Sahwin's hideous hand shot toward the surface as if to reach out and grab her. Nisha gasped in surprise and horror. She jumped back, just as Indy rushed forward to protect her. Bea caught a last glimpse of Sahwin laughing, before Nisha and Indy slammed into one another and then into the table. There was a loud crash as the Mirror of Avalon smashed to pieces onto the floor.

For several seconds, The Finders stood in gaping silence as the water blackened the blue carpet under their feet.

Then slowly, as if all the strength was seeping out of her, Nisha slid down to the floor. She wrapped her hands around her knees and buried her face in her arms.

Indy rushed over to her, but hesitated. "I'll, I'll get something to clean this up," he said shyly.

Bea kneeled down next to Nisha. "Are you alright? Did you hurt yourself?"

Nisha slowly lifted up her head to look at Bea.

"It's going to be okay," said Bea soothingly.

"Don't you realize what I've done?" Nisha whimpered. "Not only did I practically invite Sahwin into my living room, I've destroyed a Mirror of Avalon!"

"It's my fault," said Indy, returning with a towel, a broom

and a dustpan. "I should have stopped you."

"We're all to blame," said Bea.

Nisha shook her head. "No, it's my fault," she said resoundingly. "I can't even figure out the tarot cards. I don't know what made me think I could handle real magic. I had no idea what I was doing."

"You're not the only one who doesn't know what they're doing," said Indy.

Bea nodded. "Indy's right, none of us know how any of this works. You did what you thought had to be done to figure this thing out. Isn't that what we're supposed to do?"

"Right," said Indy, lifting the table upright. "And I think we might have learned something here. I saw us standing together in a room."

"Me too," said Bea. "It was sort of blue and misty. I think it was the Room of Truth. And if we saw it, it means that we were there or, it means that we will be there, and that's a good thing, right?"

Nisha sniffed. "It also means that Sahwin saw it too, and that means he knows at least as much as we do," said Nisha, wiping her tear-streaked face with the back of her sleeve. "And what am I going to tell Faye? I mean look at this mess." She held her hands out to the broken glass and water around her. "Oh no, and my tarot cards!" she exclaimed. The cards had fallen out of the box and were scattered around the floor. She turned on her hands and knees and began to gather them together.

Indy got down on the floor as well, and began to collect the larger pieces of glass. Bea joined them with the towel, trying to soak up as much of the spilled water as she could. They worked in silence for several seconds, until suddenly Nisha made a strange gasping sound and sat up so abruptly she bumped her head on the underside of the table.

"What is it?" said Bea.

Nisha turned towards them, holding tightly to the tarot box. To Bea's surprise, she was grinning widely and a small giggle escaped from her mouth before she could answer.

Bea searched Nisha's face concernedly. "Are you sure you're

okay?" she asked.

"No, I mean yes," Nisha replied excitedly. "I mean, I found something."

"What?" Indy asked.

"The Book of Charms."

"What?" said Bea. "It was under the table?"

"Well, sort of," said Nisha, her eyes sparkling with tears and excitement.

"Well… where is it?" said Indy gently.

"Here," she said, holding out the tarot box.

Bea crawled closer to Nisha, careful not to get glass in her knees, and lifted the box from Nisha's outstretched hand. There, on the cover, was the picture she had looked at dozens of times. It showed a woman kneeling on the ground. Her arms reaching out over her head towards a bright star. On the ground beside her was the same pile of books that had been there from the beginning, but something was different. Bea lifted the picture closer to her eyes. On the spine of the book at the top of the pile were the words 'Book of Charms'.

"It's weird, isn't it?" said Nisha. "I mean, how could it have been there all this time and we're just seeing it now?"

Indy brought the lid up close to his eyes and squinted. "Well, I'm going to have to take your word for it," he said, "because I don't see anything."

"Something has to be different," said Bea thoughtfully. "Something has to have changed." She reached out and took the lid back from Indy. She peered at it again closely. But it wasn't until she saw Indy dry his hand against the leg of his jeans that she realized what had happened. "It's the water," she announced, smiling.

Indy and Nisha looked back at her blankly.

"The top of the box; it's wet," she said again. "It's the Water of the Lake that's done it. It has revealed the words."

CHAPTER 43

THE HOLE IN THE FLOOR

The Finders did their best to clean up the mess in the living room as they pondered their new discovery. However, when Nisha tried to rearrange the remaining crystal balls to cover up for the missing green one, she made another upsetting discovery. Aunt Faye's pet snake, Ice, was missing from its tank. To make matters worse, Nisha couldn't remember the last time she'd seen it. Had it escaped when the table was knocked over? She hoped not. She couldn't bear to think of how Faye might react to the news that Nisha had lost her snake and the Mirror of Avalon at the same time.

Indy and Bea stayed as late as they could, not wanting to leave Nisha alone. Bea even tried to convince Nisha to spend the night at her house, but Nisha insisted on staying home to wait for Gloria.

There was very little food in the cabinets, but Nisha managed to find an old, mealy apple and the end of a loaf of grainy bread. Gloria was supposed to be taking care of her but the truth was that Gloria hadn't been to the market in days. In fact Gloria hadn't done much of anything since she'd moved in, and it seemed that the closer they got to Passage Day, the more withdrawn she had become. Most of the time, she just sat and stared out the front window, pursing her lips and mumbling at the sky.

When Nisha finished her meager meal, she washed her dish at the sink and stared out into the blackness of the backyard. She knew she should try to be hopeful, especially since they'd found The Book of Charms, yet each step forward seemed too small. How would they ever get everything figured out in time?

Nisha considered for a moment going outside. She had always been fond of the nighttime. There was a different feeling to the air at night, a buzzing sensation as though all the energy of the earth was connected together. Nisha loved to sit out under the stars and feel it hum around her. But tonight the air was thick and starless and her head and heart were heavy with worry.

Instead, she wandered into her room and sat on her bed. She picked up the tarot box and ran her fingers over the new words. She sighed. Tears slid down her cheeks, but she barely had the energy to wipe them away. It wasn't enough, she thought. This little clue wasn't enough to stop Sahwin; not when he had The Coin.

She lay back and closed her eyes and listened for the familiar sounds of the city, but they were strangely muffled and far away. There were no lights on and her room was shadowy and quiet. She whispered, "I'm sorry" into the darkness, "I'm sorry we didn't find the answers." It was an apology sent out to her Aunt Faye, to Bea, to the mother she'd never met, to no one and everyone at the same time.

The sound of someone rattling around the kitchen woke her up. A momentary surge of hope swelled up in Nisha at the thought of seeing Faye, but to both her relief and disappointment, it was only Gloria.

"Good morning and happy birthday," Gloria said, attempting a smile. Nisha tried to smile in return but she could not.

"What time is it?" she asked, glancing out the back door and studying the sky. It wasn't quite as dark as night but it didn't look like day either. Dull curtains of grey gloom hung over everything and it seemed to Nisha as if the greyness was seeping in through the window frames and under the doors.

"It's about ten in the morning. How are you?" Gloria asked.

Nisha said nothing but shook her head. How could she have let herself sleep so late?

"Sit down and have something to eat," Gloria suggested.

"I can't," Nisha replied. "Not when there's so little time."

"Sit," Gloria commanded. "I have something to tell you." Gloria slid some fried eggs on Nisha's plate along with a toasted corn muffin. Then she poured her a large glass of juice and joined her at the table.

"You may have noticed I've been distracted these last several days," Gloria began. Nisha nodded and picked at her food. She knew she should eat something but she didn't have the stomach for it.

Gloria continued. "You see, we haven't been able to find the other Caretakers, and when it became clear to us that you might not retrieve The Coin in time, Faye and Graydon decided that they had to do something. So they set out to find Sahwin. I'm sorry to say that they did not succeed."

"Find Sahwin? Is that what they've been trying to do?" Nisha choked with surprise.

Gloria nodded.

"Are they alright?"

"Well, that's just it. You see, I haven't been able to find them. I've not gotten word from any of my sources."

"Oh no," said Nisha, standing up as if to go somewhere.

Gloria lowered her voice and took Nisha's hand. "I'm afraid it gets worse. I've heard rumors that Sahwin has been crossing over into The Other World bringing…" Gloria caught her breath, "sacrifices." Then she cleared her throat and sat up straighter. "I didn't want to tell you because I'm still not sure if any of it is true. However now that Passage Day is upon us, you might as well know what I know."

Nisha did not know how to respond. Slowly, she sunk back down into her chair.

"There is a small piece of good news," said Gloria, trying to sound hopeful. "The birds say that Sahwin is having some troubles of his own, although I can't get much more from them than that. You know how birds are, just repeating the same things back and forth to one another. It's almost impossible to get a full thought out of them."

At that moment, the doorbell rang and Nisha jumped.

Gloria looked at her curiously. "I assume it's the other Finders," she said. "Didn't you expect them?"

"No… I mean, yes, I guess I knew they would come," said Nisha. "Will you get the door while I change my clothes?"

Nisha dressed quickly and brought her tarot cards out to the front room, where she found Bea and Indy waiting for her on the couch. Both of them stood up when she walked in.

"Are you okay?" said Indy. He sounded genuinely concerned, which to Nisha's dismay, made her blush. If they made it through this whole thing, Nisha swore to herself, she'd find some magic that would make it stop.

"I'm fine," she said.

"And how about Gloria?" said Bea, with a nervous glance at the empty spot on the back table where the green ball had been.

"She's fine," said Nisha reassuringly. "She told me some stuff though." Nisha went on to fill Indy and Bea in on Gloria's news.

"This thing is getting really…" Indy began.

"Scary," Nisha finished.

Bea nodded. "It's interesting about Sahwin though. Maybe he doesn't know as much about The Coin as we think he does."

Gloria came bustling back into the room and interrupted them. She had a bag of birdseed in one hand and a raw steak in the other. "I'm going to the park to see if I can get more information. I'll be back in a little while. Please try and stay out of trouble."

"Too late for that," said Indy, as soon as the door shut behind her.

"It's too late for everything," said Nisha, walking over to the table to put the tarot box down. She ran her finger over the book in the picture. "I'm so tired," she said, her voice cracking with tears. "I wish my Aunt was here."

Bea walked over to stand next to her. "I know," she said, "but we can't give up. Besides, The Mirror said we're going to end up in The Room of Truth somehow, right? And this was a serious breakthrough," she added, tapping the box of cards. Before Nisha could respond, Bea pulled her hand away with a start. "What was that?" she said, her eyes wide.

"What was what?" said Nisha.

"I felt something!" said Bea. "I felt something under my fingers when I touched the box." Bea picked up the lid and gasped. "Look, look! The book it's open!"

Nisha took the lid from Bea and her eyes widened.

"Again," Bea demanded. "We have to try it again."

Nisha put the lid back on the box and placed her hand on it. Then Bea carefully put her hand next to Nisha's. Suddenly the pages of the book fluttered.

"Now what?" whispered Nisha, afraid to take her hand away.

"What are you guys doing?" said Indy, coming over to the table. "You're so quiet."

Nisha hadn't realized it until that moment, but she and Bea hadn't been speaking aloud.

"Look at the image!" Nisha said. "When Bea and I touch the box at the same time, the pages of the book move."

"That's cool," said Indy. "It would be cooler if I could see it but…wait! I can!" He leaned over the box. "Right there, I see the book right there. He reached out his hand and touched the fluttering pages with the tip of his finger. The moment he made contact, the box fell from Nisha's hand and right through the tabletop and three of them jumped back, startled.

Indy stepped forward and lifted the tablecloth, and all three Finders knelt down. The box was gone, and in the very spot where it should have been was a hole in the floor. A strange blue mist wafted up from the opening and curled like smoke into the room.

"Okay," said Indy, nodding enthusiastically, "now that's cool!"

Bea leaned over the hole and peered in.

"Careful!" said Indy.

"It's a staircase!" said Bea excitedly, her voice echoing slightly in the opening.

"It must lead to the Room of Truth!" said Nisha.

"I'll go first," said Indy, without hesitation. He shifted himself so he was closer to the hole and slid his foot close to the edge.

"Wait!" said Nisha urgently. "We're going right now? But what if…what if…"

"What if what?" said Bea. "What if it's dangerous?"

"Or if Sahwin's down there?" said Indy.

"Or we can't get back?" Bea added.

"Umm…or all of the above," said Nisha.

"Yup, all possible," said Indy, "but unless you have something better to do today, I'm thinking we should try and save the world."

Nisha leaned over the hole and breathed in the mist. The smell was dank and familiar and instinctively she knew what it was. "The Mists," she whispered. Then she sat up slowly and looked at Bea and Indy. "I want you to know that you don't have to do this. You don't have to risk yourselves. It's my risk to take, for my mother and the people of Avalon."

"That's not true. It matters to me too," said Bea. "This whole thing started because my father has been looking for this The Coin my entire life!"

"I didn't mean that it wasn't important to you," said Nisha. "It's just that you shouldn't feel obligated just because of The Prophecy. You should think of yourselves and your families."

"We are thinking of our families, Nisha," said Indy. "Everyone is in danger. And after all this time, we're not going back out now." He checked his neck for The Kiss and his pocket for Drae Mord then said, "Bea, do you have The Minute?"

She nodded, then checked her watch. "It's already after eleven. We've got less than thirteen hours to figure this out. I'm going to set my watch alarm for five minutes until midnight just in case."

275

"Just in case," repeated Nisha nervously.

"Okay," said Indy, "I'm first, then Bea, then Nisha. Clear?"

"Yes sir," said Bea.

Indy moved carefully to the side of the opening and swung one leg over, letting his foot find the first stair. "Strange," he said, "the step feels sort of bouncy, like it's suspended in the air." He slid himself down slowly and in a moment he had disappeared through the hole.

"Whoa!" he called up to the girls, "This is wild. Come on!"

CHAPTER 44

THE ROOM OF TRUTH

Something about the mists was pleasing to Bea. Perhaps it was the salty smell in the air or maybe it was the way the dewiness felt cool on her skin. It reminded her of something long ago; a beach or ocean bluff she had visited as a small child. She felt oddly calm as she breathed in the scent and listened to the sound of Nisha's light footsteps behind her.

It hadn't taken long to get used to the soft blue light, but even with her eyes adjusted, she still couldn't really understand where they were. There was nothing visible beyond the grey-blue fog that surrounded them. The only thing Bea was sure of was that they were on a path of stepping stones which were floating miraculously like small rafts in an ocean of mist. At first they moved carefully, for there was no railing or wall around them, but once they gained their footing, they forged ahead at a steadier pace, descending ever deeper into the misty air. The hole above them, from which they had come, had long since been swallowed by soft clouds of dew.

The only other sound besides their footsteps was the echo of water dripping from somewhere far above or perhaps below. They moved without speaking, as there was little to say. While Bea concentrated on not slipping, Indy seemed to find the experience exhilarating. He bounded down the stairs like a puppy twitching with energy. Bea kept a close eye on him, calling for him to slow down whenever he got too far ahead and disappeared into the fog. She'd given up turning around to check on Nisha. Whenever she did, it filled her with anxiety. For each time Nisha vacated a stone, it drifted away behind her, leaving no possibility of returning the way they had come; a realization Bea kept to herself.

They continued stone by stone for what seemed like ages, yet time was flying by. Bea checked her watch every few minutes only to find hours had passed. It was after eight when Bea finally began to notice a change. The air around them was getting brighter. Indy appeared to sense it too, for he began moving more quickly.

"I see something," he said over his shoulder. And, after another few steps, he stopped abruptly. Bea and Nisha quickly caught up to him.

"I think it's a beach," he said, stepping carefully forward onto what appeared to be the shore of an island. "It is!" he said excitedly. "It's sand."

Bea and Nisha followed Indy onto the waterless shore, and as they did, the last stone floated away into the mist. No one said anything, but Bea could tell by Indy and Nisha's faces that they were absorbing what she already knew. They would have to find another way back home.

"It must be an island of some kind," said Nisha.

"An island in the mists," said Bea. "Do you think we're in Avalon?"

"Or under it," Nisha finished breathlessly.

The Finders walked up the beach until the line of a low dense forest could be seen. The trees were old and bent, their branches knotted together to form a dark pavilion. Bea couldn't discern a path or any sign of life. All that was visible amidst the trees was a low mist creeping between the trunks. Somewhere deep within, the sound of dripping water persisted.

"So, now what?" asked Indy.

"Maybe we should say something," suggested Nisha.

"Yes," Bea agreed. "Perhaps we should ask permission, like with The Mirror of Avalon." She turned to Nisha expectantly and Nisha shrugged with the understanding that this job fell to her.

Bea nodded, "Go on, then," she said encouragingly.

Nisha sighed with her usual quiet resignation and closed her eyes. She let her arms drop to her sides, palms open and out like Faye's when she called the names of The Nine Daughters.

"Room of Truth," said Nisha softly, "I am Nisha, Caretaker of the Third Coin. Grant us permission to enter."

"Well that was easy enough," said Indy, a moment later, "look."

Bea turned towards the fog in the direction he was pointing. Set just inside the forest was a clearing that hadn't been there before. The Finders stepped through the low growth until they stood at the edge of the glade. A perfect circle of trees lined its perimeter, and pale shafts of sunlight pushed through the heavy leaves above. The ground was covered with a soft, spongy carpet of moss.

In the center of the glade stood a blue stone archway, its weatherworn surface covered with carvings of serpents and hideous sea creatures. A dark green slime crept up the side of its walls and clung to the stone with vine-like fingers. It was so large that it appeared to be the entrance to a great castle. Yet oddly it stood alone, no wall or building attached.

"Hold on," said Indy, raising his hand in caution. "I'm going to go first. Then you can follow when I give you the signal that all is clear."

"All clear of what?" asked Bea, peering through the opening in the arch. "There's nothing on the other side but more mist."

"Mmmm," said Indy, scratching his head as if thinking deeply. "It does appear that way, doesn't it? But I've got a hunch…now stay with me on this…I'm thinking it might look like your ordinary, everyday blue stone archway in a clearing in the woods on a mystical island at the end of a floating staircase, but maybe not. Maybe it's something unusual, you know?"

"You may have a point," Bea agreed, grinning, grateful as

always that Indy could keep his head no matter the situation.

"Okay, I'm going in," he said, his tone turning serious. "Remember, don't come after me until you hear me whistle. Got it?"

Bea and Nisha nodded in silent agreement while Indy bravely stepped through the portico. Then he was gone, as if the mists had swallowed him whole.

Bea and Nisha were still and silent as they waited. As the seconds turned slowly into minutes, the tension tightened in Bea's throat. Nisha's heart pounded anxiously, and Bea could feel it as if it were her own. After another minute crawled by, Nisha said, "I can't...we just can't ..." Her voice quivered slightly.

"You're right. We have to go in there."

"But he said to wait. He hasn't signaled us," said Nisha.

"Or he can't signal us."

Nisha nodded. "I feel something...someone is here...or maybe in there."

Bea looked around. There was no evidence of another person, yet she too sensed someone else was near. "I feel it too," she admitted. "That's why we have to go in. We can't leave him in there alone."

Without further discussion, the girls stepped together into the archway.

At first nothing changed, only the sound of the water grew louder and Bea felt a soft breeze push past her cheek. Then a moment later, the breeze broke through the foggy stillness in front of her and she saw that they were no longer in the clearing but had entered a room. It was large and round, approximately the size and shape of the clearing. However, instead of earth and trees, the room was made entirely of stone. Around the perimeter of the room was a river of murky water that encircled the floor, forming an island of stone in the center. Bea and Nisha stood on a footbridge, which provided the only passage over the water.

Placed at four equidistant points around the room were four elaborate fountains, each built out from the wall and up from the floor, allowing the river to flow freely beneath. The fountains stood dry. No water ran from their metallic spouts, and even from a distance they looked cracked and tarnished.

Directly in the center of the room was a fifth fountain, different from the others, for its basin was sunken into the floor. Several enormous stone, buttress-like arches stretched from the center of the bowl and curled back in on themselves, reminding Nisha of waves on the beach. Like the others, the central fountain was in a state of decay; a green rusty color stained its bowl and only a small trickle of water dripped from its pipes.

Together, the girls crossed the small footbridge and stepped tentatively onto the floor. Nisha moved left towards one of the fountains and Bea followed her. The fountain's intricate carvings depicted a life-sized woodland scene. A large thicket of stone trees climbed up the sides and branches of carved rock stretched out above them. A deer and fawn were poised to drink from a small waterfall, now dry and brown with rust.

Bea left Nisha and wandered over to the fountain across the way. It showed two naked lovers wrapped in an embrace; a circle of spouts surrounded them at their feet. Had the water been flowing as it was meant to, the figures wouldn't be so exposed, but without the streams of water to hide them, the statues were shockingly bare. Bea turned, expecting a comment from Indy, but then, with a jolt, she remembered he was missing.

She tossed her hair back and looked around with purpose, but she could find no sign of him. Nisha was across the room in front of a fountain that portrayed the solar system. Streaky stains of mineral slime ran over the rounded curve of Jupiter.

"I think this one is Time," Nisha said, and Bea knew instantly what she meant: there was a fountain to represent each Coin.

"These first two must be Life and Love," she called back.

"Shhhhh," said someone from the center of the room. It was Indy.

Bea sighed in relief. "Why? Where are you? What's wrong?" she said. Indy stepped out from behind the center fountain and signaled for them to come closer. When they were both beside him, he whispered, "I was attacked by bugs."

"Bugs?" said Nisha, looking around warily. "They don't seem to be bothering us now."

"No, they don't," said Indy, his eyes darting around the room. "They must only be after me."

No sooner were the words out of his mouth than a bright green luminescent bug appeared in front of him. He tried to move away from it but it zipped between Bea and Nisha, and with a snapping sound and a small burst of light, it stung him on the cheek then disappeared.

Indy rubbed his cheek, "Darn things really hurt."

"Remarkable," said Bea.

"Yeah," said Indy, "remarkably painful."

"Are you alright?" asked Nisha, moving closer to him to examine his skin.

Indy stuck out his chin like a comic book hero. "I'll be okay," he said.

"Oh please," said Bea, with a laugh. "It's strange, I'll give you that, but it was just a silly little bug." Suddenly, out of the air, another bug appeared. This time it went after Bea and stung her on the neck.

"Yow!" she yelped. "That smarts!"

"Told you," said Indy.

"Is this why you didn't call for us," asked Bea, "because of these bugs?"

"Well, yes. I wanted to make sure they weren't really dangerous and because well…" Indy lowered his voice. "I feel something. Like maybe there's someone else here."

Bea glanced over at Nisha, and Nisha nodded solemnly. They could all feel it. "Did you find anything else?" asked Bea, looking around warily.

Indy nodded and pointed to the fountain in the center of the room. Despite its worn appearance, it was still impressive. Grand arches of stone stretched above their heads, and Bea could imagine how impressive it must have been with water rushing from its many spouts. Without the water, however, Bea could see what would normally be hidden. In the very center of the fountain was a round platform. A pedestal stood in the middle with a basin upon it that looked to Bea like a birdbath. Bea circled the fountain until she found a small path of stone steps leading in. Nisha and Indy followed her, and in a few seconds all three of them stepped through a flourish of stone and onto the platform itself.

On closer inspection, the birdbath wasn't a birdbath at all but an oversized cauldron, made of greenish blue glass very much like Faye's Mirror of Avalon, but far larger. A heavy wrought-iron grate with a tightly knotted pattern of bars covered the surface. Bea leaned forward and peered through the iron grille. There was a small puddle of blackened water at the bottom. To her surprise, she saw something glinting in the darkness. She leaned in closer to get a better look.

"It's The Coins," Indy said. "They're all here, except one." Again, a green light bug appeared just next to Indy's head. It was bigger than the last one, and it bit him with a snap on the ear. "Yowza! That was a nasty one," he said, irritated. "I think they're getting worse."

Bea looked around suspiciously, and then turned to Indy. "Less talking," she suggested. "They seem to be reacting to what we're saying."

Indy nodded. "You could be right. I was sort of talking to myself when I first got in here, you know, thinking out loud, and that's when they started biting. But why are some of the things we say okay and others aren't?"

"It's The Room of Truth," said Nisha looking at Bea and Indy expectantly as if this explained everything.

"Which would mean…?" Bea asked.

"Which would mean that they're…I mean, it's hard to believe but….they must be lie flies."

"What?" Bea and Indy said together.

"You know, lie flies," said Nisha, "as in, 'don't lie or the lie flies will get you.'" When Bea and Indy looked at her blankly, her cheeks went pink. "I guess you've never heard of them."

"Sure, I've heard of them," said Indy, nodding, but as soon as he said it a tiny green bug appeared and stung him on the elbow.

He started to swear but held it in. Instead, he said, "Okay, so I've never heard of lie flies before, but I wasn't lying about The Coins. The Third Coin isn't here." Yet as the words came out of his mouth a lie fly appeared and stung him soundly on the forehead.

"Enough!" he said in exasperation.

"They bite you when you're lying," said Nisha, "even if you don't know you're lying, and, according to Faye; 'the bigger the lie, the bigger the fly'."

"You'll just have to stop lying," said Bea.

"I told you. I wasn't …" Indy began, but stopped himself before the words were out. A lie fly appeared and hovered by his left ear before fading again into the air.

"You realize," Bea whispered, leaning towards Nisha and Indy, "that if we're right about the lie flies, it means The Coin must be here. They appeared when Indy said it wasn't."

Nisha face darkened. "Do you think that means that Sahwin is here too?" she asked, scanning the fog as she spoke. When neither Bea nor Indy answered, she turned and looked them, her eyes wide and shining with fear.

"I think we should focus on getting this grate open," said Bea. "If he is here, maybe we can somehow get The Coin from him and put it back where it belongs."

"Good idea," said Indy, and when Nisha nodded, Bea slid the slim diamond band off her finger. Nisha removed her necklace and slowly slipped the delicate ruby pendent off its chain. She handed it to Bea, who carefully arranged the two circles so they overlapped. Click. They set together seamlessly, forming a tiny replica of the pattern on the grate. She held it up.

"The key's ready," she announced.

"Looks good," said Indy, "but we've got a little problem. I already looked, and couldn't find a keyhole."

"Not to worry," replied Bea confidently. "Remember the prophecy – 'One to see what cannot be seen.' That means Nisha will be able to find it." However, just as she finished her sentence, a small lie fly bit her on her thumb.

Nisha shrugged and walked around the cauldron, examining

the grate carefully. "Well, the lie fly was right, I don't see a keyhole," she said. "It doesn't make sense though. Why have a key if it doesn't open the grate?"

Bea shook her head. "You'd probably have learned about this if you had kept up with your studies," she said thoughtfully. Her comment was meant as a simple observation; but as soon as it was out she realized that it sounded like an accusation.

Nisha's cheeks turned pink. "Thanks for bringing that up. Don't you think I feel badly enough about this already?"

"Of course," Bea replied. "Er, I mean, I didn't mean for it to sound that way, I …"

"Not another argument," interrupted Indy loudly. "Please, I'd rather be attacked by an army of lie flies than listen to another argument between you two." To the girls' amusement, as soon as he finished his announcement, a lie fly appeared and stung him on the jaw.

"C'mon," Indy said angrily into the air, "I was exaggerating. Don't you have a sense of humor?" Indy rubbed his cheek where the bug had stung him. "Useless flies," he mumbled under his breath. Yet once again, just as the words passed through his lips another, larger fly appeared and caught him soundly on the wrist. Indy groaned in frustration.

Despite Indy's obvious discomfort, Bea could have clapped. "That's it!" she exclaimed. "The flies aren't useless at all. They can tell us when we're right or wrong. You know, process of elimination. We can use them to figure out how to open the grate. We might have to suffer through a few stings but at least we have some kind of guide."

Nisha nodded slowly in understanding, and then Indy did too.

"I'll go first," said Bea excitedly. "Our key is meant to open this grate." When no fly appeared, she went on. "The keyhole is somewhere on the grate," she said into the air. Unfortunately, a lie fly appeared and stung her arm.

"I'll give it a try," said Nisha thoughtfully. "The keyhole is somewhere on the cauldron." She was rewarded with a sting on her chin.

Indy shrugged. "Uh, there is no keyhole," he said, his eyes darting around looking for the incoming fly. None appeared.

"Interesting," Bea said. "If there's no keyhole, there must be another way."

"Probably," Nisha said, sighing in exasperation. "But what? For all we know, we should just toss the key in the cauldron."

Bea looked at Nisha, expecting a lie fly to appear, but none did. The Finders looked from one to the other, and Indy raised an eyebrow questioningly.

"We should drop Vesica's Key into the cauldron," he said again. They all looked around for flies. None appeared.

"Amazing," said Bea, handing the key to Nisha. "I'm pretty sure you should do the honors here."

Nisha nodded and took the key from Bea. Then she moved closer to the edge of the cauldron and positioned her hand over the very center of the grate.

"Ready?"

Bea and Indy nodded in unison.

Bea held her breath as Nisha let the key slip from her fingers. She was worried it would fall through the grate and they would lose it along with The Coin. To her surprise and relief however, it didn't fall at all; at least, not as it should have. Instead, it appeared to sink slowly through the air as if through thick syrup, and as it was about to drop through the ironwork, it stopped.

"You should say something," Bea suggested, "chant, maybe."

When no lie flies appeared, Nisha nodded and stretched her arms out over the basin. Quietly, she began the list of ancient names that Bea had grown familiar with.

"I call to the Goddesses of the Other World: Keridwen and Ana, Cerridwen and Morgana, Hecate and Morrigeu, Igraine, Elaine and Lunesa." As Nisha spoke, the grate began to turn in one direction and the key in the other. At the same time, the ironwork of the grate moved, slowly unknotting itself until the pattern was no longer intricate but two simple circles overlapping. When the transformation was complete, the grate stopped spinning and turned from black to a bright gleaming gold. Then, in a blink, it vanished entirely.

"Very cool!" said Indy, nodding enthusiastically.

Nisha smiled and retrieved the key from the air. Then all three Finders leaned over to see inside.

The glass sides of the cauldron were smooth and unadorned, but at the bottom were five circles, arranged like a five on the side of a die. The middle circle was empty, but the other four held four of the most remarkable coins any of them had ever seen.

The first one seemed to be made of a rough, coppery-green metal. Threads of a translucent emerald stone ran through it to form a tree. Its roots curved up from the bottom to touch the wide curving branches above. Bea recognized the symbol. It was the tree of life; very appropriate, she thought, for The Coin of Life.

The Second Coin, The Coin of Death, was dark and made of a hard gray metal Bea hadn't seen before. Its surface was intricately carved to look like feathers. Pressed into its center was what appeared to be the eye of a crow, black and shiny as if wet. It was incredibly fierce and lifelike and so complete in its detail that Bea could have sworn it blinked slightly when she moved her glance away.

The next coin, The Coin of Love, was made of a dark red stone. It somehow looked familiar to Bea, though it wasn't until Indy nudged her and pointed to his neck that Bea placed it. It was the same material as The Kiss, the bead Bridget had given Indy at the flea market. In the water, the color looked like blood flecked with shimmering gold specks. Inlaid in its center was a fat golden apple. Oddly, the longer she looked at it the more she desired to reach out and touch it. It took some effort for her to force her gaze away and when she did, she felt a strange sadness as if she'd lost something precious.

As Bea's gaze fell on The Fifth Coin, however, she instantly felt better. It was made of a pale white material that reminded Bea of opals. Deep within its layers were light, translucent colors that appeared to shift and illuminate in the soft light of the room. Tiny gems were set around the edge like numbers on a clock and she thought that perhaps The Coin of Time was the most exquisite of all.

The three of them stood mesmerized for several seconds. "They're beautiful," Nisha whispered. But before Bea could respond, Nisha held her hand up to silence her. Her eyes were as round as The Coins themselves and Bea knew without a doubt that Sahwin was there.

CHAPTER 45

THE FIGHT

Nisha actually smelled Sahwin before she saw him. A sickening stench of living death drifted over the floor on a rolling ball of mist. When she turned and lifted her eyes towards the source, he was there, standing on the small footbridge, the dim blue light reflecting off his black coat, making him look as if he were carved out of metal. A crow sat on his shoulder, its head deformed and its remaining black eye staring intently at Indy. Then he spoke and his voice made her stomach double over.

"They are beautiful, it's true, Miss Lakewood; but beautiful as they are, without this one to recharge their powers…" he held up the Third Coin between his fingers, "they're useless. Just like the three of you."

A lie fly appeared in the air and headed straight for Sahwin's face. He batted it away with an impatient snort, but the crow on his shoulder cawed loudly and flew to a safer perch on The Fountain of Love.

"I speak the truth," he called out into the air. "They are Finders who lost The Coin. It is disgraceful. Luckily, I found it."

Nisha watched as another two luminous bugs, larger than the

first one, soared towards Sahwin. Despite their speed, he easily flicked them away, red sparks flickering from his fingertips. In fact, pale and thin as he was, he seemed to crackle with power. *Has he tricked us into coming here?* She wondered. *He had The Coin, what else could he want?*

Sahwin took several steps forward and stopped at the end of the footbridge. At the same time, Indy began to move as well. He jumped off the platform, then over the side of the basin, and landed on the floor in front of the fountain. Without a discussion, Nisha and Bea quickly followed him.

"Well, I see you were able to unlock Vesica's Gate," said Sahwin with amusement. "Good for you. But still, no Coin; it must be terribly frustrating."

"So that's it? You needed us to open the gate?" said Bea. "Well it's open now, why don't you put The Coin where it belongs?"

"Always trying to be clever, aren't you?" said Sahwin nastily. "You think I need you to open The Cauldron of Coins? Don't be foolish. How do you think the other coins got in there? Every Caretaker has a key and they were all more than happy to oblige me." He turned to Nisha, "But only The Caretaker of Third Coin can make The Cauldron work, isn't that right, Miss Lakewood?"

Nisha was stunned for a moment. Was she really necessary to make it all work? She didn't know. She hadn't had the training. Her heart pounded.

Don't panic. He's bluffing. He's afraid of the lie flies. That's why he asked a question rather than making a statement. He doesn't know how it works and he thinks you do.

Nisha was careful not to react to Bea's thought. She suspected Sahwin could sense them when they spoke without words. She watched as his eyes shifted around the room as if trying to find the source of the energy.

Okay, Nisha thought, with a deep breath, *if he's bluffing, I can bluff too.*

She opened her mouth to speak but hesitated. If she made something up, the lie flies would give her away.

Luckily, Indy stepped in, giving her time to think.

"Why should she help you?" he said moving bravely towards Sahwin.

"Because I'm asking her to do what we all know needs to be done," said Sahwin, with a sly smile. "If she refuses, The Lost will break through and the world you know will be destroyed. So really, it is you that needs her help, not me. I am protected by Avalloc, King of the Otherworld. My safety is guaranteed. It is you and everyone else that will suffer."

Several lie flies both small and large circled around Sahwin's head. He waved his hand at them irritably.

"And if we activate The Coin? What then?" Bea asked.

"Well, Miss Brightman, it's quite simple. The Lost remain in the Darkness of the Other World, you get to live and I get The Coins."

More lie flies attacked Sahwin but bounced off his leather coat.

"I'm not sure I like that arrangement," said Nisha, who suddenly felt a fierce protectiveness for The Third Coin.

Sahwin laughed. "Oh really?" he said mockingly. "And who should have them; The Caretakers? You and the others have proven you don't deserve them. It was far too easy for me to take them from you. I found all of them, with nothing more than some money from that idiot Wang and a little help from Miss Brightman's tedious, know-it-all of a father."

"My father would never help you!" Bea exclaimed, but when she did a rather large lie fly appeared and stung her on the shoulder. She looked down at it, confused.

"He was quite accommodating, really," Sahwin replied, "hunted down every lead, never asking for money or even an explanation. Moved anywhere I told him to." Sahwin's shook his head. "It's sad really, how he never seemed to give a thought to how difficult it must have been for you."

Nisha looked nervously at Bea. Although lie flies appeared around Sahwin, Nisha could see that his words had stung her more than any fly could.

Keep it together, she thought to Bea. *He's trying to get to you just like he did in class. If your father did help him, I'm sure he didn't know what he was doing.*

It was obvious Sahwin was enjoying Bea's growing anger and Nisha could almost feel Bea's blood heating up. She had to intervene before Bea did something she'd regret. Nisha stepped forward but it was Indy who spoke.

"Leave her alone," he said.

"Or what?" Sahwin asked, glaring back at Indy. "Go on," he pressed. "Challenge me. Be the fool you were born to be." Indy hesitated for a moment and Sahwin laughed.

"Just as I suspected; a fool and a coward just like your ancestors, charging into battles you have no chance of winning." The flies came at him from different directions, but Sahwin took no notice.

"You don't know anything about my ancestors, Skull-face," Indy said, sounding less afraid than Nisha thought he should. A lie fly appeared and stung him. But Indy didn't move.

"On the contrary, I am an expert in your ancestry. I teach classes on it, in fact," he added with a grin. "And I can tell you one thing for certain: the gene pool is quite consistent; arrogant, silly boys who manage to get themselves in way over their heads."

A large lie fly appeared and hung in the air right in front of Sahwin's nose. With a lightning-fast movement, Sahwin grabbed it out of the air and crushed it in his hand, wiping the bug's glowing green guts on the sleeve of his jacket.

"What are you talking about?" Indy said, looking both miffed and annoyed.

"Don't try and pretend you don't know who you are," Sahwin barked. "What other possible reason could there be for you to be chosen as a Finder?"

"Wait," said Bea. "Are you saying that Indy is a Finder because he's related to King Arthur?"

Sahwin rolled his eyes. "*King* Arthur? How many times do we have to have this conversation, Miss Brightman?

"But you admit Arthur was a real person?"

Sahwin snorted indignantly. "He lived, yes, and he was real

enough to destroy the glory that was once Avalon. But he was no king, no great warrior as the stories say. He was a stupid, lucky boy." Two lie flies appeared but Sahwin zapped them away with a snap of his fingers. "But that nonsense is over now," he continued, grinning. "The time of Man Kind's rule ends today. Now is the time for Avalon to ascend again. It's time for a man of the Island to do the job our pathetic Lady of the Lake could not."

"And," he said, turning to Nisha, "It begins with you Miss Lakewood, Daughter of Caitria. Bring The Waters to life now and we all live. Disobey me and I'll send you to Avalloc with the other Caretakers."

As Sahwin spoke lie flies appeared so quickly, Nisha couldn't tell what was true and what was not.

"So that's where they are?" Bea asked. "You've sent them to Avalloc?"

"And why not? It's only fair he gets something. And it's been The Caretakers keeping him and his kind out of The Light for so long." Sahwin's eyes found Nisha's. "But he won't be happy until he has all five."

Nisha shook her head. Had she understood him right? Had he really given living people to the King of the Other World as some kind of payment for his own safety? Did that mean all The Caretakers were dead?

Then suddenly Indy was in front of her, Drae Mord flashing in his hand. The crow cawed viciously at the sight of the knife. "You're not going to give him Nisha or anyone else for that matter," Indy said defiantly, and Nisha almost smiled when no lie fly appeared.

"Oh don't be ridiculous, boy," said Sahwin, laughing, "Do you really think you can protect her from me using that old Goblin knife?"

Indy said nothing, but stood his ground.

Sahwin took several more steps across the misty floor.

"Stop," Indy shouted, bending his arm back as if ready to throw.

Sahwin slowed, but did not stop. "Please, throw the knife.

I've been hoping to get it back in my family's possession for years."

"I'm warning you," said Indy.

Sahwin took another step forward and another. Nisha held her breath. She could see Indy's hand shaking ever so slightly.

"Coward," said Sahwin and one of the green lights appeared just over his head. The distraction was what Indy had been waiting for. He threw the knife straight at Sahwin's neck. But Sahwin was faster. He caught the knife just as the tip of it pricked his skin. A single drop of black blood slid down his throat and into the collar of his coat.

"You should not have done that," said Sahwin, his face even more hideous as it contorted with anger. He came towards Indy faster than Nisha had ever seen anyone move and grasped him by the throat. Indy struggled furiously but he could not free himself. Sahwin dragged Indy over to the edge of the stone floor, knelt down and pulled Indy to his knees. Then he forced Indy's face into the river. Indy's scream was drowned out by the water, but Nisha could see his body writhing in pain. She knew contact with the waters of Avalon could hurt and even kill ordinary people.

"Ah, The River of Sadness; never a favorite with Man Kind," said Sahwin offhandedly, as if holding Indy's head underwater required no effort at all. "Burns with the fire of hell and fills their heads with the most hideous visions."

Bea pushed forward, but Nisha stepped in front of her.

"Leave him alone," said Nisha, surprised at the strength of her own voice.

"Show me how to activate The Coin."

"If I do, will you spare his life?" Nisha asked, trying to keep the desperation out of her voice.

"Don't forget, we can tell if you are lying," Bea called out from just behind Nisha's shoulder.

"Is that all it takes?" said Sahwin, yanking Indy from the water by his hair and carelessly tossing him to one side. Indy's body crumpled to the floor.

"Oh don't look so distressed," said Sahwin lazily. "He's

unconscious, but he's not dead." He waved his spidery fingers around his head. "See, no flies. Now, I have spared him, tell me how it works."

Nisha stared at Indy's limp body for a moment and swallowed hard to keep her composure. Then she lifted her eyes to meet Sahwin's. "Give me The Coin and I will show you." She held her breath waiting but no flies appeared.

Sahwin's face contorted again and he grabbed Indy by the hair "Don't test me, Miss Lakewood," he hissed.

Nisha raised her hands in surrender. "Bring The Coin to The Cauldron and we'll do it together," she said.

Sahwin flicked his long coat behind him as he strode towards them. At the same time, his hideous crow flew across the room and perched itself on Sahwin's shoulder.

"After you," he said, pushing Nisha up the small stones to the platform. "You too." He shoved Bea after her. When they were all standing at The Cauldron's edge he glared at Nisha expectantly.

Do you know what you're doing? Bea asked silently.

I don't know. Maybe.

"And?" said Sahwin, his eyes darting back and forth between the girls.

"And The Coin must be returned to its place in The Cauldron of Coins," said Nisha, her confidence growing when again no lie flies appeared. Then she climbed the stairs to the platform and pointed. "Right here, in the middle."

"I've already tried that," said Sahwin impatiently. "It would be a grave mistake to think you can trick me."

"I am not lying," she said, gesturing to the air around her. "See, no flies."

Sahwin nodded as he considered her words. Slowly, he pulled The Coin of Balance from his sleeve.

Just then, Bea's watch began to beep; five minutes remained before midnight.

"Five minutes," Bea said quietly.

Sahwin looked back and forth between the two girls suspiciously. "So you have some sort of plan, do you? Well, I can fix that." He grabbed Bea and pushed her roughly up against Nisha so they were standing with their backs pressed together. Then, he produced a thin black chain from his coat and looped it around them. "Be still," he commanded, and instantly neither girl could move.

At the same time, Nisha realized she could hear every thought in Bea's head.

"Sit," he ordered, and the girls slid, back to back, down to the floor, unable to resist his orders.

"What is it?" asked Bea, struggling against the thin shackle.

"It's a Chain of Command," said Sahwin, and again he smiled grotesquely, causing the cut in his neck to ooze. "It's a delightful piece of dark magic. No one really knows why it works." Then he turned back to The Cauldron and both girls held their breath. With no ceremony at all, he pushed The Third Coin into its place in the circle. He waited a moment but nothing happened. Then he turned back to Nisha with one eyebrow raised.

What's supposed to happen? Bea thought anxiously.

I don't know… something must be wrong, answered Nisha. *The Third Coin is supposed to connect the others together. It's the flow between the coins, the connection makes them powerful.*

Seconds ticked by, and still, nothing.

Nisha did her best to control the panic rising in her chest. She cleared her throat and said,

"It doesn't work until the stroke of mid…"

"Shut up!" Sahwin hissed, and, like a flash, he was next to her. She could smell the scent of rot on his breath mixing with the stench of the crow's oily feathers. Drae Mord was in his hand, and he pressed the blade into the skin just under her chin.

"Children," Sahwin whispered with contempt, "every one of you a selfish, lying, treacherous creature." A large green lie fly appeared at near his left eye and he let it sting his cheek without flinching.

"So tell me, Miss Lakewood, who dies first: the boy or your friend Miss Brightman? Personally, I'd like to get Miss Brightman out of the way. I've always found her irritating."

"Put the knife down," said a voice from across the room. It

was Aunt Faye.

At first Nisha couldn't see her because she couldn't move her head, but then Aunt Faye came into view. She was wearing her summoning gown but it was dirty and torn, a small leather pouch hung at her hip. Nisha could see the weariness in her Aunt's face. However when their eyes met, Nisha saw a fierceness in Faye that she had never seen before. Also, there was something glowing and silver wound around her arm like a vine.

To her surprise, the bracelet began to move, and it took Nisha a moment to understand what it was. It was Ice, her aunt's pet snake. It must be a SpellSpitter, she thought. How had she not realized it before? She had read about SpellSpitters when she was a little girl, but it never occurred to her that they were real or that Ice was one of them. Spellspitters were the only weapon the Daughters of Avalon allowed themselves. The snakes could spit Lake pebbles with tremendous force. The women would collect the stones and enchant them with spells, then feed them to the snake. In this way, the women could cast their curses from a great distance.

As soon as Sahwin saw Faye, he leapt from the platform and onto the floor. He grabbed the crow from his shoulder and threw it like a spear toward Faye's small frame. She dodged the bird with more agility than Nisha had imagined she had. The bird hit the blue stone wall behind her and fell to into the water, dead from a broken neck.

Faye did not let the bird distract her. She aimed her snake-wrapped arm and with a silent command, Ice spit out a stone which rocketed towards Sahwin. Amazingly, the pebble grew in size and increased in velocity. By the time it hit Sahwin it was a rock the size of a baseball, hurtling with great force into his stomach. He doubled over from the blow.

Nisha heard footsteps and tried to turn, but could not, still paralyzed by the chain wrapped around her. Then she heard, rather than saw, someone tackle Sahwin while he was still on the ground. It was Indy. She could hear them grunting and twisting until their struggle brought them into her line of sight.

Indy had Sahwin by the throat this time, his thumb pressing into the open wound in Sahwin's neck. Blood pushed out over Indy's hands, but it was not enough to stop Sahwin. With incredible strength, he rolled Indy over so that he was on top of him, and grasped Indy's throat with his bony fingers. Unable to breathe, Indy could not hold on. His grip failed him and he looked as if he were about to pass out. At that moment, another large rock came hurtling towards them and hit Sahwin squarely in the head. A large gash gushed black blood over his eye and down his cheek, making him look more horrifying than ever.

And then another rock was upon him but he was ready. He rolled off Indy and away, and caught it in one hand. As he climbed back to his feet, he brought the rock to his lips and whispered a curse. Then he sent it hurdling back at Faye. Faye moved quickly, and it landed at her feet, but then suddenly burst into flame, catching the hem of her skirt and forcing her to rush to the river to put it out.

Sahwin took the opportunity to attack. He was nearly on top of Faye before Nisha even had a chance to call out. Fortunately, Faye must have heard him coming, for she was ready. As he reached out for the back of her neck, she whirled around to face him and with one arching motion, brought a huge swell of water from the river crashing down over his head. It knocked him down and sent him sliding across the slick floor. He recovered quickly, and cast a curse at Faye that pushed her backward with incredible force. Her head hit the Fountain of Life and she was knocked unconscious.

At that moment, Indy ran up from behind Sahwin and tackled him. Again, they struggled in the flood for several seconds, though Indy had little chance. The burning of the water weakened him. Sahwin easily overwhelmed him and with a shove of his boot, pushed Indy off the wet stone floor and into the river itself.

Nisha gasped in terror and frustration, but there was nothing she could do. The more she struggled, it seemed, the less she could move. Then Sahwin was back in front of her; Drae Mord at her throat again.

"Stay where you are or I will kill her," he said, calling out to Faye, who was slowly coming to.

Nisha struggled more urgently, trying to somehow back away from the knife that was pressed into her neck. Then a thought crashed loudly through her mind. *Stop moving, would you? I've almost got it.*

CHAPTER 46

THE STROKE OF MIDNIGHT

Come on, come on, Bea thought as she struggled to get the small piece of metal into her fingers. *Just about...almost....*

"I'm afraid you're out of time," said Sahwin, smiling cruelly at the girls. Then he pressed the knife further into Nisha's skin, drawing blood. Both Nisha and Bea gasped at the pain of it.

Then, finally, Bea felt her fingertip touch the end of the metal.

"Just a minute," she said. It came out less forcefully than she intended but it didn't seem to matter. The moment the words were out of her mouth, everything froze; everything except for her and Nisha. Even the river stopped moving. Faye was caught in mid-stride, anger hardened on her face.

"Bea, you did it!" said Nisha, her whispery voice loud in the still air.

"Yes, but now what? How do we get out of this? Where's Indy?"

"I'm here," Indy called out weakly from the other side of the room. "The river must have carried me around." He coughed several times as he crawled towards them.

"What a relief," said Bea expressing what she knew Nisha was also feeling. "Are you okay? Can you cut us out of this?"

Bea counted the seconds waiting for Indy. What was taking him so long? However, just as she opened her mouth to shout at him to hurry, he came into view. His face was pale with pain and his body was bruised and bloody. His clothes hung from him as if he'd been starved.

Indy hauled himself to his knees next to Sahwin and struggled to wrench the knife from Sahwin's bony grip.

Bea felt a strong wave of concern rush through her and she knew that it had come from Nisha. Being this close to her, Bea could feel Nisha's feelings along with her thoughts, and it occurred to her that the closer they were together the more their thoughts and feelings mixed.

With a rough tug, Indy pulled the knife out of Sahwin's fist. Drae Mord sliced effortlessly through The Chain of Command and Bea and Nisha scrambled to their feet.

As soon as the girls were separated, Bea's ability to hear Nisha's thoughts was diminished. And suddenly, as if she'd known it all along, Bea understood what needed to happen. She spoke out loud. "Nisha, when the clock starts again, we have to be here together at The Cauldron of the Coins."

Nisha frowned in confusion.

"It's us. We're the connection. We make The Coin work like we did at the Flea Market," said Bea.

A look of comprehension passed across Nisha's face and she smiled as she positioned herself at the edge of The Cauldron.

Indy stationed himself behind Sahwin, Drae Mord poised at Sahwin's throat. "You know I'm going to have to do whatever it takes," Indy said.

But before they girls could reply, everything was moving again. How many seconds did they have left?

Sahwin eyes blazed with the realization of what had happened, and despite the threat of Drae Mord, he attacked. He spun around to face Indy, the knife leaving a shallow slit around his throat. He grasped Indy by both wrists and shoved him backward so they stood face to face, both surging forward with all their strength. For several seconds, they were so evenly matched they barely moved. Indy's face was contorted with

301

effort. He pushed the entire weight of his body against Sahwin. Sahwin pressed back, but his injuries had weakened him

"Let the boy go," Faye commanded as she rushed up behind Sahwin, a small dagger in her hand.

"As you wish," cackled Sahwin, and with a sudden movement he threw himself out of the way, releasing Indy from his control.

The unexpectedness of Sahwin's release made it impossible for Indy to stop himself. The force of his efforts against Sahwin propelled him forward. He hit Faye with his full strength, toppling her backward onto the stone floor. Bea was relieved to see Faye's dagger fly out of her hand and clamor to the ground behind her. But her relief was short lived. Something was wrong. Faye wasn't moving.

With only a second left until midnight, Bea grabbed Nisha's hand to keep her from rushing to her Aunt's side. She pulled Nisha's hand into the Cauldron and together they touched the Third Coin.

Then the dark blue room was ablaze with a blinding silvery-gold light that shot out from the Cauldron in every direction. Bea could feel the energy of the Coins pumping through her like blood. Her hair and Nisha's braids floated strangely around their heads as if they were being electrocuted in slow motion. The fountains gushed into life.

When the silvery light dimmed and the mist cleared, Bea pulled her hand out of the bowl and Nisha did the same. The Passage was complete.

Nisha scrambled out of the fountain and ran to her Aunt's side. It was then that Bea saw what had happened. Drae Mord was lodged deep in Faye's shoulder. Indy was kneeling beside her, his eyes wide in disbelief.

Bea looked around for Sahwin, but he was gone. She scrambled over the side of the fountain and followed Nisha to where Faye lay.

"Kiss her!" Nisha commanded, falling to her knees next to Indy. "Kiss her!" Nisha commanded again when Indy's face showed his confusion.

"She's still alive. Use The Kiss and kiss her right now!"

"But…but I don't love her. Didn't Bridget say I had to love the person for the stone to …"

"You do love her!" Nisha insisted, her eyes full of tears. "You have to. You have to love her because… because I love her. Please, Indy, please try…" Tears streamed down Nisha's face and Bea kneeled beside her. She put her hand on Nisha's shoulder and said, "Try, Indy. For Nisha and me. Please save Aunt Faye."

CHAPTER 47

THE SNOW

Nisha couldn't breathe. It was as if she had forgotten how. Time had slowed and yet it felt like minutes were passing as she watched Indy hunt around beneath the collar of his t-shirt to find The Kiss. After an eternity, he produced the small stone.

Then he reached out and slowly pulled Drae Mord from Faye's shoulder. Nisha felt herself grow weak and dizzy. She knew Bea was saying something, she could feel the urgent tone of Bea's words pressing through the wooziness in her head, but the meaning was lost. Perhaps Bea was reminding Indy how to work The Kiss. *Get on with it,* Nisha wanted to shout, but without breath there were no words.

Indy leaned over Faye, holding the stone to his lips. Then he looked up into Nisha's eyes; his long black eyelashes were wet and stuck together. *From the river? From tears?* Still looking at her, he kissed the stone gently. Then he turned and placed his lips against Aunt Faye's.

Instantly, the old woman's face twitched into life. The color came rushing back to her cheeks, and she took a small, sharp breath. Then she sat up so suddenly she smacked her forehead into Indy's. Indy looked stunned for a moment but then his eyes rolled up in his head and he fell backward on to the floor, pretending to be knocked out by the blow.

Perhaps it was Bea who started to laugh first. Nisha couldn't be sure, but then they were all laughing. Nisha laughed so hard she cried, or maybe she was crying already but it didn't matter. Aunt Faye was alright.

Faye was the first to regain her composure. She struggled to her feet and Indy jumped up to help her, looking as if he too had recovered some. She looked around the room and nodded solemnly. "Sahwin escaped," she said with a frustrated sigh. Then she turned to Indy. "Help me to The Cauldron, dear boy."

Together, they walked slowly up the small path to the platform. Faye grasped the edge of The Cauldron and carefully peered over the side.

"Just as I suspected," she said, turning back the girls. "He took them all."

Nisha wanted to say something, to offer some kind of apology, but Bea spoke first. "All except this one," she said, holding up The Third Coin.

Faye nodded. "Good girl. At least we have one, and that is enough for now." She shook her head and said, "Though it's going to be difficult to tell The Council that the other four are missing."

"It's going to be more difficult than you think," said Indy. "Sahwin told us that he gave the other four Caretakers to Avalloc in exchange for his safety."

Faye nodded slowly. "I was worried it might be something like that. The Caretakers have been missing for some time now."

"What does it mean?" Nisha asked.

"And what can we do about it?" Indy added.

"It means we're going to have to find them," said Faye.

"So they're not …dead?" Nisha asked.

"No, dear," said Faye with a sad smile. "They are worth much more to Avalloc alive. Passage Day can't happen without them. But that is a lesson for another day. What matters is that you kids did it. The gateway between this world and The Other World has been resealed and The Lost cannot escape. The

Passage is done and it cannot be undone until the next Passage Day."

"When is that?" asked Indy.

"Passage Day comes when a Caretaker is ready to hand down her Coin to her chosen successor. Only The Council can tell us who is next and when. Even more reason for us to head home."

"I would like that very much," said Bea, "but we barely found our way in. I have no idea how to get out."

"Yes, it was tricky getting here," said Faye. "Graydon and I tried everything we could think of but it wasn't until I got back to our apartment that I actually figured it out."

"So you found the hole in the floor?" Indy asked.

"There's a hole in my floor?" said Faye, sounding alarmed. "I didn't see any. In fact the only unusual thing I found was Indy's skateboard and that's when it occurred to me that the entrance has been just outside my door all along. Come, I'll show you."

Faye climbed down from the center fountain and headed over to the Fountain of Love. Then she hiked up her gown, which was soaked with water and some of her own blood, and climbed over the rim of the basin.

"It's just back here," she said.

"You're not going to make me go through the water again, are you?" Indy groaned as they followed her towards the now gushing fountain. Some of the water splashed up over the edge, and Indy jumped back.

"Just take a hold of one of us and you'll be fine. You can't be hurt if you're escorted by a daughter of the Lake."

"But what about Bea?" Indy asked.

"Yes, she'll do," said Faye. Indy looked at Bea quizzically and Bea shrugged in return.

Faye climbed up over the side of the Fountain, and tromped through the water, past the embracing couple whose nudity was now covered by the jets of fountain water. Faye sloshed her way toward the back of the fountain, where an apple tree was carved into the bluish wall. Nisha could see the chubby feet of a fat stone cupid dangling from the marble branches above Faye's head. A small stone ladder leaned up against the tree trunk.

"Come along," said Faye, signaling for them to follow her.

Bea went first, bravely stepping in to the churning water, and Nisha was surprised to see that she did not react other than to turn and smile back at her. Nisha went next and had to push herself up over the rim as she was too short to swing her leg over. Indy immediately hurried to help, lifting her up easily by the waist and placing her in the fountain. He was rewarded with a huge splash of water.

"Any pain?" Faye shouted to be heard over the churn of the water.

"Nope, nothing," Indy said, grinning.

"Good. Keep a firm grasp on Nisha and you'll be fine."

Indy looked up at Nisha, who was standing in the fountain, and with a blinding smile he held out his hand to her. She willed herself not to blush as she threaded her small fingers through his.

"This way," Faye said once they were all crowded at the back of the fountain. She tugged at her sopping skirt and stepped up onto the first rung of the short ladder.

Nisha almost laughed. The stone ladder was no more than seven or eight rungs.

However, when Faye reached the branches above her, she simply kept climbing, and in seconds, she had disappeared. Bea went after her followed by Nisha and Indy.

After only a few more steps, Nisha's head cleared the top of the branches and she found herself climbing up the side of a dirty, foul-smelling hole.

"Where are we?" Indy asked. "And what is that delightful odor?"

Faye didn't answer. Instead she stopped climbing and said, "Give me a moment to check the traffic."

"Check for traffic?" Indy asked Nisha, but again before anyone could answer him, Faye called down to them.

"Looks clear," she announced cheerfully. Then Nisha heard the heavy scraping of metal and suddenly they were bathed in a strange light. Something wet and cold was falling down on them.

Nisha climbed up the last several rungs of the ladder to find herself standing next to the manhole cover in the middle of their street, just outside of her apartment. It was early morning, and it was snowing.

CHAPTER 48

THE HOMECOMING

"Bianca?"

"Father?"

Bea was only just absorbing the shock of climbing out of a manhole into the middle of her street at dawn. To see her father sitting on their front stoop with her notebook in his hands was almost too confusing.

"What is going on here?" he said, standing up abruptly.

"I thought you were away..." Bea said, realizing it was the wrong thing to say only after she said it.

"And that's an excuse to stay out all night?" He walked towards them. Bea looked down at her wet dirty clothes, and glanced nervously at Faye whose gown was covered in blood. "And what in the name of God were you doing in a ..." Then he stopped. He was looking at Nisha.

"Captain?" said Faye, "you're alive?" Bea's father slowly pulled his gaze away from Nisha and looked at Faye. An expression of recognition crossed his face, followed by one of disbelief.

A car horn blasted and they all looked up.

"Get outta the road!" the cab driver shouted. "Whaddaya, nuts?"

Bea, her father, Indy, Nisha, and Faye all hurried over to Bea's front stoop where a light dusting of snow had started to accumulate.

When they were safely out of the street, Bea's father turned to Faye and said, "I don't understand. What is going on here?"

"I'm not sure," said Faye. "I... we thought you were dead, lost at sea or perhaps killed by..."

"Sahwin..." Father said, finishing Faye's sentence. He cleared his throat and shook his head. "No. We never found him. As soon as I realized that my daughter was on board, we headed to the nearest port so she would be safe. We had no choice; I had no choice."

Faye looked from Bea to Nisha and then back to Bea's father, and a slow, tentative smile spread across her face. "Incredible," she said, shaking her head.

"What is, Aunt Faye?" said Nisha.

"Danu's plan," said Faye. "She tricked us; this whole time, she tricked us. I thought the baby was with me and your father thought the baby was with him. That's why he never came looking for you, Nisha. Why would he, if he didn't know you existed?"

"What trick? What are you talking about? My daughter was with me. She's right here."

Looking back and forth between her father and Faye made Bea feel as if her brain was on fire. How could it be that her father was talking to Faye as if he knew her, and talking about Sahwin and even Danu?

"Yes, she is," said Faye, her eyes filling with tears as she grasped Bea's pale fingers in her knobby brown hand. "I knew it and yet I denied my inner voice..." Then she turned to Nisha and grasped her hand as well. "Oh, the thought ran through my mind a dozen times especially when I realized you girls could Thought Share, but I never let myself really believe it was possible."

"What are you talking about Auntie?" Nisha said, sounding as confused as Bea felt.

"Twins, my darling child; you and Bea are twins. Danu split

you up without telling anyone. She must have done it as a precaution, to keep you safe from Sahwin." Then she smiled again. "But I believe it was your mother's magic that kept The Coin safe, for it must have been she who transferred The Coin's powers into the two of you."

"You mean… we're sisters?" asked Nisha.

"You mean we're the Third Coin?" asked Bea.

"Yes, and yes or more specifically you're the magic that makes it work."

"That's why The Coin didn't work until we touched it," said Nisha, turning to Bea. "How did you know?"

"I didn't," Bea said with a shrug. "I only knew that when we first touched The Coin at the flea market that something happened, something powerful. I thought that maybe if we touched it again, we could create enough energy to get it to work." She shrugged again and slowly sat herself down on the wet steps. "But…" she began, looking back and forth between her father, Nisha and Faye. "I don't understand the rest of it," she said. "Nisha and I are sisters? I…but…" she started again. Finally, she turned to her father and said, "Why? Why didn't you ever tell me who my mother was? Why didn't you ever tell me about Avalon?"

Her father's eyes met hers and she could see the sadness in them. "What could I tell you, Bianca? That your mother was from a mythical island? That she was killed by a madman over a coin?"

"You could have at least told me her name," Bea said. "You told me her name was Katherine."

"No, I told you her name was Cait. You made it Katherine and I didn't correct you. I thought that the less you knew, the safer you were. It was the reasonable thing to do."

"Reasonable?" said Bea, blinking back the tears that had sprung into her eyes.

"Please understand, Bianca. When your mother died, I couldn't bear it. I thought I would lose my mind. All I had left was you. I had to protect you." Then he turned and looked at Nisha. "Yet, somehow all the while I felt that there was something missing; something more I needed to know. To think, all this time I thought it was The Coin…I thought that was the missing piece, your mother's Coin. That's why I searched endlessly, risked everything to find it. I never imagined…" Then he turned back to Bea and said, "I hope you can forgive me."

Tears ran down her cheeks, but they weren't tears of anger. Somehow, she felt relieved as though she too had been looking for something they had finally found. She sighed. "Of course I can forgive you, but you have to promise never to withhold the truth from me again," she said meeting his tentative eyes.

"I only did it for your own good, and I believe you did a good deal of withholding yourself, young lady," he said with an eyebrow raised.

"Promise," Bea demanded.

"Fine, but I'll expect the same from you," he replied.

"Agreed. Oh, and another thing," Bea said, standing up. "Nisha and Aunt Faye have to come and live with us."

"Well… I can't… that will have to be…"

Before he could get his sentence out, the front door opened with a loud bang.

"How about some breakfast?" said Nana Anna, who must have been listening from just inside the door. "It seems there are things to be worked out and some eggs would do you all some good. You're wet and it's snowing, for heaven's sake."

It was snowing. Large white flakes drifted down around them. Bea was suddenly aware of how cold she was, but at the same time she didn't care. It felt wonderful to be cold and wet and home.

Somehow, Nana Anna managed to get them all into the house and dry. The rest of the morning was spent around the dining room table. They ate and talked and slowly until they fit all the pieces of the story together. Nisha and Father were shy with each other but Bea was certain it wouldn't last long. Conversely, she and Nana Anna were like old friends reunited. She had liked the old woman right from the start, and it now it felt as if they'd always known each other. Nisha was amused when she realized that Bea's crazy grandfather was also her own, but the discovery that Mr. Morton and Sahwin were the same person was horrifying for Father.

As the hours passed, arrangements were discussed, plans suggested and finally the decision was made that Faye and Nisha would move in. By the time the noon sun had climbed to the top of the sky, the snow had stopped and Bea felt for the first time in her life as if everything was right.

While Father and Aunt Faye continued to talk over tea, Bea, Indy and Nisha pulled on some coats and went out to the stoop. The air was crystal clear and the sun blazed brightly in the sky. The three Finders stood listening to the bustling sounds of the city.

"I knew it the whole time," Indy announced.

"You did not," said Nisha, laughing.

"Yes I did. Only sisters fight as much as you two."

"Well, that's because sisters know they'll always be connected, even if they fight," said Bea matter-of-factly.

"Exactly… that's how I knew."

"You didn't know…" said Nisha and Bea together.

Just then, a woman's voice called out from down the block. "Charlie? Charlie? Is that you?

"Oh no," Indy said. "I forgot to call my mother."

"Your name is Charlie?" Bea asked, surprised at herself for not having thought to ask before.

"Wait a minute," said Nisha. "You're not…"

"Charlie Campbell, you get over here this instant," Indy's mother called out.

Nisha and Bea looked at each other in amazement. "You're Charlie Campbell?" Nisha said.

"You mean Charlie Campbell from your kindergarten playground?" asked Bea.

"One and the same," Indy replied with a flash of his amazing grin. "But now I've *really* gotta fly," he added with a wink, and both girls couldn't help but laugh.

ABOUT THE AUTHOR

J. A. Howard is an author and marketing executive in New York. As the mother of two daughters, Howard is focused on the healthy development and empowerment of young women in all of her work. The Third Coin, Howard's first novel, aims to encourage sisterhood and compassion among middle grade girls. She lives outside Manhattan with her family.

Made in the USA
Middletown, DE
03 December 2018